by Sas Milledge

SPECIAL THANKS TO **BELLE MURDOCH** FOR FLATS
AND TO **MARIE SOLEDAD** FOR SENSITIVITY READING

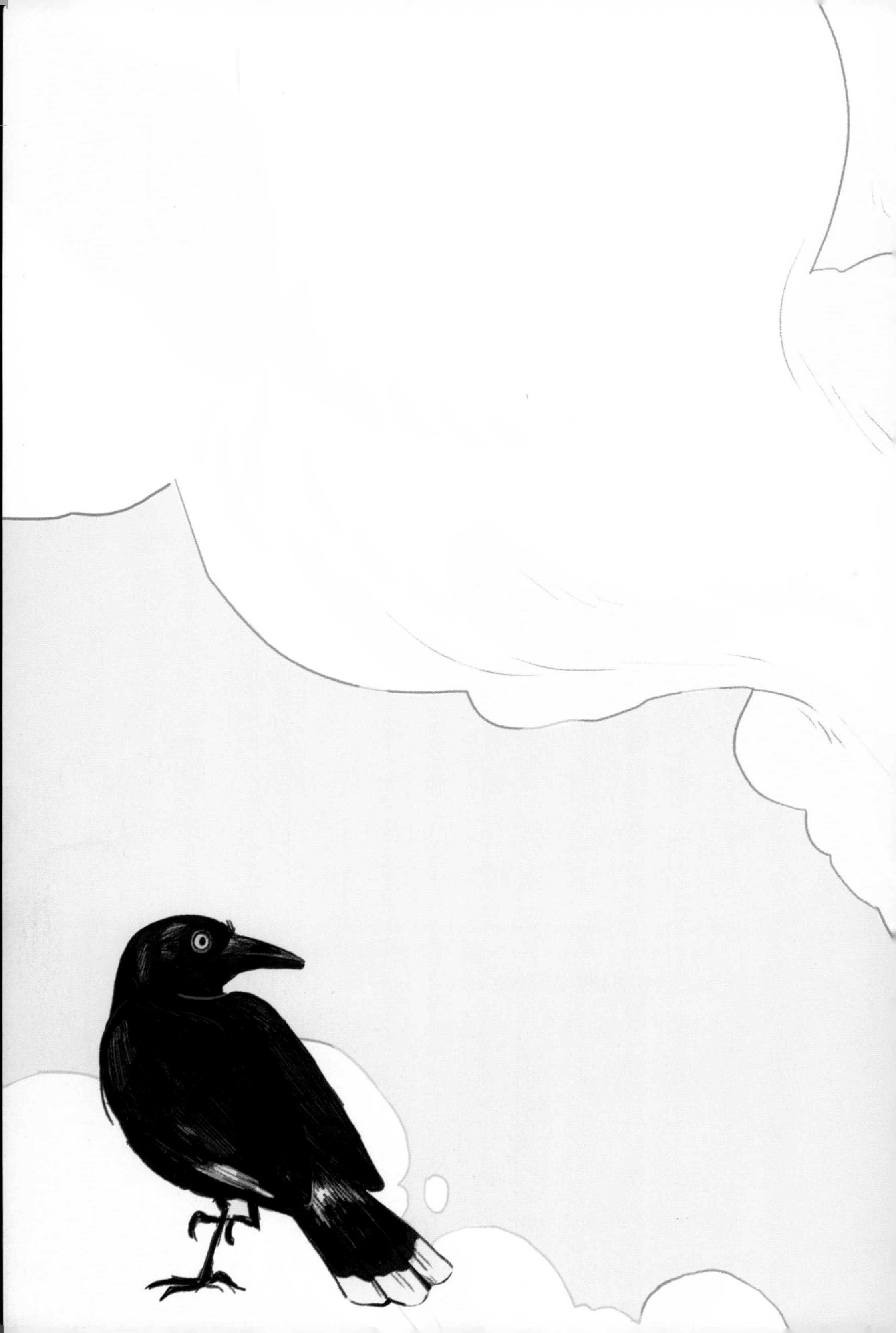

Sas Milledge

Mamo™

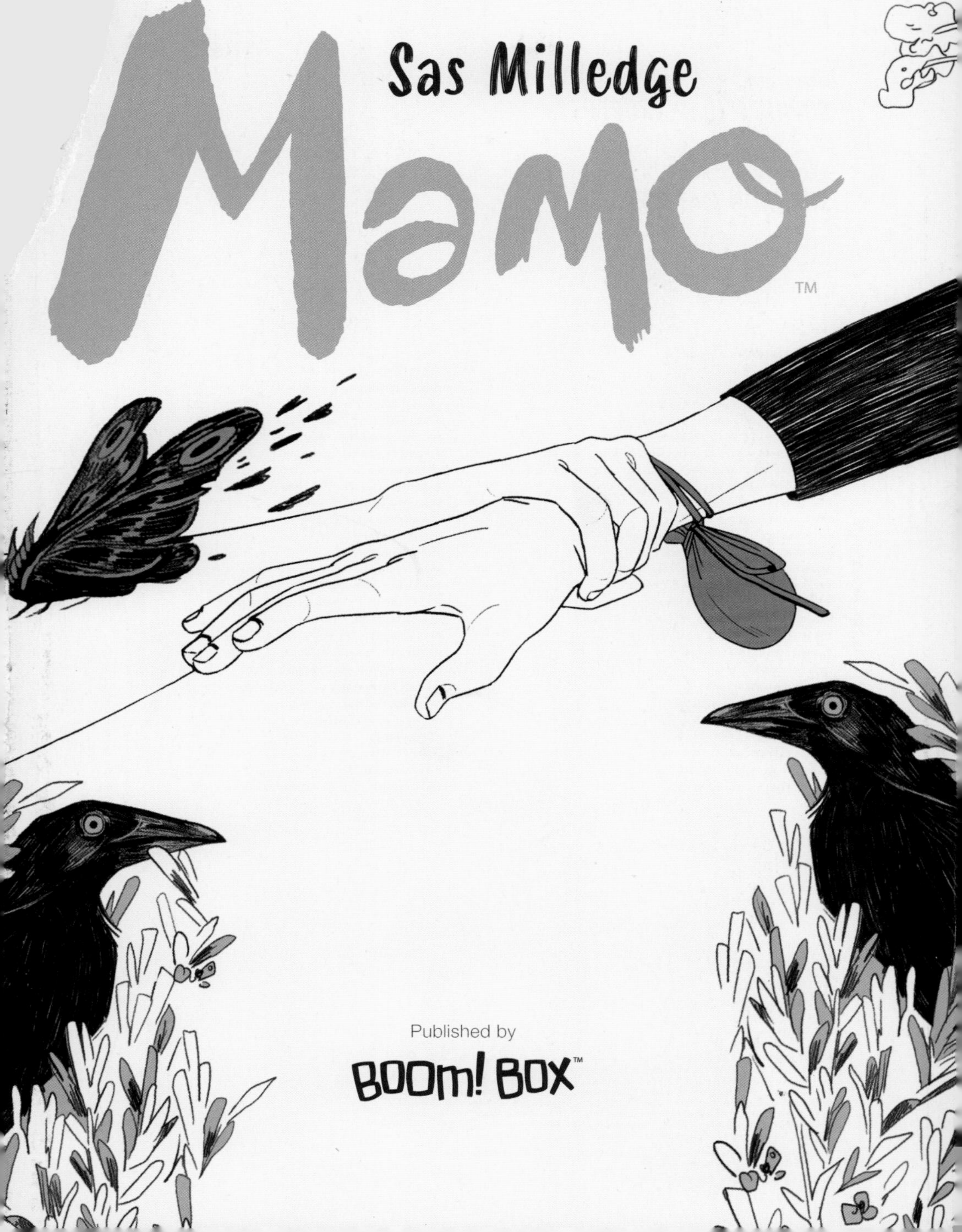

Published by
BOOM! BOX™

DESIGNER
MICHELLE ANKLEY

ASSISTANT EDITOR
KENZIE RZONCA

EDITOR
SOPHIE PHILIPS-ROBERTS

SENIOR EDITOR
SHANNON WATTERS

MAMO, July 2022. Published by BOOM! Box, a division of Boom Entertainment, Inc. Mamo is ™ &
© 2022 Sas Milledge. Originally published in single magazine form as MAMO No. 1-5. ™ & © 2021
Sas Milledge. All rights reserved. BOOM! Box™ and the BOOM! Box logo are trademarks of Boom
Entertainment, Inc., registered in various countries and categories. All characters, events, and
institutions depicted herein are fictional. Any similarity between any of the names, characters,
persons, events, and/or institutions in this publication to actual names, characters, and persons,
whether living or dead, events, and/or institutions is unintended and purely coincidental. BOOM!
Box does not read or accept unsolicited submissions of ideas, stories, or artwork.

BOOM! Studios, 5670 Wilshire Boulevard, Suite 400, Los Angeles, CA 90036-5679. Printed in Canada.
Second Printing.

ISBN: 978-1-68415-817-1, eISBN: 978-1-64668-450-2

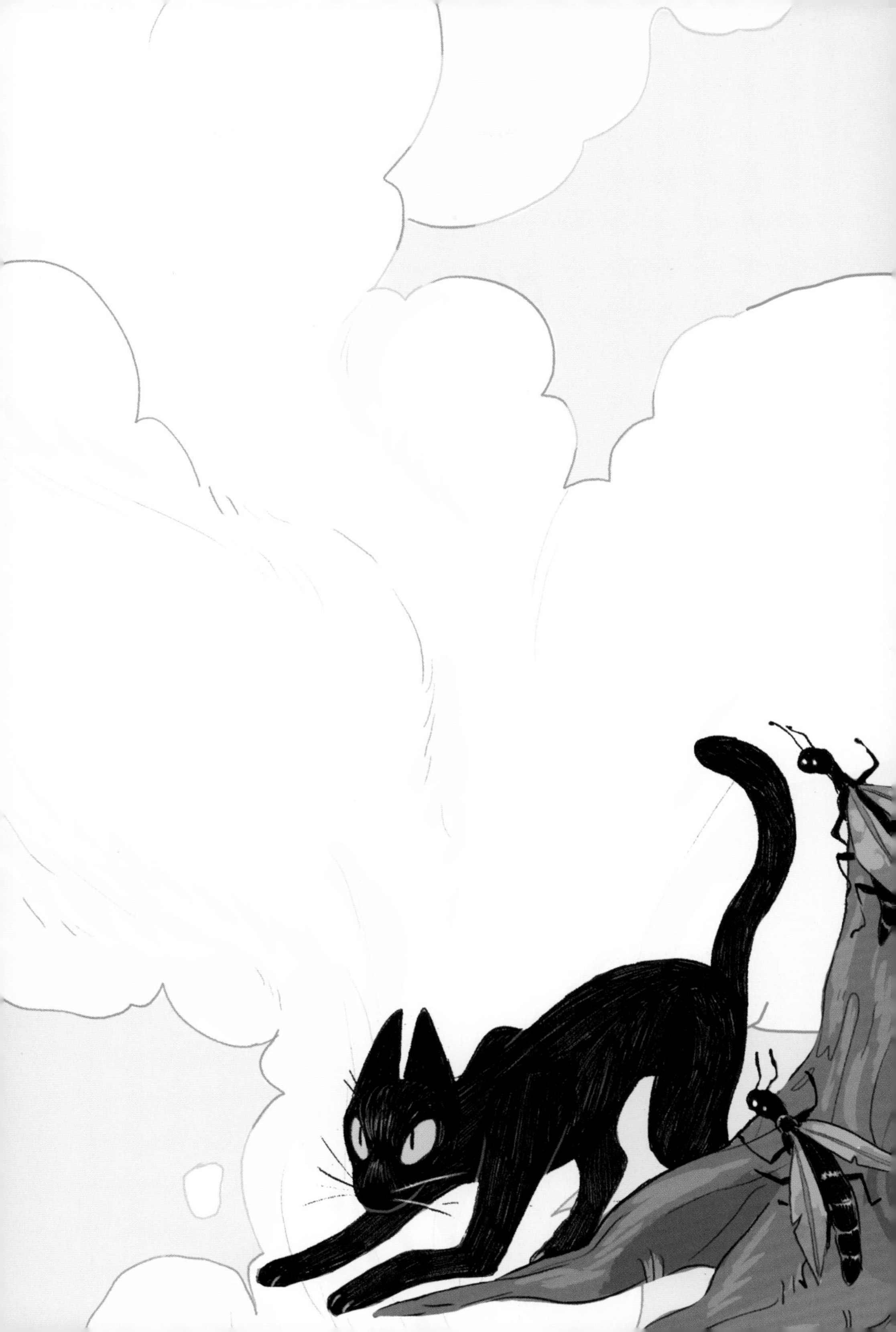

Chapter
1

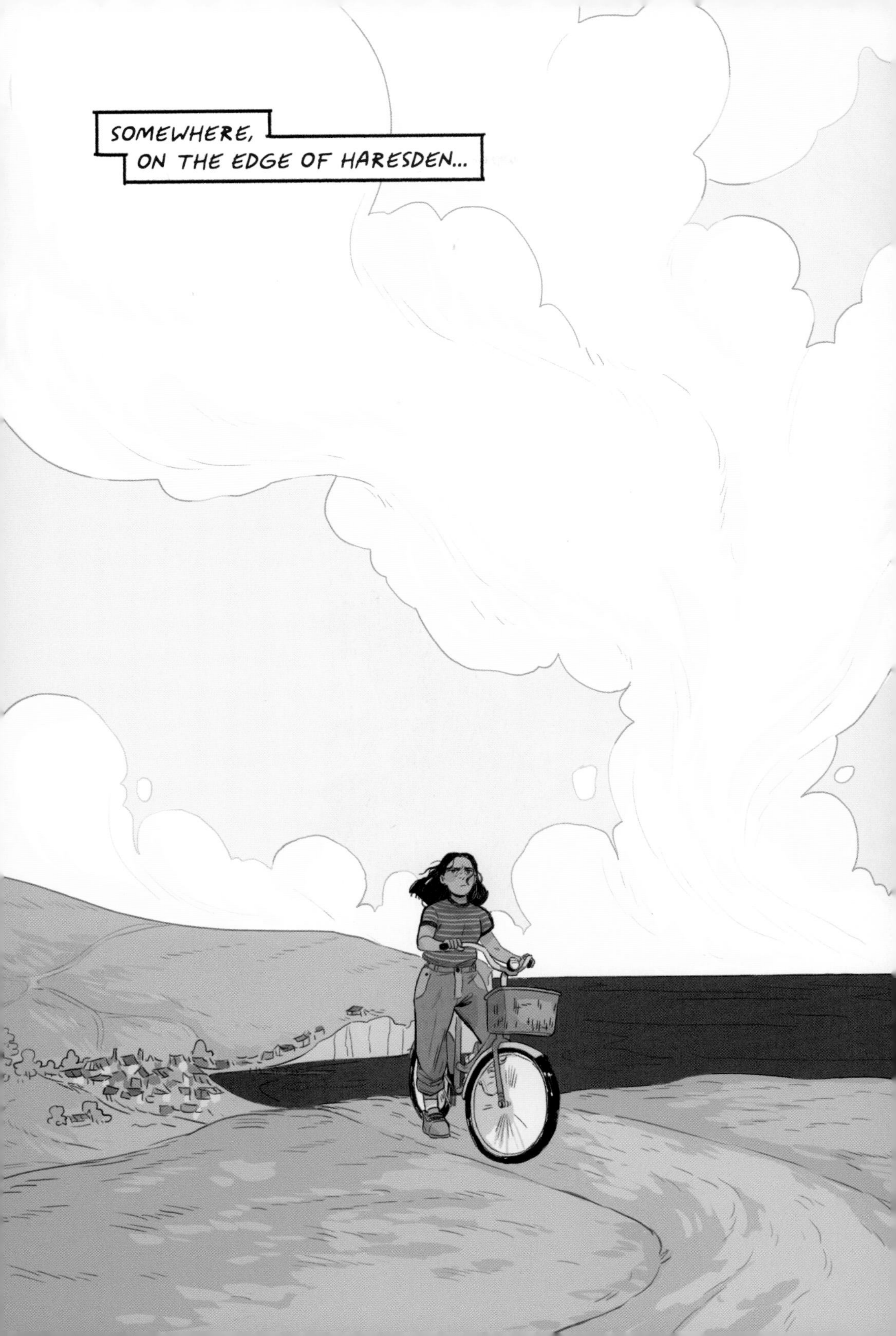
SOMEWHERE, ON THE EDGE OF HARESDEN...

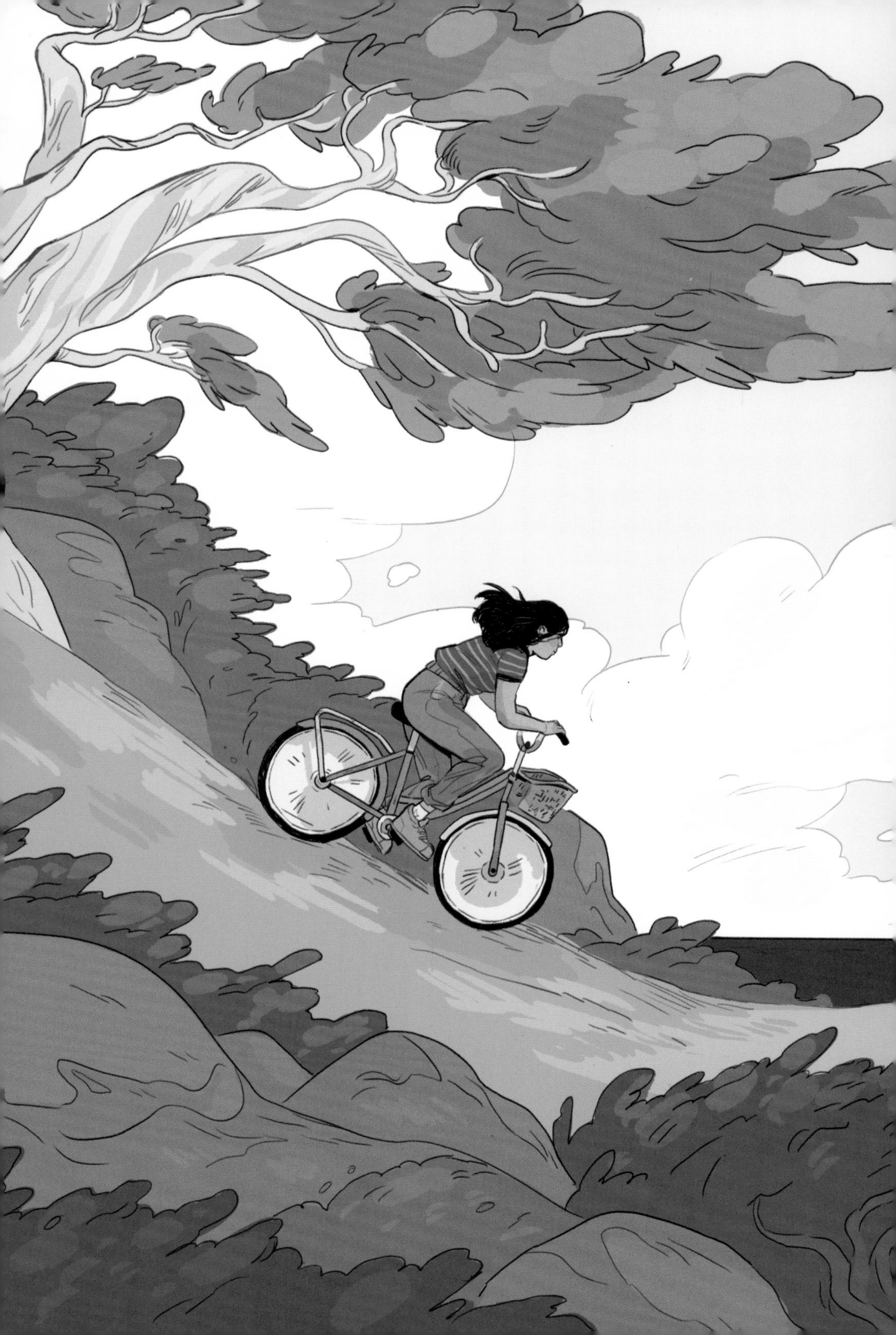

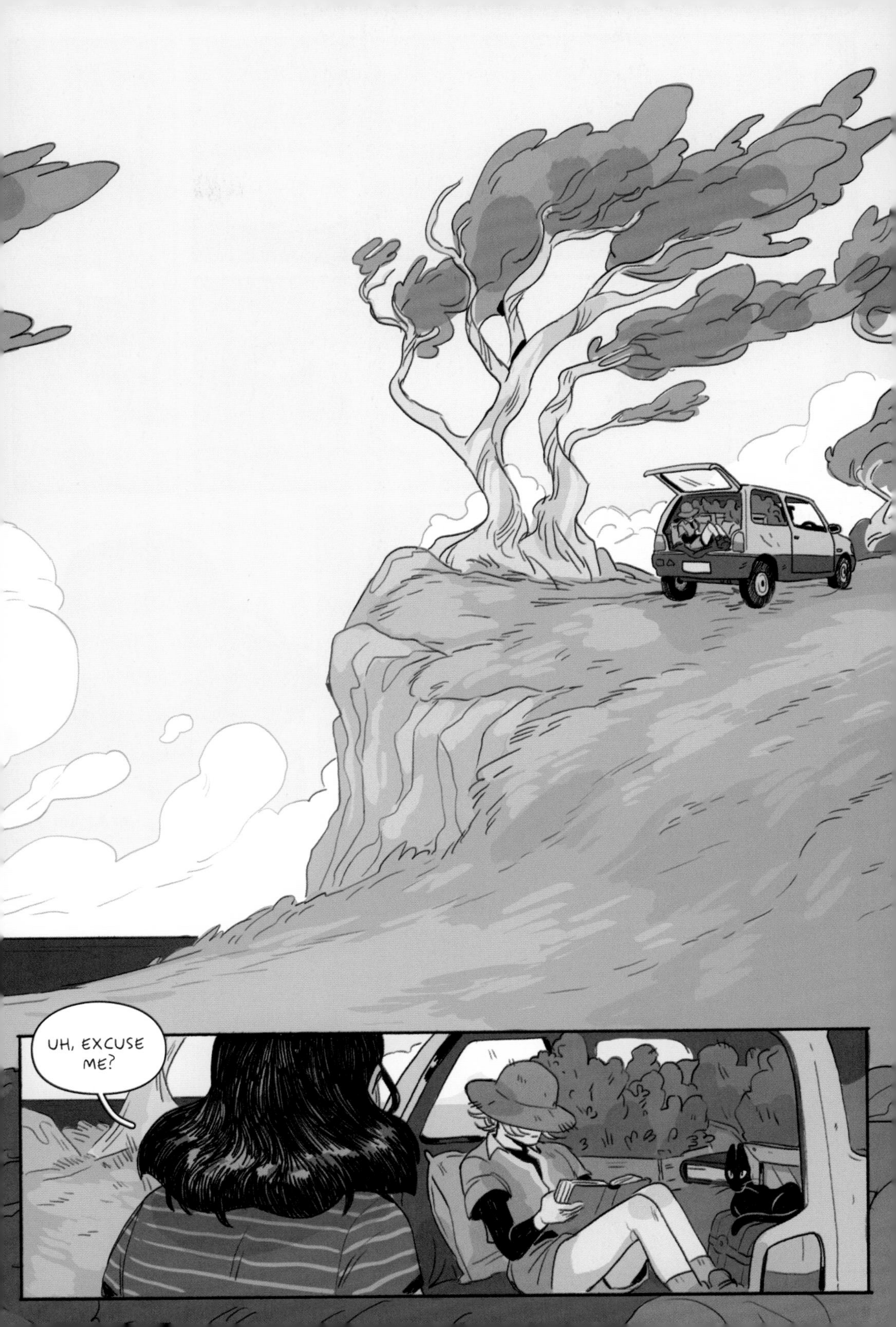
UH, EXCUSE ME?

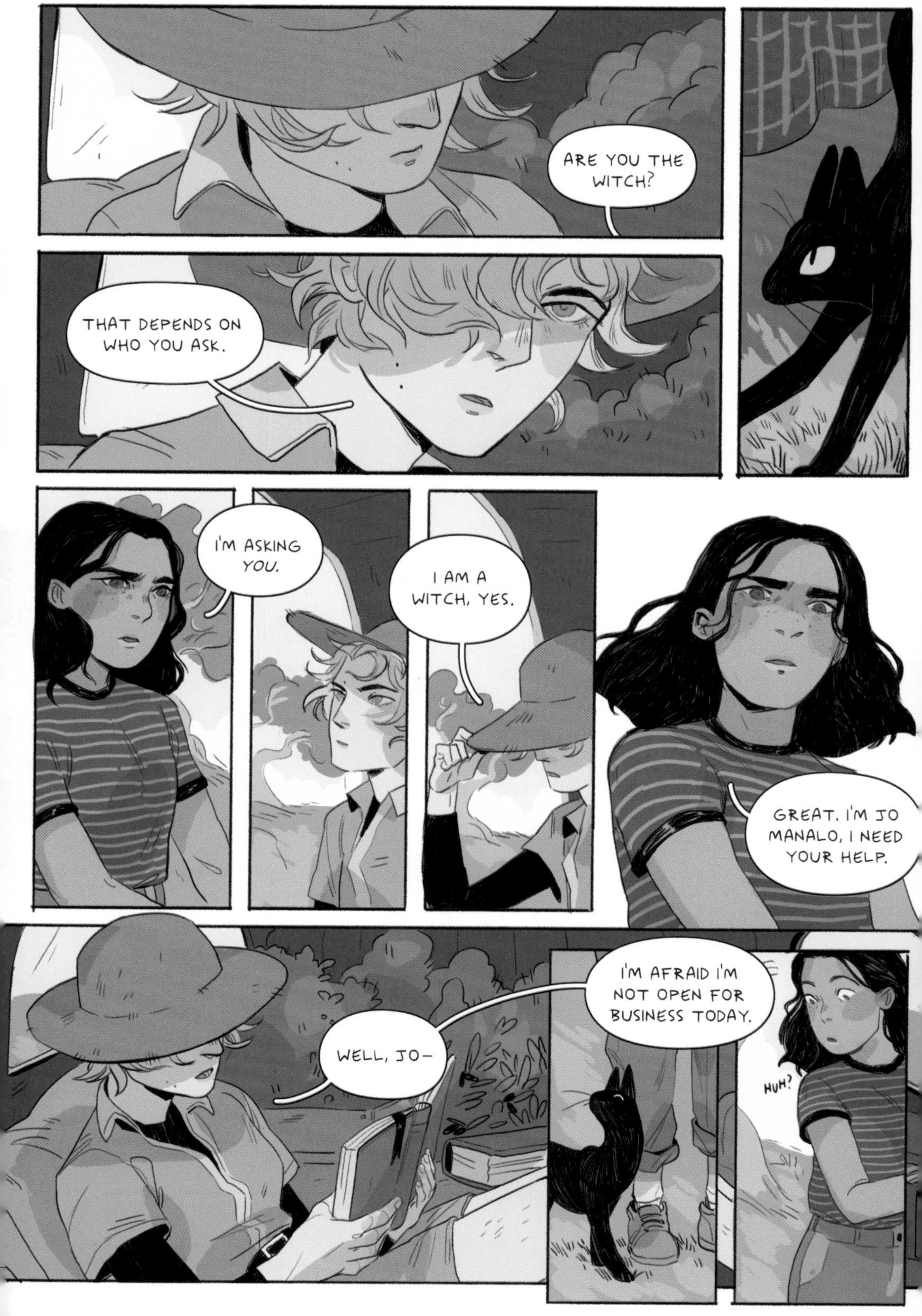
ARE YOU THE WITCH?
THAT DEPENDS ON WHO YOU ASK.
I'M ASKING *YOU.*
I AM A WITCH, YES.
GREAT. I'M JO MANALO, I NEED YOUR HELP.
WELL, JO–
I'M AFRAID I'M NOT OPEN FOR BUSINESS TODAY.
HUH?

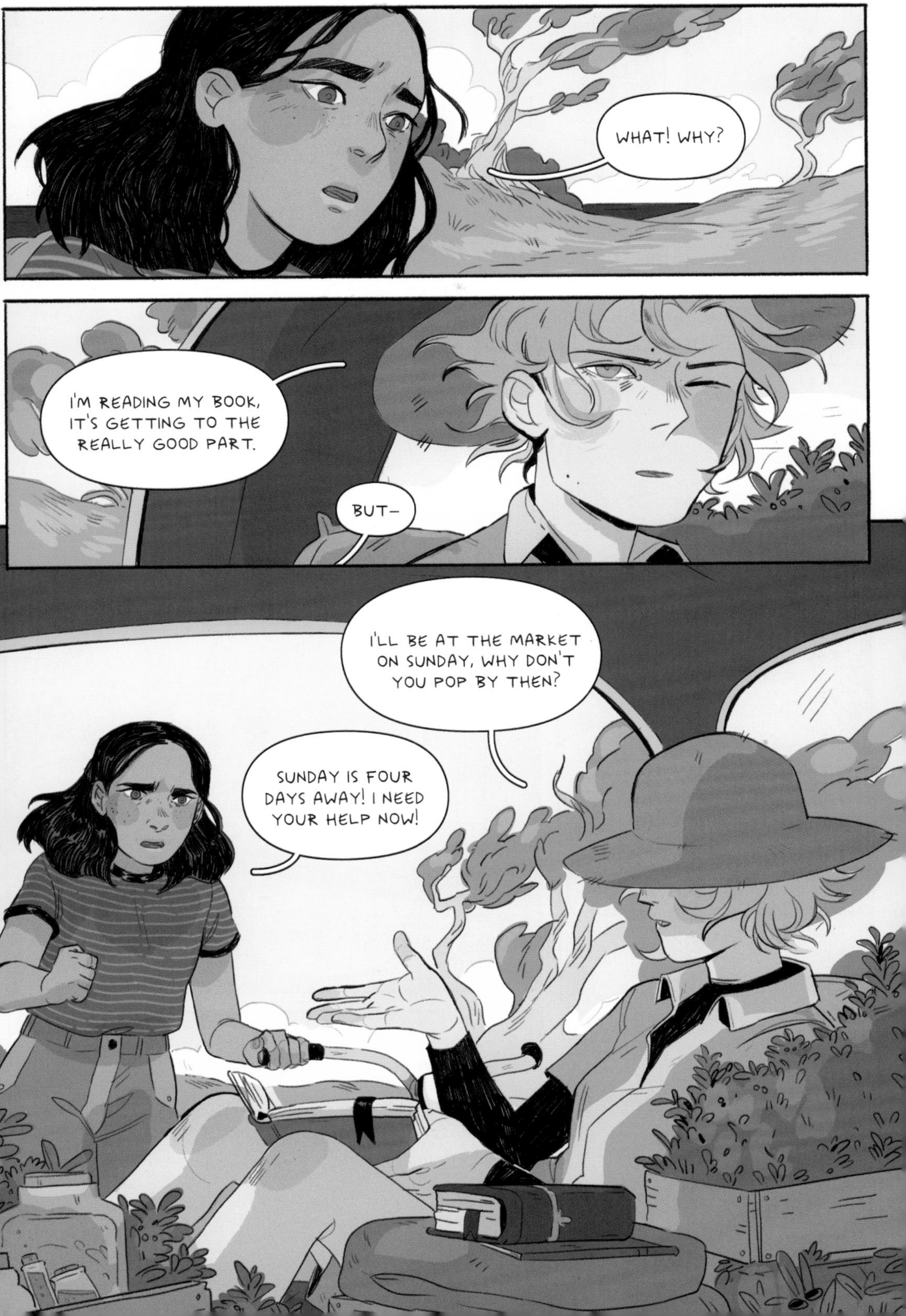
WHAT! WHY?
I'M READING MY BOOK, IT'S GETTING TO THE REALLY GOOD PART.
BUT–
I'LL BE AT THE MARKET ON SUNDAY, WHY DON'T YOU POP BY THEN?
SUNDAY IS FOUR DAYS AWAY! I NEED YOUR HELP NOW!

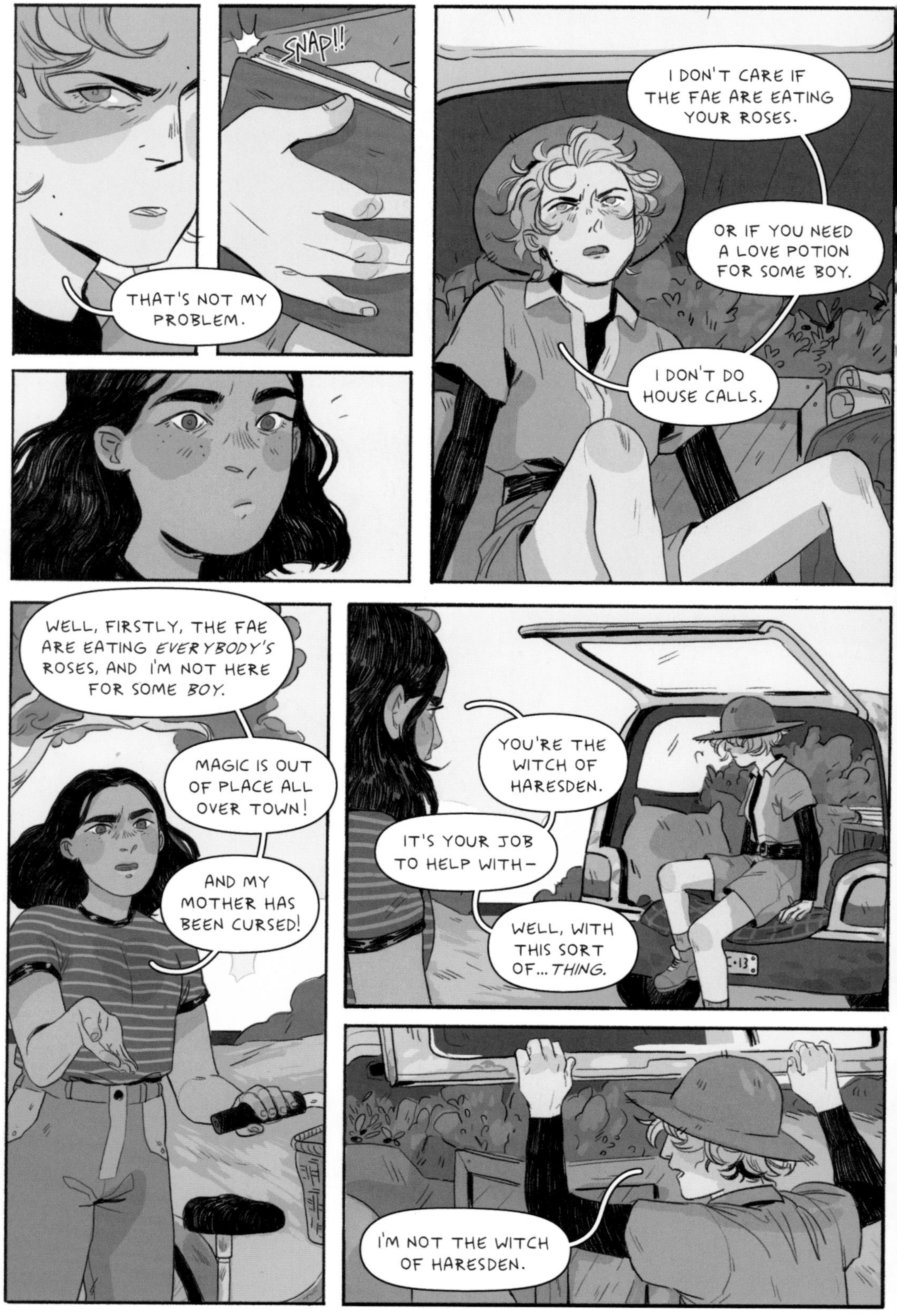
SNAP!!
THAT'S NOT MY PROBLEM.
I DON'T CARE IF THE FAE ARE EATING YOUR ROSES.
OR IF YOU NEED A LOVE POTION FOR SOME BOY.
I DON'T DO HOUSE CALLS.
WELL, FIRSTLY, THE FAE ARE EATING *EVERYBODY'S* ROSES, AND I'M NOT HERE FOR SOME *BOY*.
MAGIC IS OUT OF PLACE ALL OVER TOWN!
AND MY MOTHER HAS BEEN CURSED!
YOU'RE THE WITCH OF HARESDEN.
IT'S YOUR JOB TO HELP WITH—
WELL, WITH THIS SORT OF... *THING*.
I'M NOT THE WITCH OF HARESDEN.

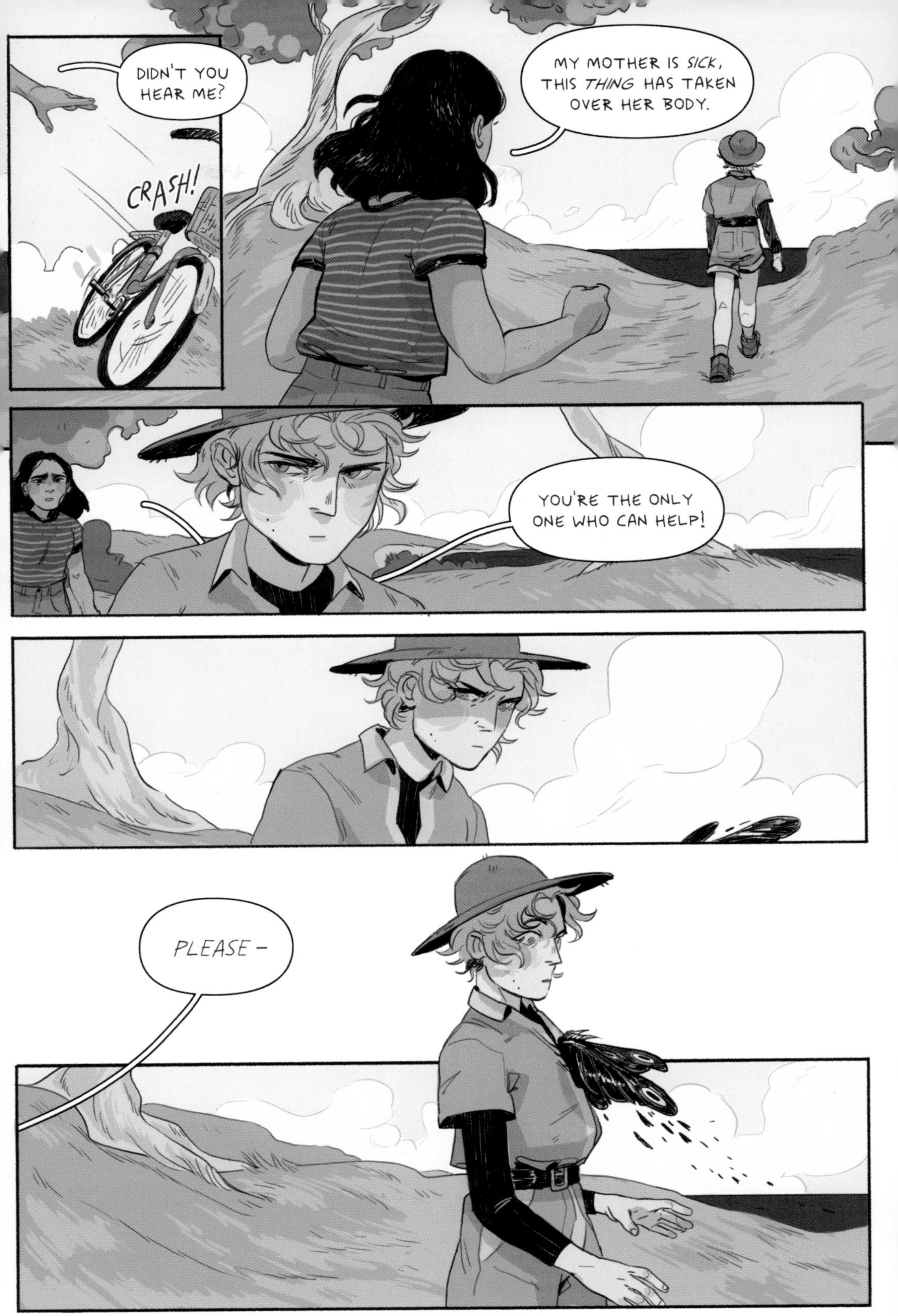
DIDN'T YOU HEAR ME?
CRASH!
MY MOTHER IS SICK, THIS THING HAS TAKEN OVER HER BODY.
YOU'RE THE ONLY ONE WHO CAN HELP!
PLEASE -

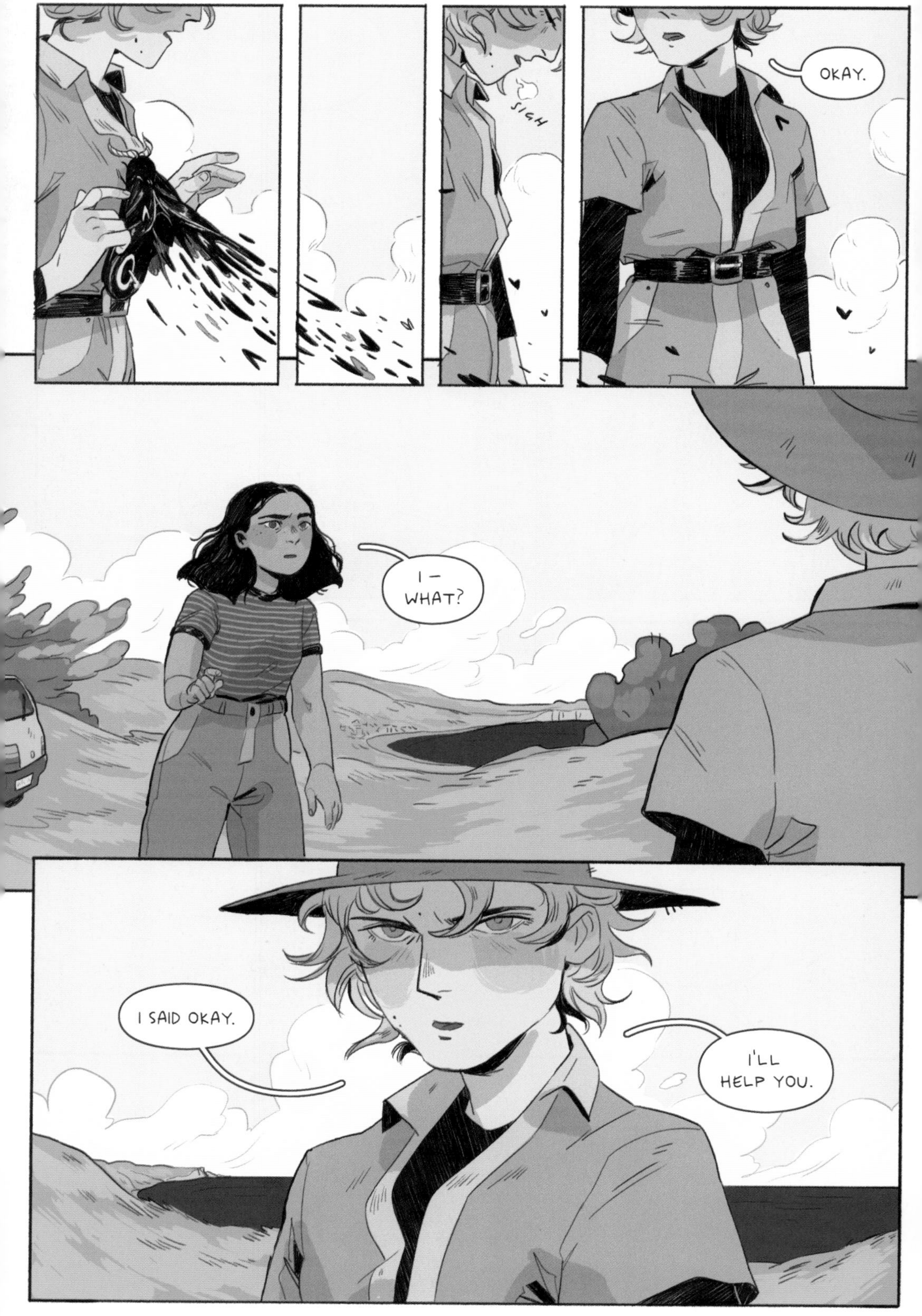
SIGH
OKAY.
I—
WHAT?
I SAID OKAY.
I'LL
HELP YOU.

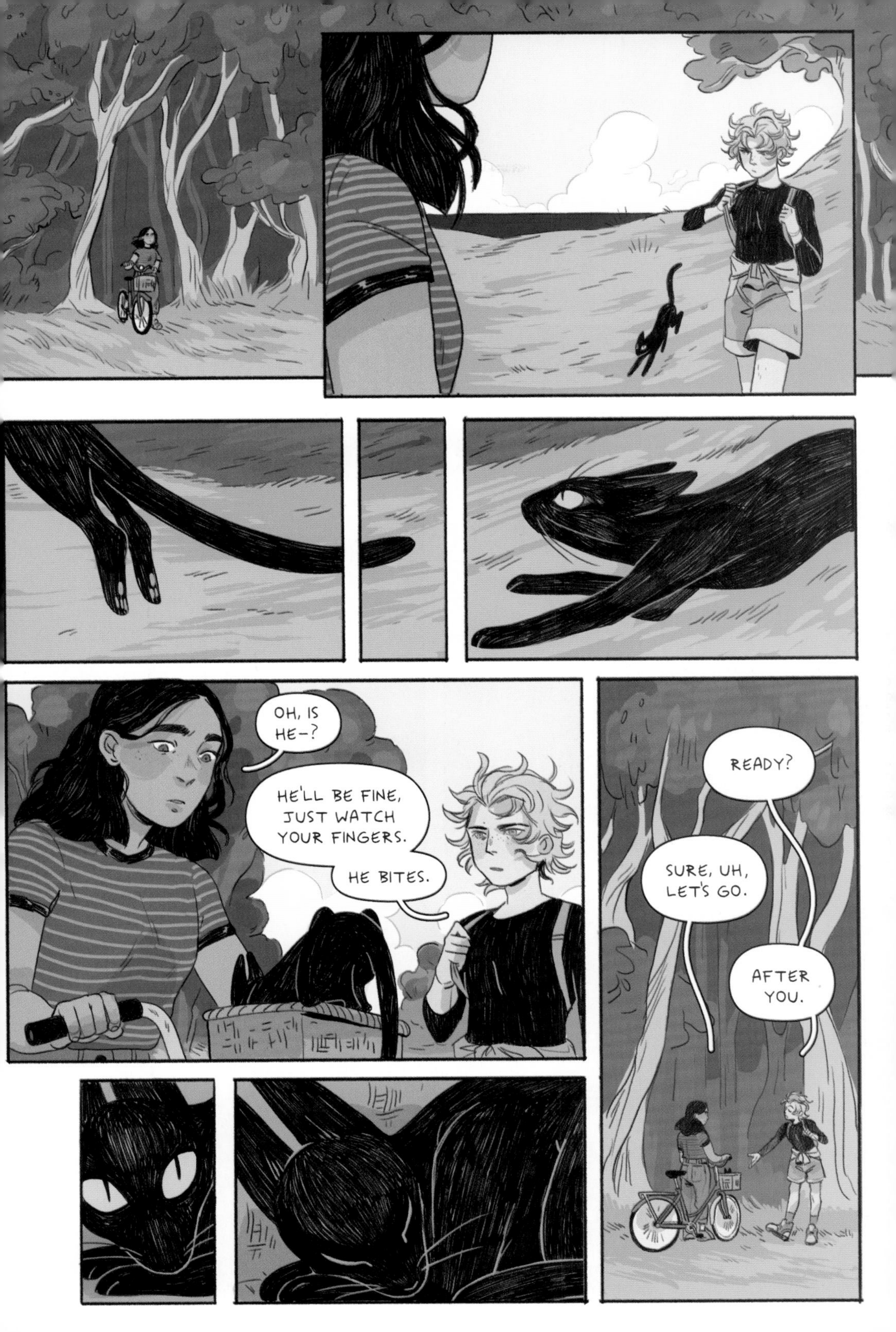
OH, IS HE–?
HE'LL BE FINE, JUST WATCH YOUR FINGERS.
HE BITES.
READY?
SURE, UH, LET'S GO.
AFTER YOU.

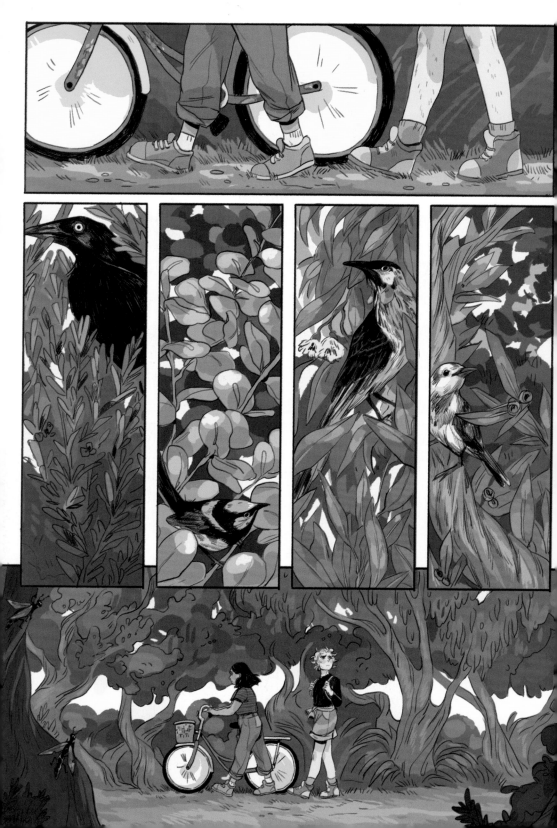

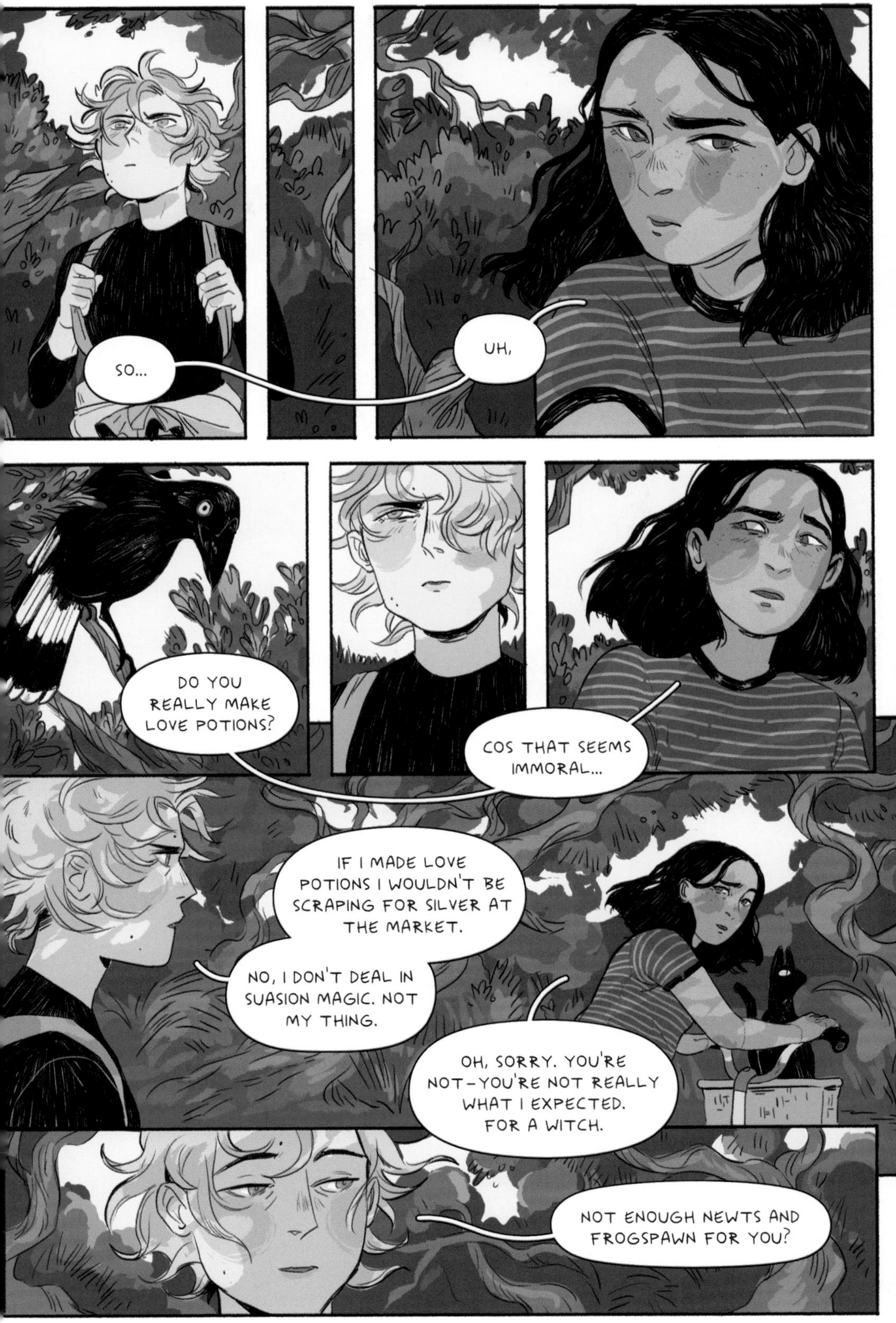
SO...
UH,
DO YOU REALLY MAKE LOVE POTIONS?
COS THAT SEEMS IMMORAL...
IF I MADE LOVE POTIONS I WOULDN'T BE SCRAPING FOR SILVER AT THE MARKET.
NO, I DON'T DEAL IN SUASION MAGIC. NOT MY THING.
OH, SORRY. YOU'RE NOT—YOU'RE NOT REALLY WHAT I EXPECTED. FOR A WITCH.
NOT ENOUGH NEWTS AND FROGSPAWN FOR YOU?

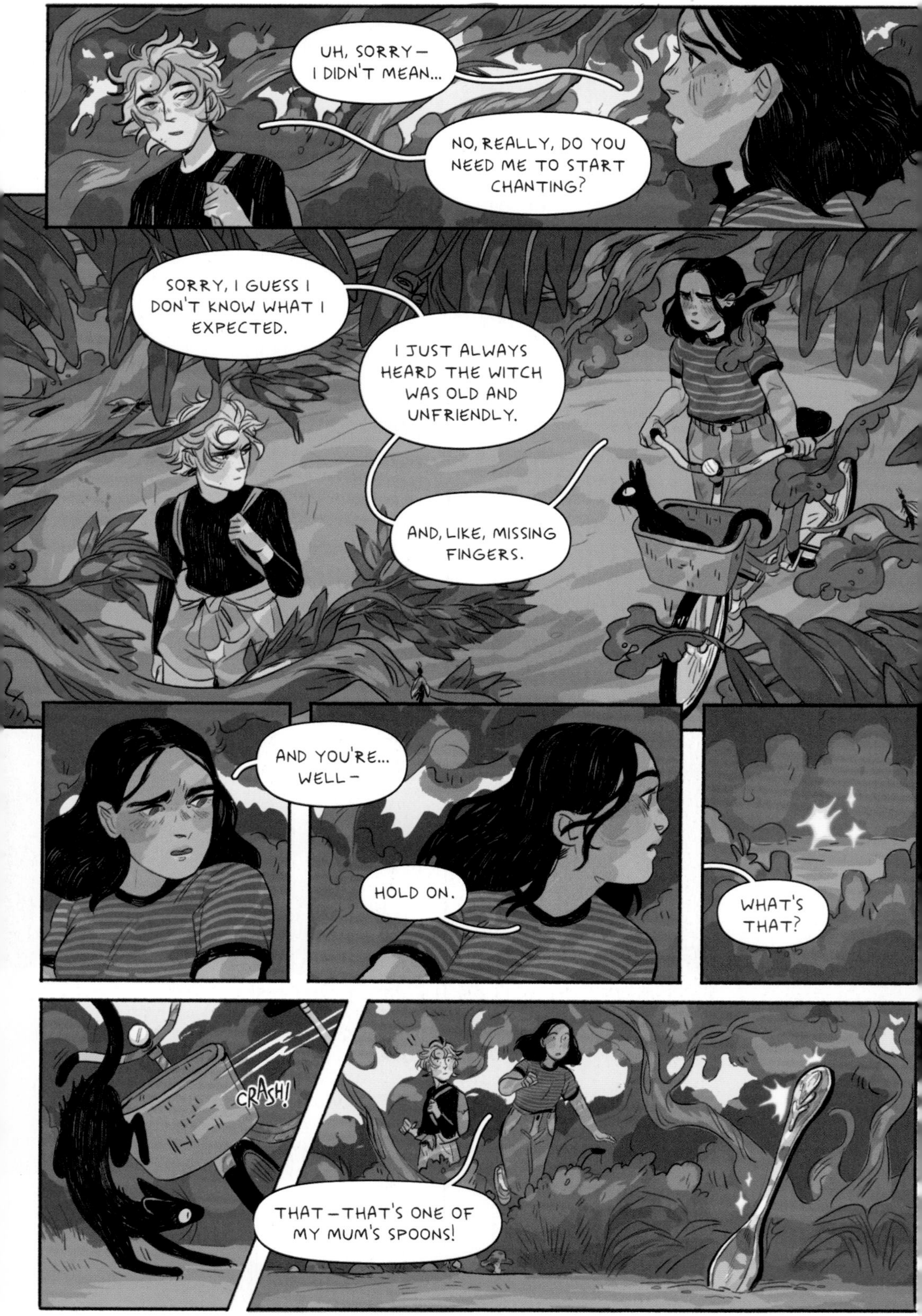
UH, SORRY— I DIDN'T MEAN...
NO, REALLY, DO YOU NEED ME TO START CHANTING?
SORRY, I GUESS I DON'T KNOW WHAT I EXPECTED.
I JUST ALWAYS HEARD THE WITCH WAS OLD AND UNFRIENDLY.
AND, LIKE, MISSING FINGERS.
AND YOU'RE... WELL—
HOLD ON.
WHAT'S THAT?
CRASH!
THAT—THAT'S ONE OF MY MUM'S SPOONS!

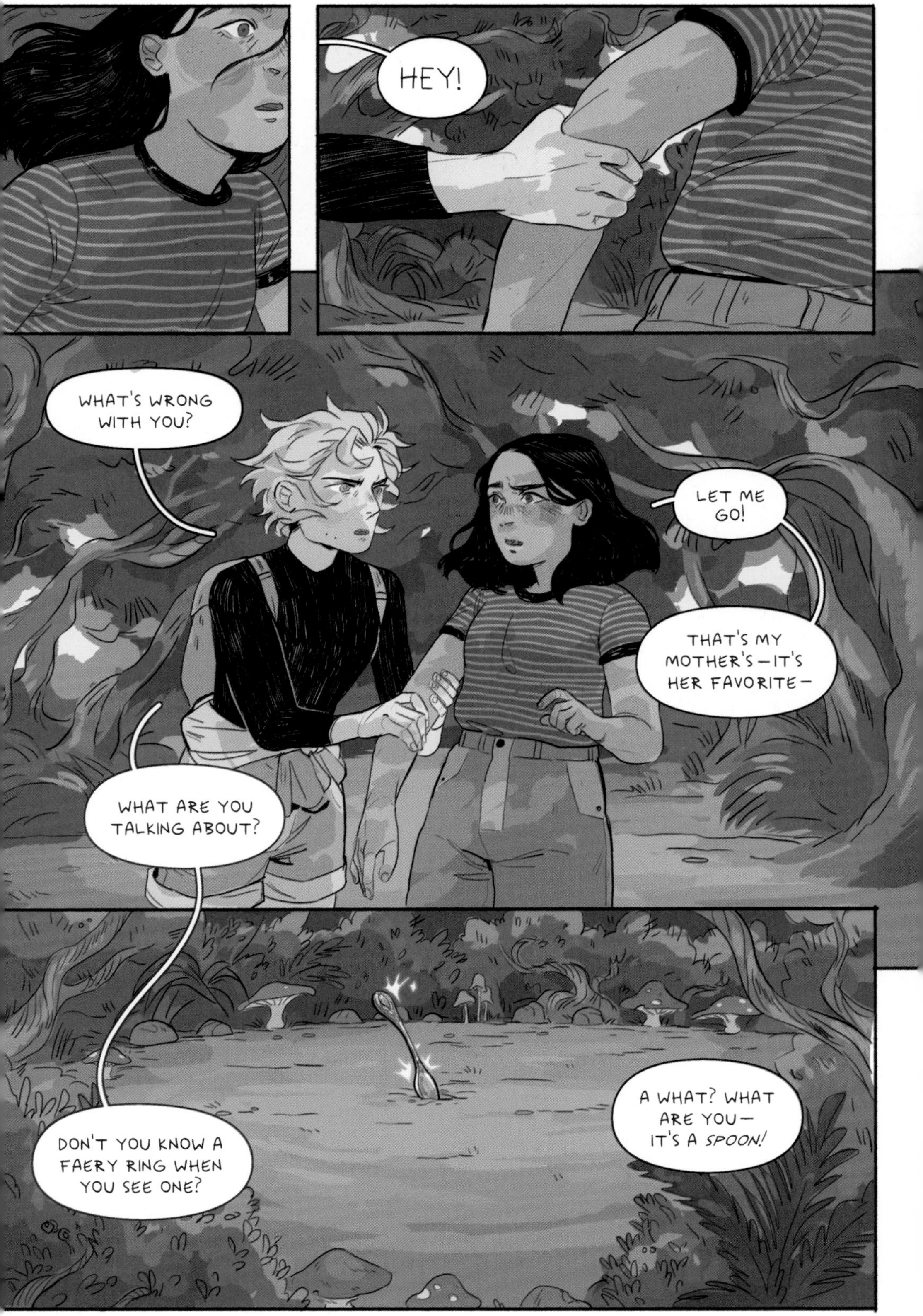
HEY!
WHAT'S WRONG WITH YOU?
LET ME GO!
THAT'S MY MOTHER'S—IT'S HER FAVORITE—
WHAT ARE YOU TALKING ABOUT?
DON'T YOU KNOW A FAERY RING WHEN YOU SEE ONE?
A WHAT? WHAT ARE YOU— IT'S A *SPOON!*

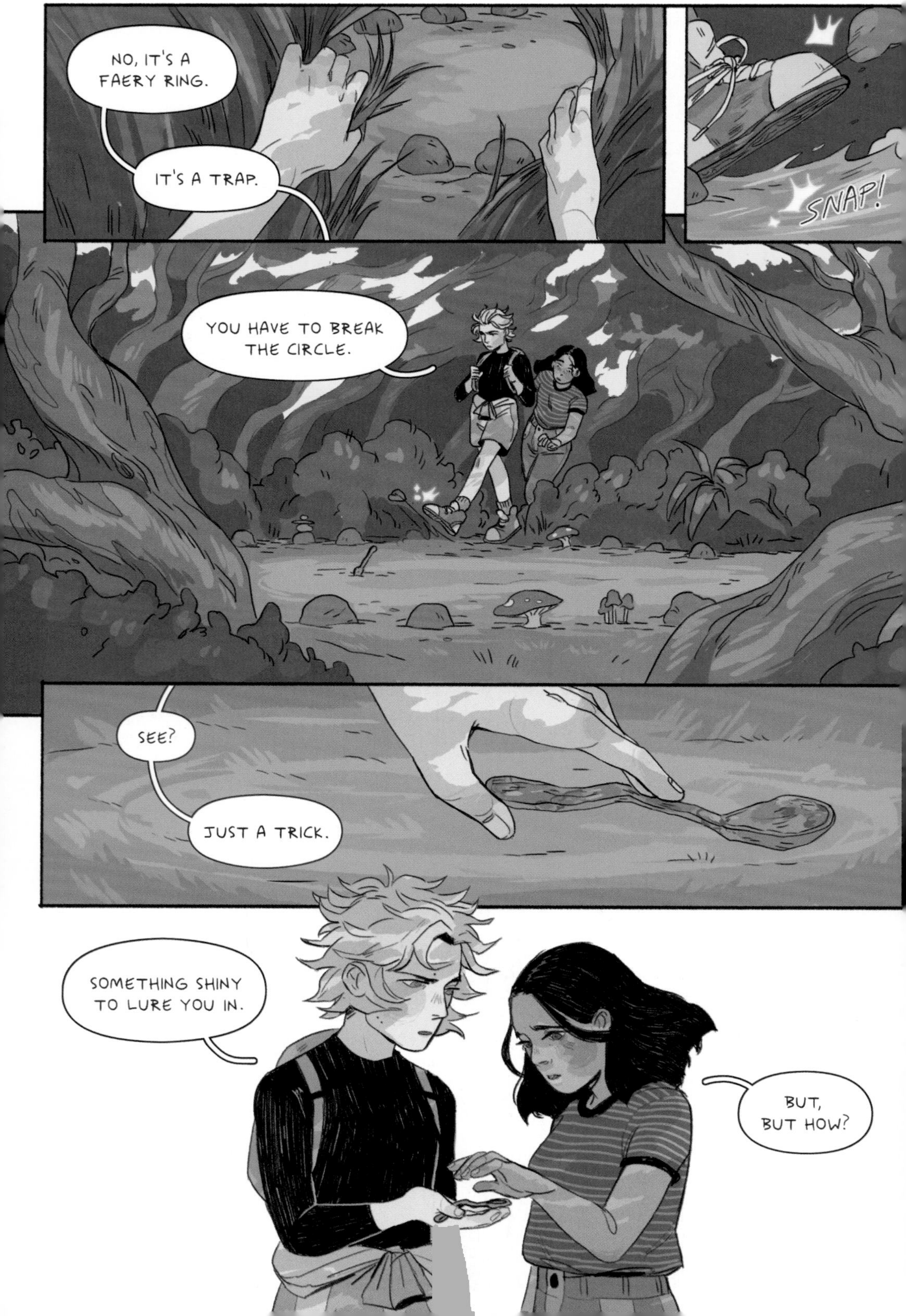
NO, IT'S A FAERY RING.
IT'S A TRAP.
SNAP!
YOU HAVE TO BREAK THE CIRCLE.
SEE?
JUST A TRICK.
SOMETHING SHINY TO LURE YOU IN.
BUT, BUT HOW?

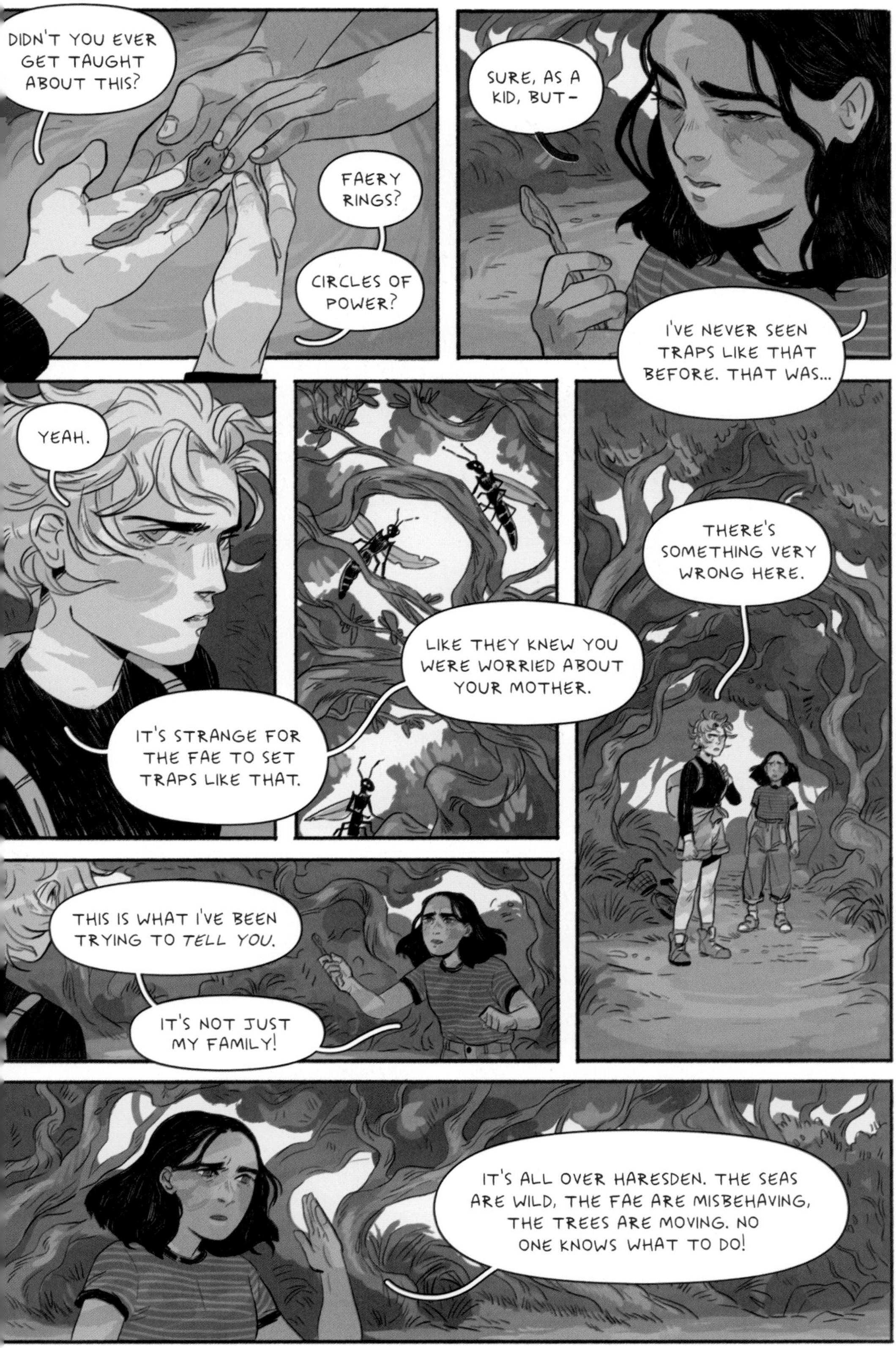
DIDN'T YOU EVER GET TAUGHT ABOUT THIS?
FAERY RINGS?
CIRCLES OF POWER?
SURE, AS A KID, BUT-
I'VE NEVER SEEN TRAPS LIKE THAT BEFORE. THAT WAS...
YEAH.
IT'S STRANGE FOR THE FAE TO SET TRAPS LIKE THAT.
LIKE THEY KNEW YOU WERE WORRIED ABOUT YOUR MOTHER.
THERE'S SOMETHING VERY WRONG HERE.
THIS IS WHAT I'VE BEEN TRYING TO *TELL YOU.*
IT'S NOT JUST MY FAMILY!
IT'S ALL OVER HARESDEN. THE SEAS ARE WILD, THE FAE ARE MISBEHAVING, THE TREES ARE MOVING. NO ONE KNOWS WHAT TO DO!

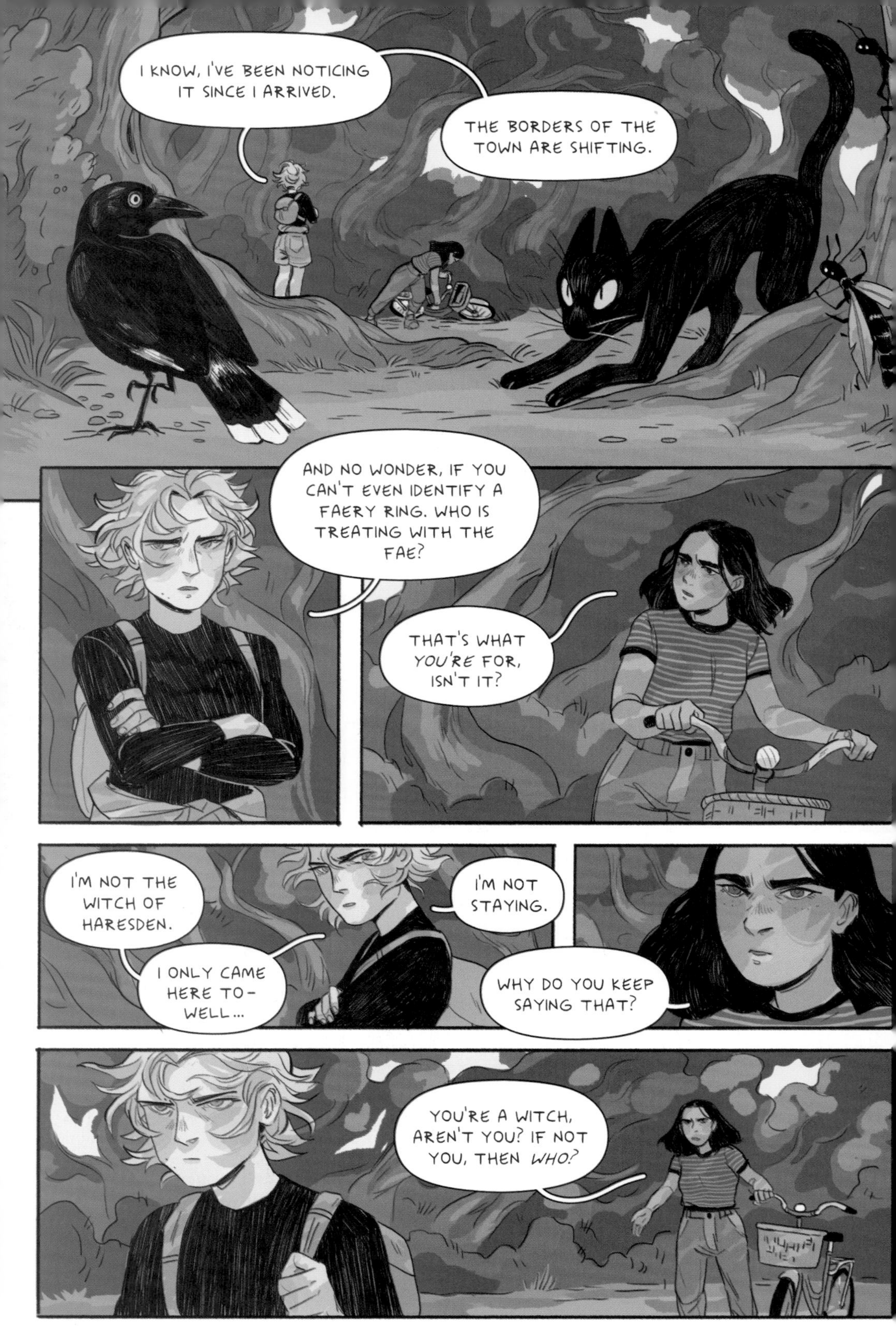

I KNOW, I'VE BEEN NOTICING IT SINCE I ARRIVED.
THE BORDERS OF THE TOWN ARE SHIFTING.
AND NO WONDER, IF YOU CAN'T EVEN IDENTIFY A FAERY RING. WHO IS TREATING WITH THE FAE?
THAT'S WHAT *YOU'RE* FOR, ISN'T IT?
I'M NOT THE WITCH OF HARESDEN.
I ONLY CAME HERE TO- WELL...
I'M NOT STAYING.
WHY DO YOU KEEP SAYING THAT?
YOU'RE A WITCH, AREN'T YOU? IF NOT YOU, THEN *WHO?*

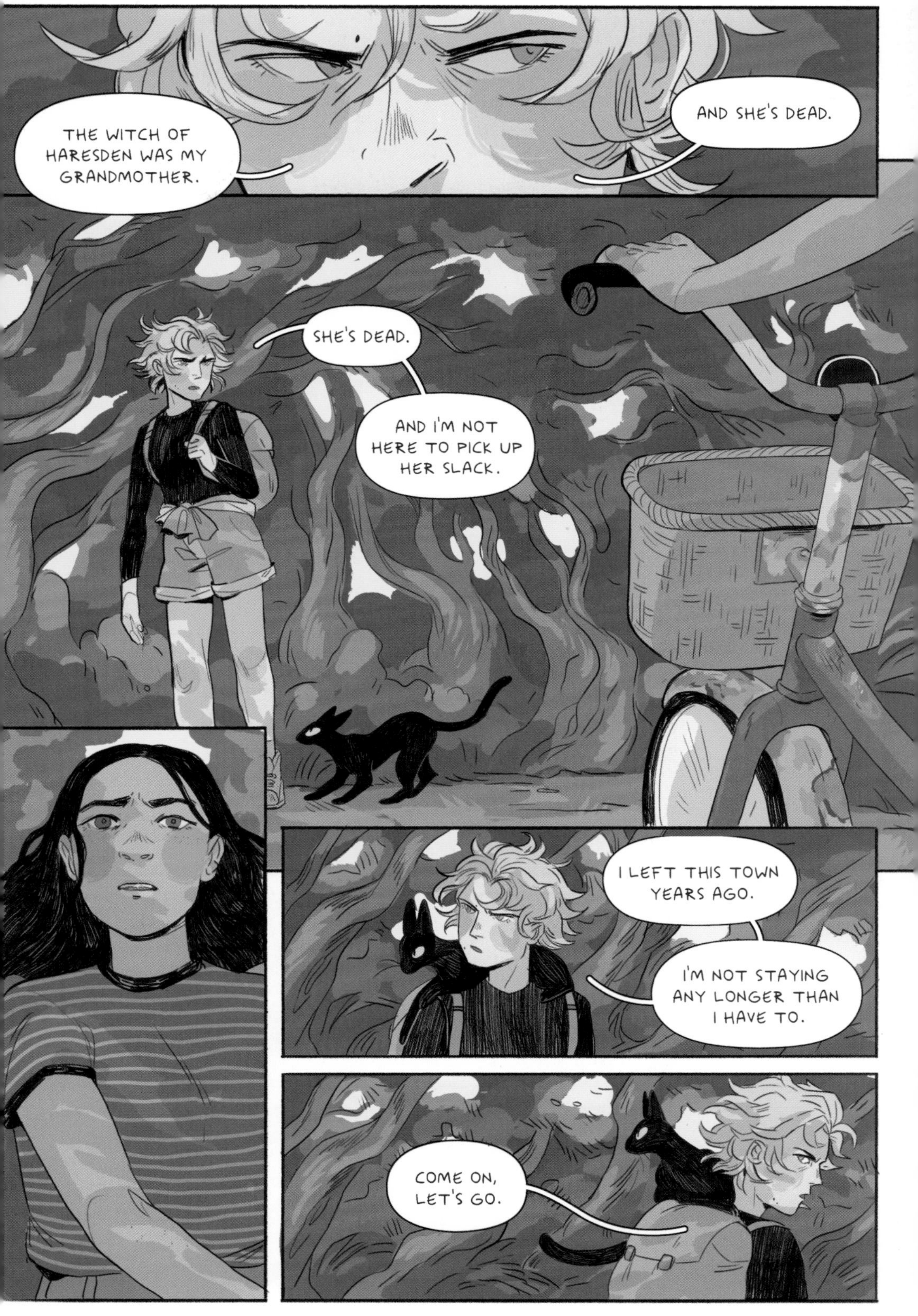
THE WITCH OF HARESDEN WAS MY GRANDMOTHER.
AND SHE'S DEAD.
SHE'S DEAD.
AND I'M NOT HERE TO PICK UP HER SLACK.
I LEFT THIS TOWN YEARS AGO.
I'M NOT STAYING ANY LONGER THAN I HAVE TO.
COME ON, LET'S GO.

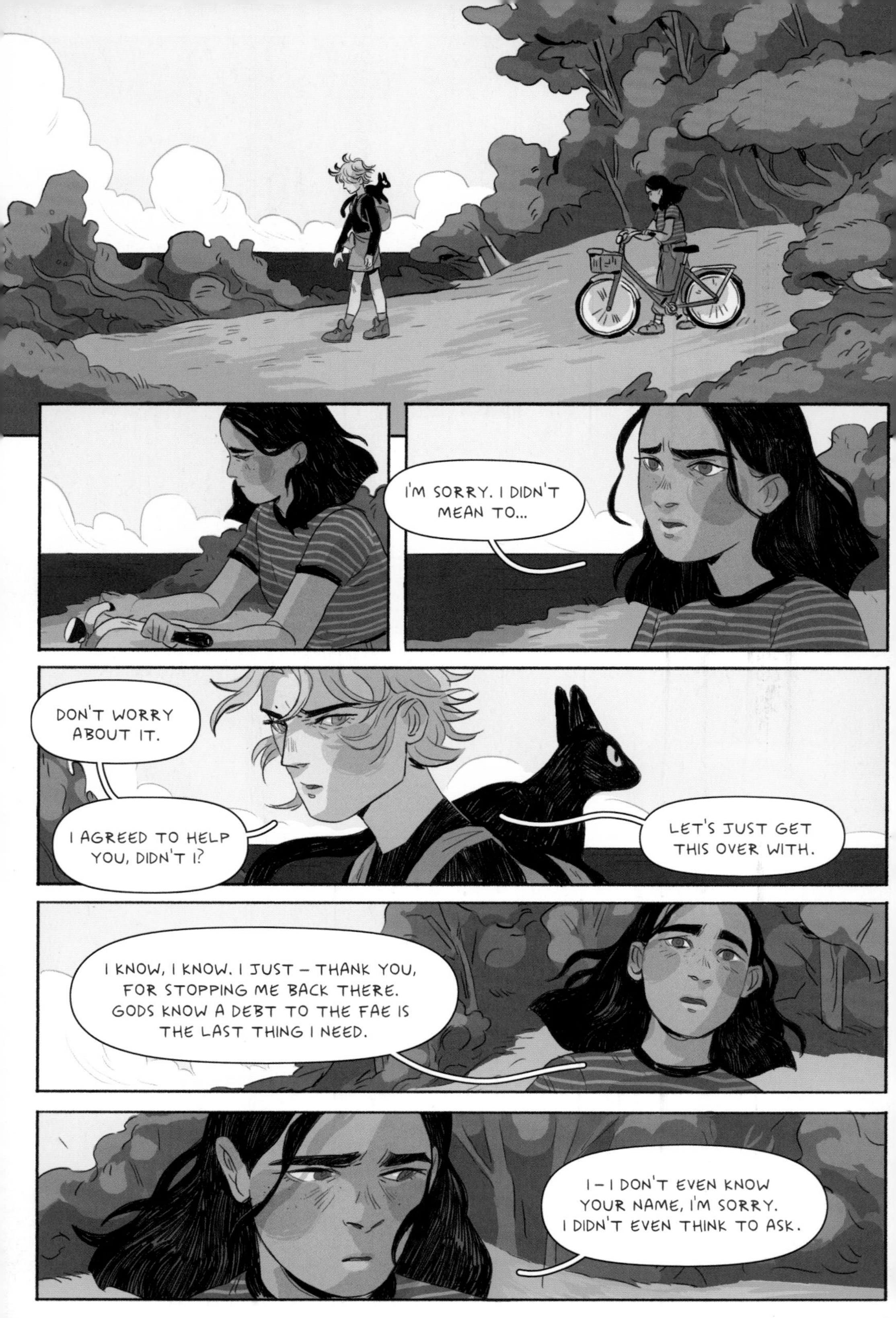
I'M SORRY. I DIDN'T MEAN TO...
DON'T WORRY ABOUT IT.
I AGREED TO HELP YOU, DIDN'T I?
LET'S JUST GET THIS OVER WITH.
I KNOW, I KNOW. I JUST – THANK YOU, FOR STOPPING ME BACK THERE. GODS KNOW A DEBT TO THE FAE IS THE LAST THING I NEED.
I – I DON'T EVEN KNOW YOUR NAME, I'M SORRY. I DIDN'T EVEN THINK TO ASK.

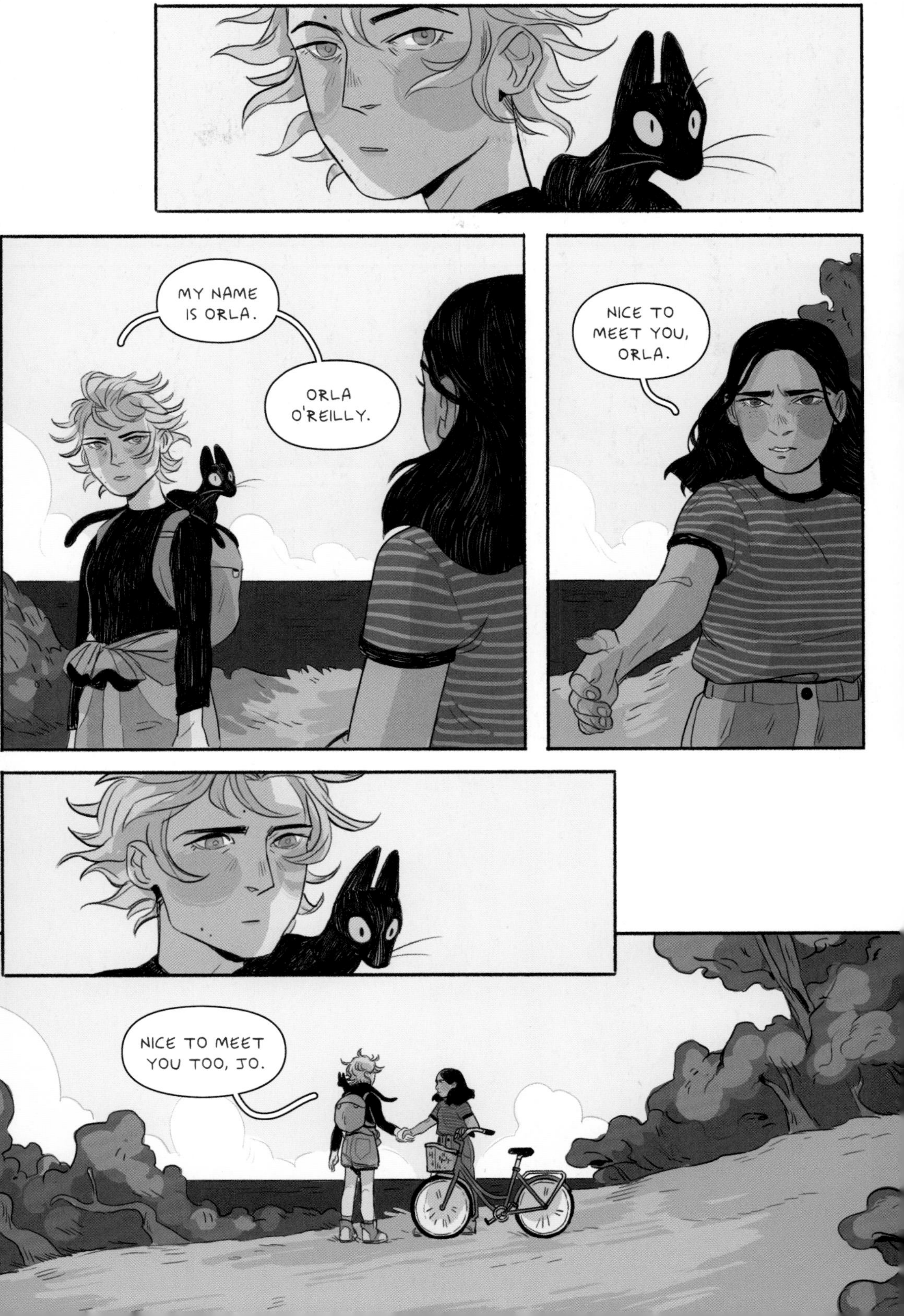
MY NAME IS ORLA.
ORLA O'REILLY.
NICE TO MEET YOU, ORLA.
NICE TO MEET YOU TOO, JO.

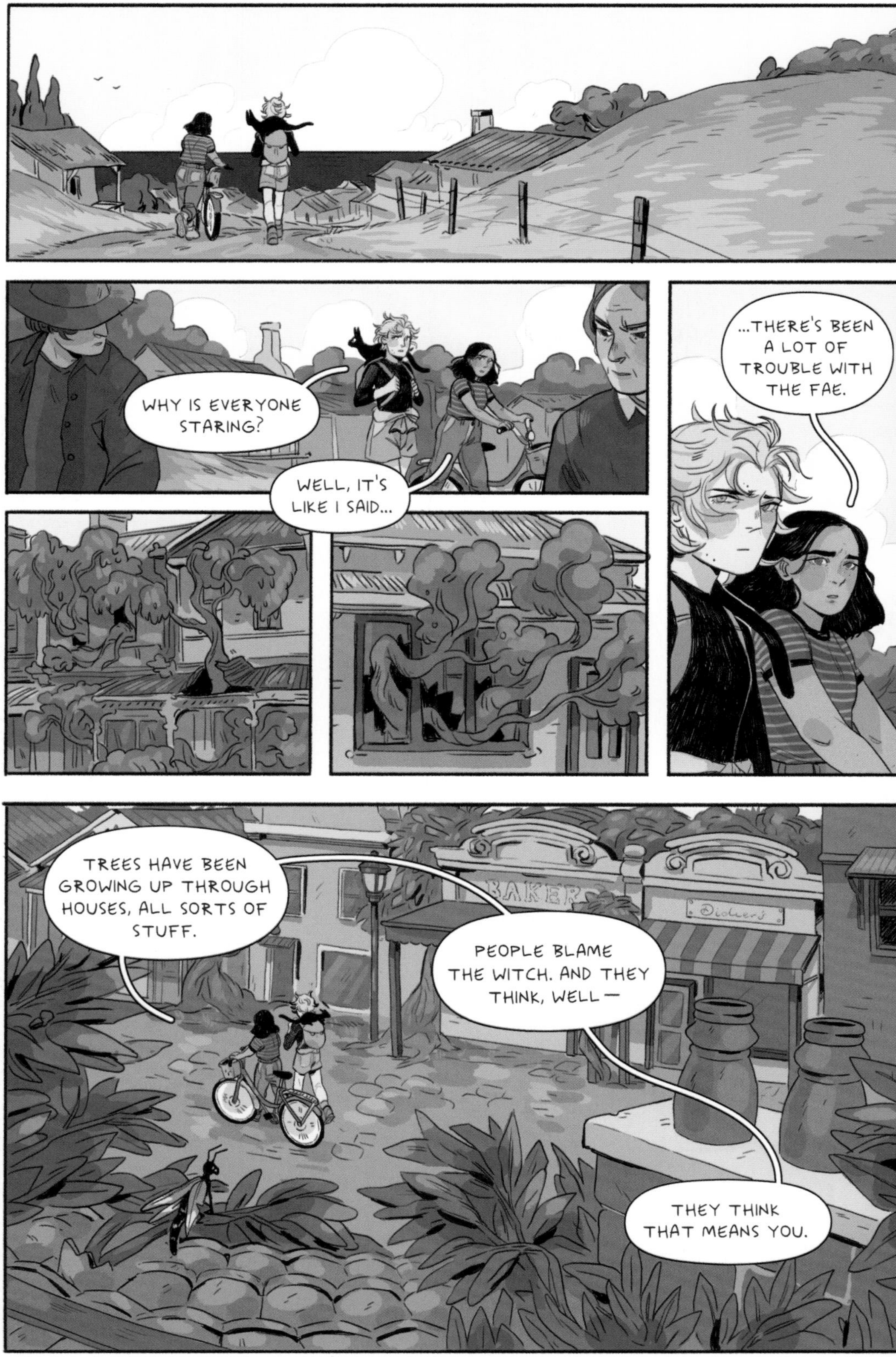
WHY IS EVERYONE STARING?
WELL, IT'S LIKE I SAID...
...THERE'S BEEN A LOT OF TROUBLE WITH THE FAE.
TREES HAVE BEEN GROWING UP THROUGH HOUSES, ALL SORTS OF STUFF.
BAKER
PEOPLE BLAME THE WITCH. AND THEY THINK, WELL—
THEY THINK THAT MEANS YOU.

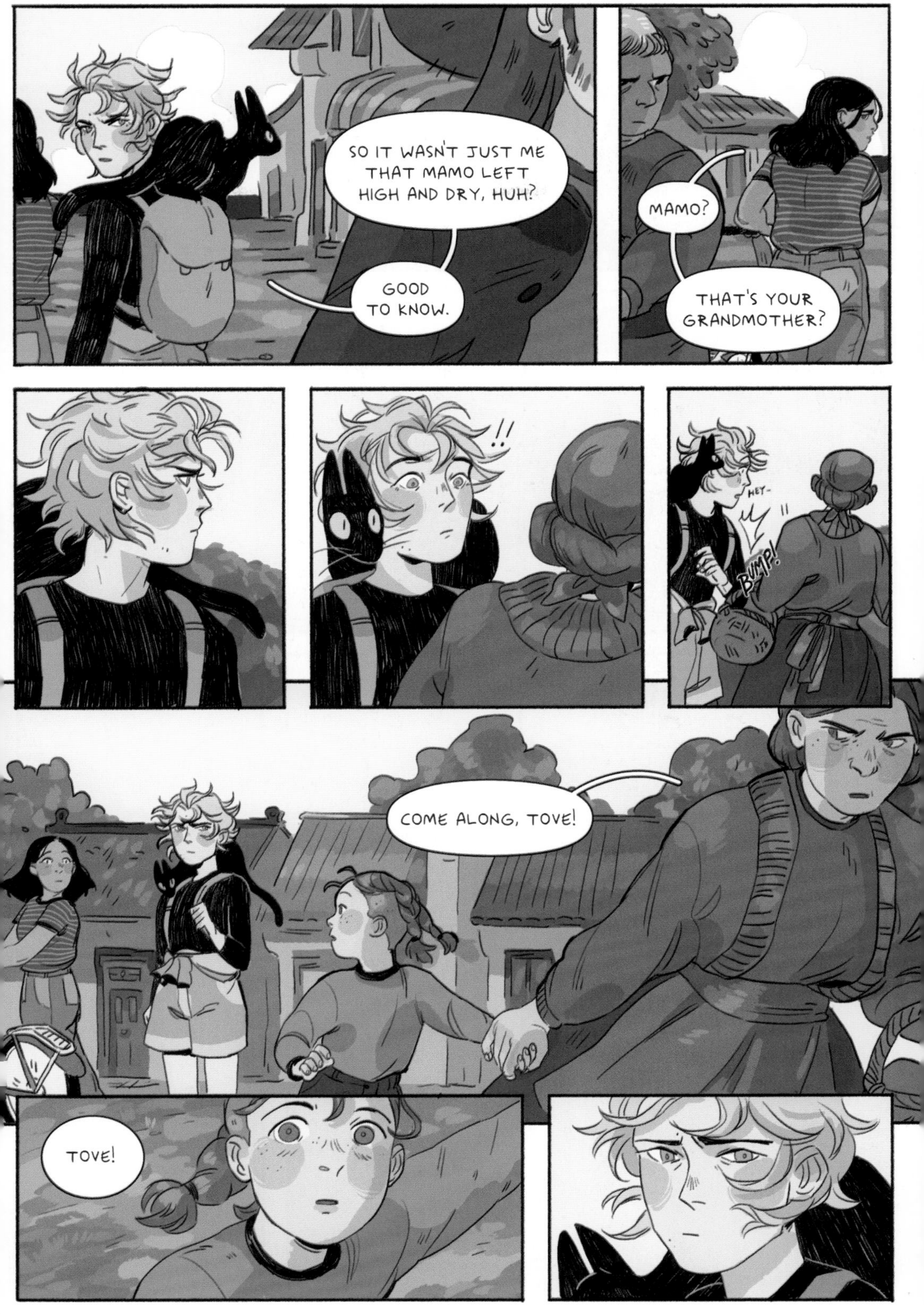
SO IT WASN'T JUST ME THAT MAMO LEFT HIGH AND DRY, HUH?
GOOD TO KNOW.
MAMO?
THAT'S YOUR GRANDMOTHER?
!!
HEY–
BUMP!
COME ALONG, TOVE!
TOVE!

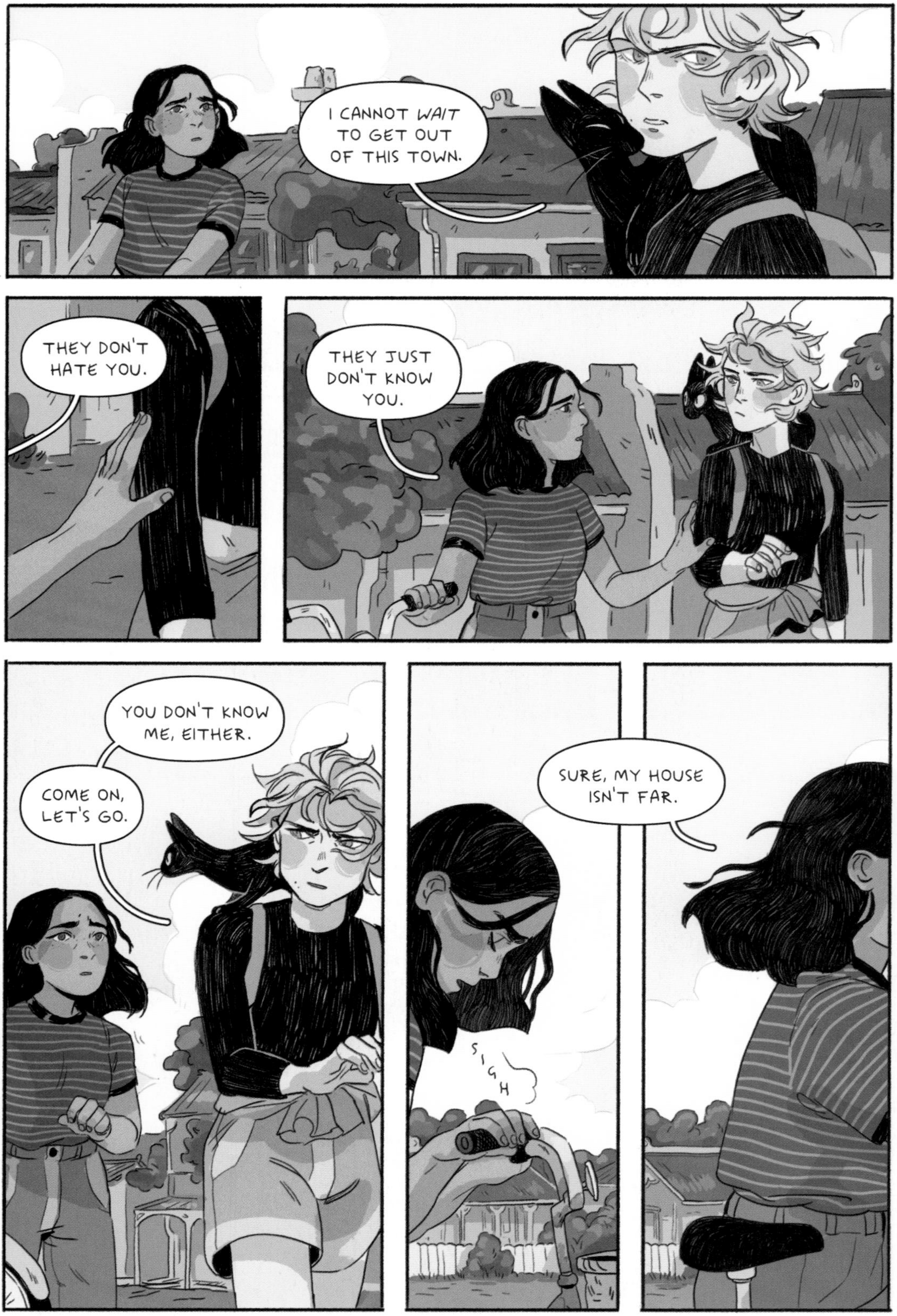
I CANNOT *WAIT* TO GET OUT OF THIS TOWN.
THEY DON'T HATE YOU.
THEY JUST DON'T KNOW YOU.
YOU DON'T KNOW ME, EITHER.
COME ON, LET'S GO.
SIGH
SURE, MY HOUSE ISN'T FAR.

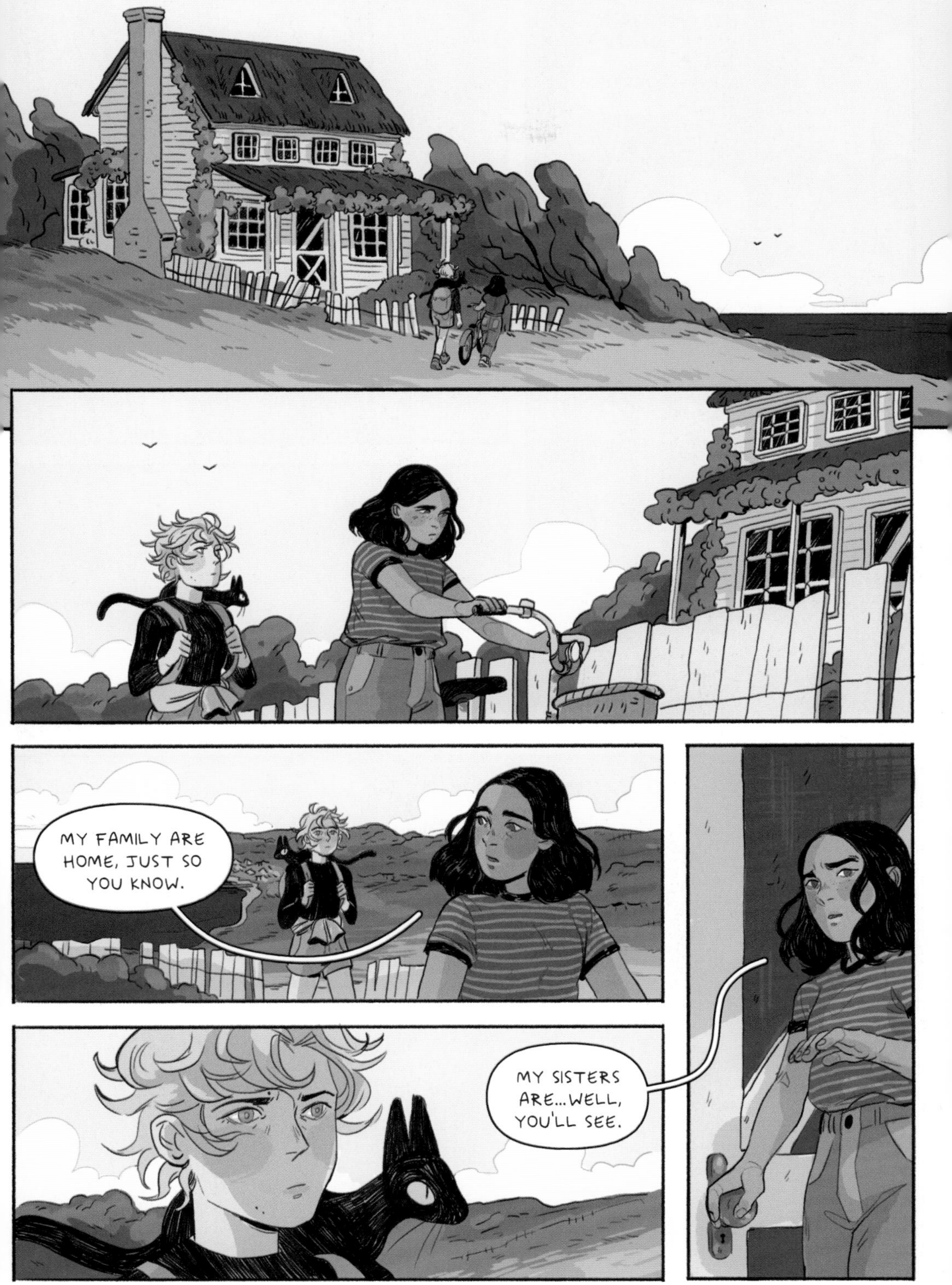
MY FAMILY ARE HOME, JUST SO YOU KNOW.
MY SISTERS ARE...WELL, YOU'LL SEE.

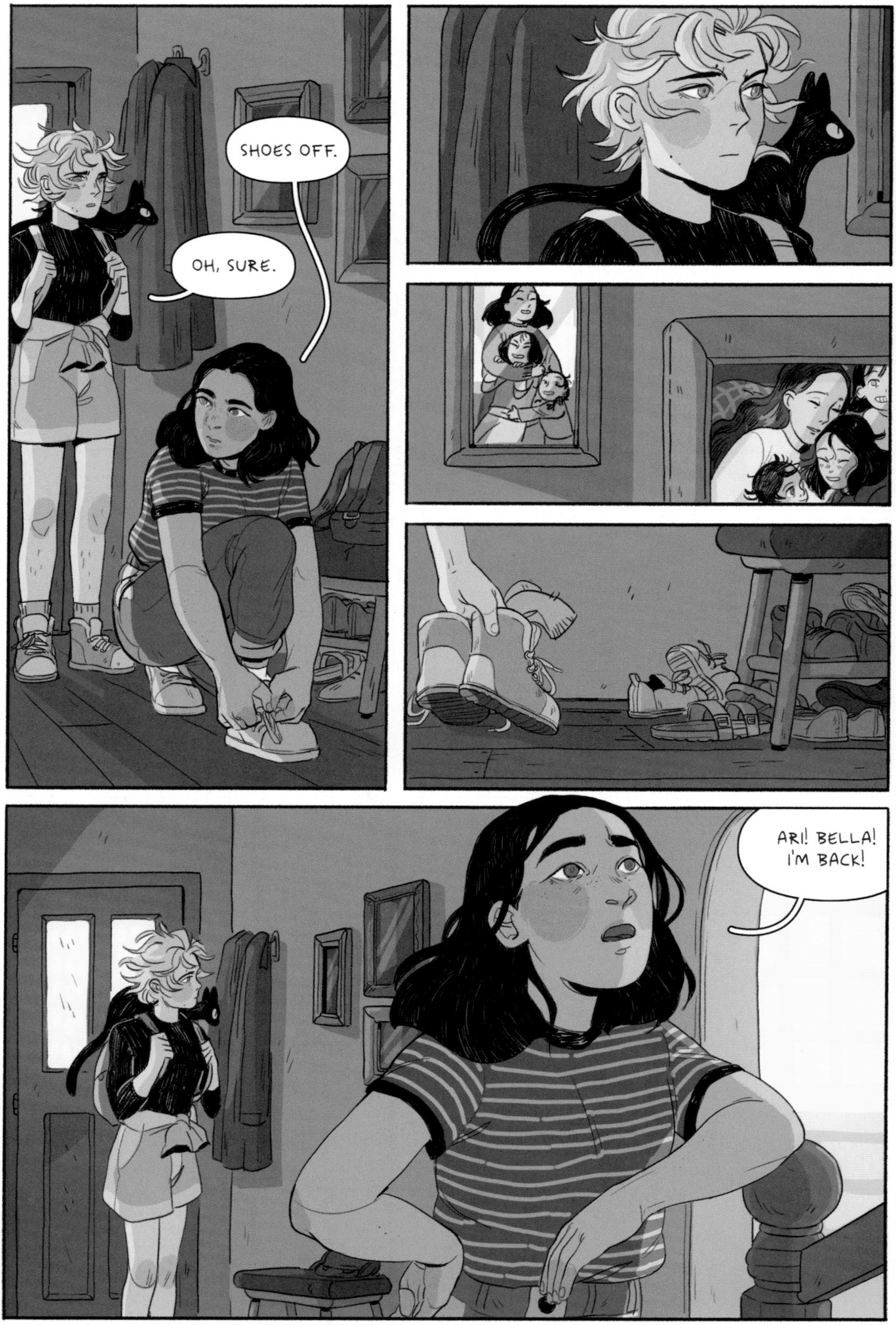
SHOES OFF.
OH, SURE.
ARI! BELLA! I'M BACK!

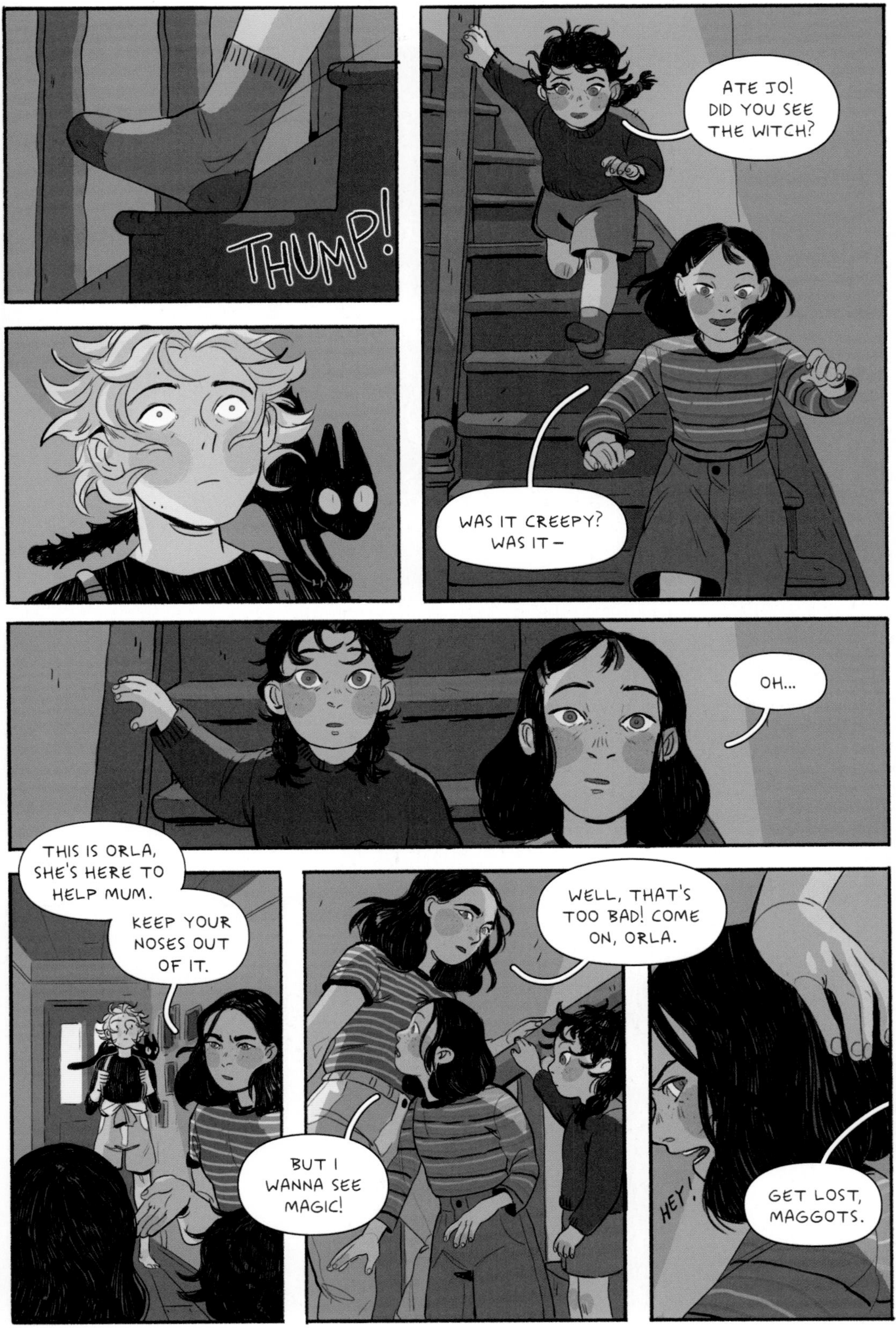
THUMP!
ATE JO! DID YOU SEE THE WITCH?
WAS IT CREEPY? WAS IT—
OH...
THIS IS ORLA, SHE'S HERE TO HELP MUM.
KEEP YOUR NOSES OUT OF IT.
WELL, THAT'S TOO BAD! COME ON, ORLA.
BUT I WANNA SEE MAGIC!
HEY!
GET LOST, MAGGOTS.

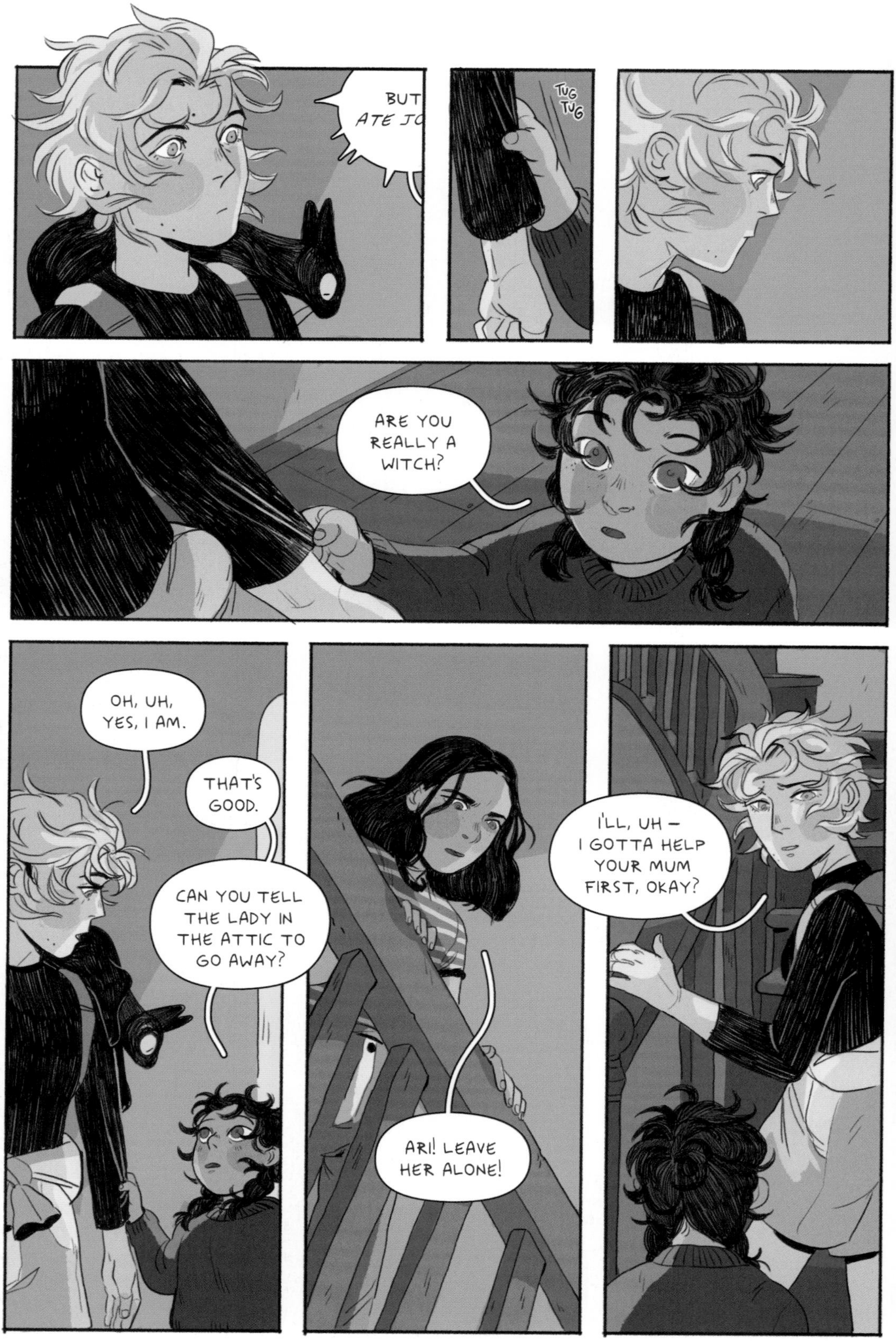
BUT
ATE JO
TUG
TUG
ARE YOU REALLY A WITCH?
OH, UH, YES, I AM.
THAT'S GOOD.
CAN YOU TELL THE LADY IN THE ATTIC TO GO AWAY?
ARI! LEAVE HER ALONE!
I'LL, UH — I GOTTA HELP YOUR MUM FIRST, OKAY?

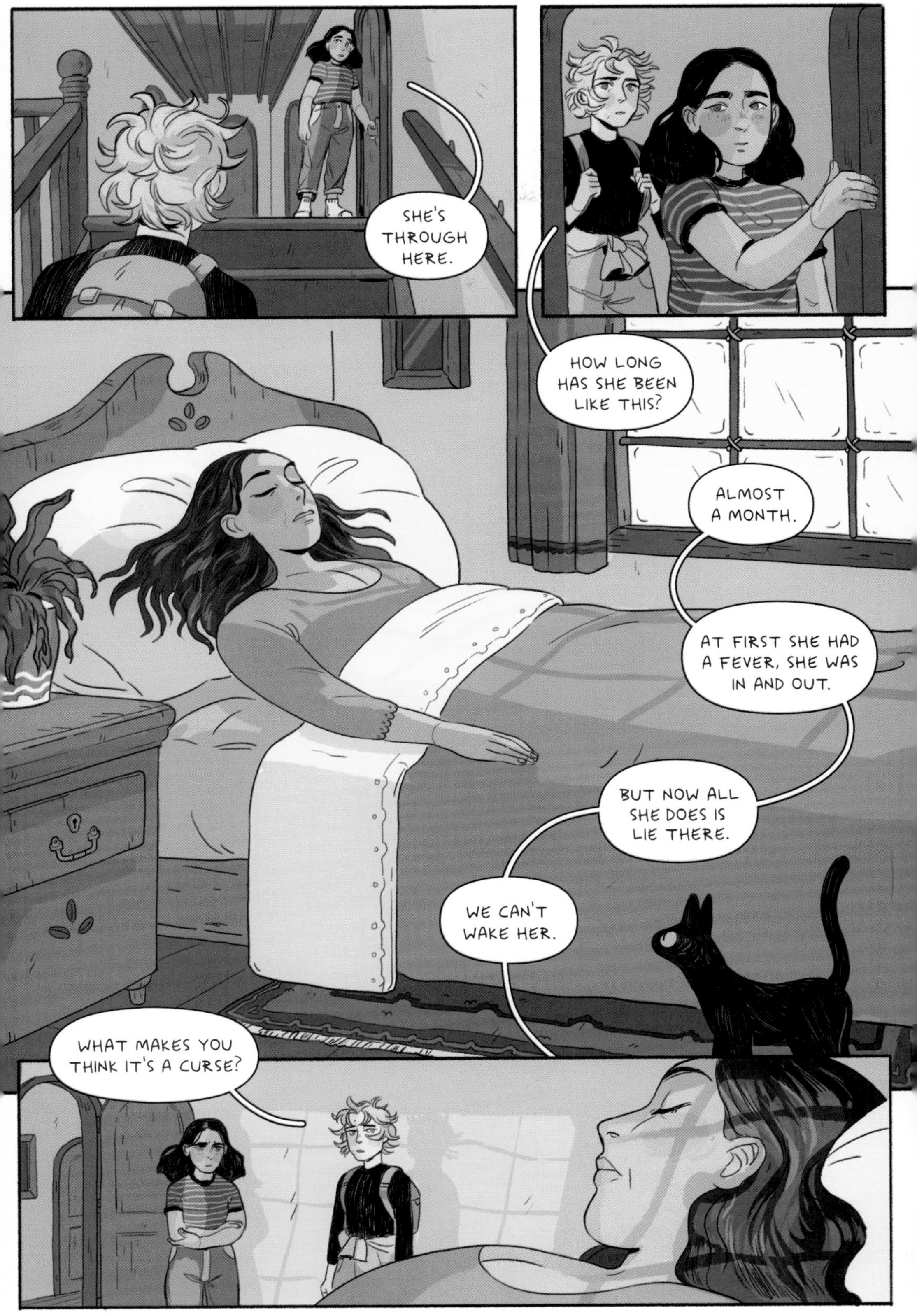
SHE'S THROUGH HERE.
HOW LONG HAS SHE BEEN LIKE THIS?
ALMOST A MONTH.
AT FIRST SHE HAD A FEVER, SHE WAS IN AND OUT.
BUT NOW ALL SHE DOES IS LIE THERE.
WE CAN'T WAKE HER.
WHAT MAKES YOU THINK IT'S A CURSE?

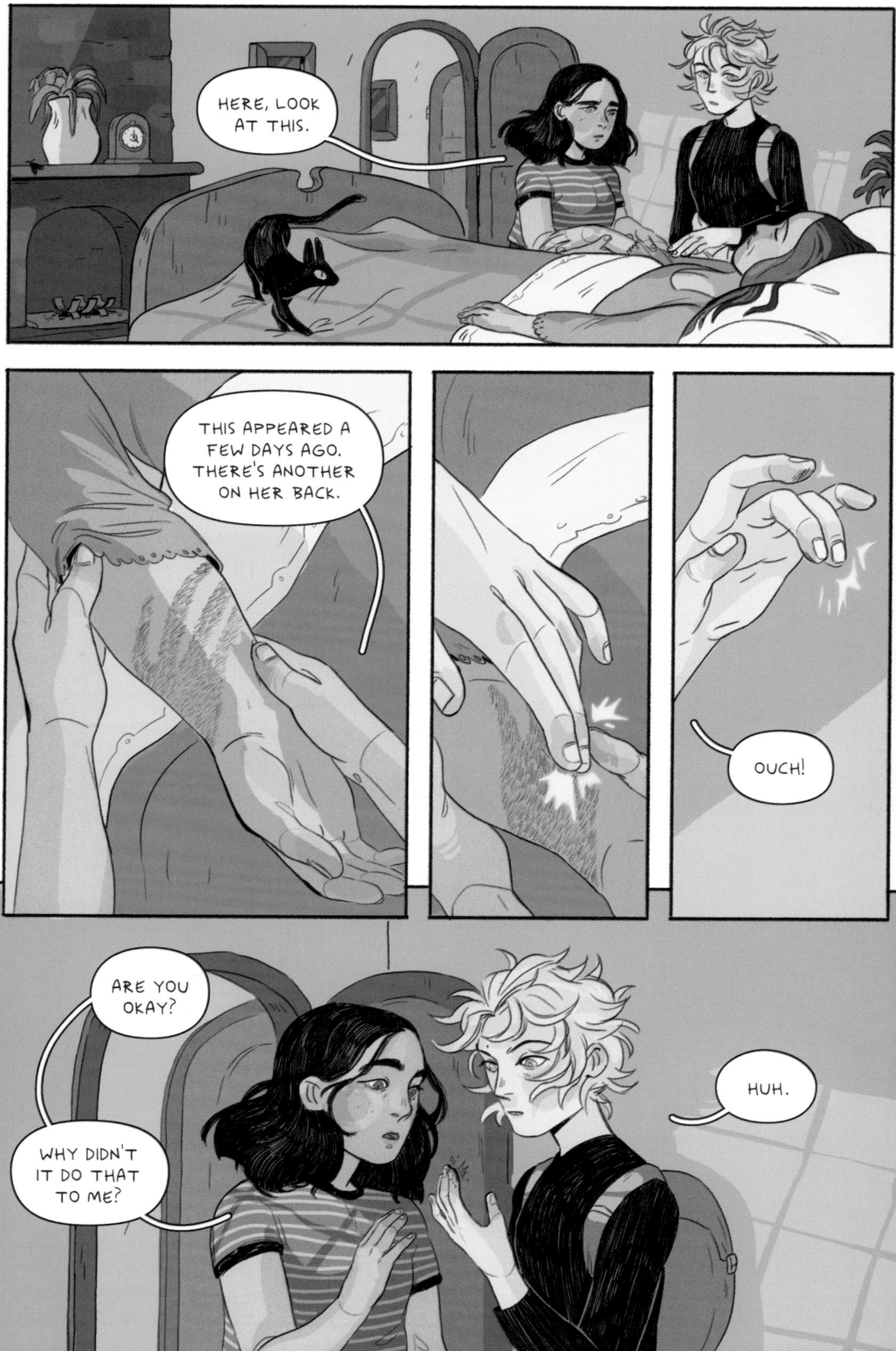
HERE, LOOK AT THIS.
THIS APPEARED A FEW DAYS AGO. THERE'S ANOTHER ON HER BACK.
OUCH!
ARE YOU OKAY?
WHY DIDN'T IT DO THAT TO ME?
HUH.

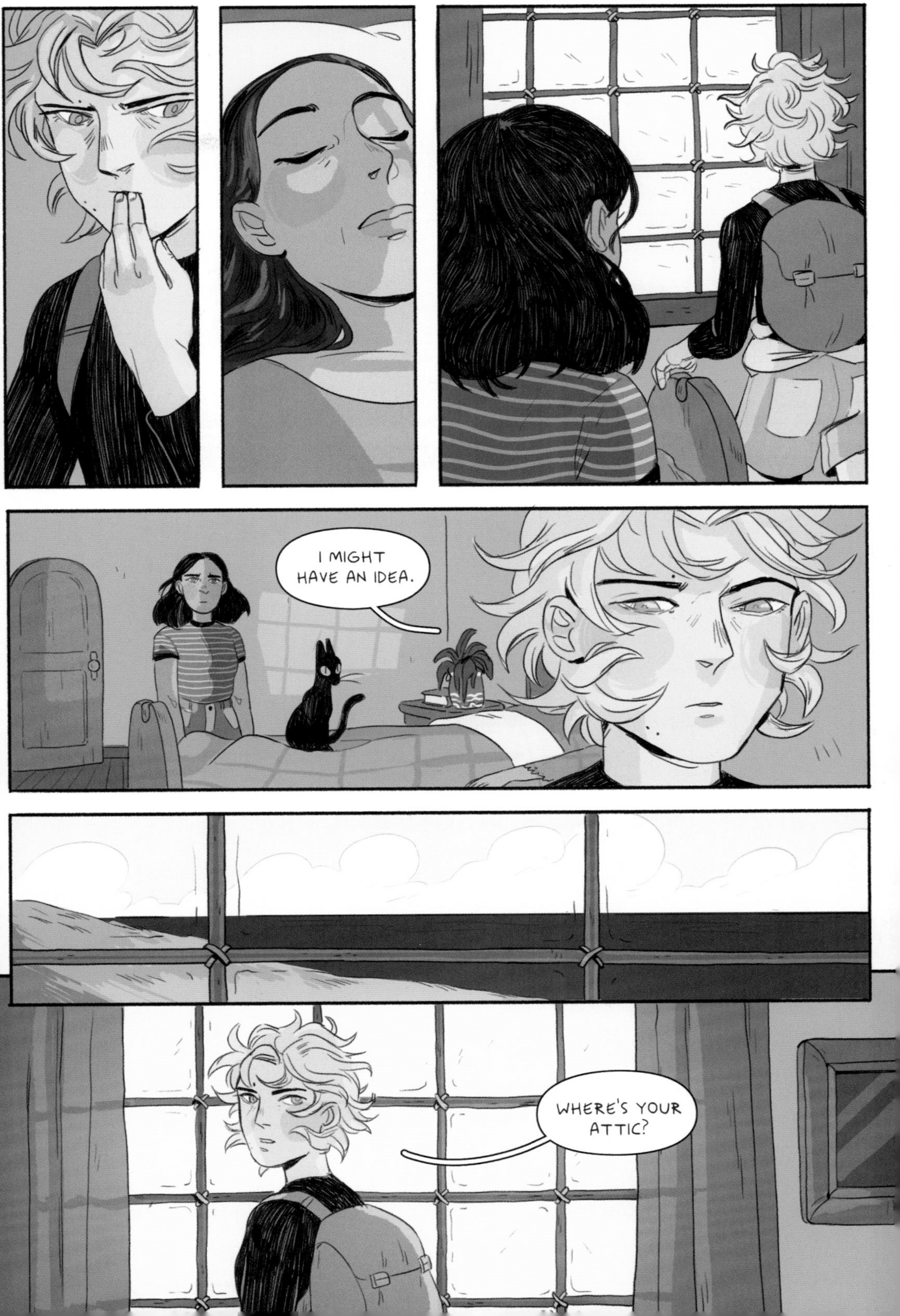
I MIGHT HAVE AN IDEA.
WHERE'S YOUR ATTIC?

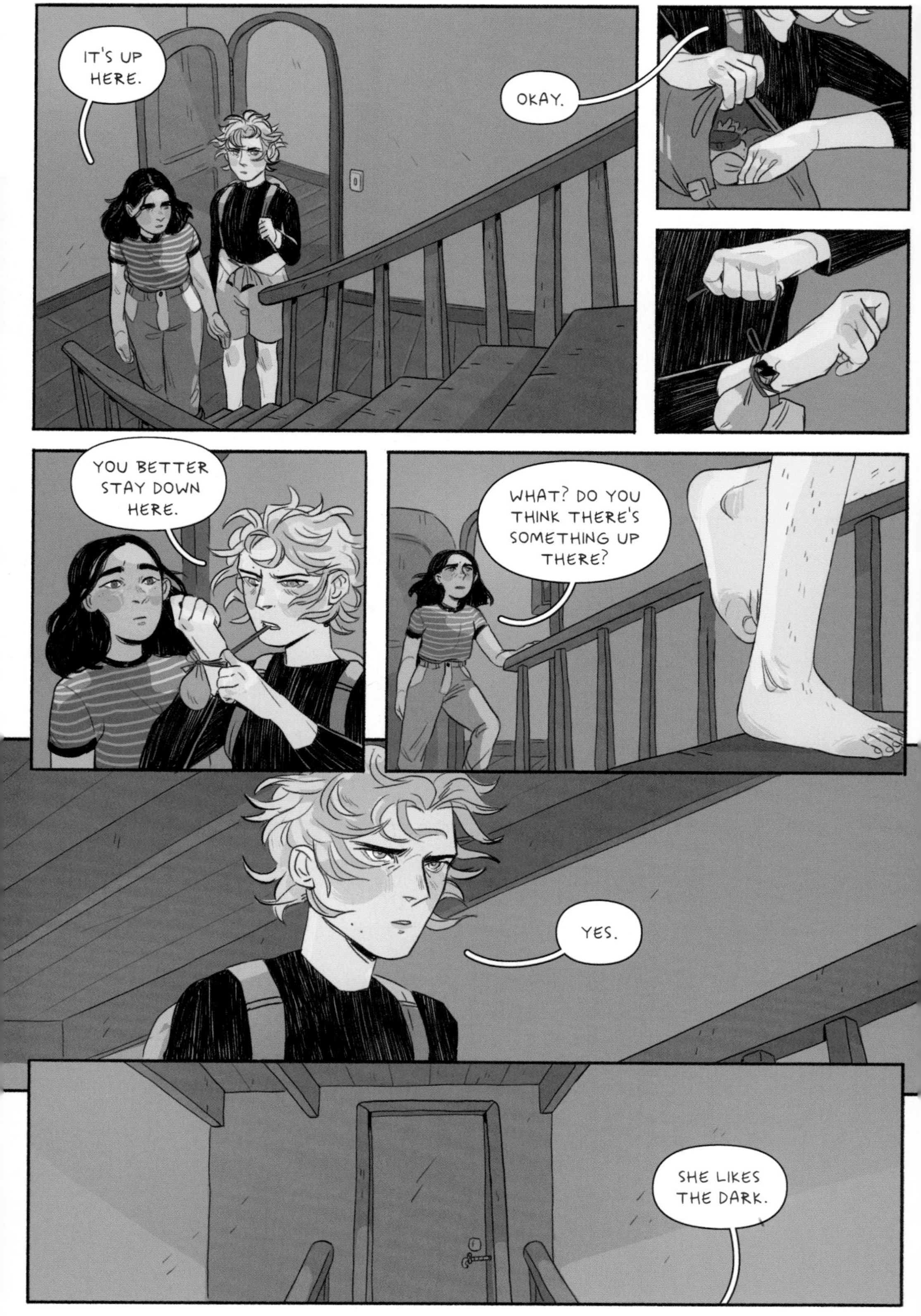
IT'S UP HERE.
OKAY.
YOU BETTER STAY DOWN HERE.
WHAT? DO YOU THINK THERE'S SOMETHING UP THERE?
YES.
SHE LIKES THE DARK.

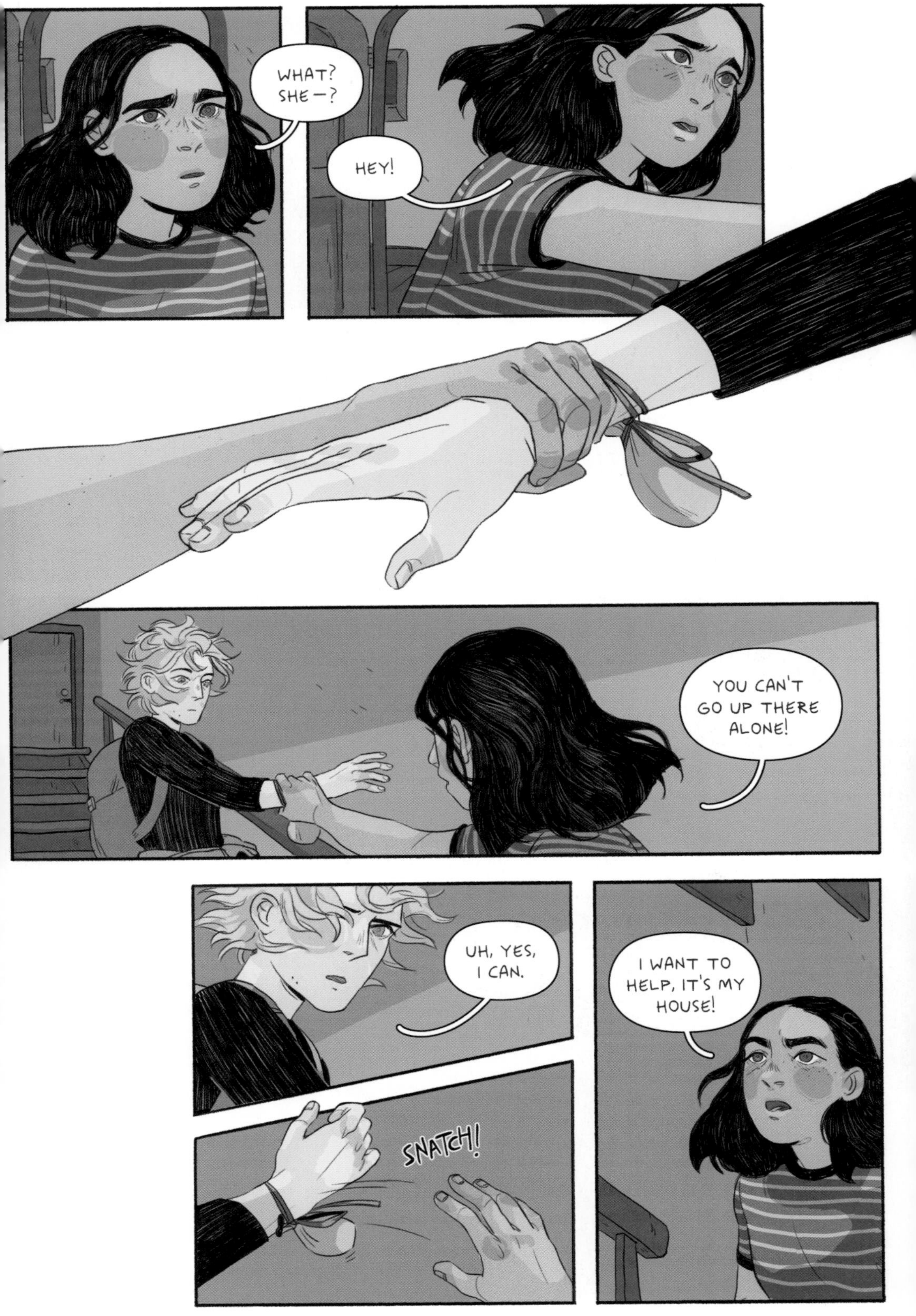
WHAT? SHE—?
HEY!
YOU CAN'T GO UP THERE ALONE!
UH, YES, I CAN.
SNATCH!
I WANT TO HELP, IT'S MY HOUSE!

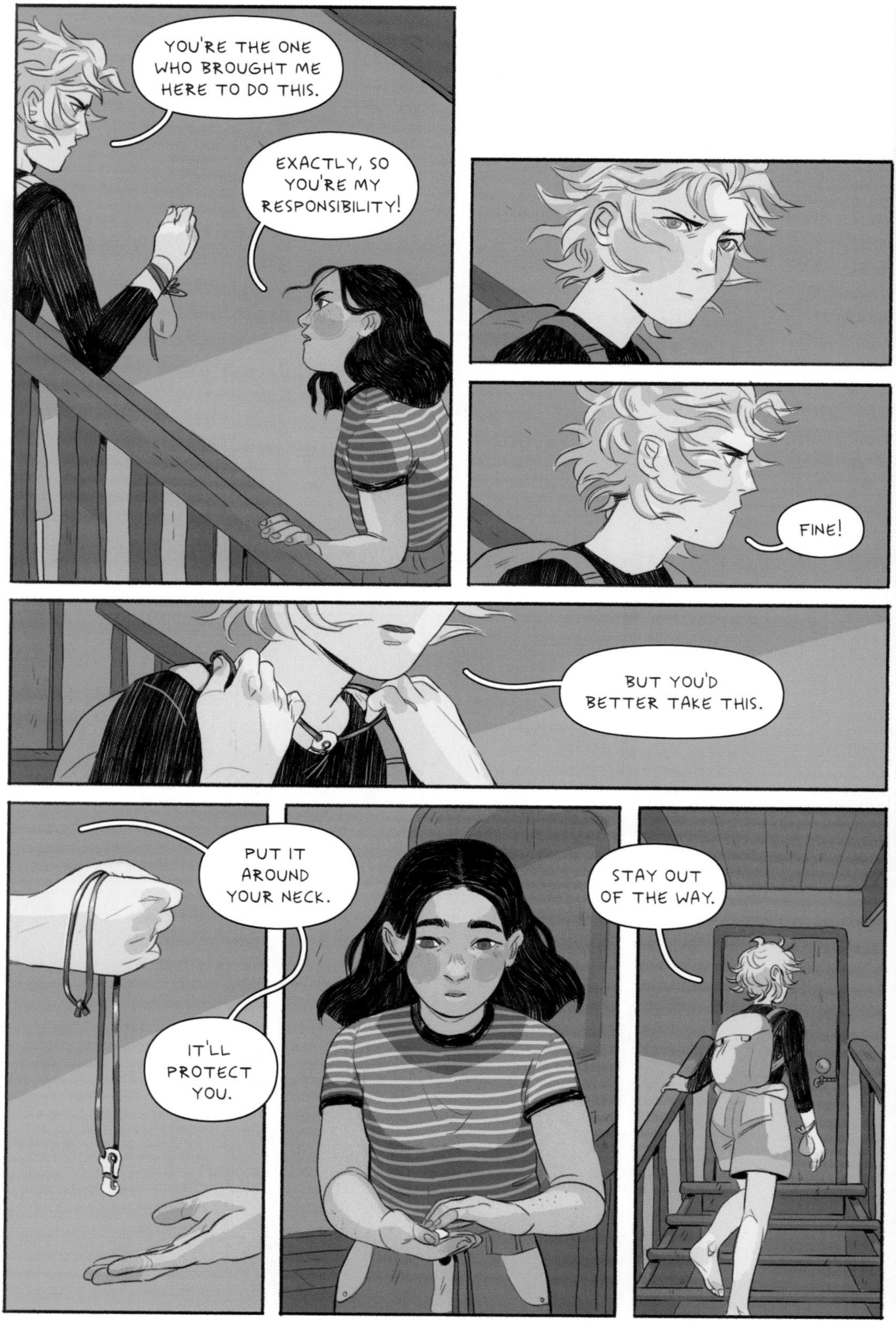
YOU'RE THE ONE WHO BROUGHT ME HERE TO DO THIS.
EXACTLY, SO YOU'RE MY RESPONSIBILITY!
FINE!
BUT YOU'D BETTER TAKE THIS.
PUT IT AROUND YOUR NECK.
IT'LL PROTECT YOU.
STAY OUT OF THE WAY.

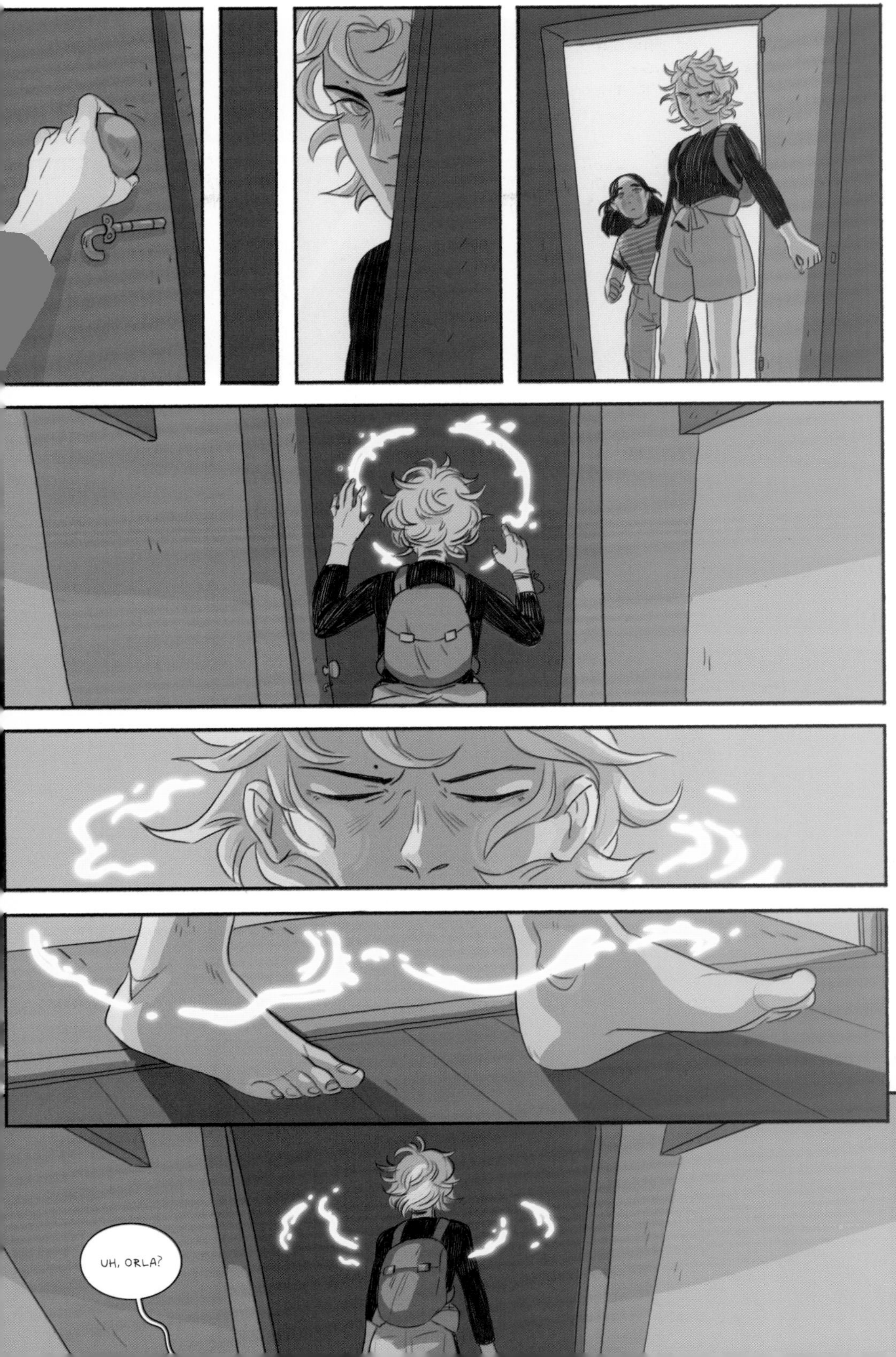

UH, ORLA?

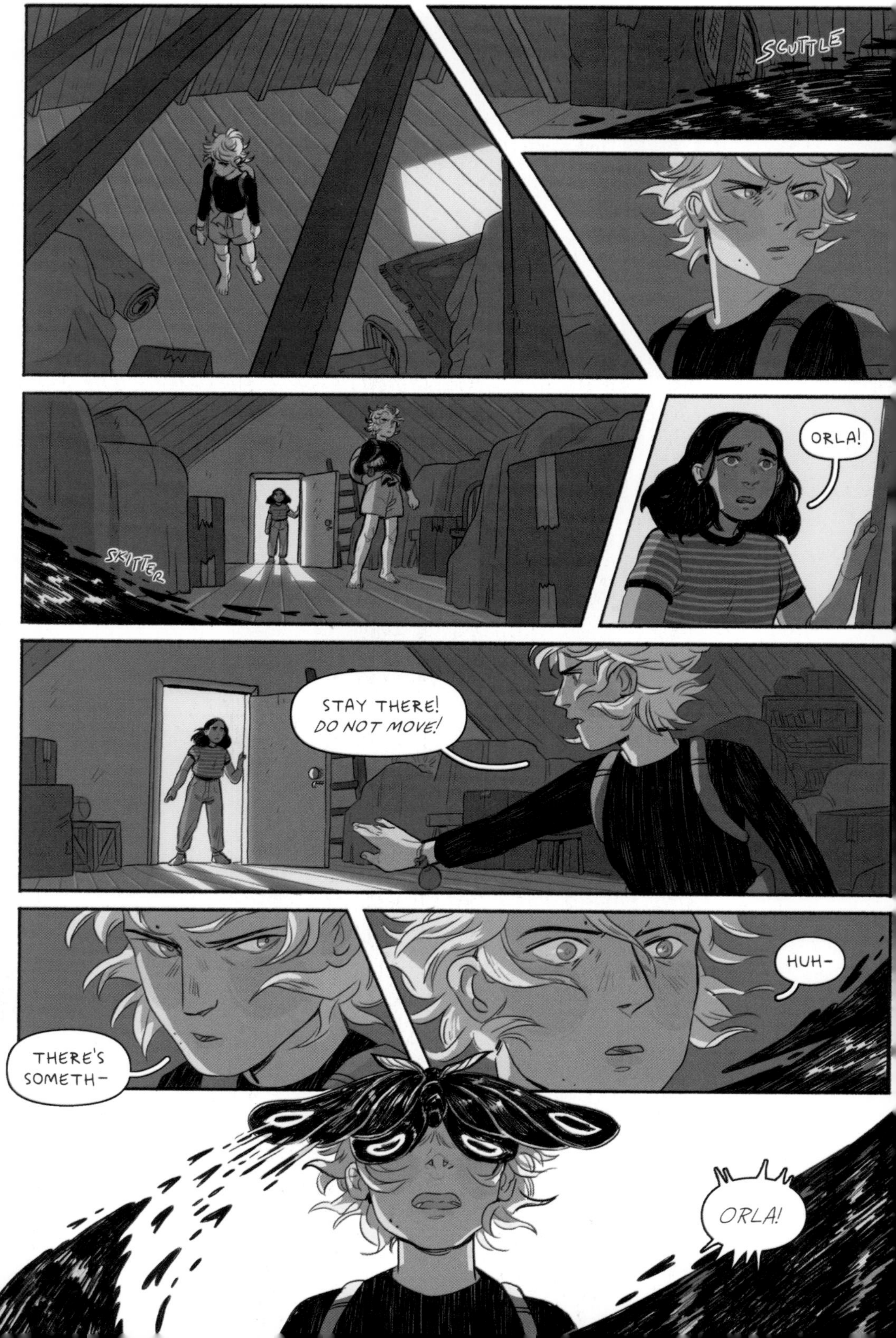
SCUTTLE
SKITTER
ORLA!
STAY THERE!
DO NOT MOVE!
THERE'S SOMETH-
HUH-
ORLA!

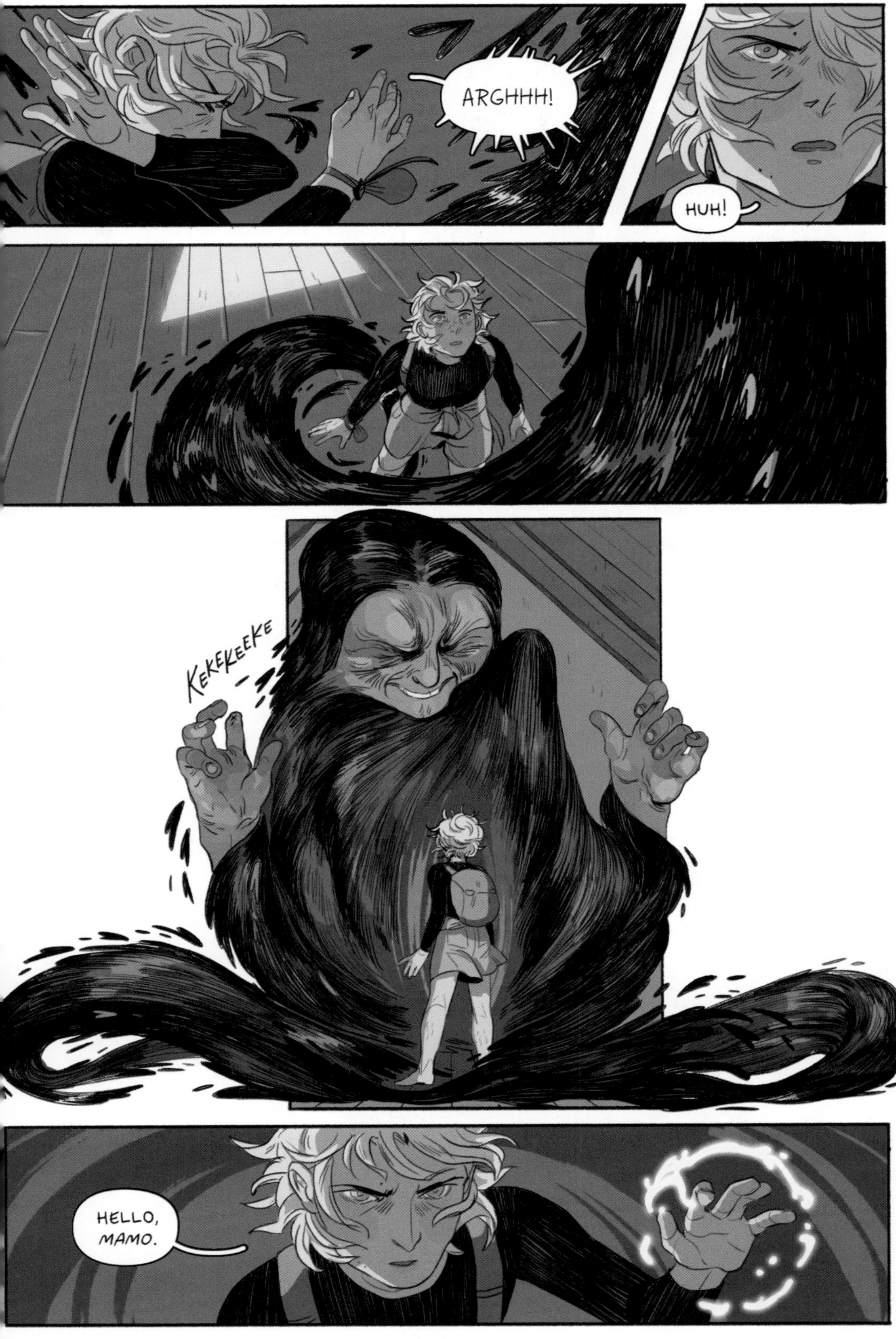
ARGHHH!
HUH!
KEKEKEEKE
HELLO, MAMO.

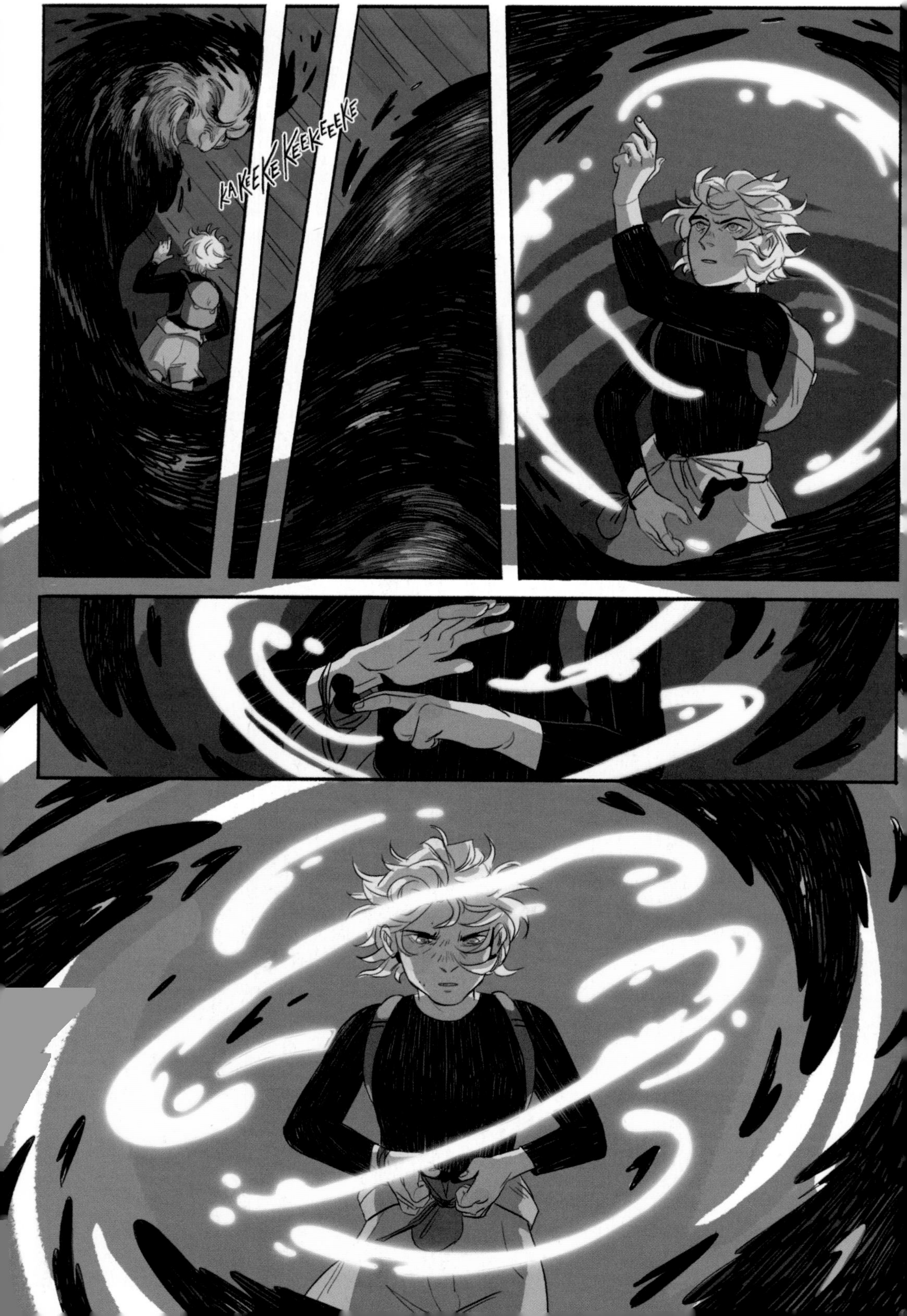
KAKEEKE KEEKEEEKE

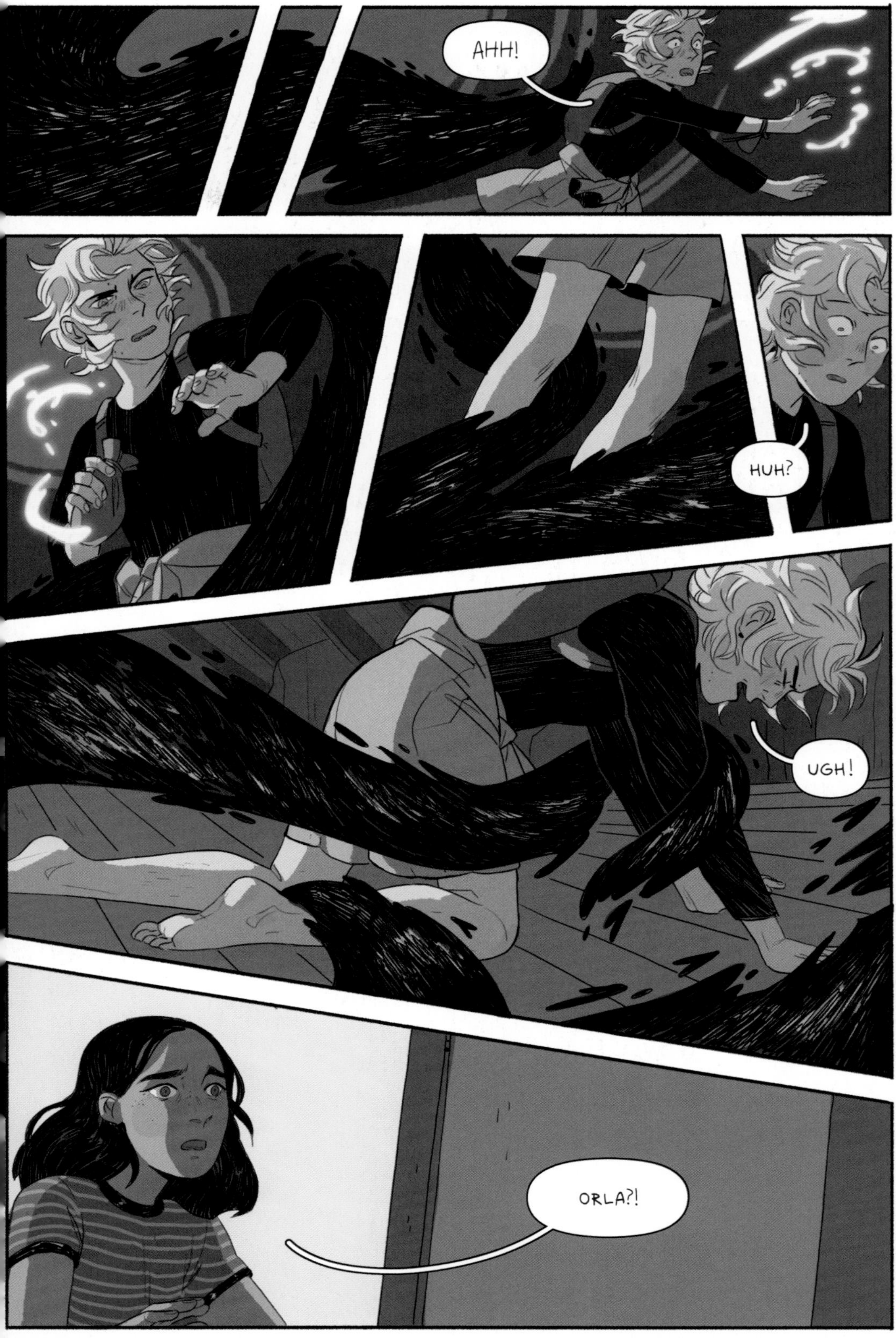
AHH!
HUH?
UGH!
ORLA?!

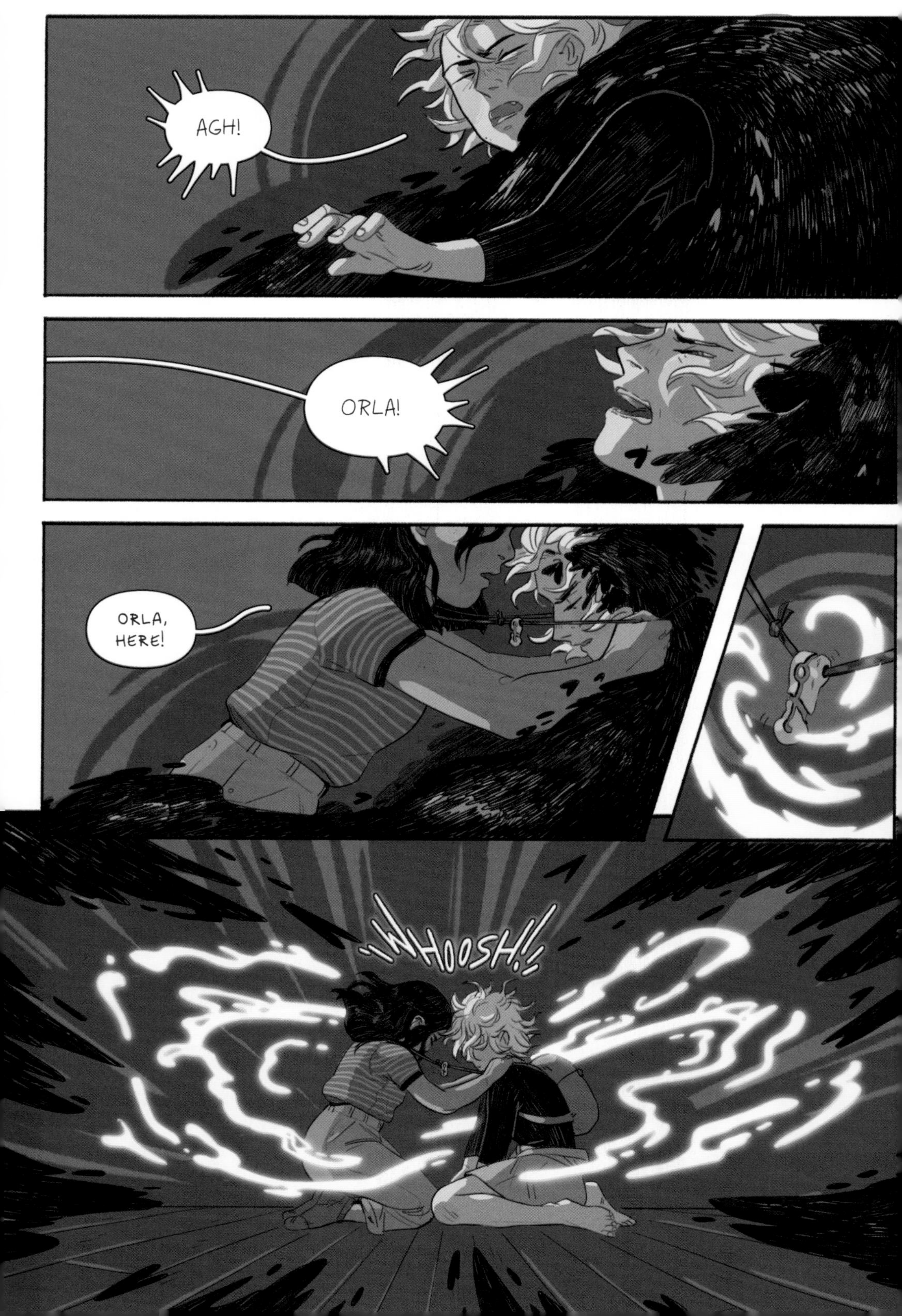
AGH!
ORLA!
ORLA, HERE!
WHOOSH!!

Chapter 2

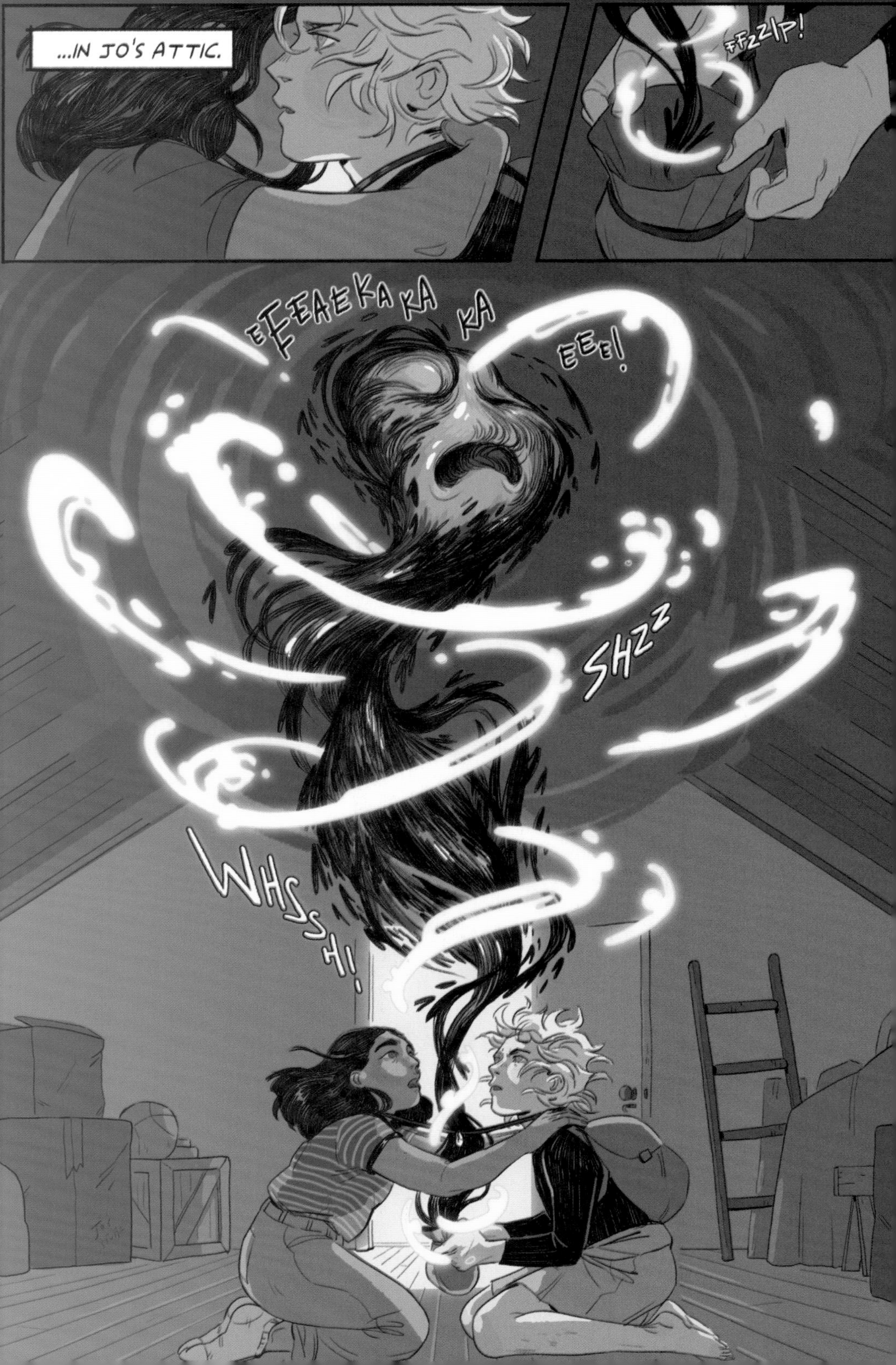
...IN JO'S ATTIC.
FFZZIP!
EEEAEKA KA KA EEE!
SHZZ
WHSSSH!

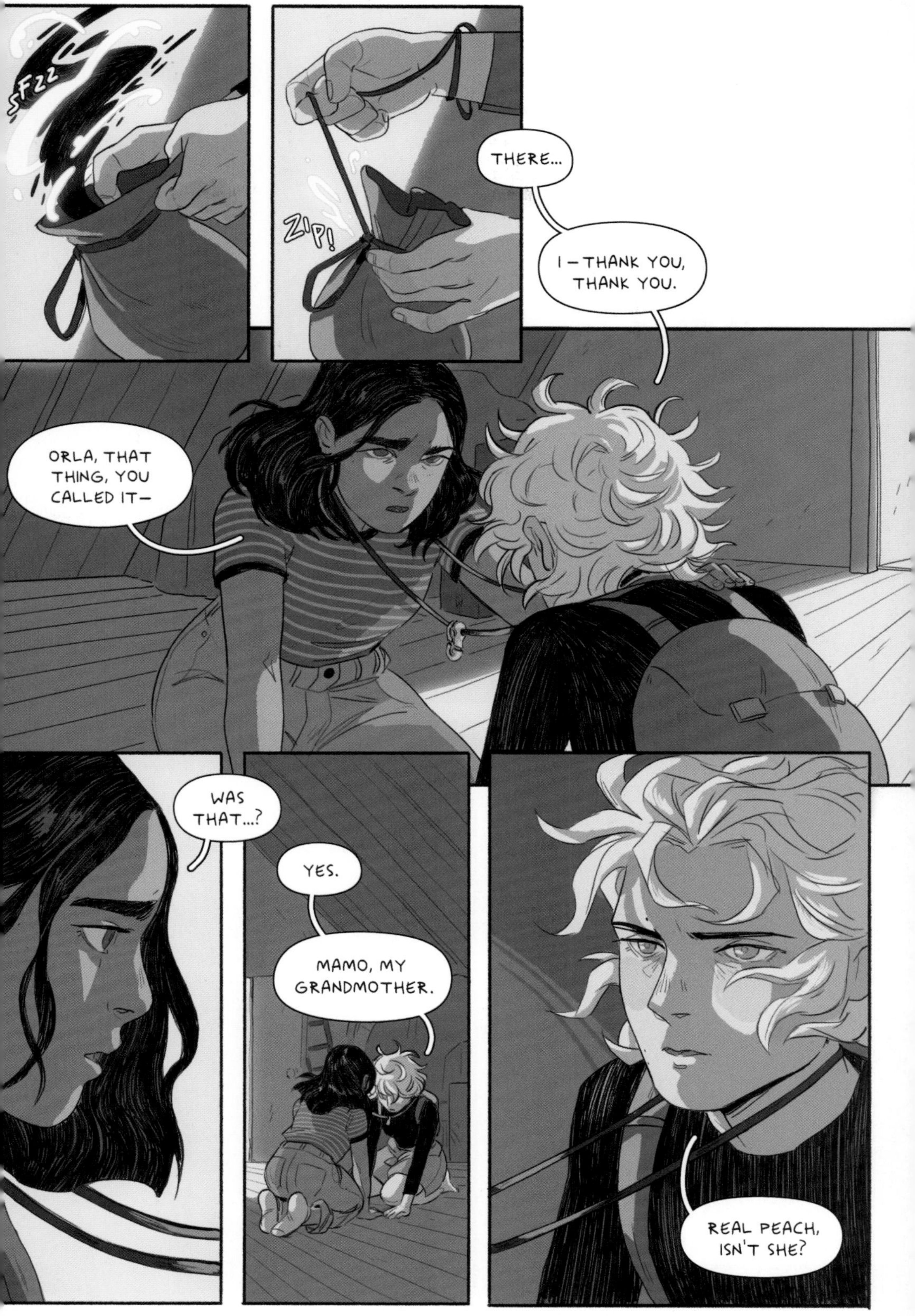
SFZZ
ZIP!
THERE...
I—THANK YOU, THANK YOU.
ORLA, THAT THING, YOU CALLED IT—
WAS THAT...?
YES.
MAMO, MY GRANDMOTHER.
REAL PEACH, ISN'T SHE?

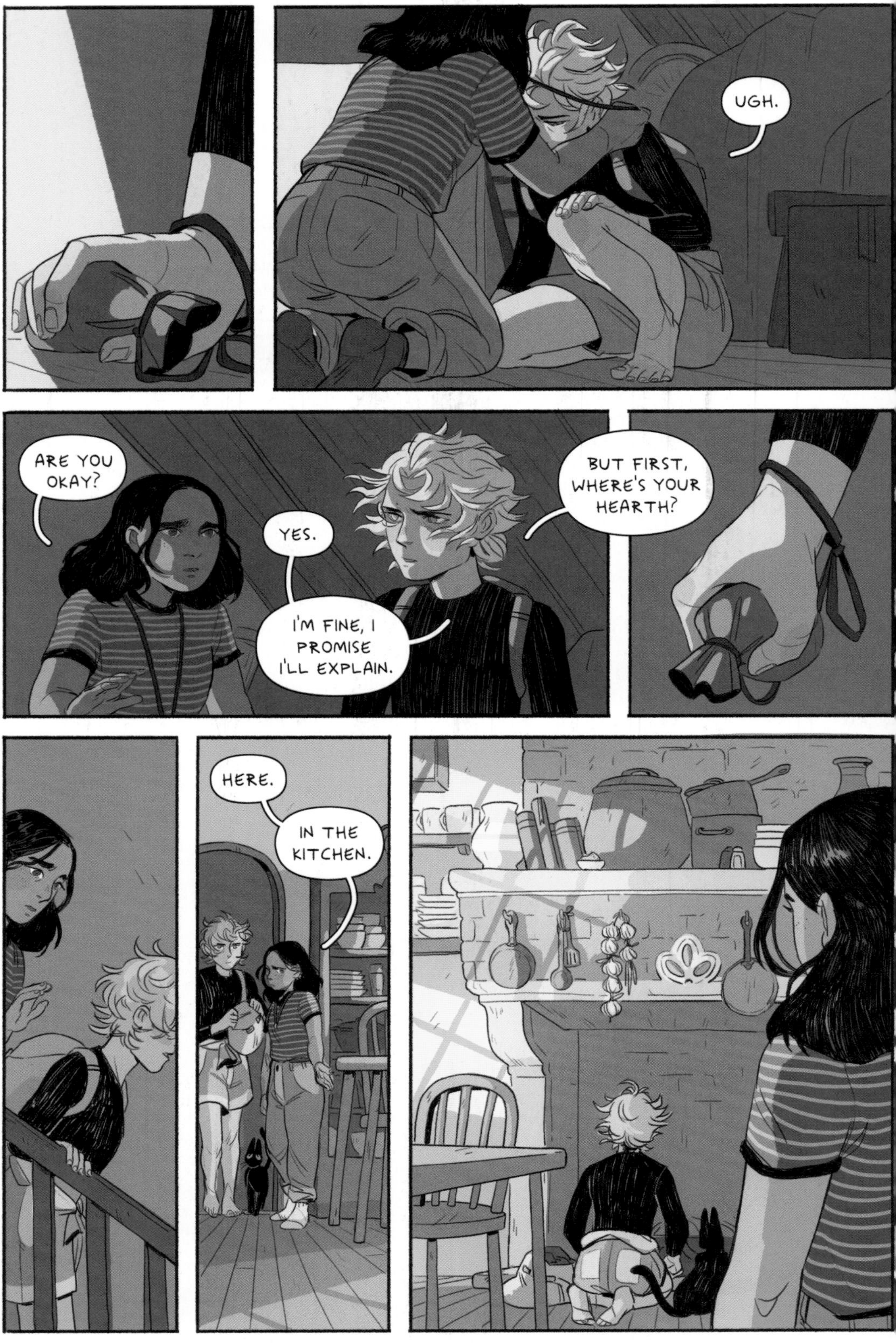
UGH.
ARE YOU OKAY?
YES.
I'M FINE, I PROMISE I'LL EXPLAIN.
BUT FIRST, WHERE'S YOUR HEARTH?
HERE.
IN THE KITCHEN.

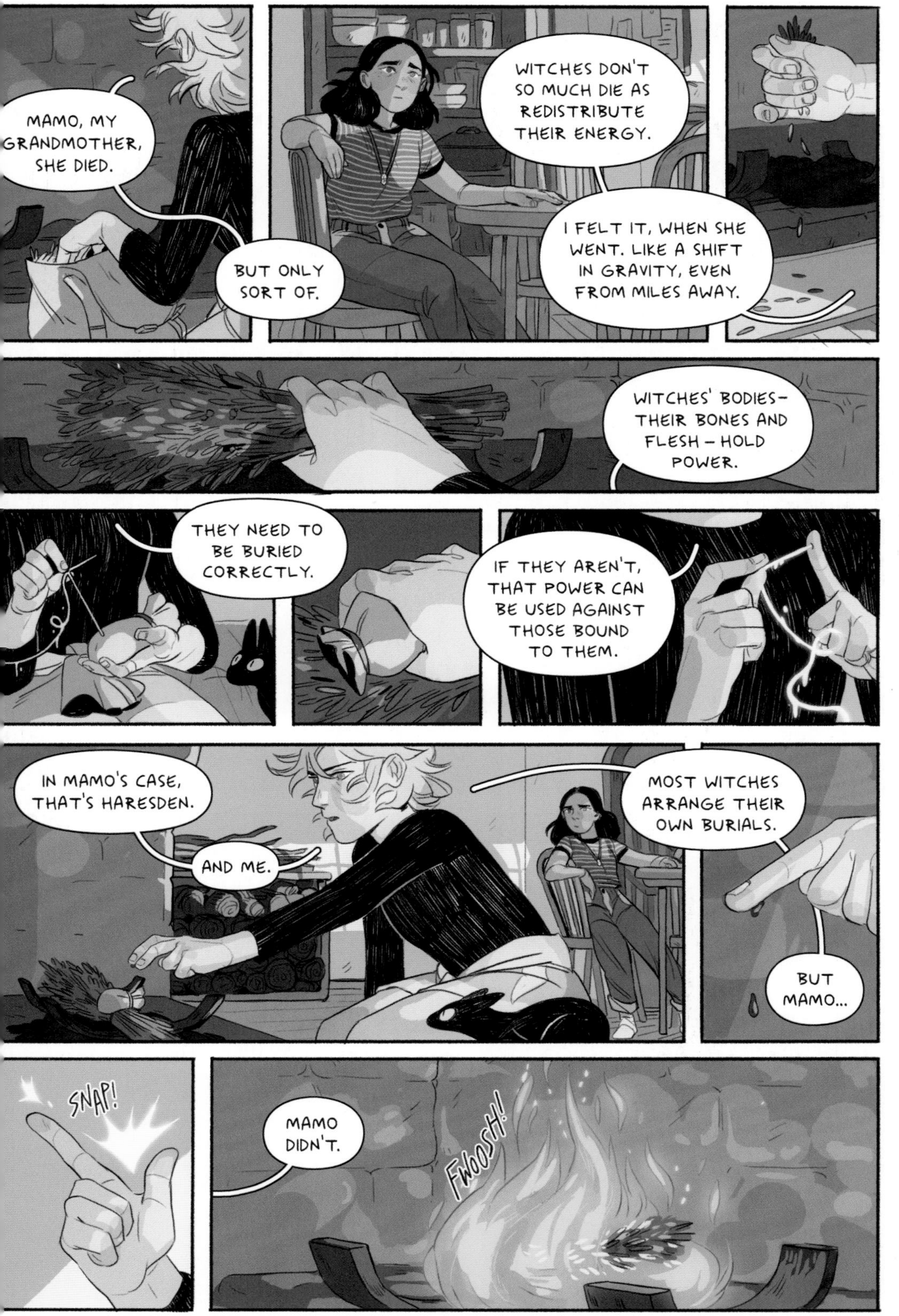
MAMO, MY GRANDMOTHER, SHE DIED.
BUT ONLY SORT OF.
WITCHES DON'T SO MUCH DIE AS REDISTRIBUTE THEIR ENERGY.
I FELT IT, WHEN SHE WENT. LIKE A SHIFT IN GRAVITY, EVEN FROM MILES AWAY.
WITCHES' BODIES– THEIR BONES AND FLESH – HOLD POWER.
THEY NEED TO BE BURIED CORRECTLY.
IF THEY AREN'T, THAT POWER CAN BE USED AGAINST THOSE BOUND TO THEM.
IN MAMO'S CASE, THAT'S HARESDEN.
AND ME.
MOST WITCHES ARRANGE THEIR OWN BURIALS.
BUT MAMO...
SNAP!
MAMO DIDN'T.
FWOOSH!

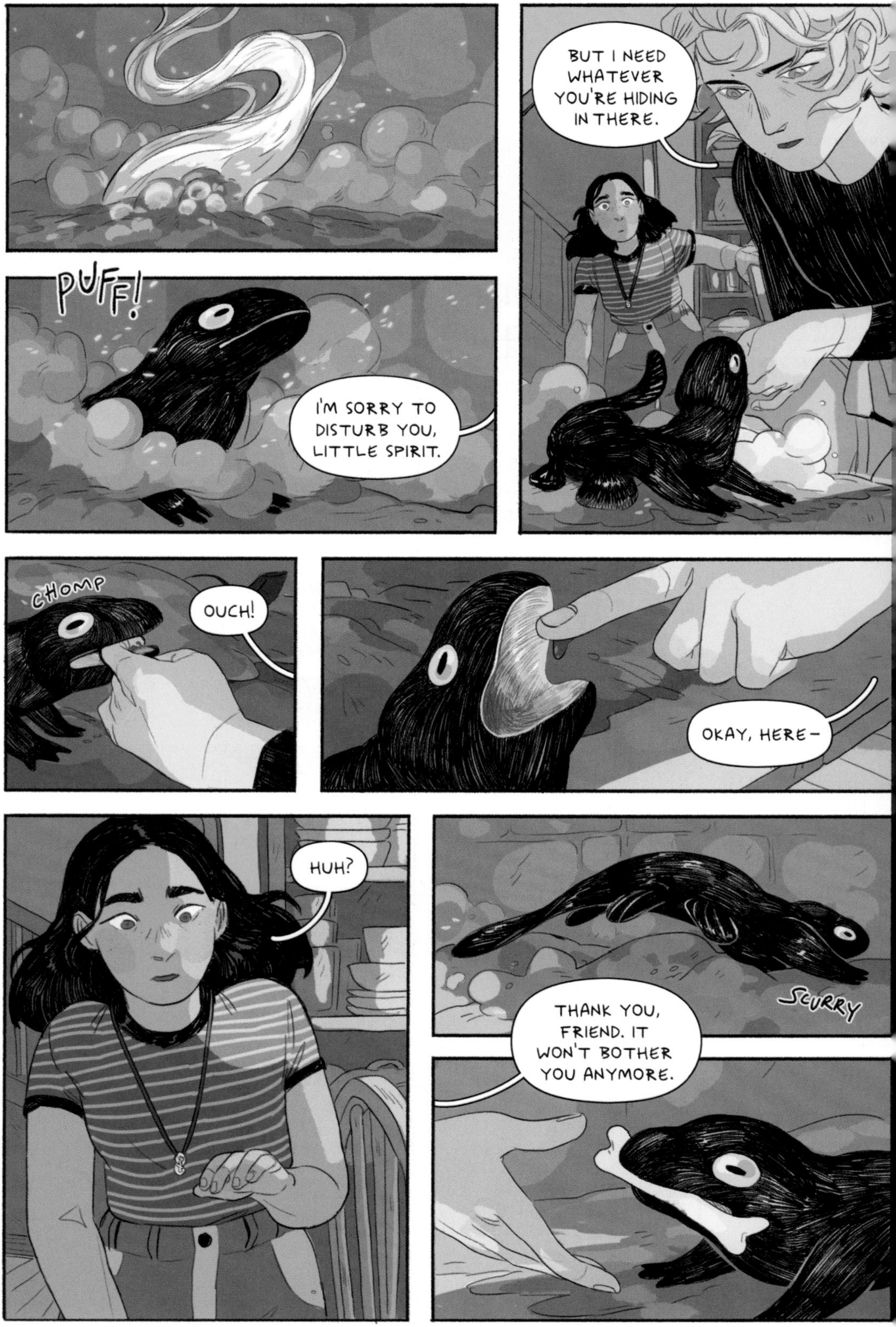
BUT I NEED WHATEVER YOU'RE HIDING IN THERE.
PUFF!
I'M SORRY TO DISTURB YOU, LITTLE SPIRIT.
CHOMP
OUCH!
OKAY, HERE–
HUH?
SCURRY
THANK YOU, FRIEND. IT WON'T BOTHER YOU ANYMORE.

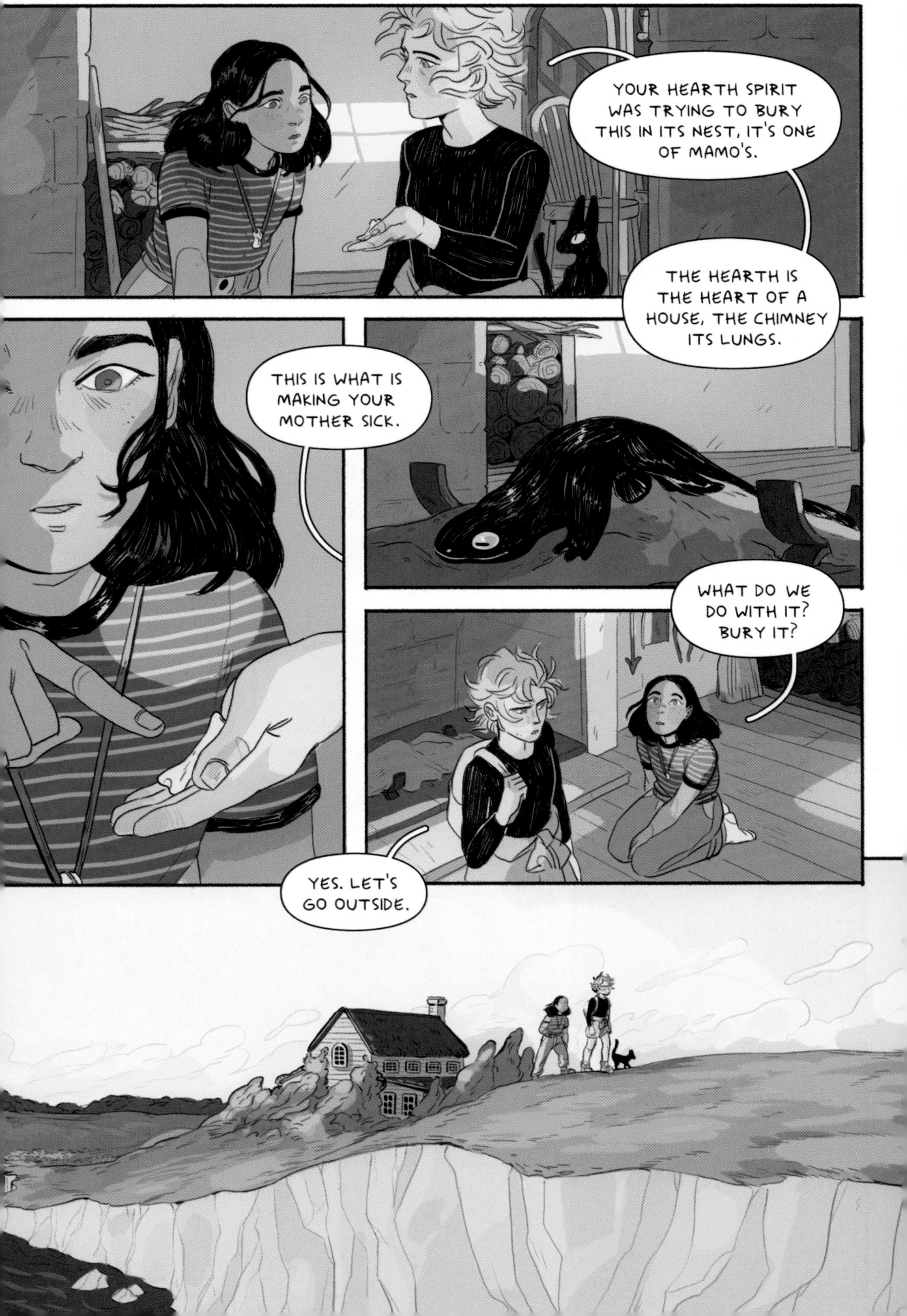
YOUR HEARTH SPIRIT WAS TRYING TO BURY THIS IN ITS NEST, IT'S ONE OF MAMO'S.
THE HEARTH IS THE HEART OF A HOUSE, THE CHIMNEY ITS LUNGS.
THIS IS WHAT IS MAKING YOUR MOTHER SICK.
WHAT DO WE DO WITH IT? BURY IT?
YES. LET'S GO OUTSIDE.

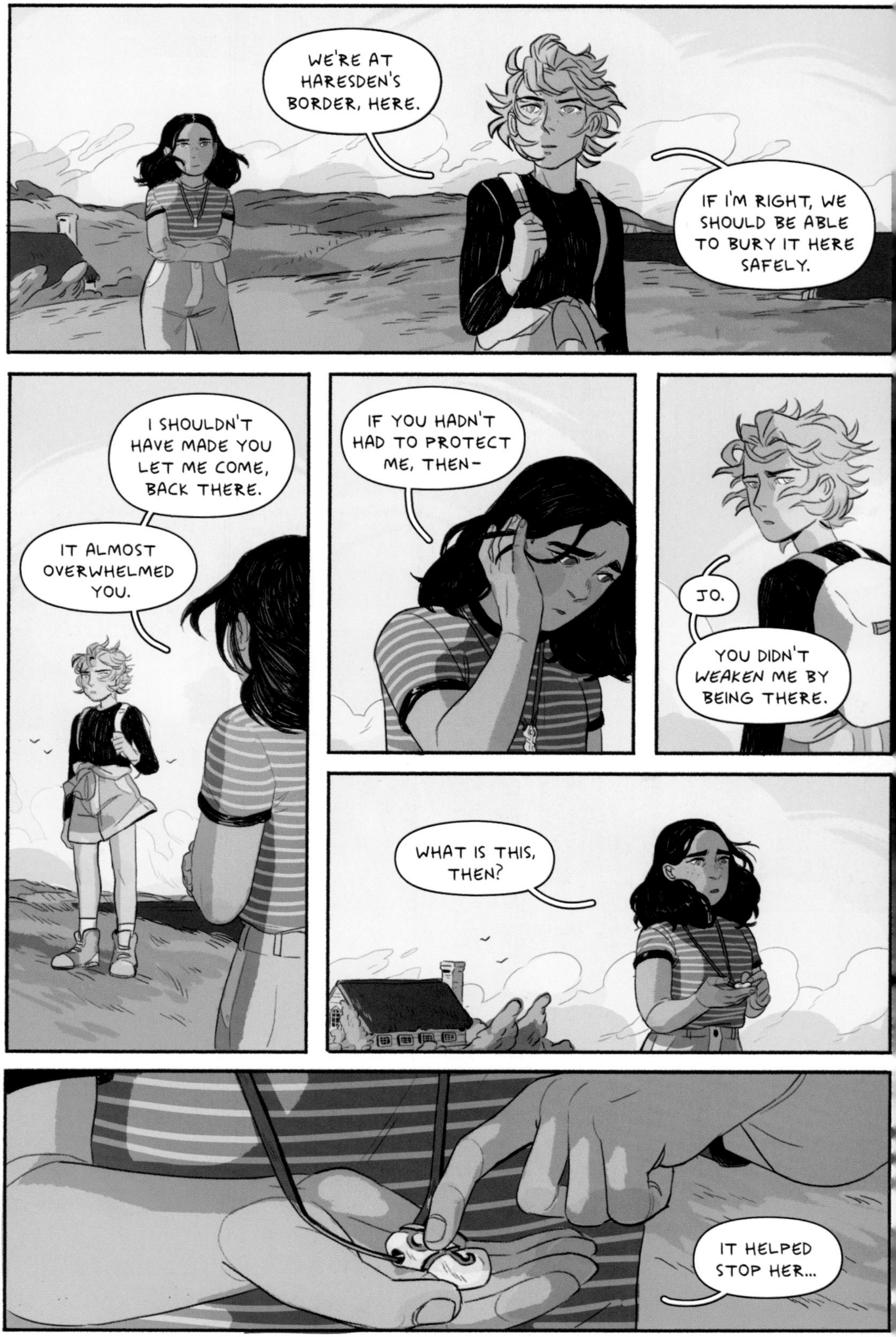
WE'RE AT HARESDEN'S BORDER, HERE.
IF I'M RIGHT, WE SHOULD BE ABLE TO BURY IT HERE SAFELY.
I SHOULDN'T HAVE MADE YOU LET ME COME, BACK THERE.
IT ALMOST OVERWHELMED YOU.
IF YOU HADN'T HAD TO PROTECT ME, THEN-
JO.
YOU DIDN'T WEAKEN ME BY BEING THERE.
WHAT IS THIS, THEN?
IT HELPED STOP HER...

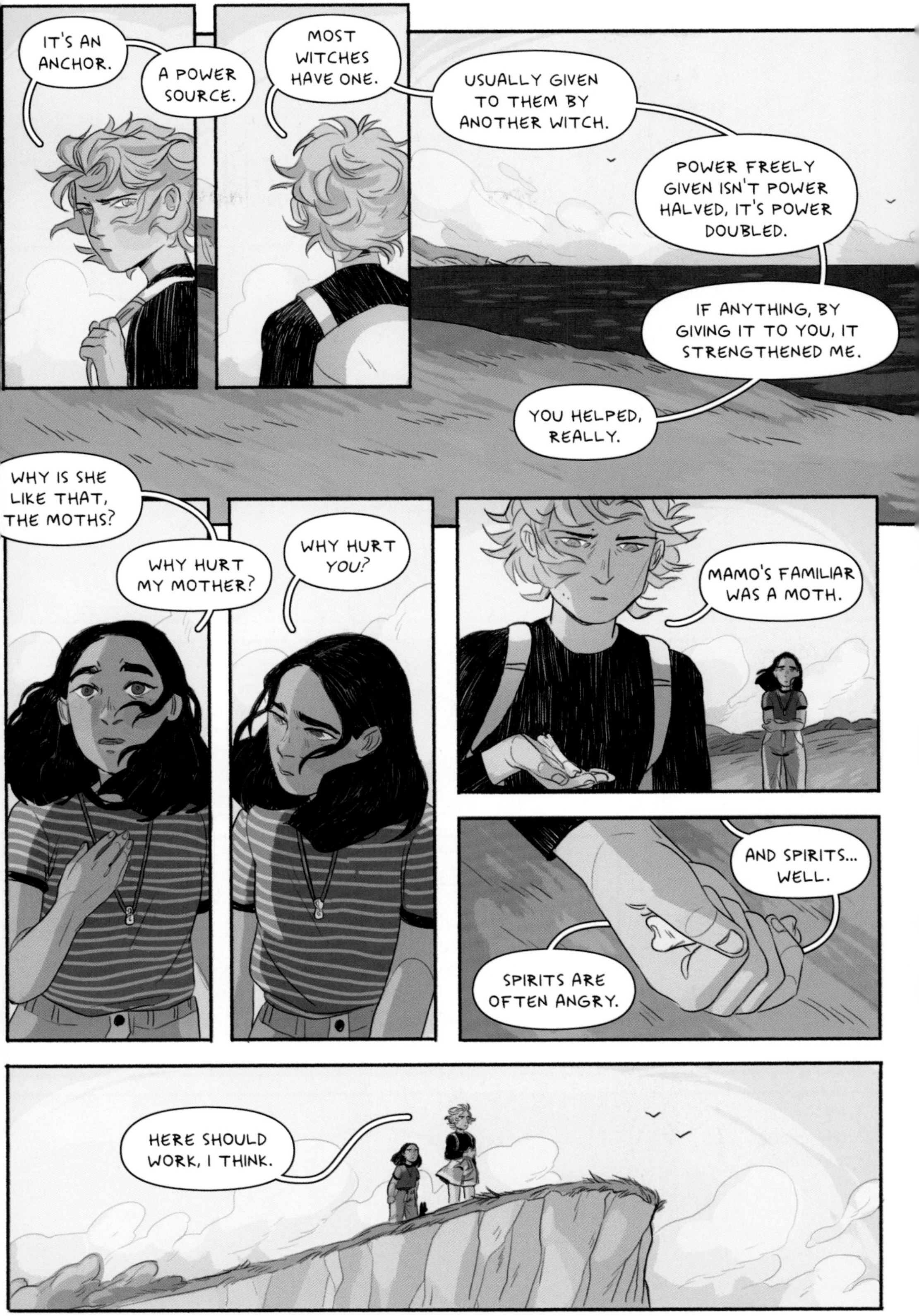
IT'S AN ANCHOR.
A POWER SOURCE.
MOST WITCHES HAVE ONE.
USUALLY GIVEN TO THEM BY ANOTHER WITCH.
POWER FREELY GIVEN ISN'T POWER HALVED, IT'S POWER DOUBLED.
IF ANYTHING, BY GIVING IT TO YOU, IT STRENGTHENED ME.
YOU HELPED, REALLY.
WHY IS SHE LIKE THAT, THE MOTHS?
WHY HURT MY MOTHER?
WHY HURT *YOU?*
MAMO'S FAMILIAR WAS A MOTH.
AND SPIRITS... WELL.
SPIRITS ARE OFTEN ANGRY.
HERE SHOULD WORK, I THINK.

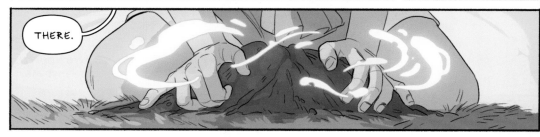

THERE.

THAT OUGHT TO KEEP IT IN PLACE.

HOW DID IT END UP IN OUR HOUSE?

I DON'T KNOW.

BUT IT EXPLAINS WHY THE WHOLE COUNTRYSIDE IS IN AN UPROAR. SHE HASN'T BEEN BURIED, SHE'S BEEN SCATTERED.

ANY MIS-BURIED BONE CAN CAUSE CHAOS, LET ALONE THE BONES OF A WITCH WHO WAS BOUND TO THE TOWN.

WHAT DOES THAT MEAN?

FOR HARESDEN?

FOR YOU?

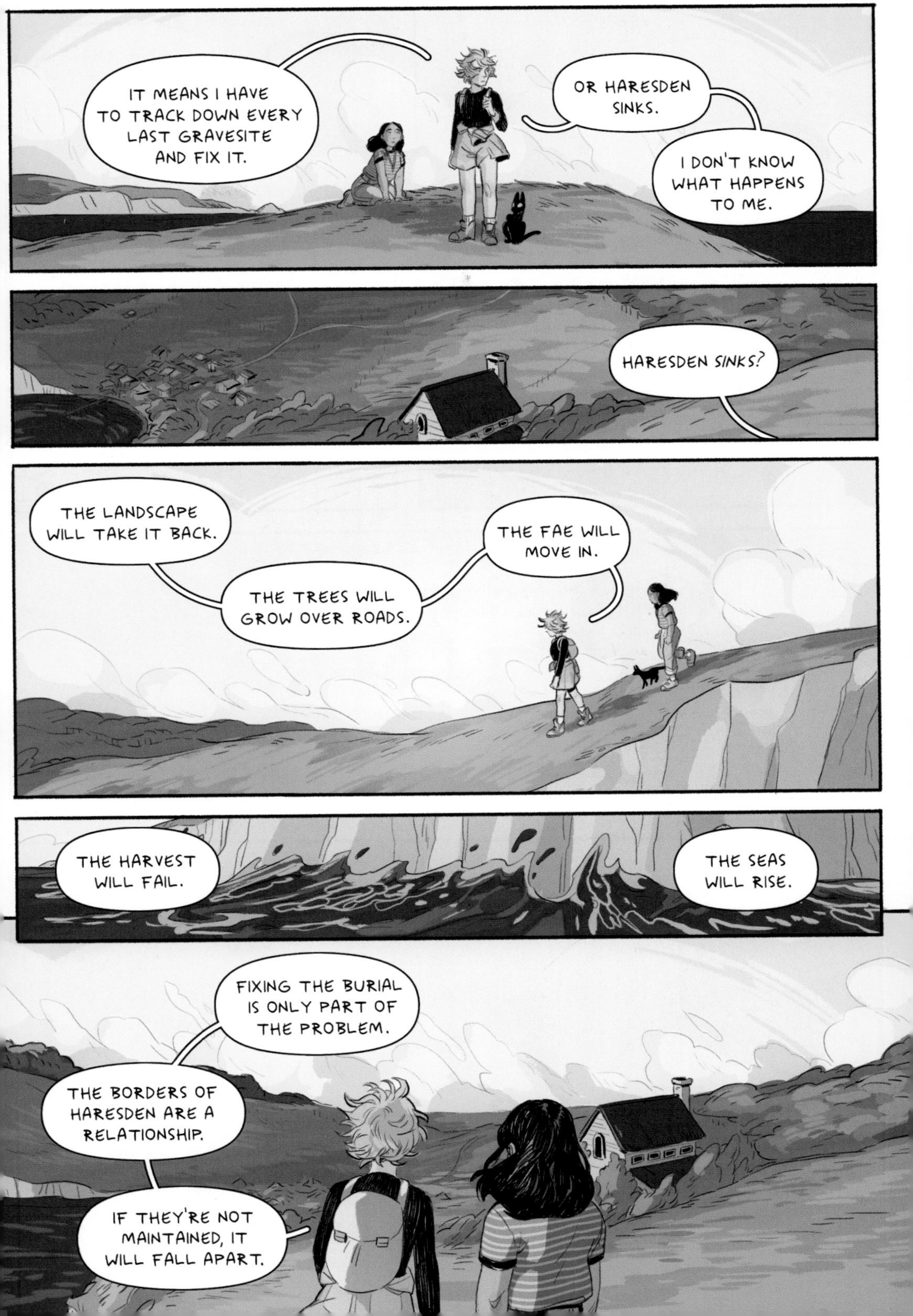
IT MEANS I HAVE TO TRACK DOWN EVERY LAST GRAVESITE AND FIX IT.
OR HARESDEN SINKS.
I DON'T KNOW WHAT HAPPENS TO ME.
HARESDEN SINKS?
THE LANDSCAPE WILL TAKE IT BACK.
THE TREES WILL GROW OVER ROADS.
THE FAE WILL MOVE IN.
THE HARVEST WILL FAIL.
THE SEAS WILL RISE.
FIXING THE BURIAL IS ONLY PART OF THE PROBLEM.
THE BORDERS OF HARESDEN ARE A RELATIONSHIP.
IF THEY'RE NOT MAINTAINED, IT WILL FALL APART.

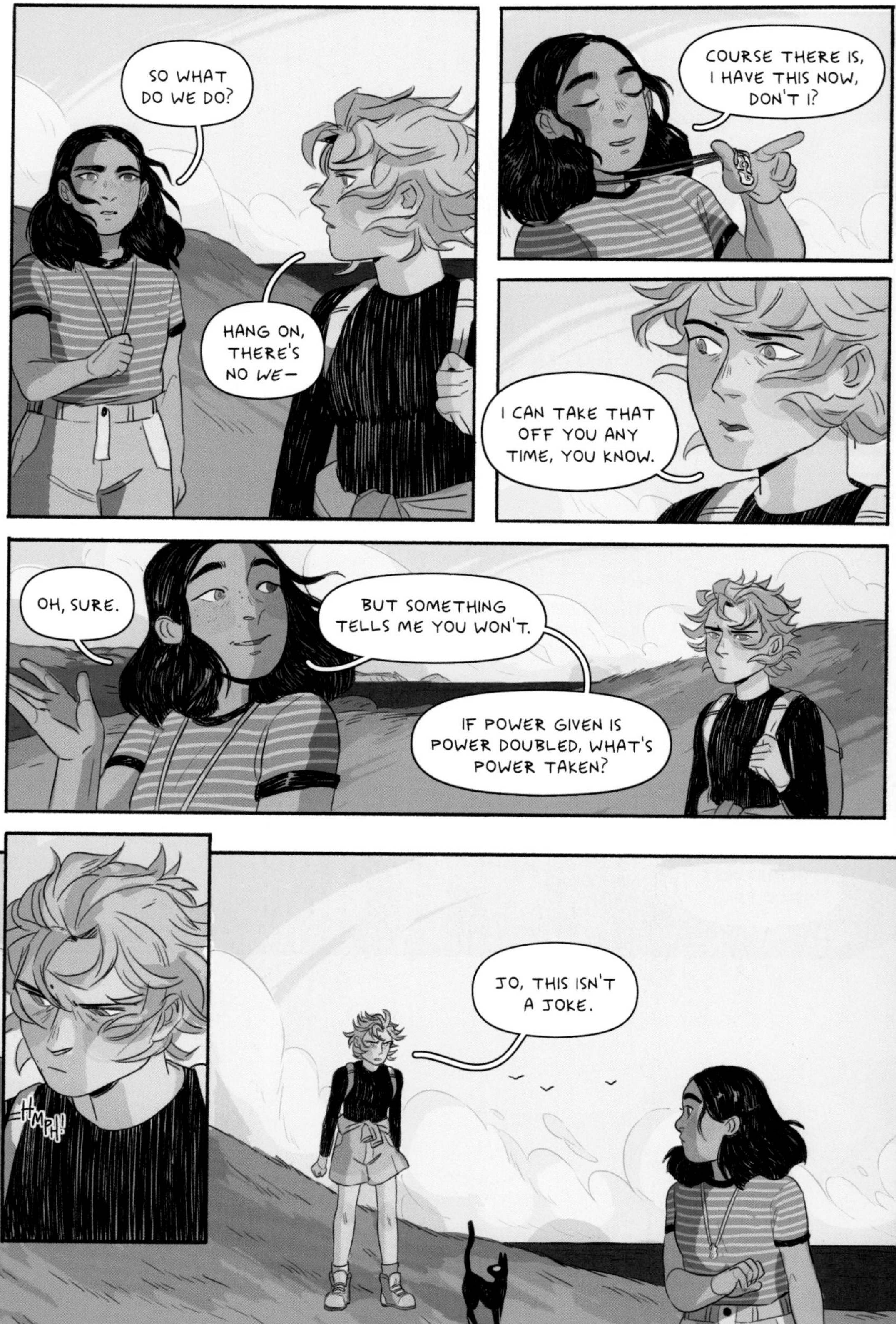
SO WHAT DO WE DO?
HANG ON, THERE'S NO WE—
COURSE THERE IS, I HAVE THIS NOW, DON'T I?
I CAN TAKE THAT OFF YOU ANY TIME, YOU KNOW.
OH, SURE.
BUT SOMETHING TELLS ME YOU WON'T.
IF POWER GIVEN IS POWER DOUBLED, WHAT'S POWER TAKEN?
HMPH!
JO, THIS ISN'T A JOKE.

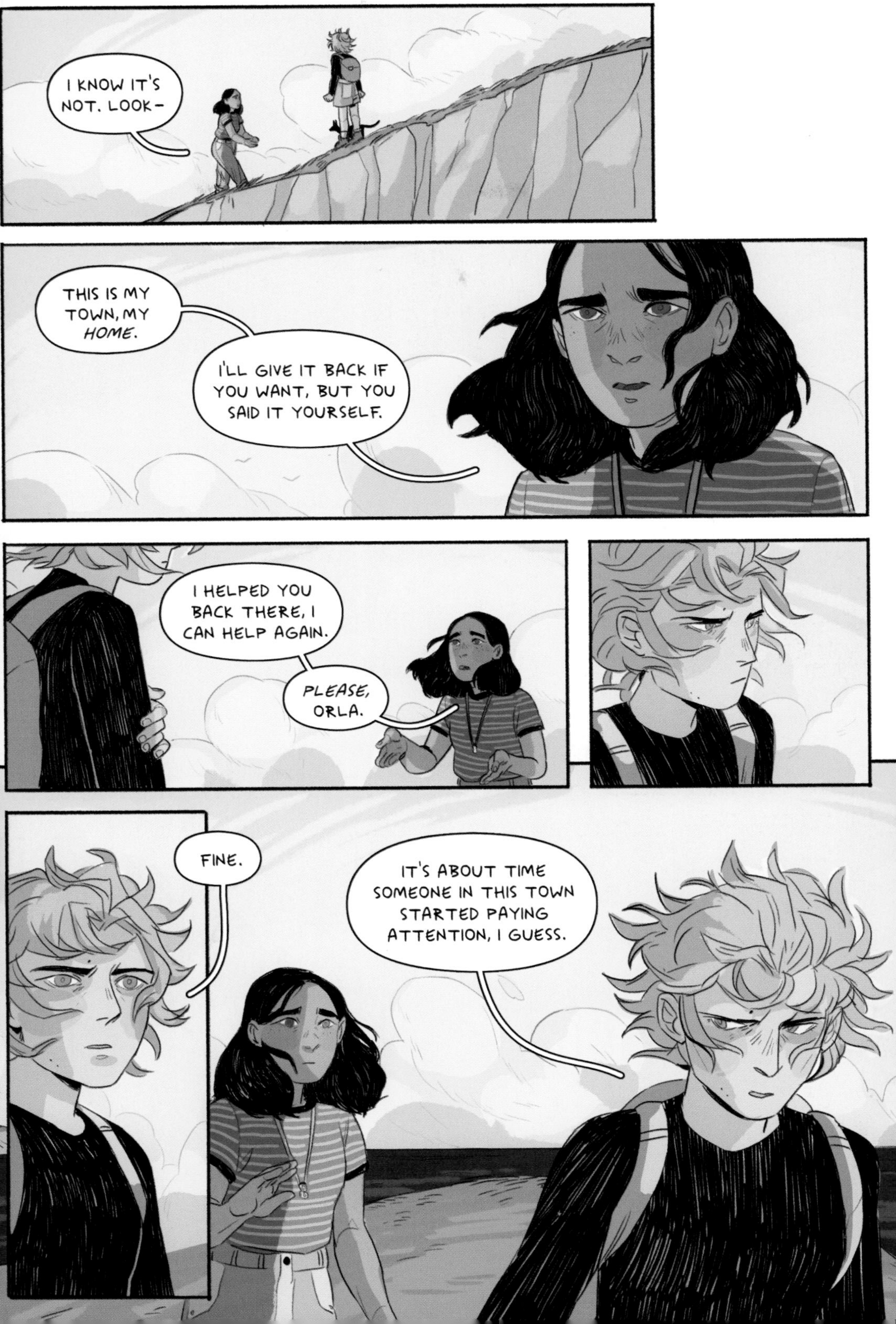
I KNOW IT'S NOT. LOOK-
THIS IS MY TOWN, MY *HOME*.
I'LL GIVE IT BACK IF YOU WANT, BUT YOU SAID IT YOURSELF.
I HELPED YOU BACK THERE, I CAN HELP AGAIN.
PLEASE, ORLA.
FINE.
IT'S ABOUT TIME SOMEONE IN THIS TOWN STARTED PAYING ATTENTION, I GUESS.

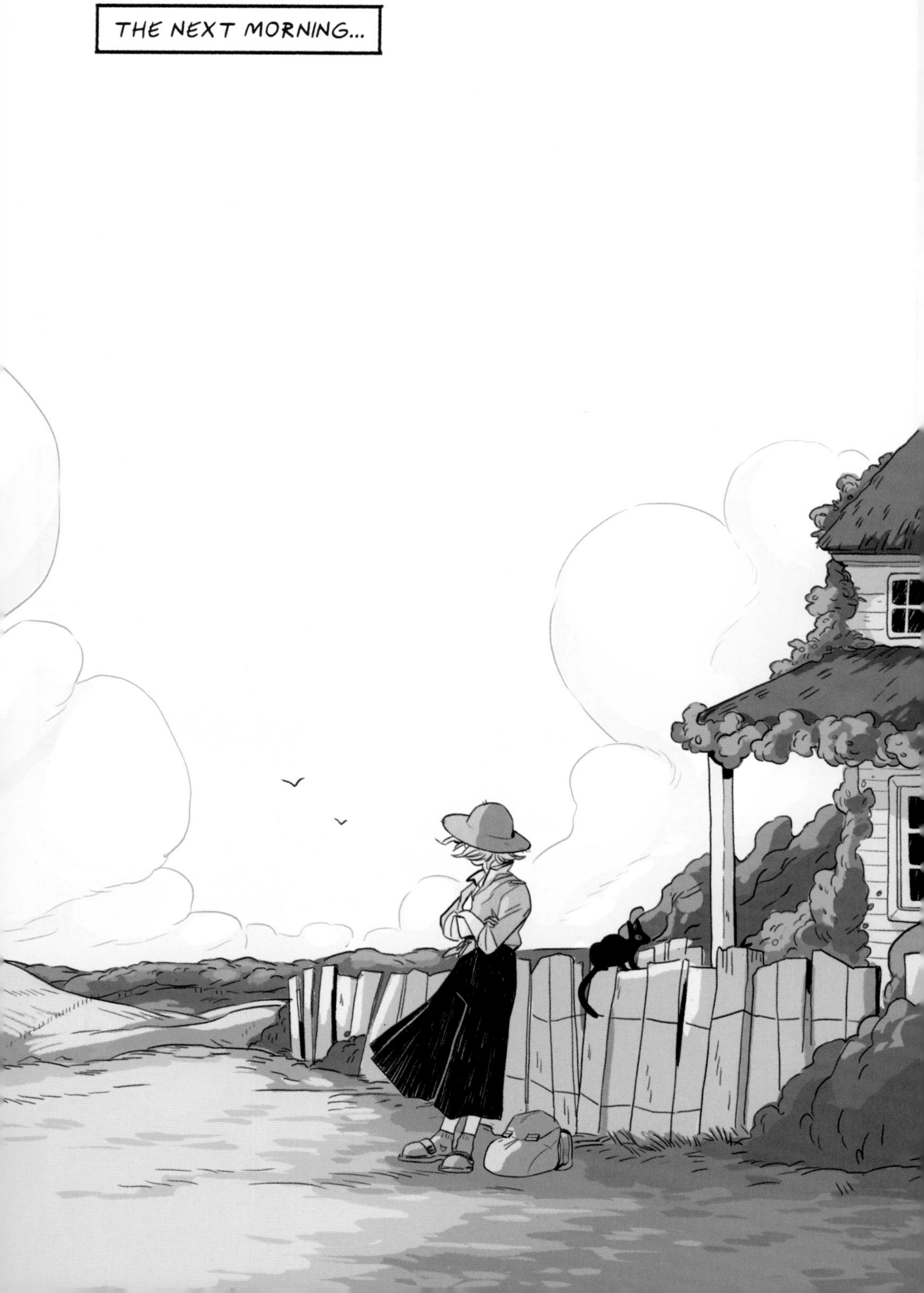
THE NEXT MORNING...

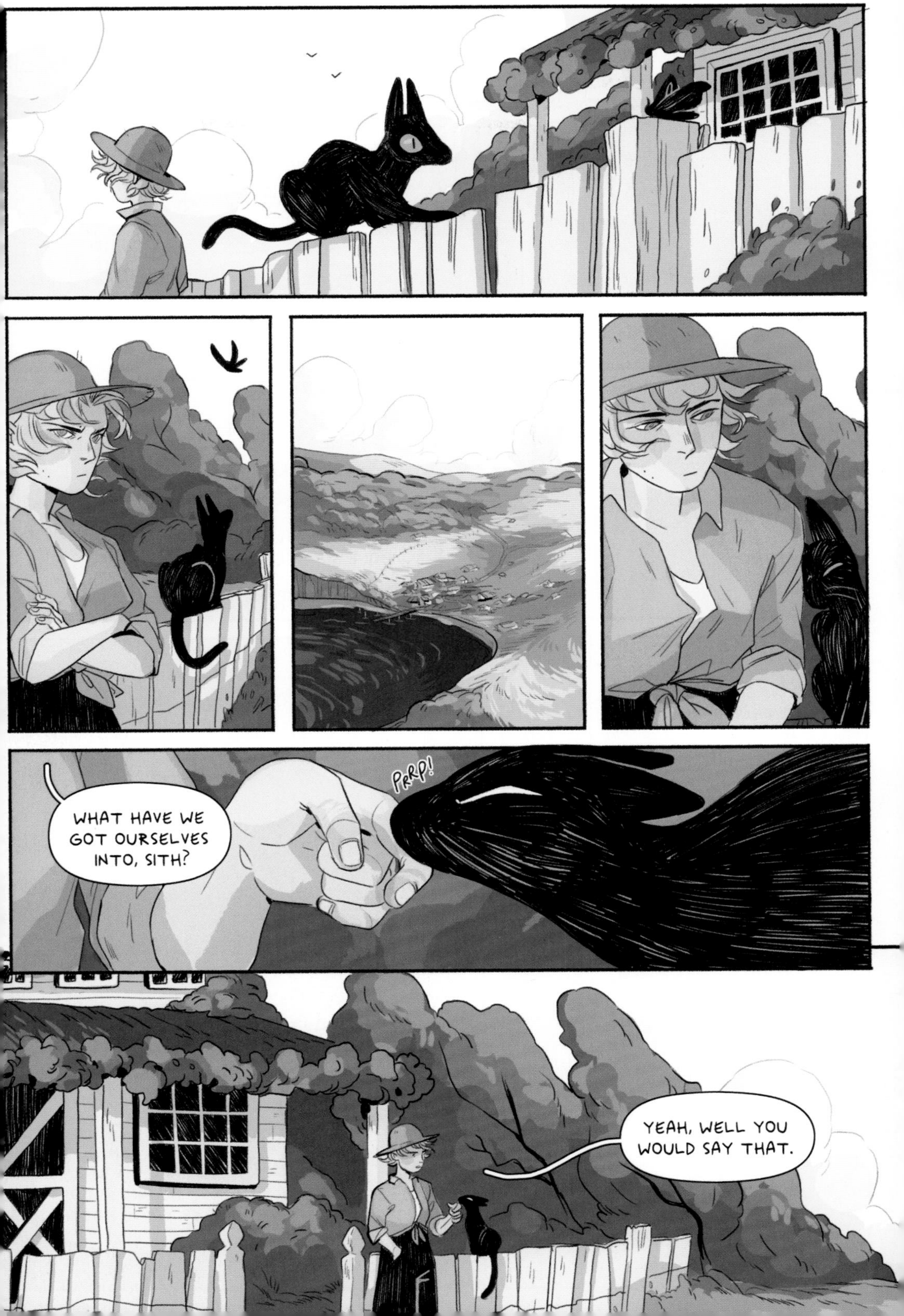
PRRP!
WHAT HAVE WE GOT OURSELVES INTO, SITH?
YEAH, WELL YOU WOULD SAY THAT.

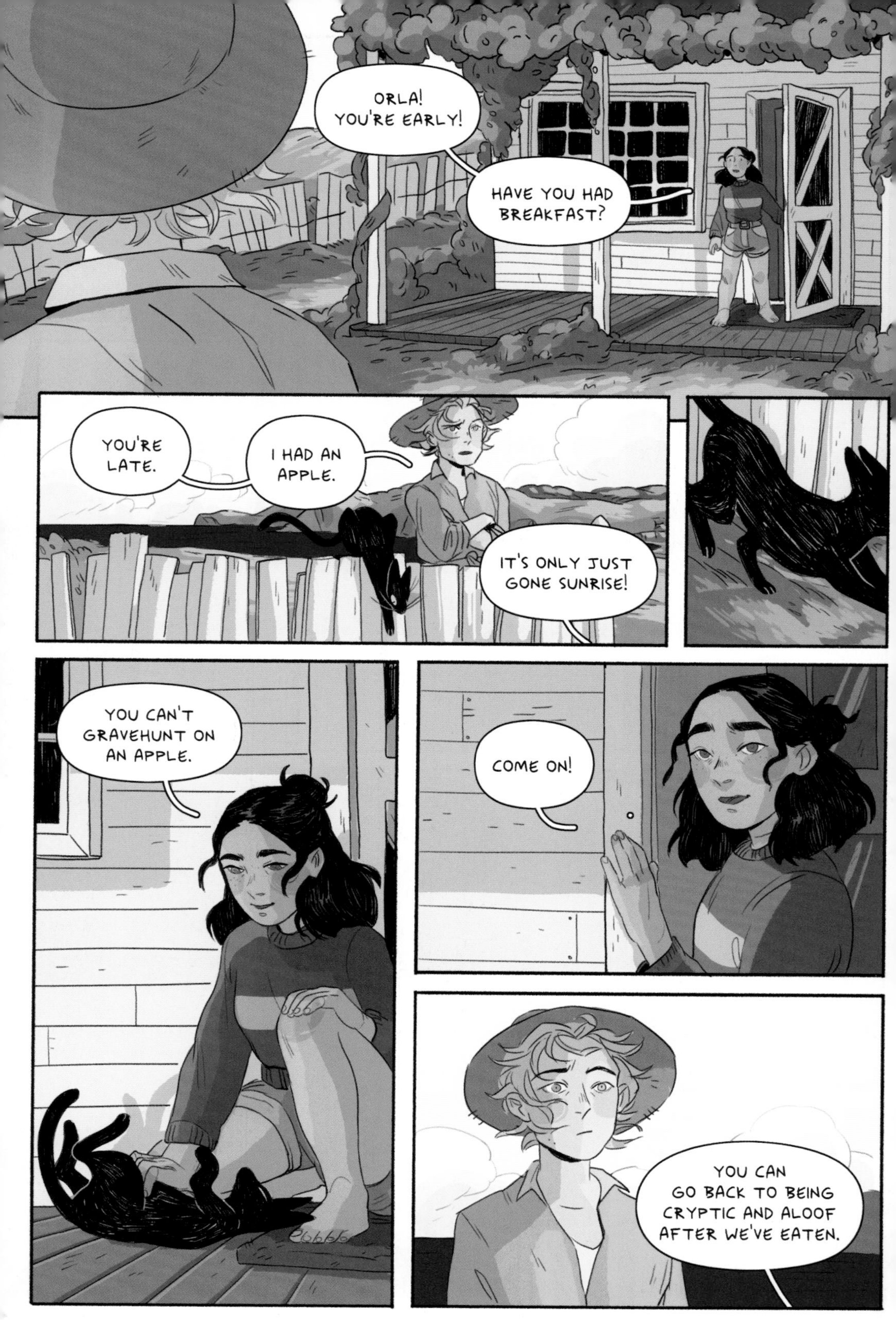
ORLA! YOU'RE EARLY!
HAVE YOU HAD BREAKFAST?
YOU'RE LATE.
I HAD AN APPLE.
IT'S ONLY JUST GONE SUNRISE!
YOU CAN'T GRAVEHUNT ON AN APPLE.
COME ON!
YOU CAN GO BACK TO BEING CRYPTIC AND ALOOF AFTER WE'VE EATEN.

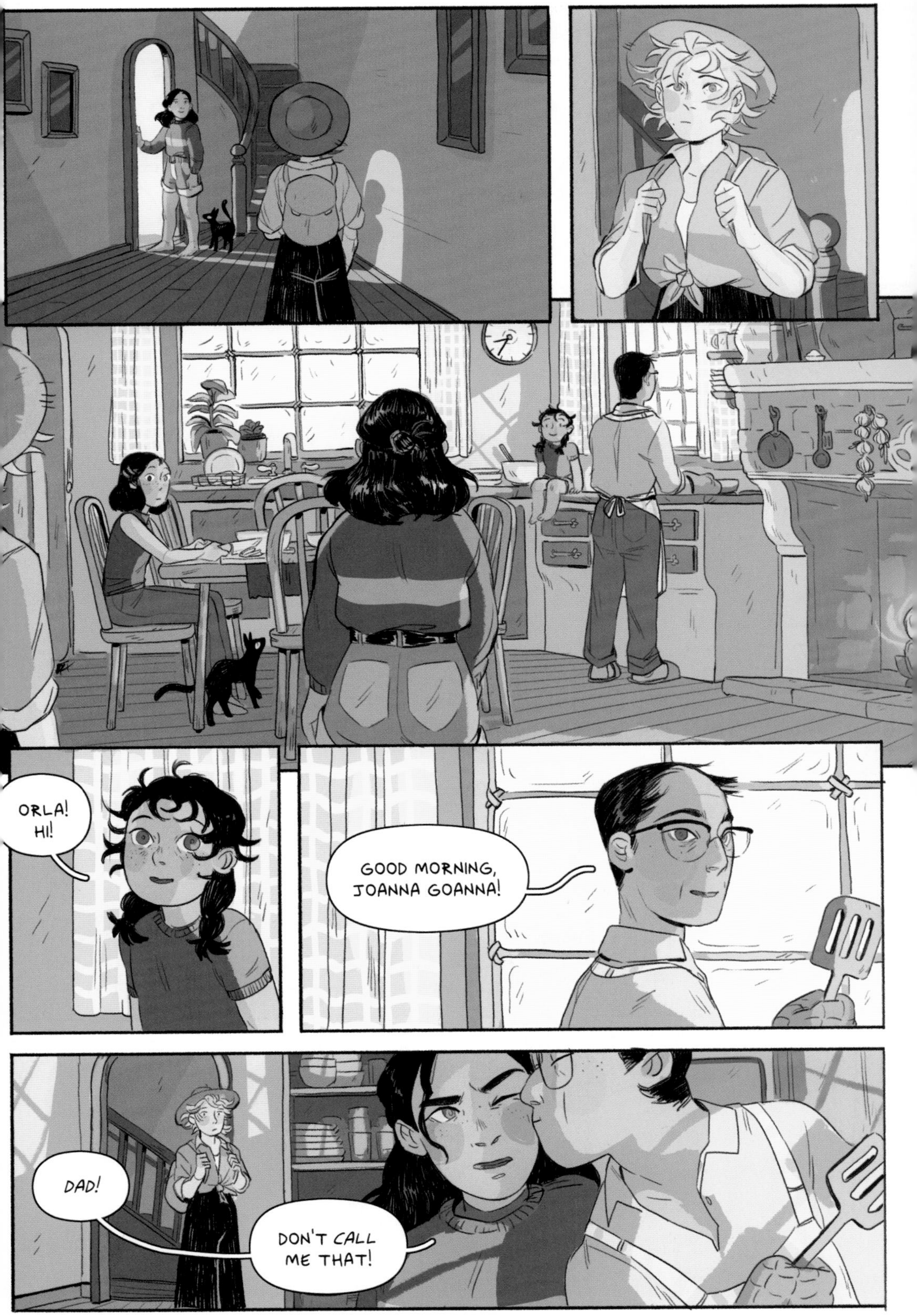
ORLA! HI!
GOOD MORNING, JOANNA GOANNA!
DAD!
DON'T CALL ME THAT!

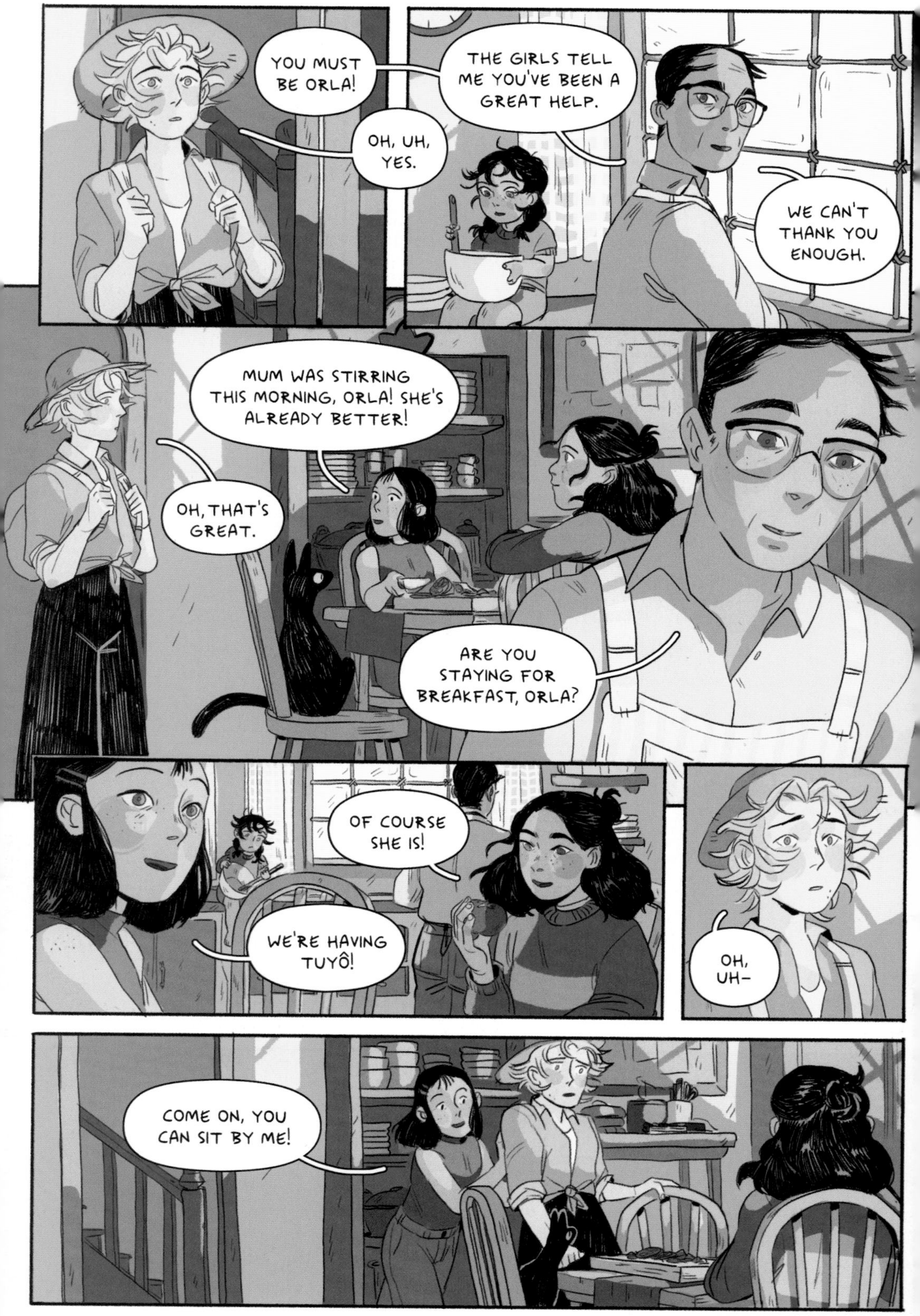
YOU MUST BE ORLA!
THE GIRLS TELL ME YOU'VE BEEN A GREAT HELP.
OH, UH, YES.
WE CAN'T THANK YOU ENOUGH.
MUM WAS STIRRING THIS MORNING, ORLA! SHE'S ALREADY BETTER!
OH, THAT'S GREAT.
ARE YOU STAYING FOR BREAKFAST, ORLA?
OF COURSE SHE IS!
WE'RE HAVING TUYÔ!
OH, UH-
COME ON, YOU CAN SIT BY ME!

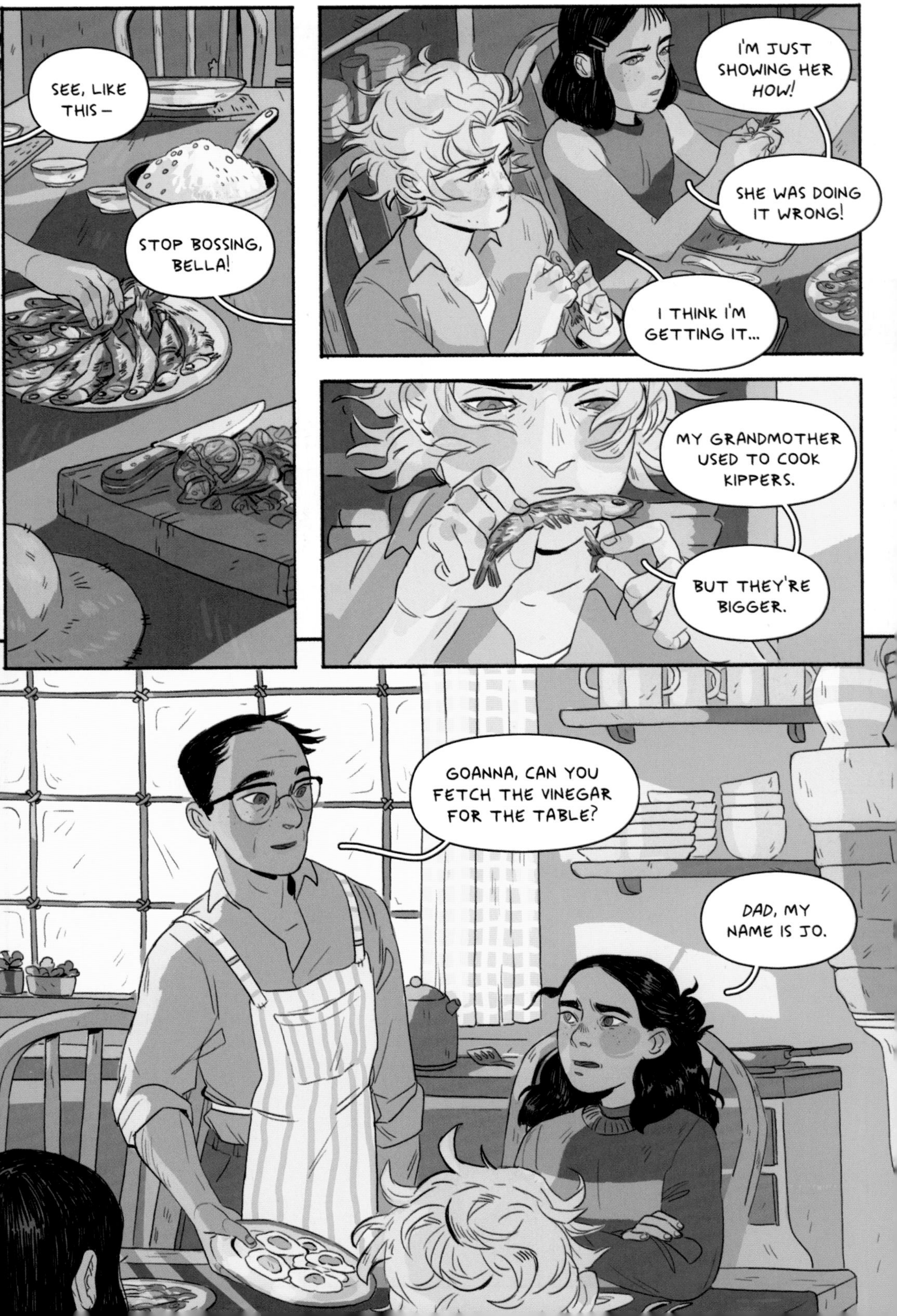
SEE, LIKE THIS –
STOP BOSSING, BELLA!
I'M JUST SHOWING HER HOW!
SHE WAS DOING IT WRONG!
I THINK I'M GETTING IT...
MY GRANDMOTHER USED TO COOK KIPPERS.
BUT THEY'RE BIGGER.
GOANNA, CAN YOU FETCH THE VINEGAR FOR THE TABLE?
DAD, MY NAME IS JO.

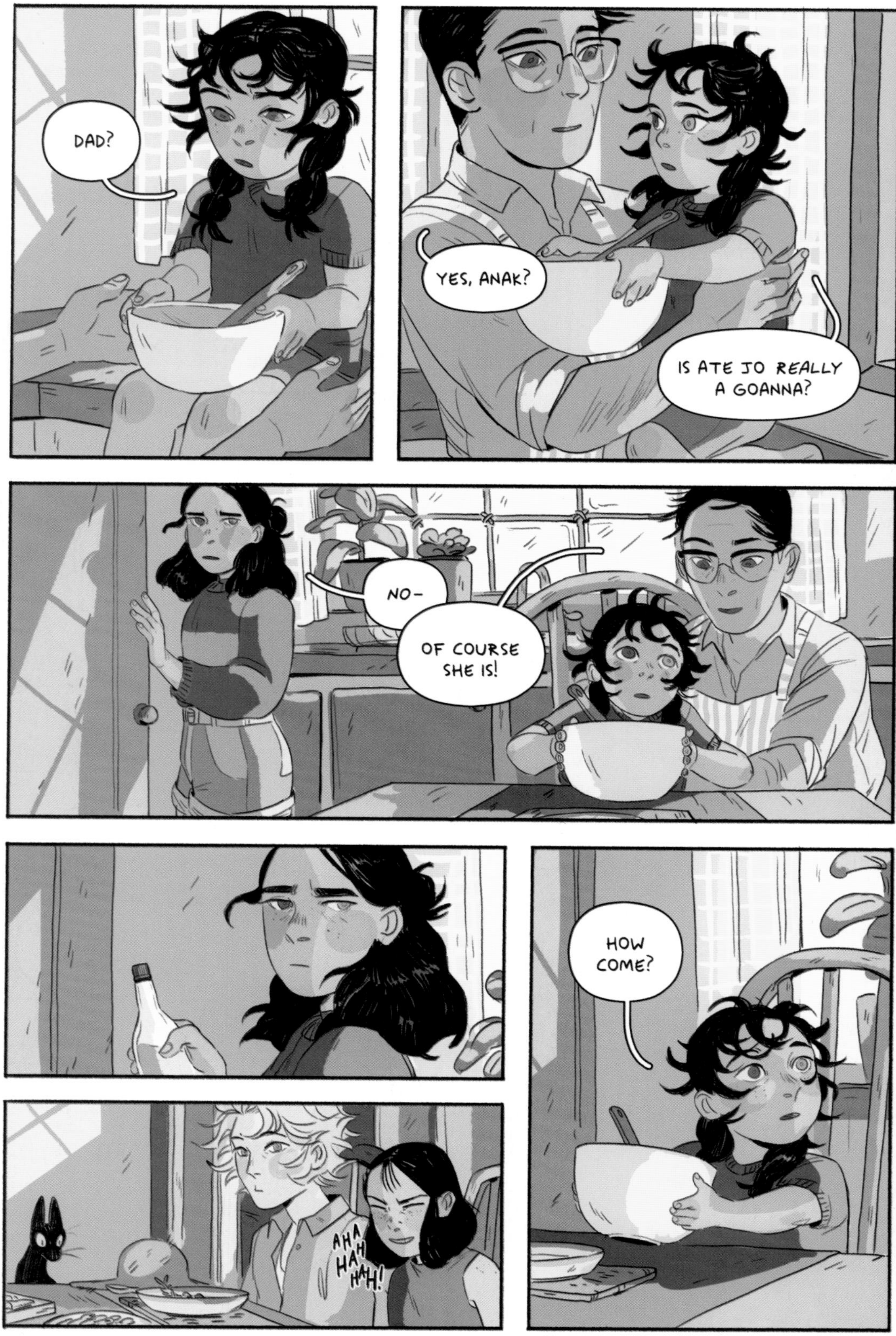
DAD?
YES, ANAK?
IS ATE JO REALLY A GOANNA?
NO-
OF COURSE SHE IS!
HOW COME?
AHAHAHAHAH!

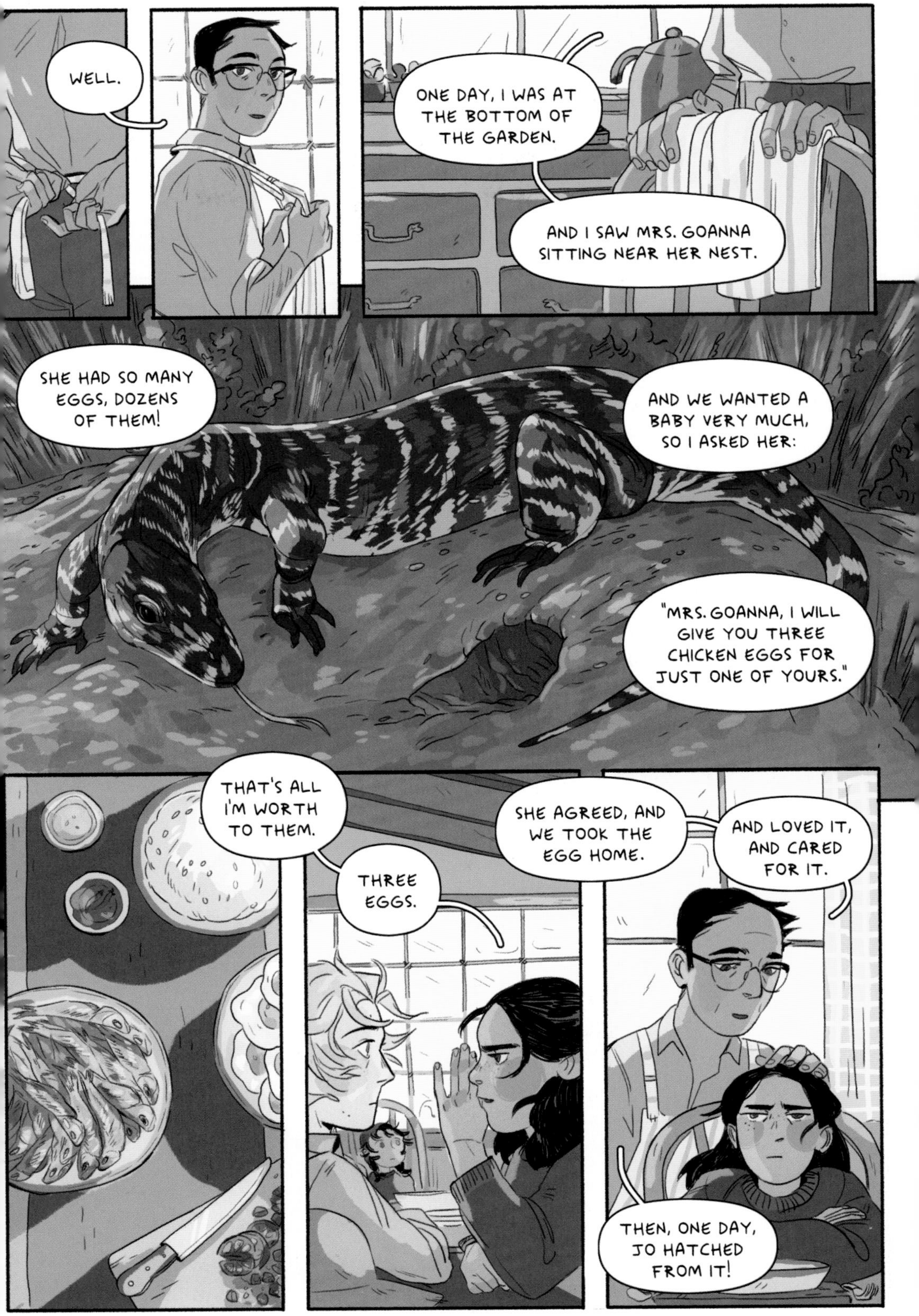
WELL.
ONE DAY, I WAS AT THE BOTTOM OF THE GARDEN.
AND I SAW MRS. GOANNA SITTING NEAR HER NEST.
SHE HAD SO MANY EGGS, DOZENS OF THEM!
AND WE WANTED A BABY VERY MUCH, SO I ASKED HER:
"MRS. GOANNA, I WILL GIVE YOU THREE CHICKEN EGGS FOR JUST ONE OF YOURS."
THAT'S ALL I'M WORTH TO THEM.
THREE EGGS.
SHE AGREED, AND WE TOOK THE EGG HOME.
AND LOVED IT, AND CARED FOR IT.
THEN, ONE DAY, JO HATCHED FROM IT!

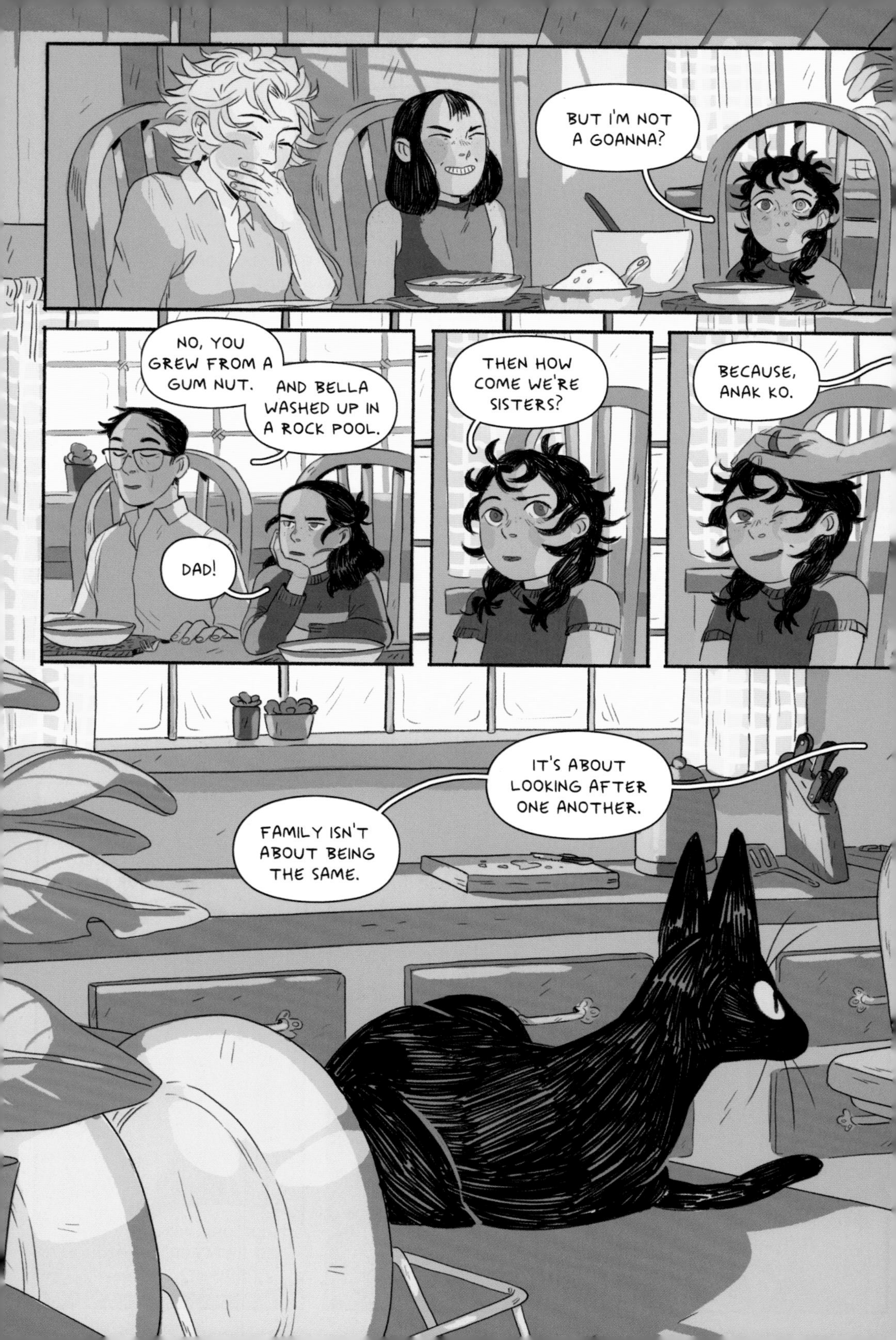
BUT I'M NOT A GOANNA?
NO, YOU GREW FROM A GUM NUT.
AND BELLA WASHED UP IN A ROCK POOL.
DAD!
THEN HOW COME WE'RE SISTERS?
BECAUSE, ANAK KO.
FAMILY ISN'T ABOUT BEING THE SAME.
IT'S ABOUT LOOKING AFTER ONE ANOTHER.

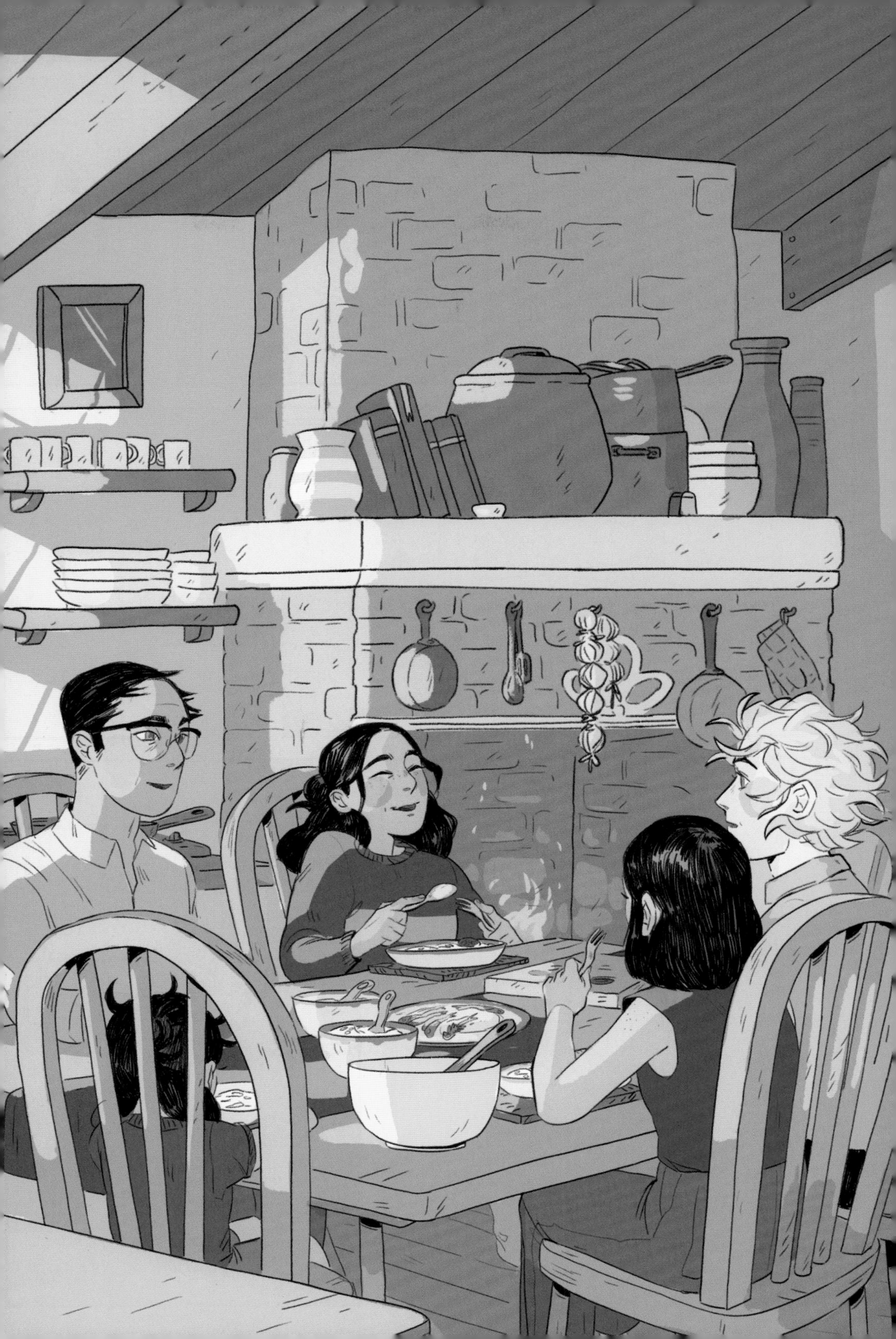

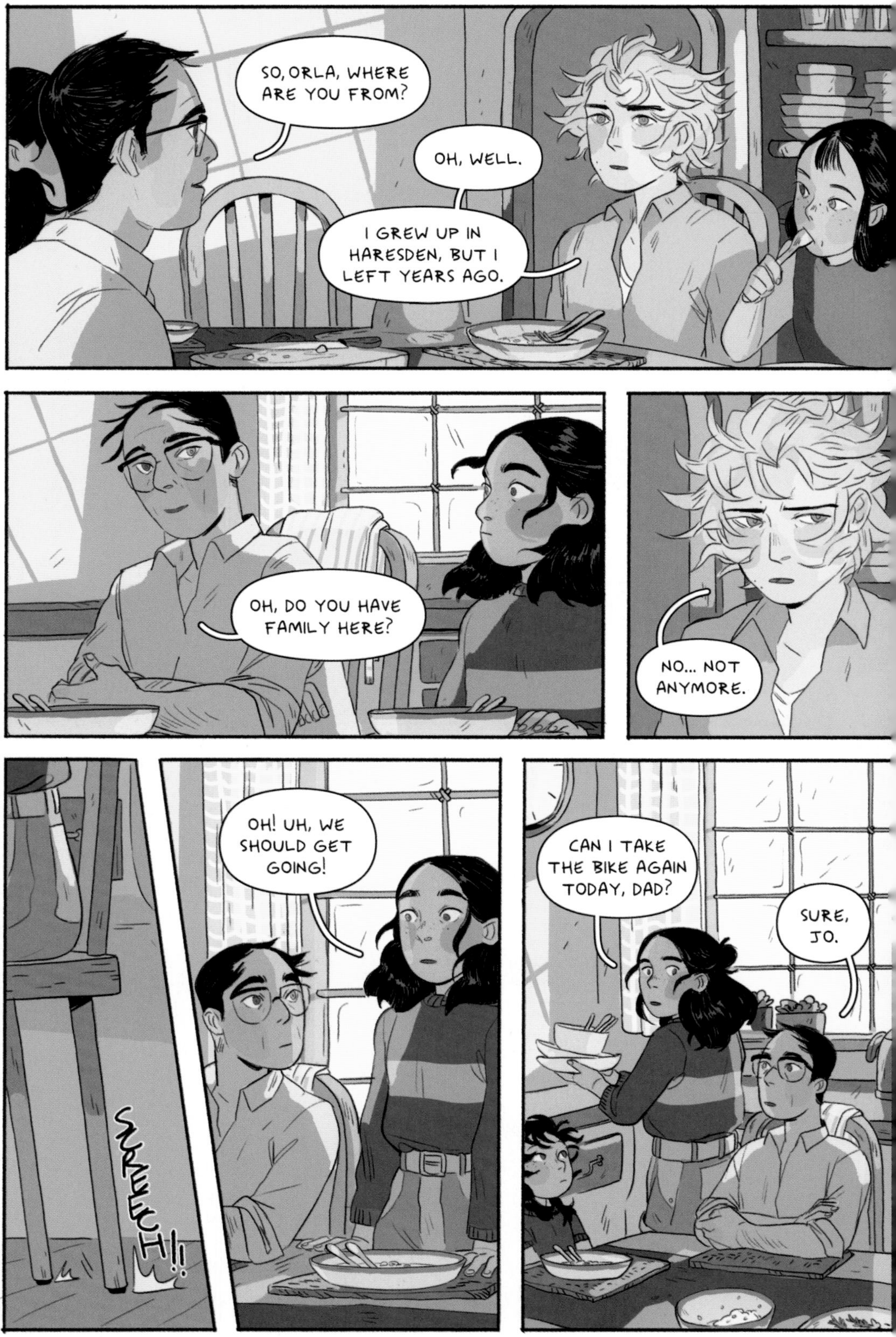
SO, ORLA, WHERE ARE YOU FROM?
OH, WELL.
I GREW UP IN HARESDEN, BUT I LEFT YEARS AGO.
OH, DO YOU HAVE FAMILY HERE?
NO... NOT ANYMORE.
SCREECH!!
OH! UH, WE SHOULD GET GOING!
CAN I TAKE THE BIKE AGAIN TODAY, DAD?
SURE, JO.

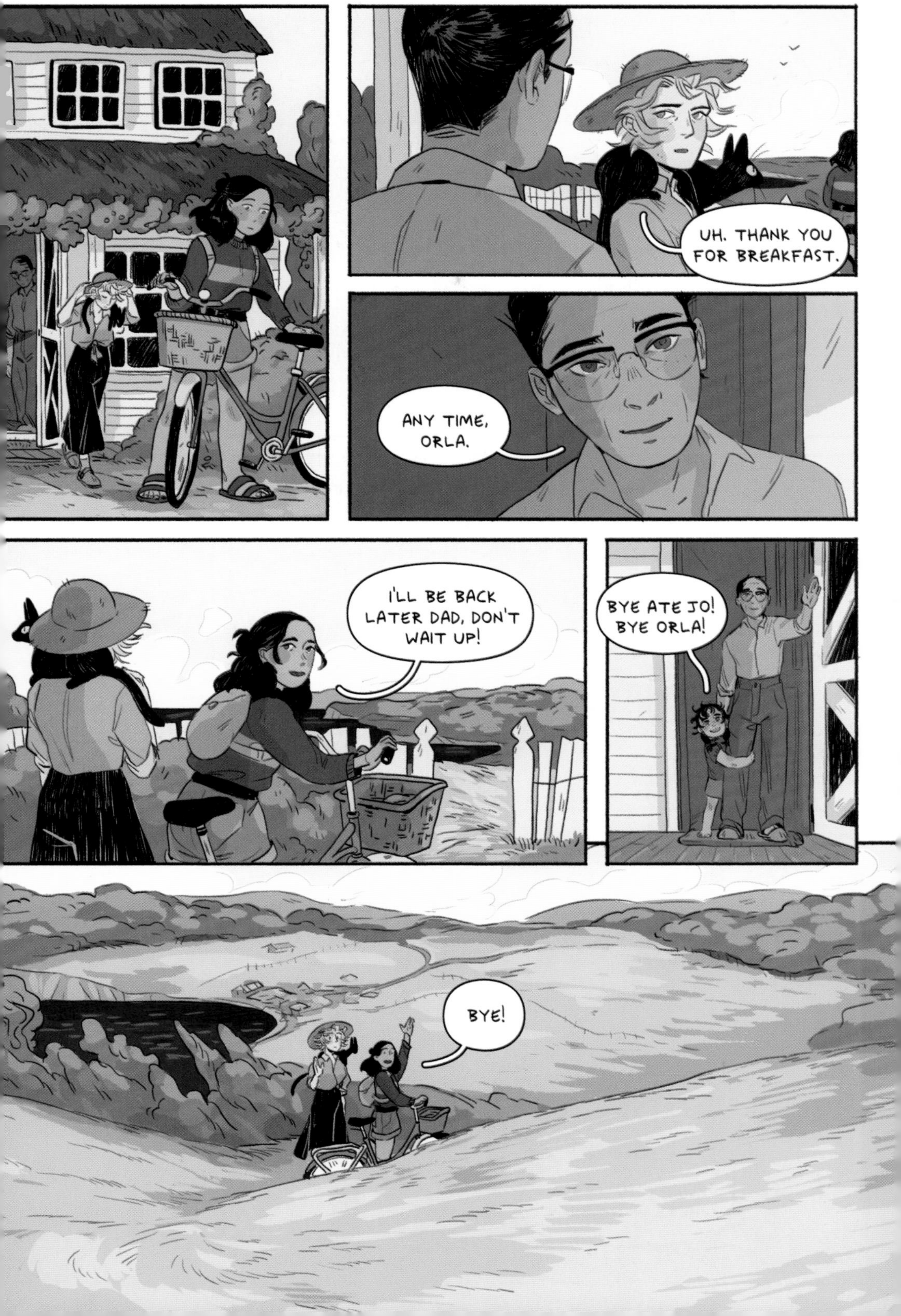
UH. THANK YOU FOR BREAKFAST.
ANY TIME, ORLA.
I'LL BE BACK LATER DAD, DON'T WAIT UP!
BYE ATE JO! BYE ORLA!
BYE!

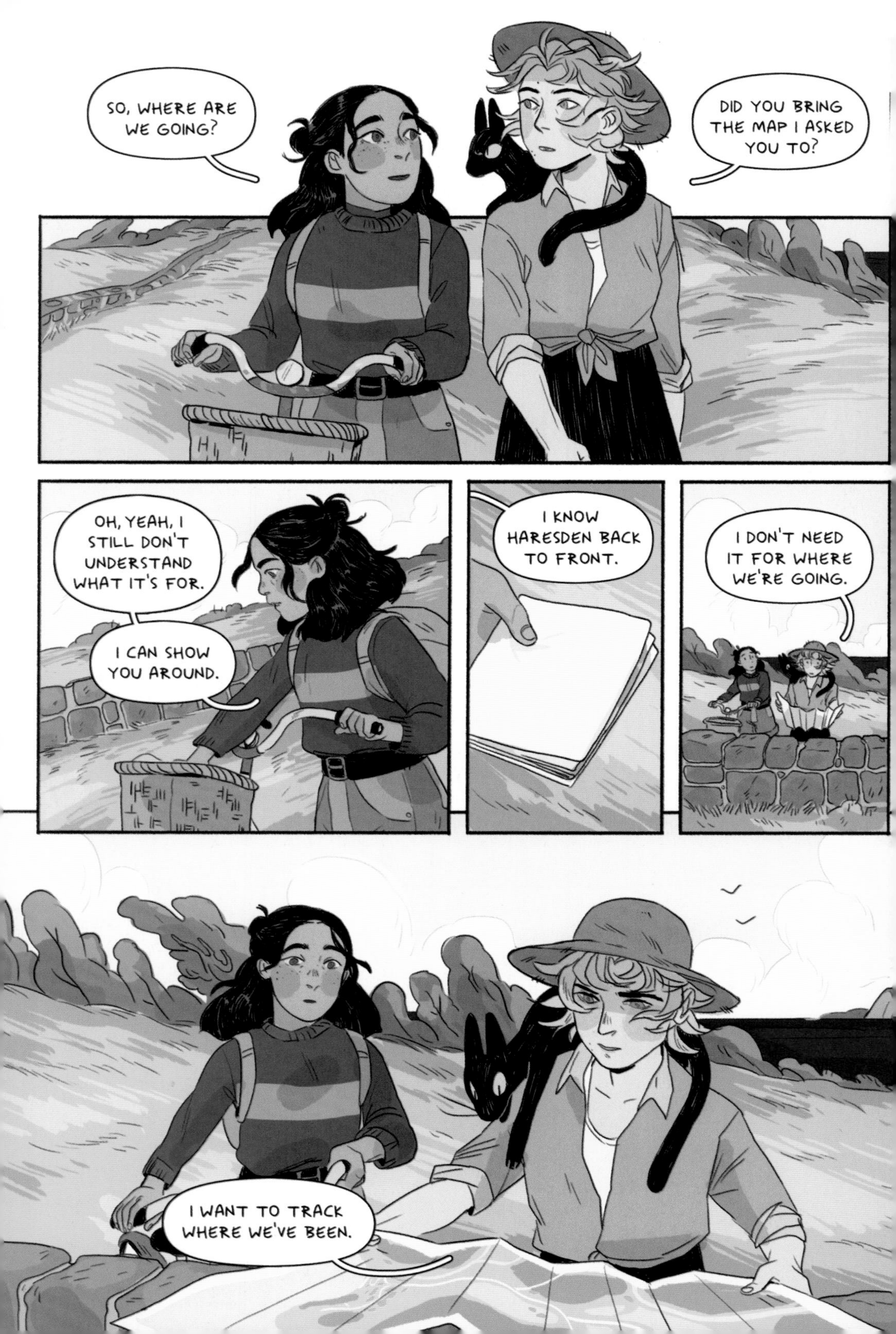
SO, WHERE ARE WE GOING?
DID YOU BRING THE MAP I ASKED YOU TO?
OH, YEAH, I STILL DON'T UNDERSTAND WHAT IT'S FOR.
I CAN SHOW YOU AROUND.
I KNOW HARESDEN BACK TO FRONT.
I DON'T NEED IT FOR WHERE WE'RE GOING.
I WANT TO TRACK WHERE WE'VE BEEN.

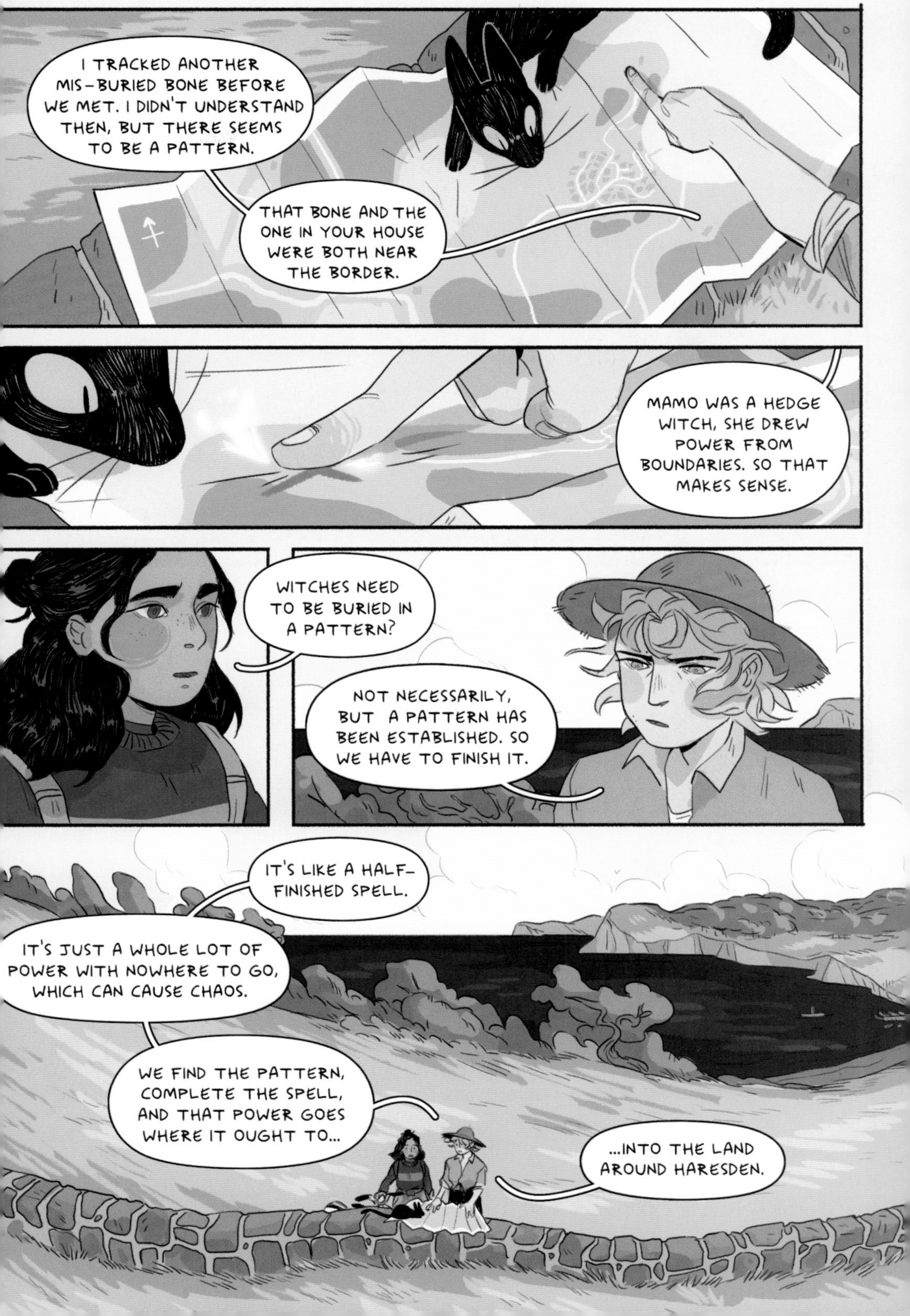

I TRACKED ANOTHER MIS-BURIED BONE BEFORE WE MET. I DIDN'T UNDERSTAND THEN, BUT THERE SEEMS TO BE A PATTERN.
THAT BONE AND THE ONE IN YOUR HOUSE WERE BOTH NEAR THE BORDER.
MAMO WAS A HEDGE WITCH, SHE DREW POWER FROM BOUNDARIES. SO THAT MAKES SENSE.
WITCHES NEED TO BE BURIED IN A PATTERN?
NOT NECESSARILY, BUT A PATTERN HAS BEEN ESTABLISHED. SO WE HAVE TO FINISH IT.
IT'S LIKE A HALF-FINISHED SPELL.
IT'S JUST A WHOLE LOT OF POWER WITH NOWHERE TO GO, WHICH CAN CAUSE CHAOS.
WE FIND THE PATTERN, COMPLETE THE SPELL, AND THAT POWER GOES WHERE IT OUGHT TO...
...INTO THE LAND AROUND HARESDEN.

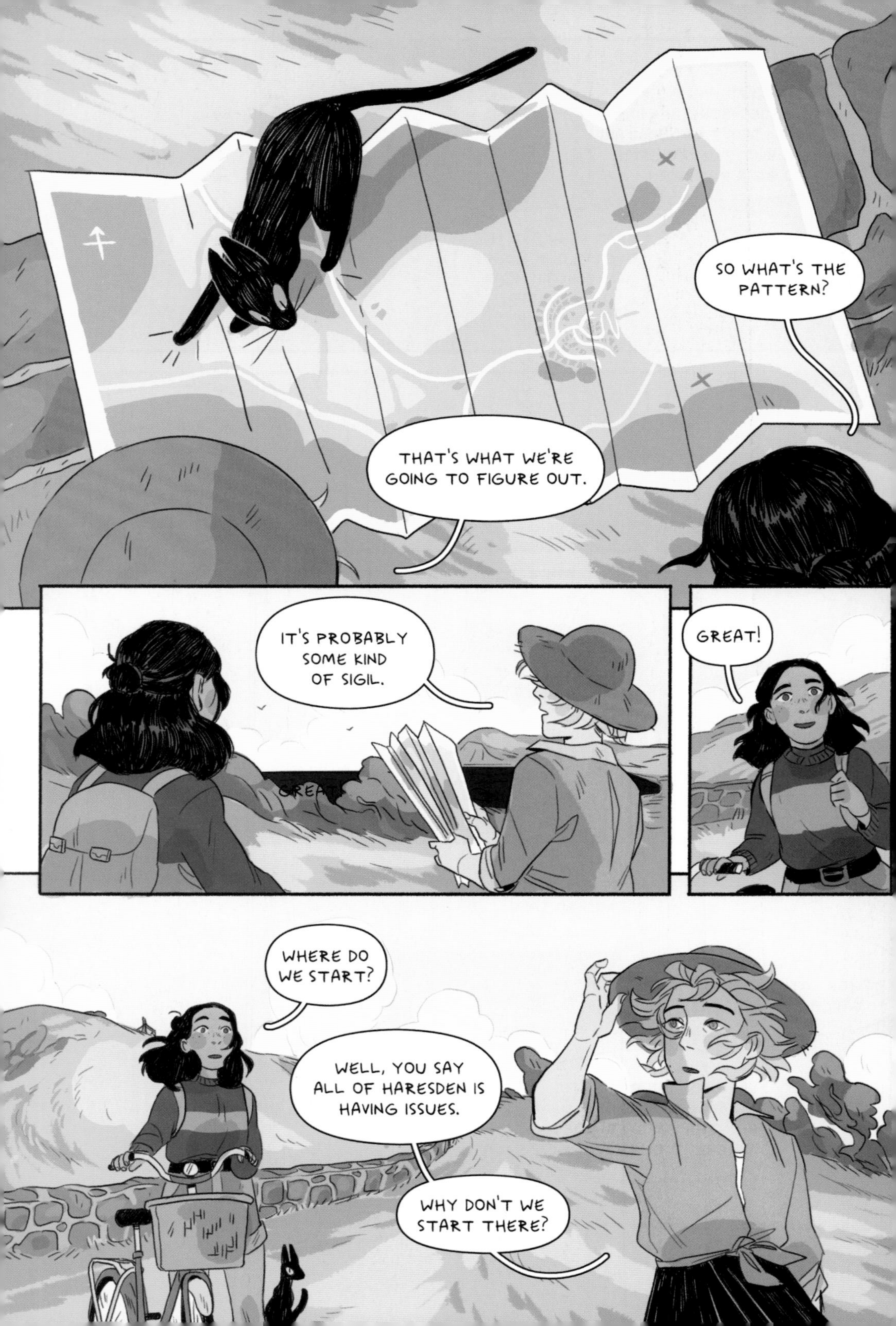
SO WHAT'S THE PATTERN?
THAT'S WHAT WE'RE GOING TO FIGURE OUT.
IT'S PROBABLY SOME KIND OF SIGIL.
GREAT!
WHERE DO WE START?
WELL, YOU SAY ALL OF HARESDEN IS HAVING ISSUES.
WHY DON'T WE START THERE?

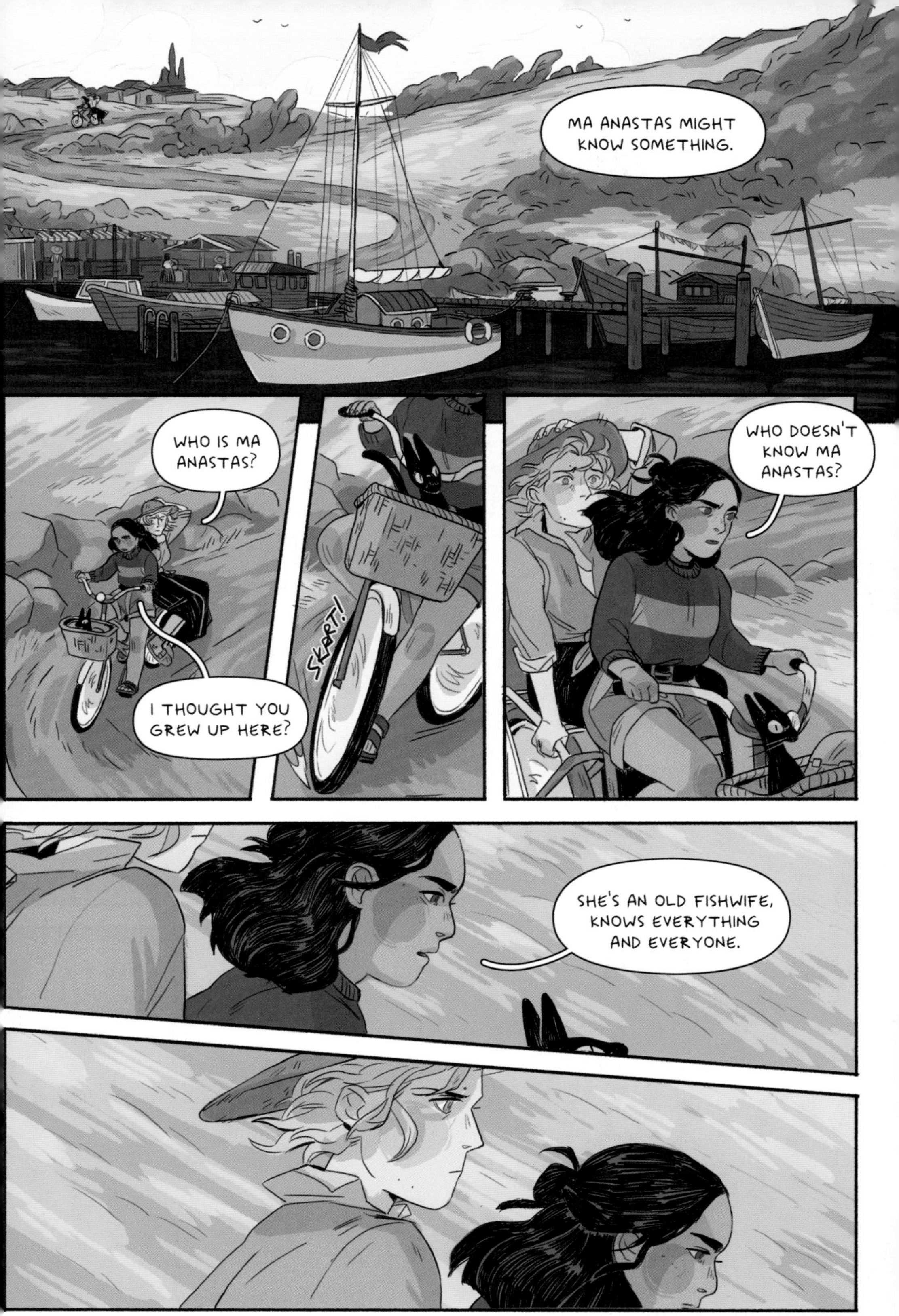
MA ANASTAS MIGHT KNOW SOMETHING.
WHO IS MA ANASTAS?
I THOUGHT YOU GREW UP HERE?
SKRRT!
WHO DOESN'T KNOW MA ANASTAS?
SHE'S AN OLD FISHWIFE, KNOWS EVERYTHING AND EVERYONE.

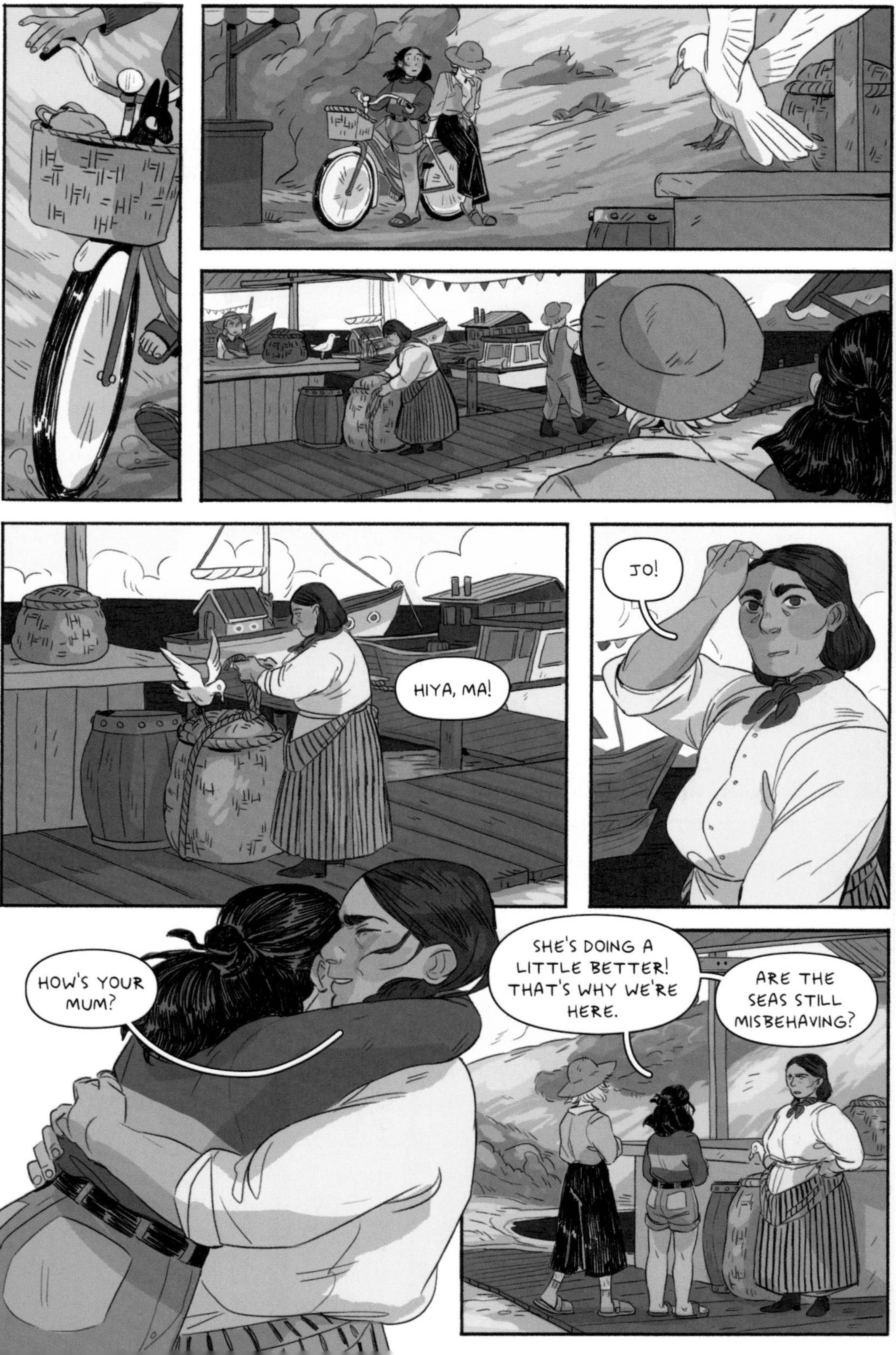
HIYA, MA!
JO!
HOW'S YOUR MUM?
SHE'S DOING A LITTLE BETTER! THAT'S WHY WE'RE HERE.
ARE THE SEAS STILL MISBEHAVING?

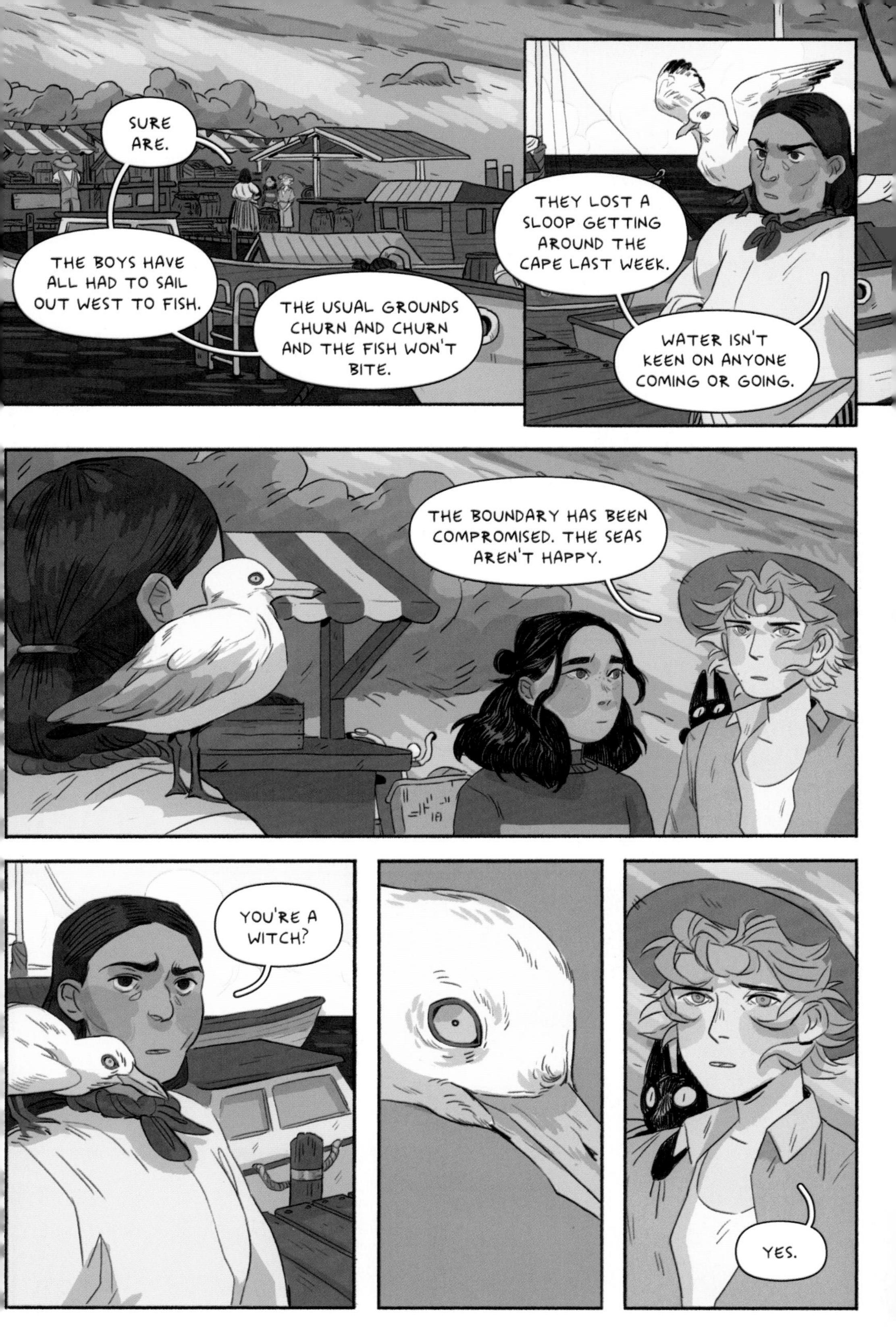
SURE ARE.
THE BOYS HAVE ALL HAD TO SAIL OUT WEST TO FISH.
THE USUAL GROUNDS CHURN AND CHURN AND THE FISH WON'T BITE.
THEY LOST A SLOOP GETTING AROUND THE CAPE LAST WEEK.
WATER ISN'T KEEN ON ANYONE COMING OR GOING.
THE BOUNDARY HAS BEEN COMPROMISED. THE SEAS AREN'T HAPPY.
YOU'RE A WITCH?
YES.

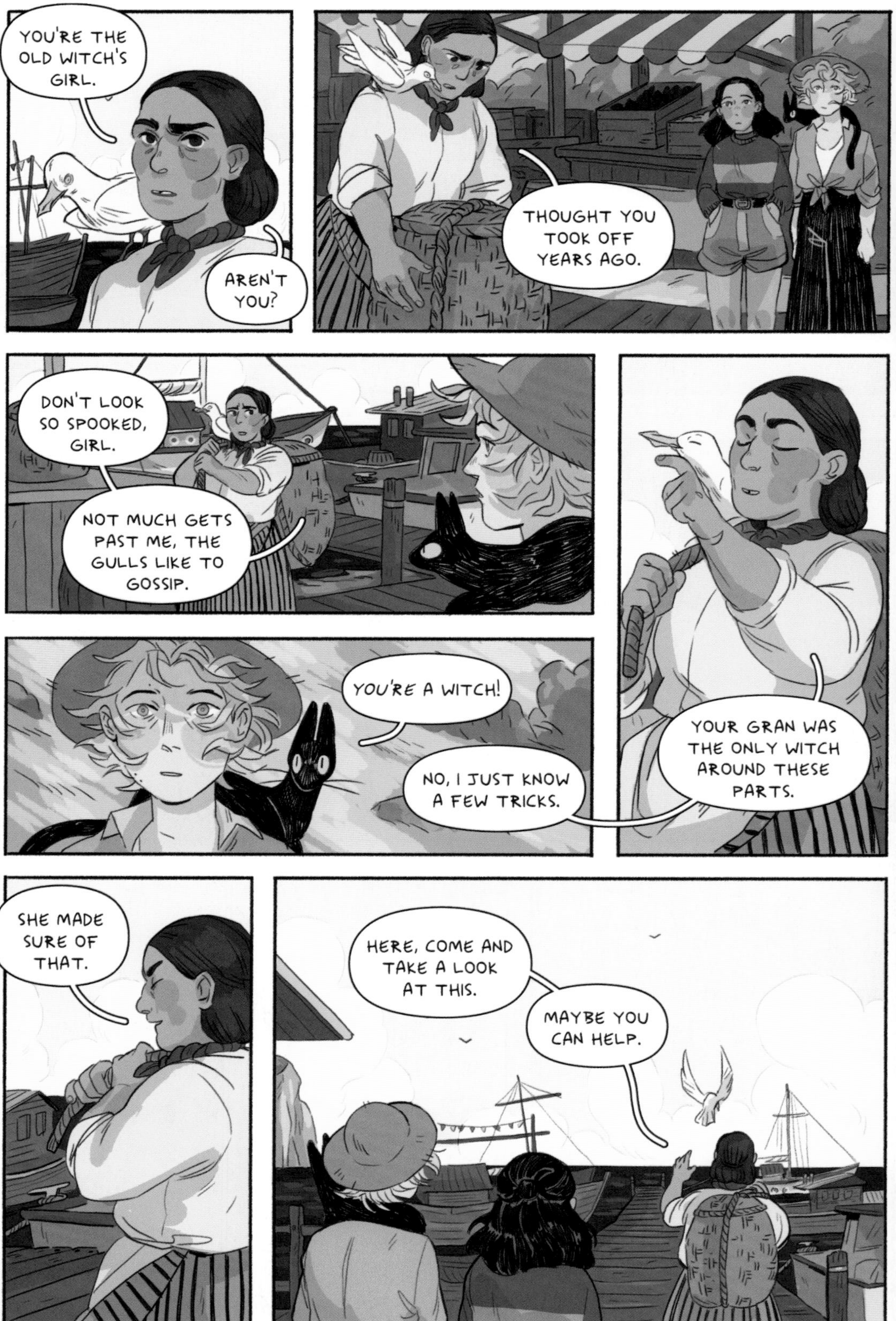
YOU'RE THE OLD WITCH'S GIRL.
AREN'T YOU?
THOUGHT YOU TOOK OFF YEARS AGO.
DON'T LOOK SO SPOOKED, GIRL.
NOT MUCH GETS PAST ME, THE GULLS LIKE TO GOSSIP.
YOU'RE A WITCH!
NO, I JUST KNOW A FEW TRICKS.
YOUR GRAN WAS THE ONLY WITCH AROUND THESE PARTS.
SHE MADE SURE OF THAT.
HERE, COME AND TAKE A LOOK AT THIS.
MAYBE YOU CAN HELP.

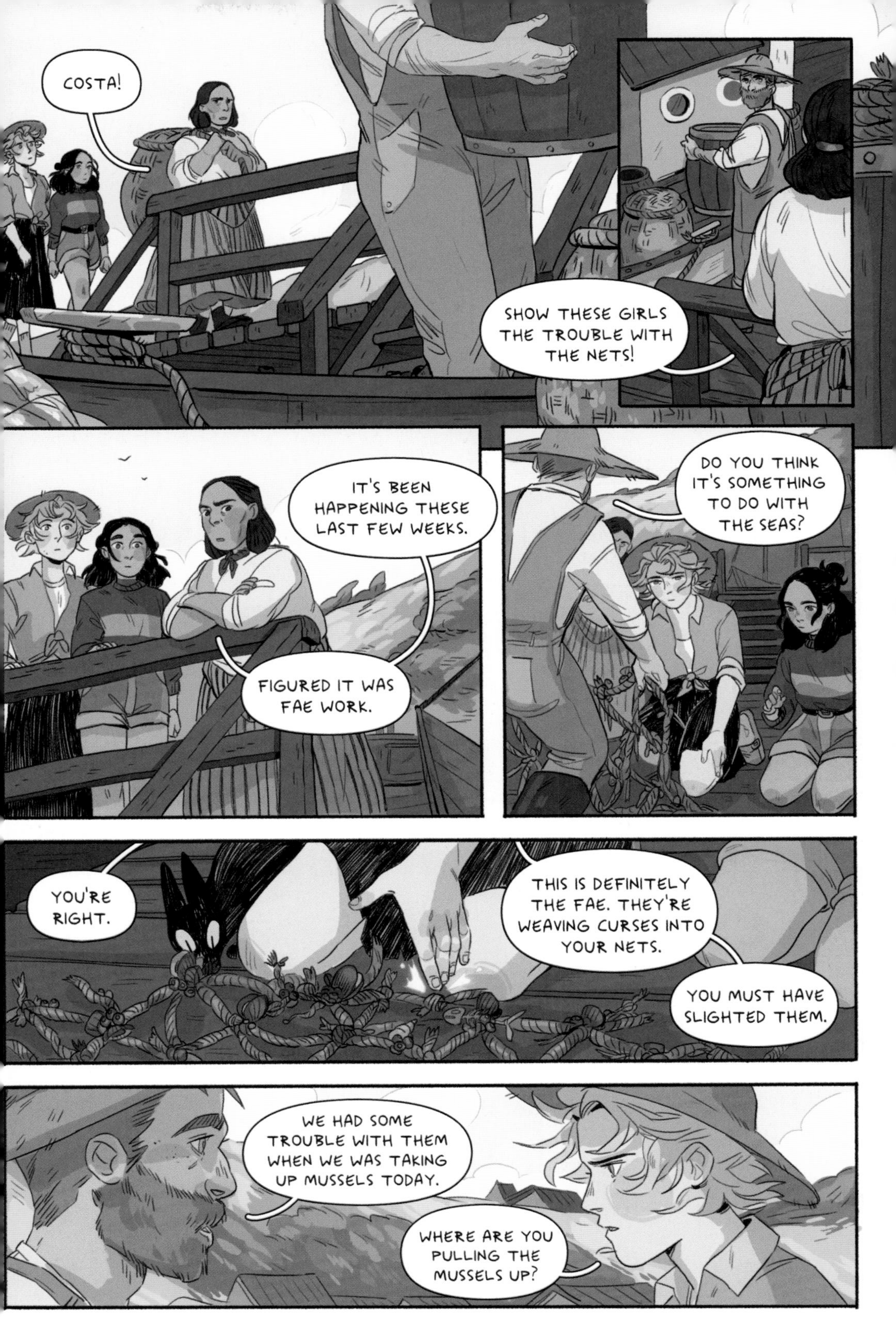
COSTA!
SHOW THESE GIRLS THE TROUBLE WITH THE NETS!
IT'S BEEN HAPPENING THESE LAST FEW WEEKS.
FIGURED IT WAS FAE WORK.
DO YOU THINK IT'S SOMETHING TO DO WITH THE SEAS?
YOU'RE RIGHT.
THIS IS DEFINITELY THE FAE. THEY'RE WEAVING CURSES INTO YOUR NETS.
YOU MUST HAVE SLIGHTED THEM.
WE HAD SOME TROUBLE WITH THEM WHEN WE WAS TAKING UP MUSSELS TODAY.
WHERE ARE YOU PULLING THE MUSSELS UP?

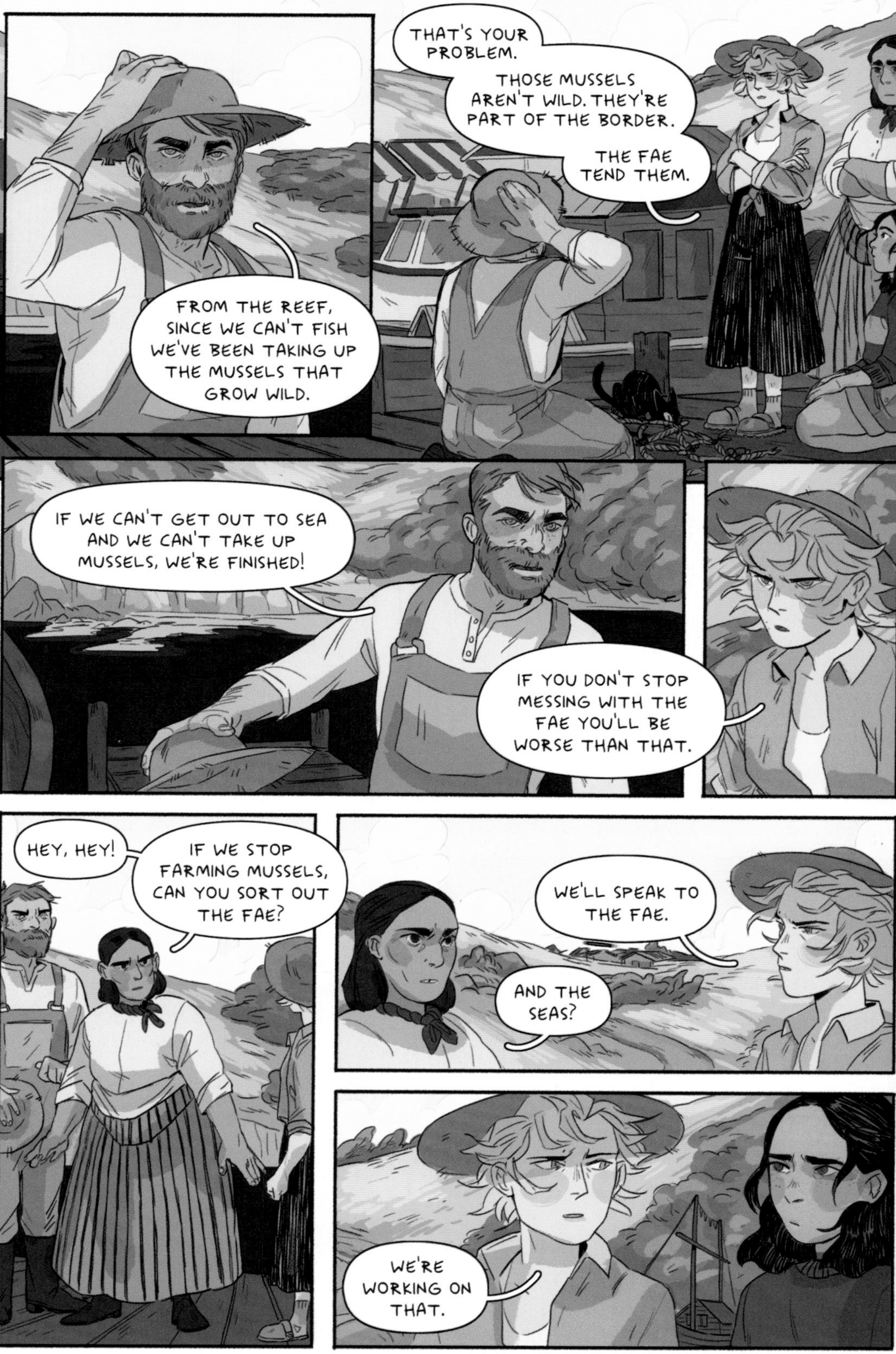
FROM THE REEF, SINCE WE CAN'T FISH WE'VE BEEN TAKING UP THE MUSSELS THAT GROW WILD.
THAT'S YOUR PROBLEM.
THOSE MUSSELS AREN'T WILD. THEY'RE PART OF THE BORDER.
THE FAE TEND THEM.
IF WE CAN'T GET OUT TO SEA AND WE CAN'T TAKE UP MUSSELS, WE'RE FINISHED!
IF YOU DON'T STOP MESSING WITH THE FAE YOU'LL BE WORSE THAN THAT.
HEY, HEY!
IF WE STOP FARMING MUSSELS, CAN YOU SORT OUT THE FAE?
WE'LL SPEAK TO THE FAE.
AND THE SEAS?
WE'RE WORKING ON THAT.

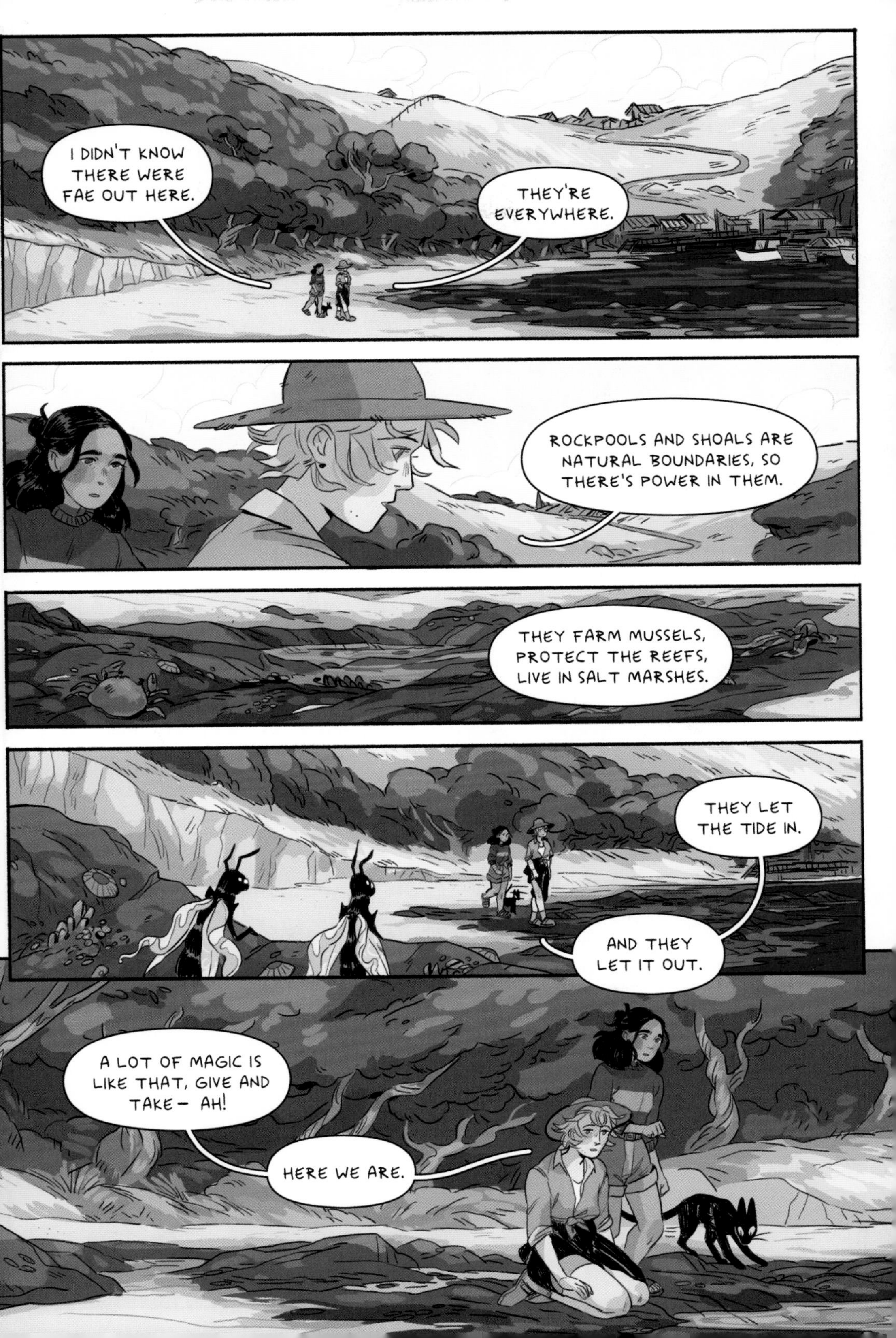
I DIDN'T KNOW THERE WERE FAE OUT HERE.
THEY'RE EVERYWHERE.
ROCKPOOLS AND SHOALS ARE NATURAL BOUNDARIES, SO THERE'S POWER IN THEM.
THEY FARM MUSSELS, PROTECT THE REEFS, LIVE IN SALT MARSHES.
THEY LET THE TIDE IN.
AND THEY LET IT OUT.
A LOT OF MAGIC IS LIKE THAT, GIVE AND TAKE— AH!
HERE WE ARE.

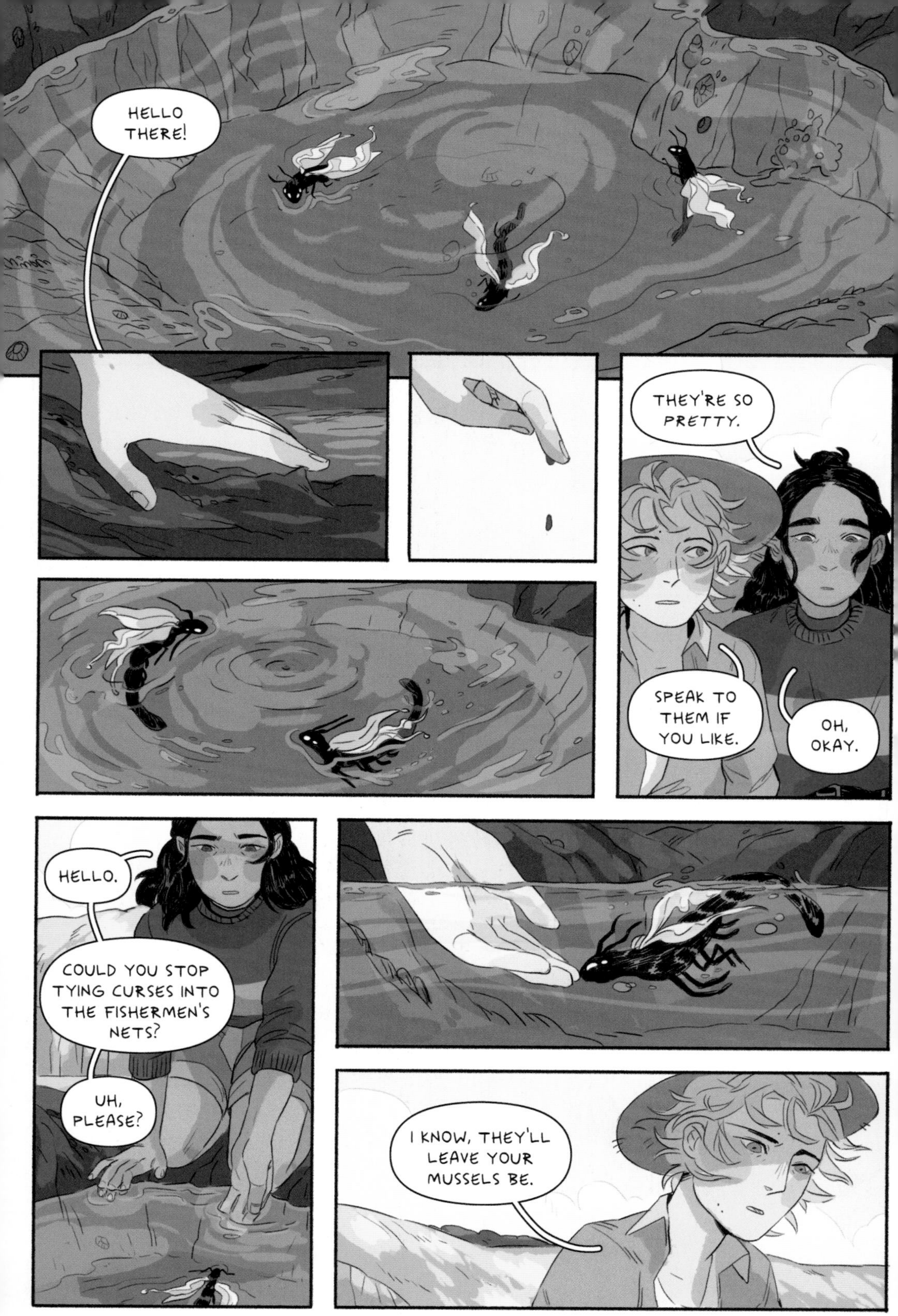
HELLO THERE!
THEY'RE SO PRETTY.
SPEAK TO THEM IF YOU LIKE.
OH, OKAY.
HELLO.
COULD YOU STOP TYING CURSES INTO THE FISHERMEN'S NETS?
UH, PLEASE?
I KNOW, THEY'LL LEAVE YOUR MUSSELS BE.

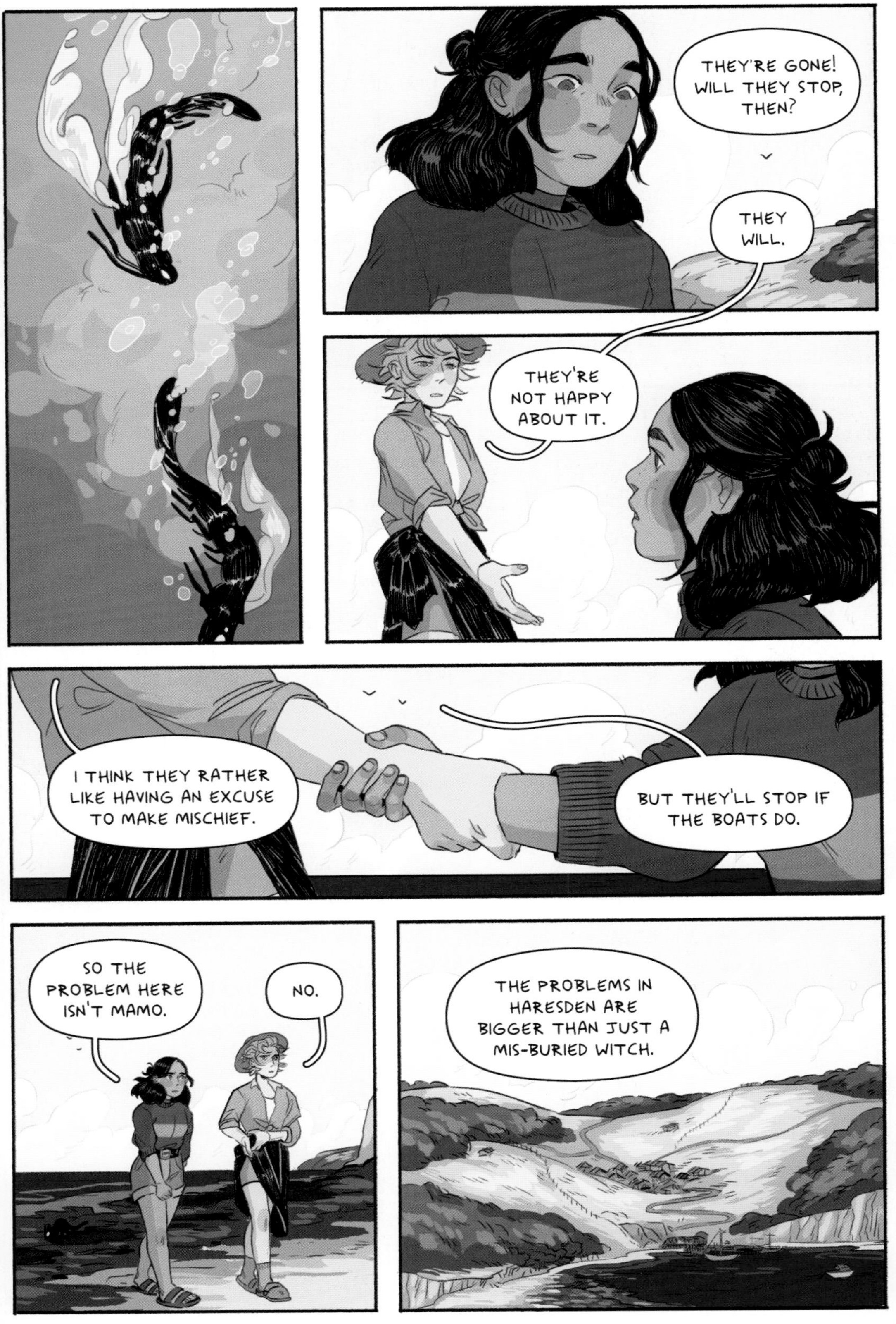
THEY'RE GONE! WILL THEY STOP, THEN?
THEY WILL.
THEY'RE NOT HAPPY ABOUT IT.
I THINK THEY RATHER LIKE HAVING AN EXCUSE TO MAKE MISCHIEF.
BUT THEY'LL STOP IF THE BOATS DO.
SO THE PROBLEM HERE ISN'T MAMO.
NO.
THE PROBLEMS IN HARESDEN ARE BIGGER THAN JUST A MIS-BURIED WITCH.

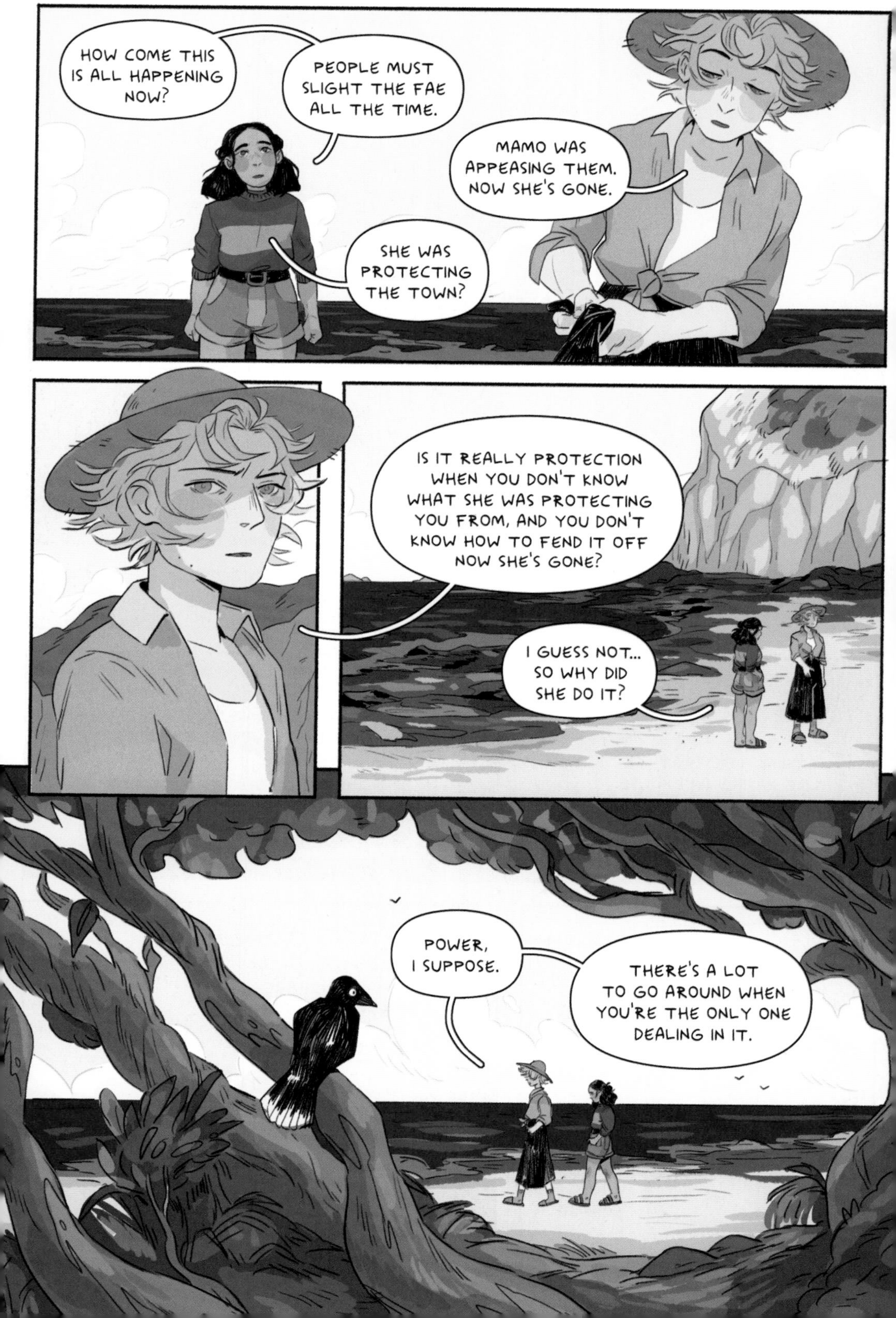
HOW COME THIS IS ALL HAPPENING NOW?
PEOPLE MUST SLIGHT THE FAE ALL THE TIME.
MAMO WAS APPEASING THEM. NOW SHE'S GONE.
SHE WAS PROTECTING THE TOWN?
IS IT REALLY PROTECTION WHEN YOU DON'T KNOW WHAT SHE WAS PROTECTING YOU FROM, AND YOU DON'T KNOW HOW TO FEND IT OFF NOW SHE'S GONE?
I GUESS NOT... SO WHY DID SHE DO IT?
POWER, I SUPPOSE.
THERE'S A LOT TO GO AROUND WHEN YOU'RE THE ONLY ONE DEALING IN IT.

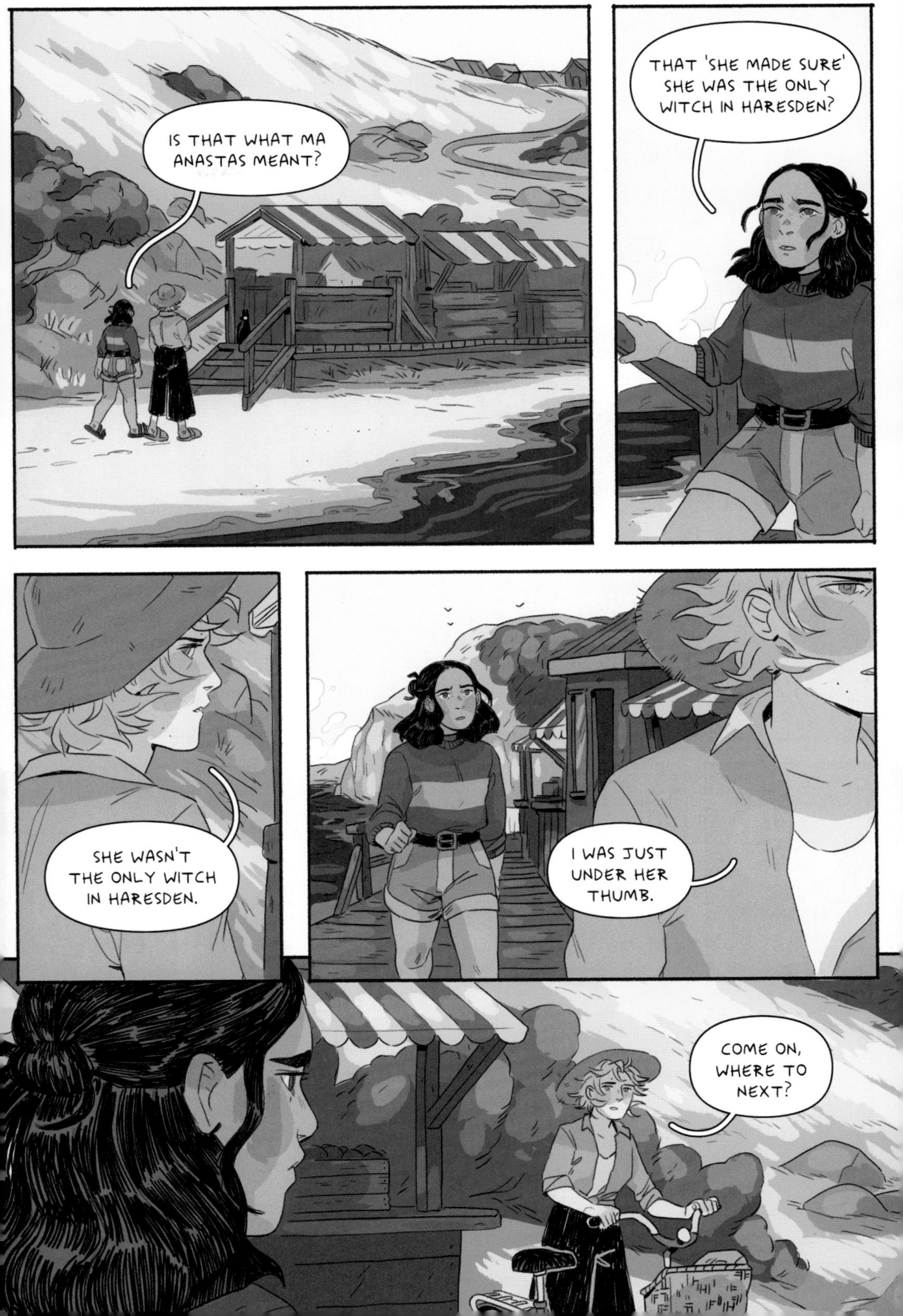
IS THAT WHAT MA ANASTAS MEANT?
THAT 'SHE MADE SURE' SHE WAS THE ONLY WITCH IN HARESDEN?
SHE WASN'T THE ONLY WITCH IN HARESDEN.
I WAS JUST UNDER HER THUMB.
COME ON, WHERE TO NEXT?

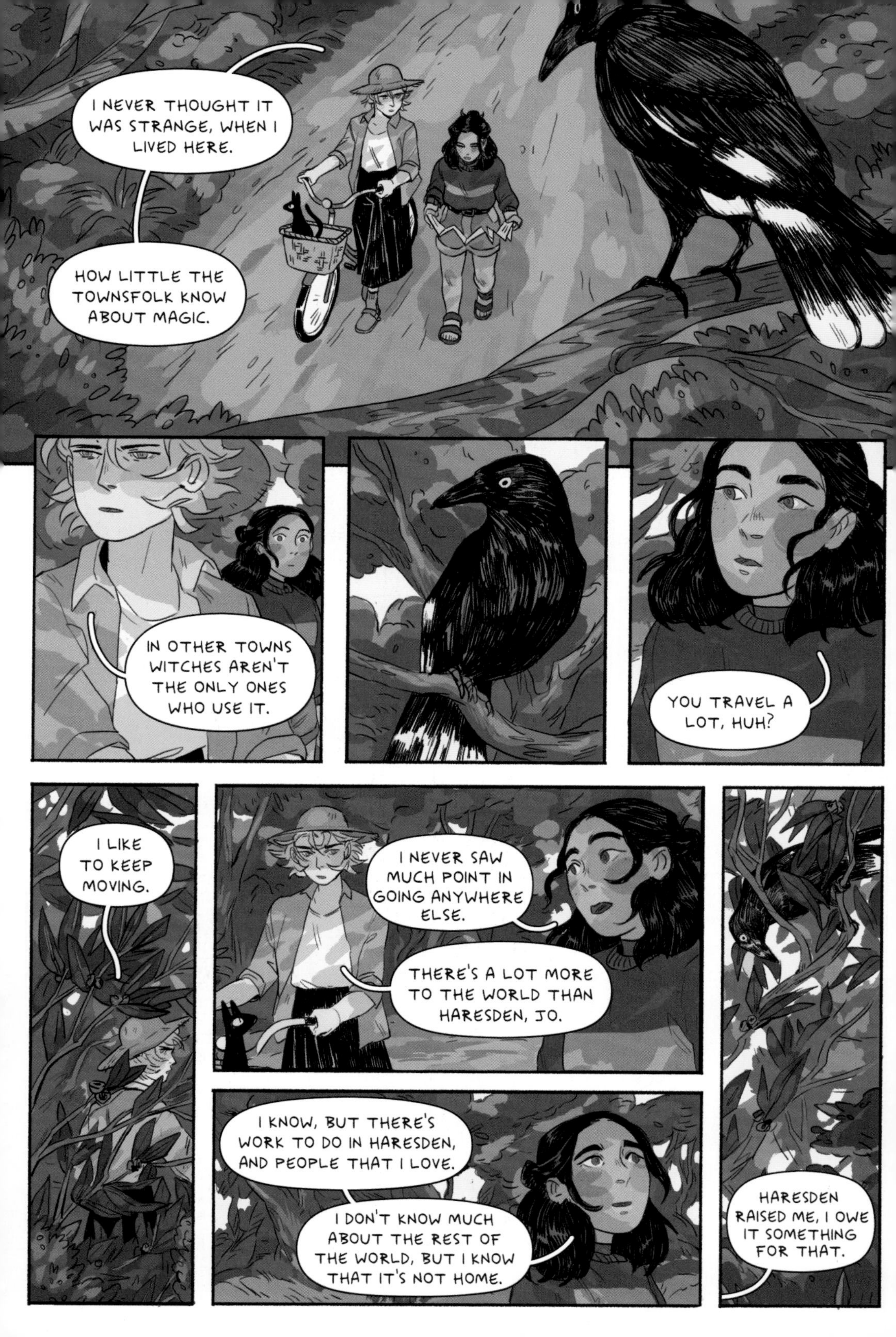
I NEVER THOUGHT IT WAS STRANGE, WHEN I LIVED HERE.
HOW LITTLE THE TOWNSFOLK KNOW ABOUT MAGIC.
IN OTHER TOWNS WITCHES AREN'T THE ONLY ONES WHO USE IT.
YOU TRAVEL A LOT, HUH?
I LIKE TO KEEP MOVING.
I NEVER SAW MUCH POINT IN GOING ANYWHERE ELSE.
THERE'S A LOT MORE TO THE WORLD THAN HARESDEN, JO.
I KNOW, BUT THERE'S WORK TO DO IN HARESDEN, AND PEOPLE THAT I LOVE.
I DON'T KNOW MUCH ABOUT THE REST OF THE WORLD, BUT I KNOW THAT IT'S NOT HOME.
HARESDEN RAISED ME, I OWE IT SOMETHING FOR THAT.

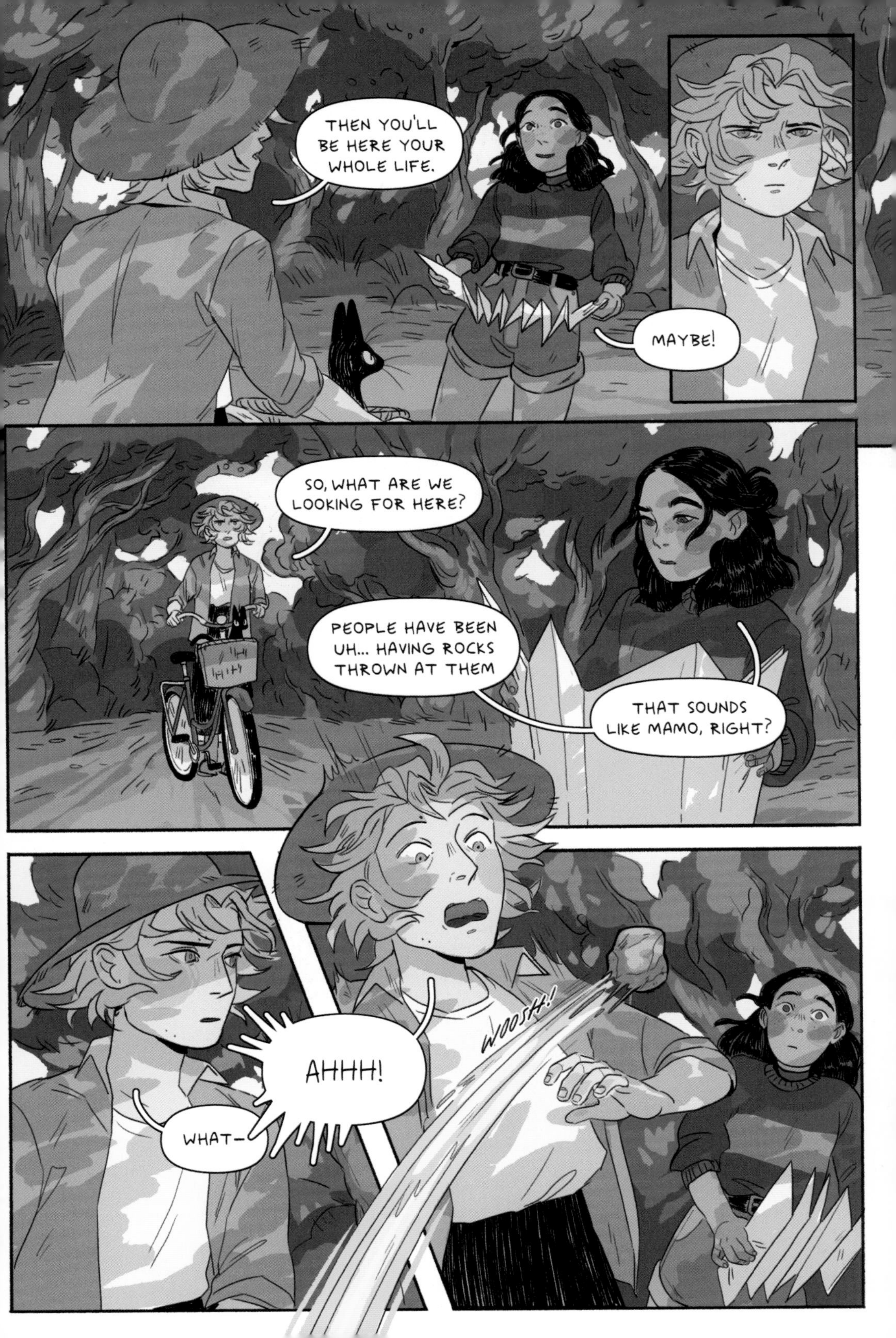
THEN YOU'LL BE HERE YOUR WHOLE LIFE.
MAYBE!
SO, WHAT ARE WE LOOKING FOR HERE?
PEOPLE HAVE BEEN UH... HAVING ROCKS THROWN AT THEM
THAT SOUNDS LIKE MAMO, RIGHT?
AHHH!
WHAT-
WOOSH!

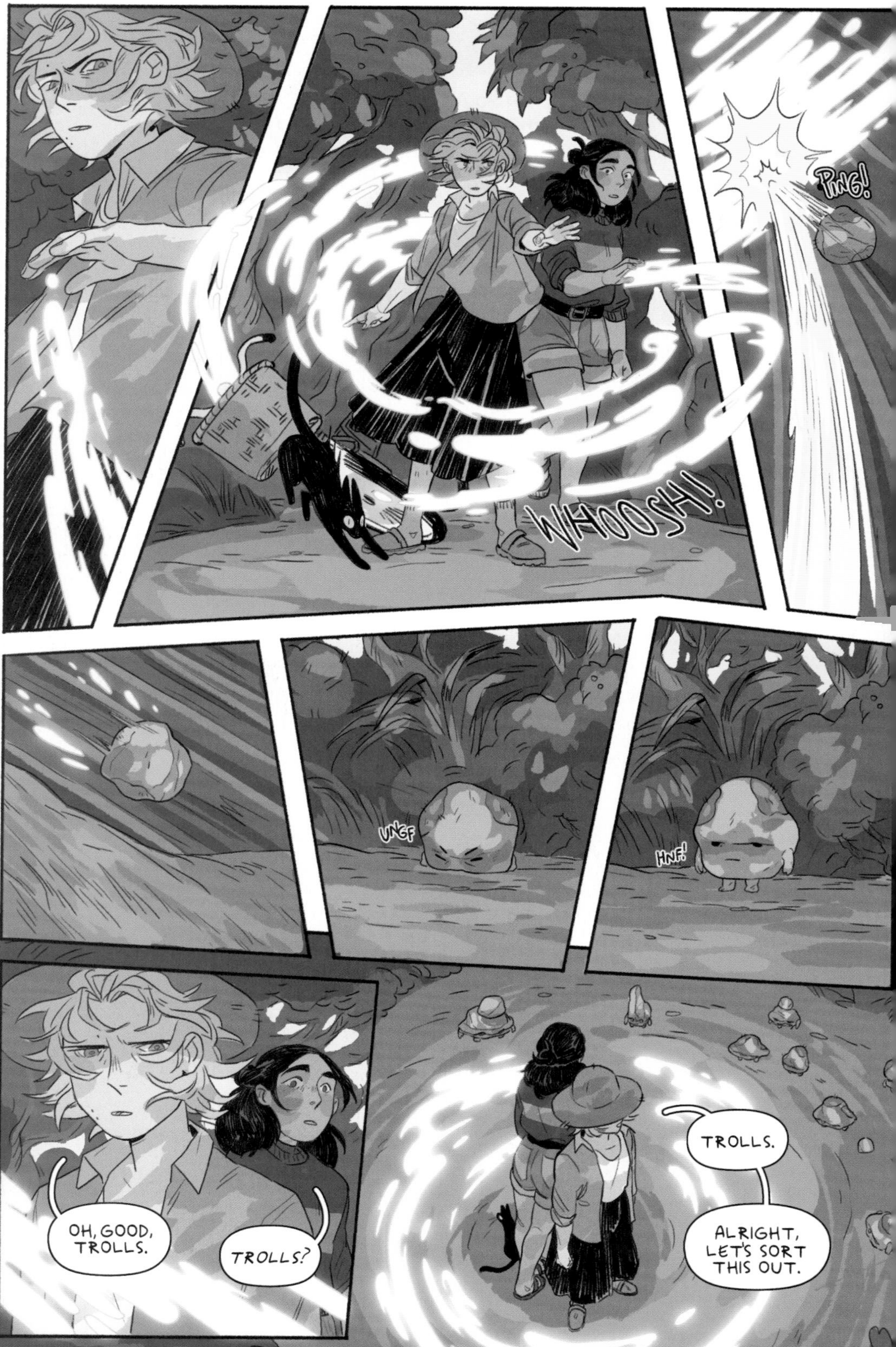
PING!
WHOOSH!
UNGF
HNF!
OH, GOOD, TROLLS.
TROLLS?
TROLLS.
ALRIGHT, LET'S SORT THIS OUT.

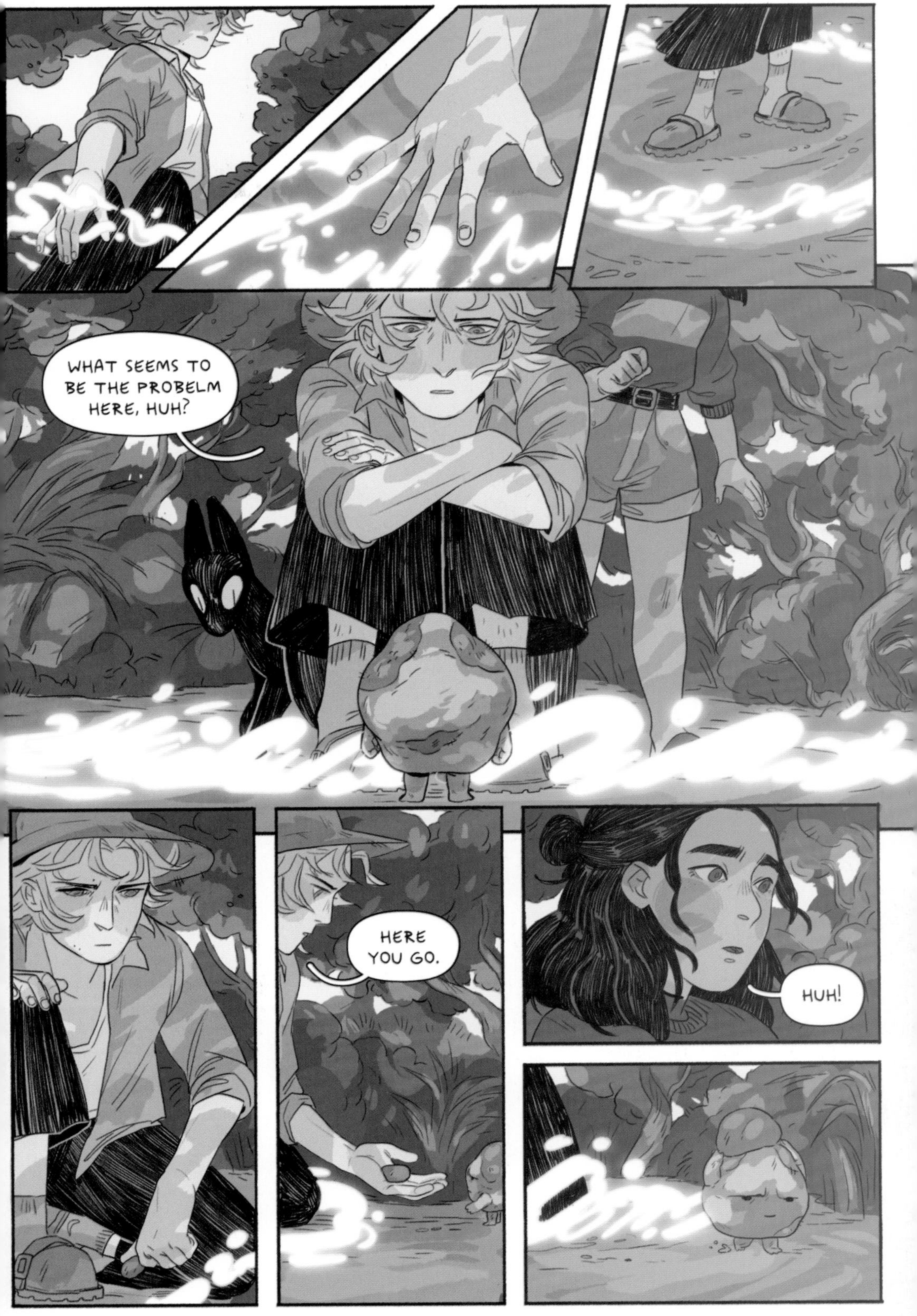
WHAT SEEMS TO BE THE PROBELM HERE, HUH?
HERE YOU GO.
HUH!

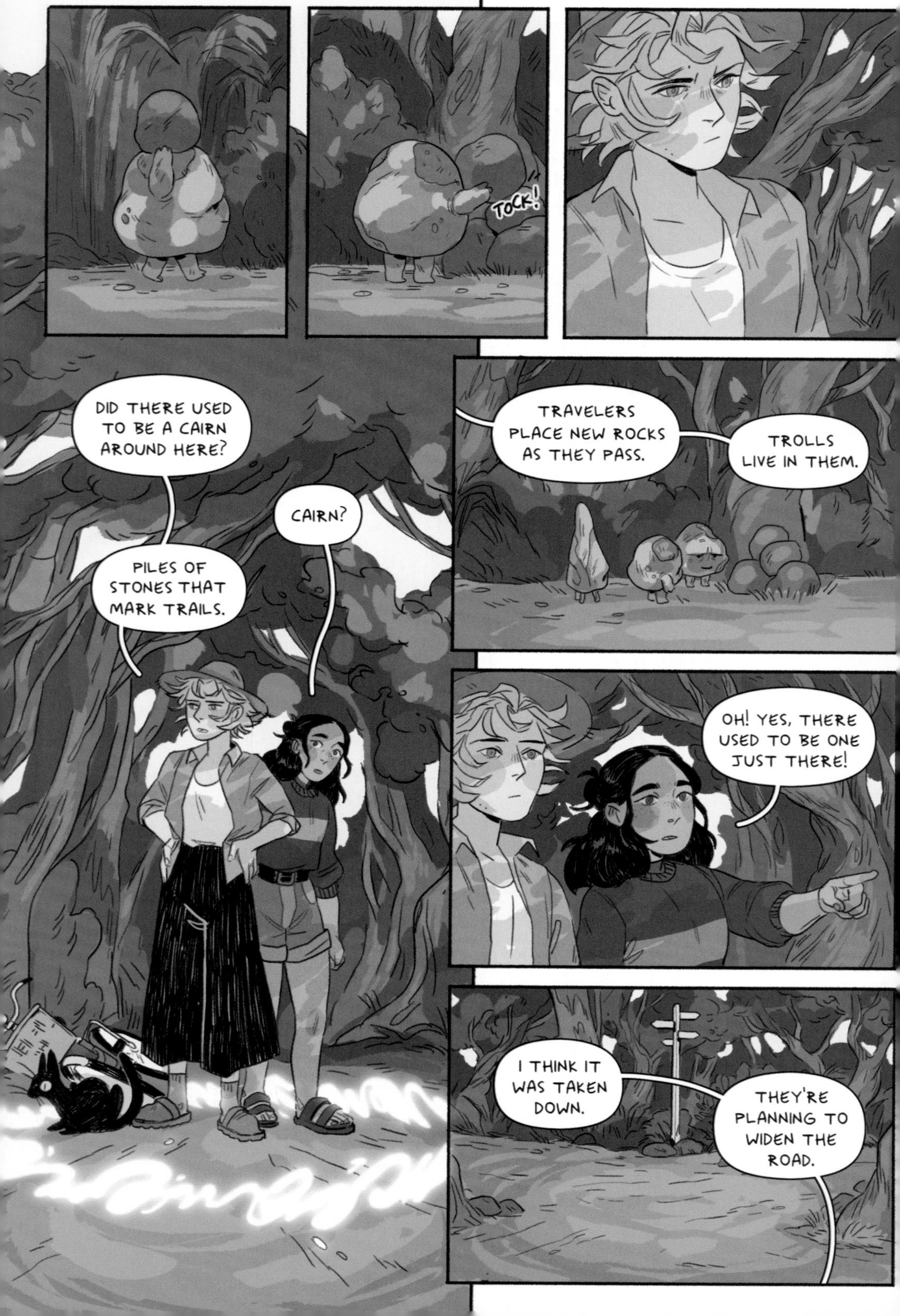
TOCK!
DID THERE USED TO BE A CAIRN AROUND HERE?
CAIRN?
PILES OF STONES THAT MARK TRAILS.
TRAVELERS PLACE NEW ROCKS AS THEY PASS.
TROLLS LIVE IN THEM.
OH! YES, THERE USED TO BE ONE JUST THERE!
I THINK IT WAS TAKEN DOWN.
THEY'RE PLANNING TO WIDEN THE ROAD.

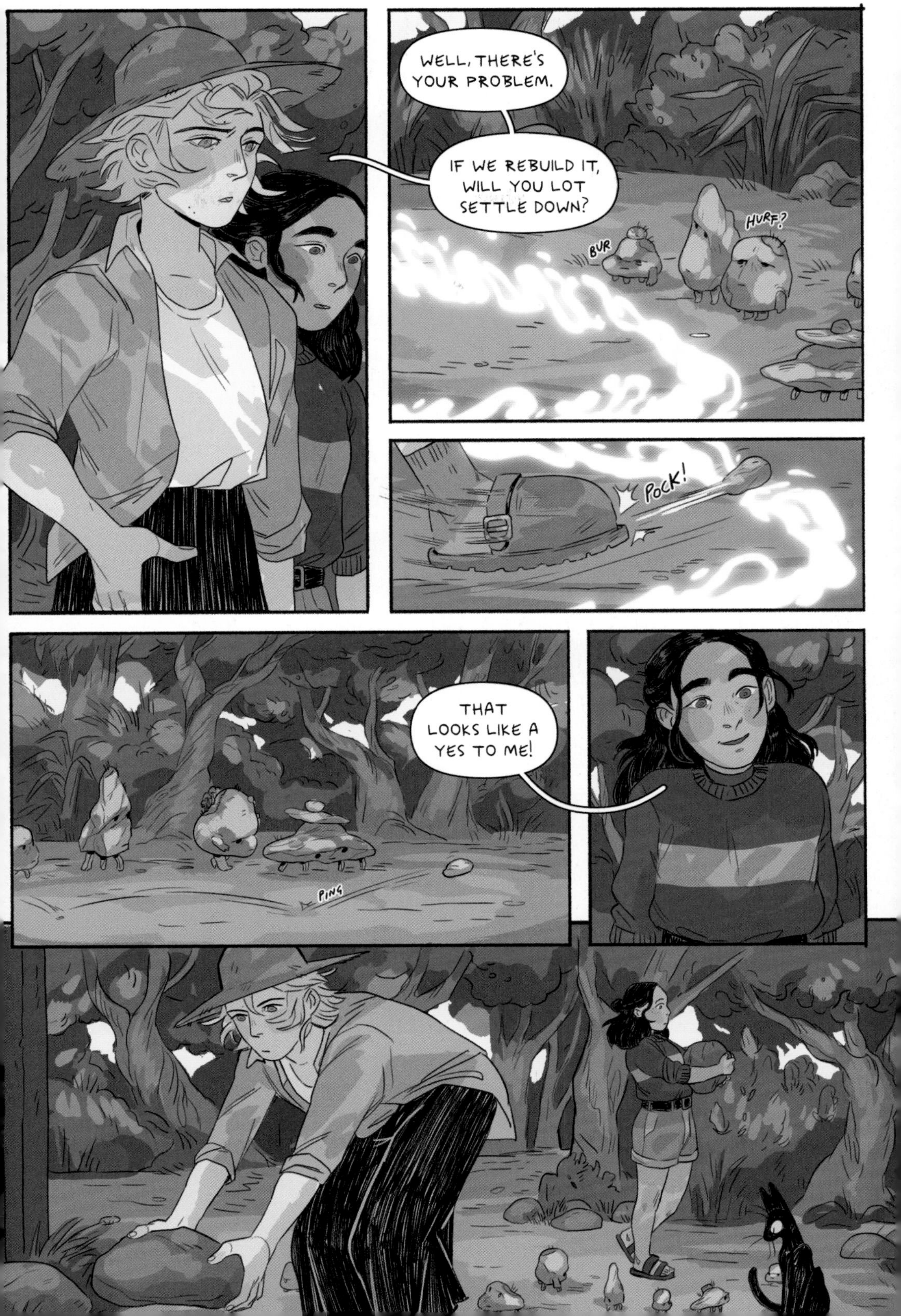
WELL, THERE'S YOUR PROBLEM.
IF WE REBUILD IT, WILL YOU LOT SETTLE DOWN?
BUR
HURF?
POCK!
PING
THAT LOOKS LIKE A YES TO ME!

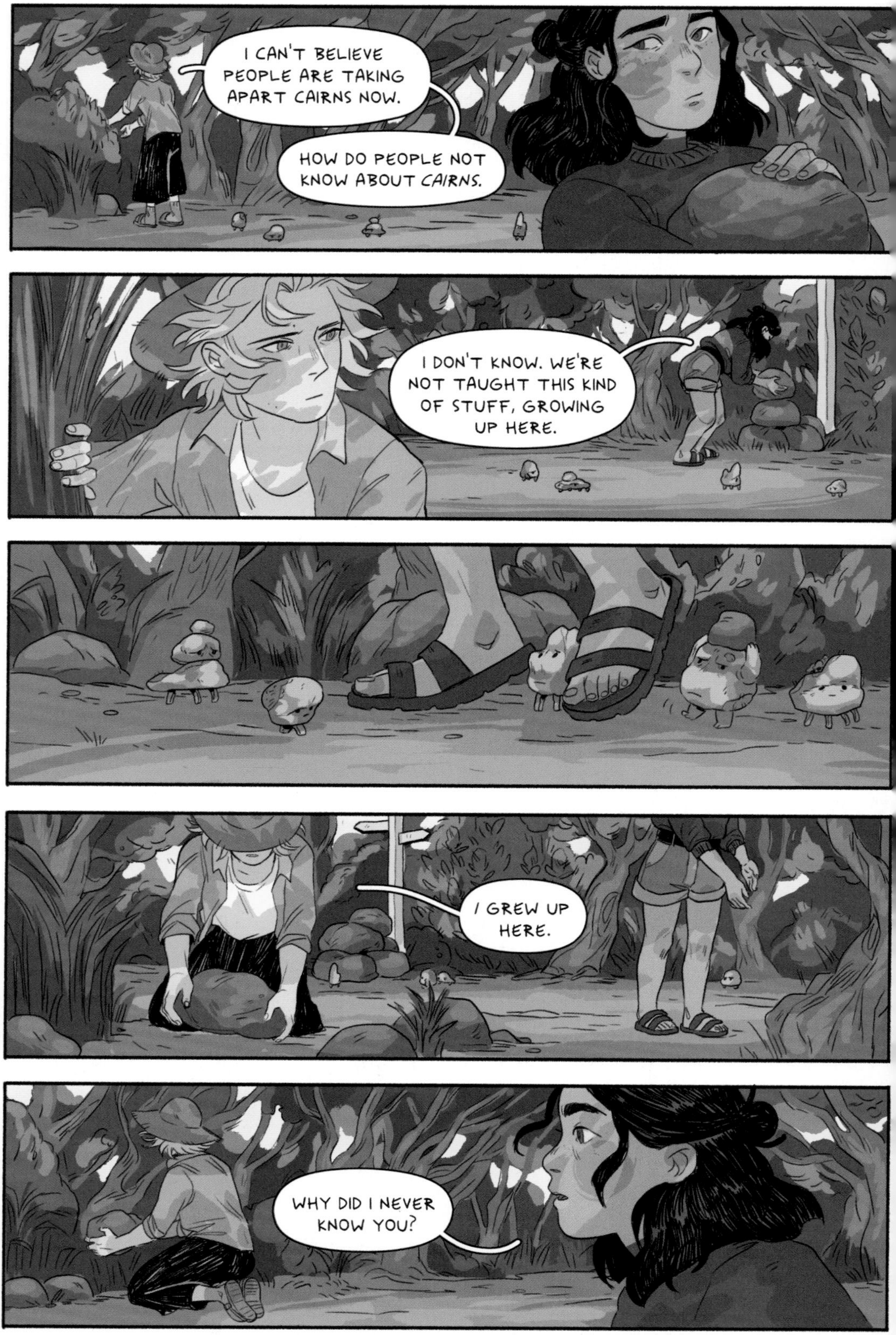
I CAN'T BELIEVE PEOPLE ARE TAKING APART CAIRNS NOW.
HOW DO PEOPLE NOT KNOW ABOUT *CAIRNS.*
I DON'T KNOW. WE'RE NOT TAUGHT THIS KIND OF STUFF, GROWING UP HERE.
I GREW UP HERE.
WHY DID I NEVER KNOW YOU?

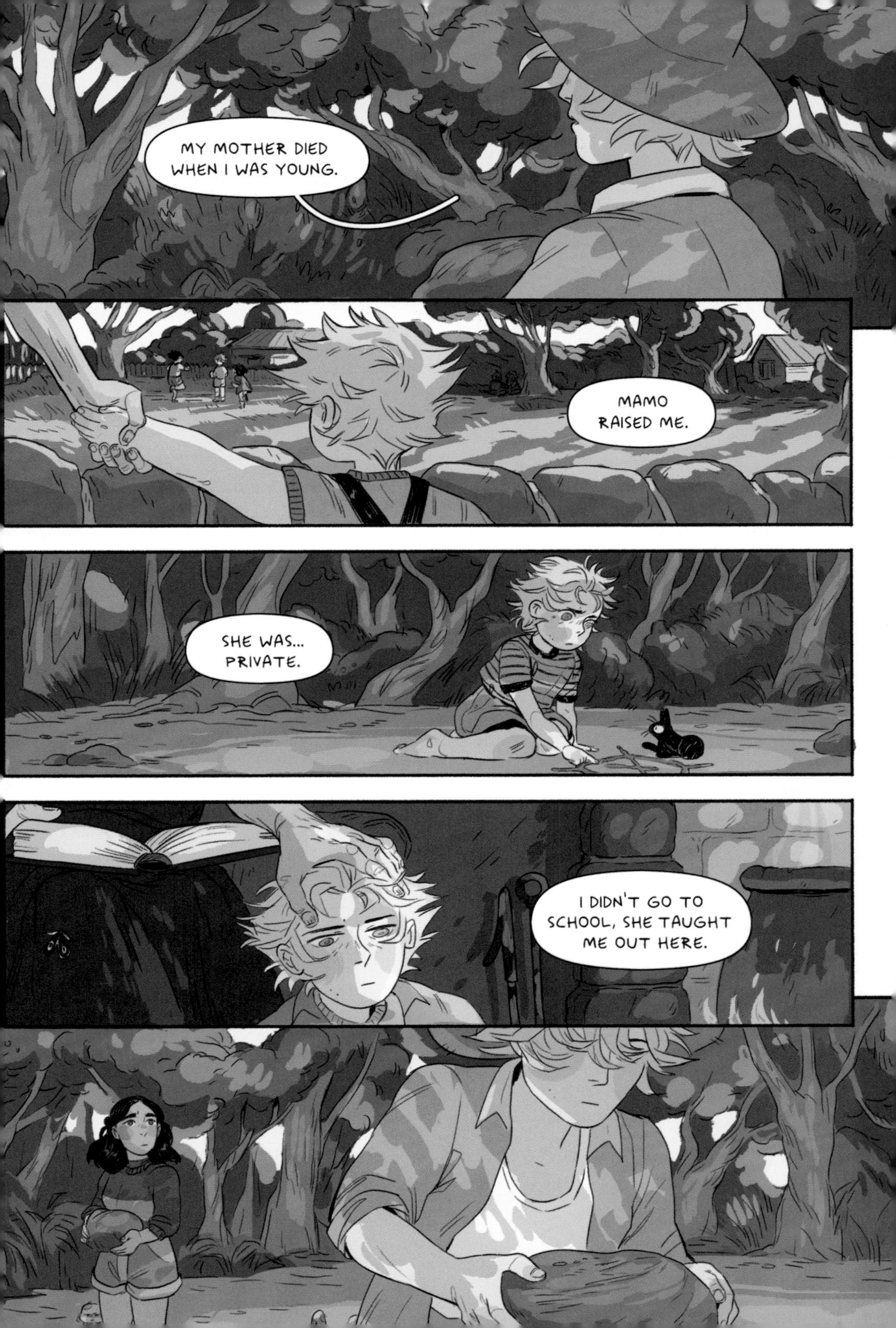
MY MOTHER DIED WHEN I WAS YOUNG.
MAMO RAISED ME.
SHE WAS... PRIVATE.
I DIDN'T GO TO SCHOOL, SHE TAUGHT ME OUT HERE.

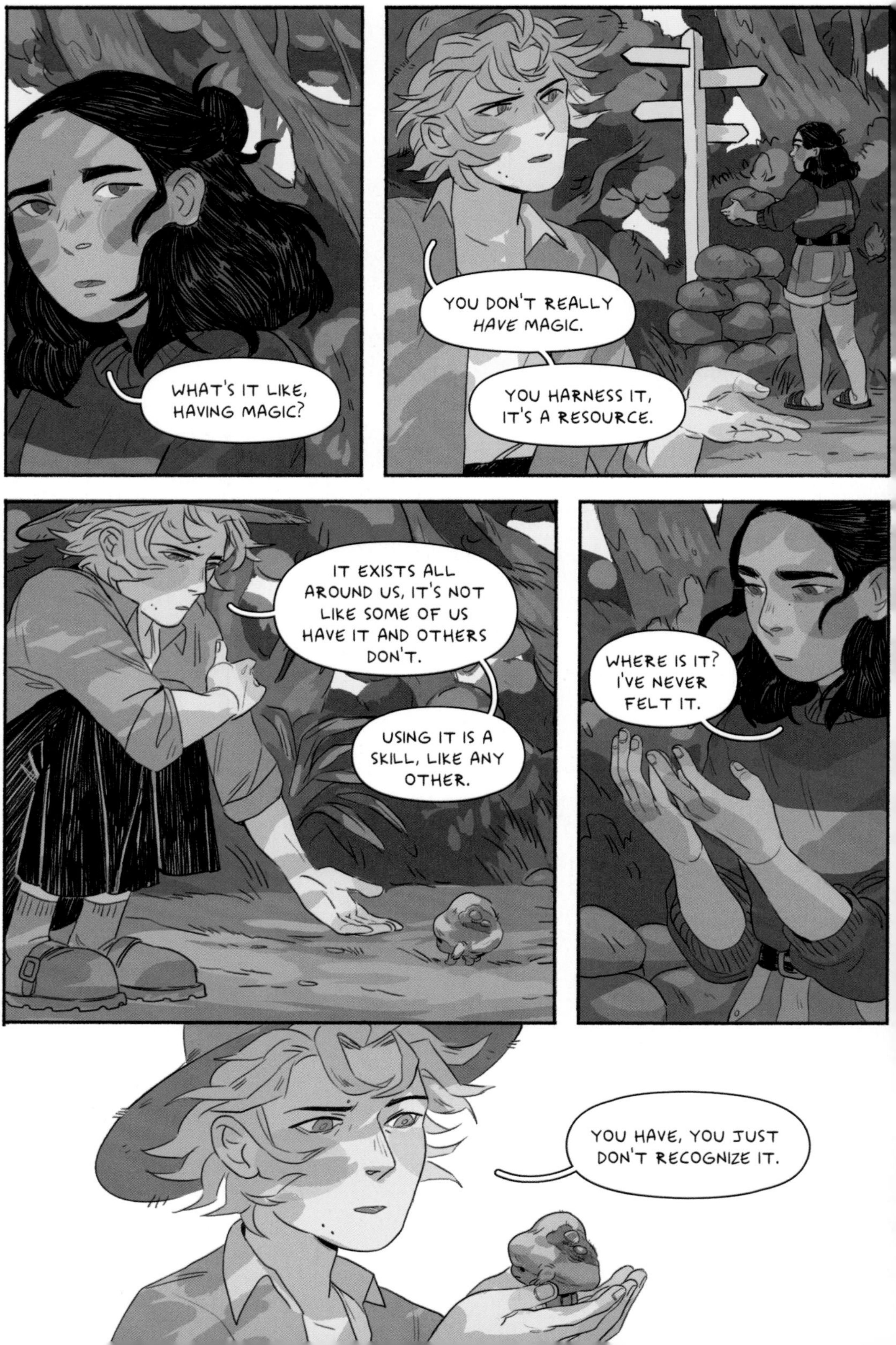
WHAT'S IT LIKE, HAVING MAGIC?
YOU DON'T REALLY *HAVE* MAGIC.
YOU HARNESS IT, IT'S A RESOURCE.
IT EXISTS ALL AROUND US, IT'S NOT LIKE SOME OF US HAVE IT AND OTHERS DON'T.
USING IT IS A SKILL, LIKE ANY OTHER.
WHERE IS IT? I'VE NEVER FELT IT.
YOU HAVE, YOU JUST DON'T RECOGNIZE IT.

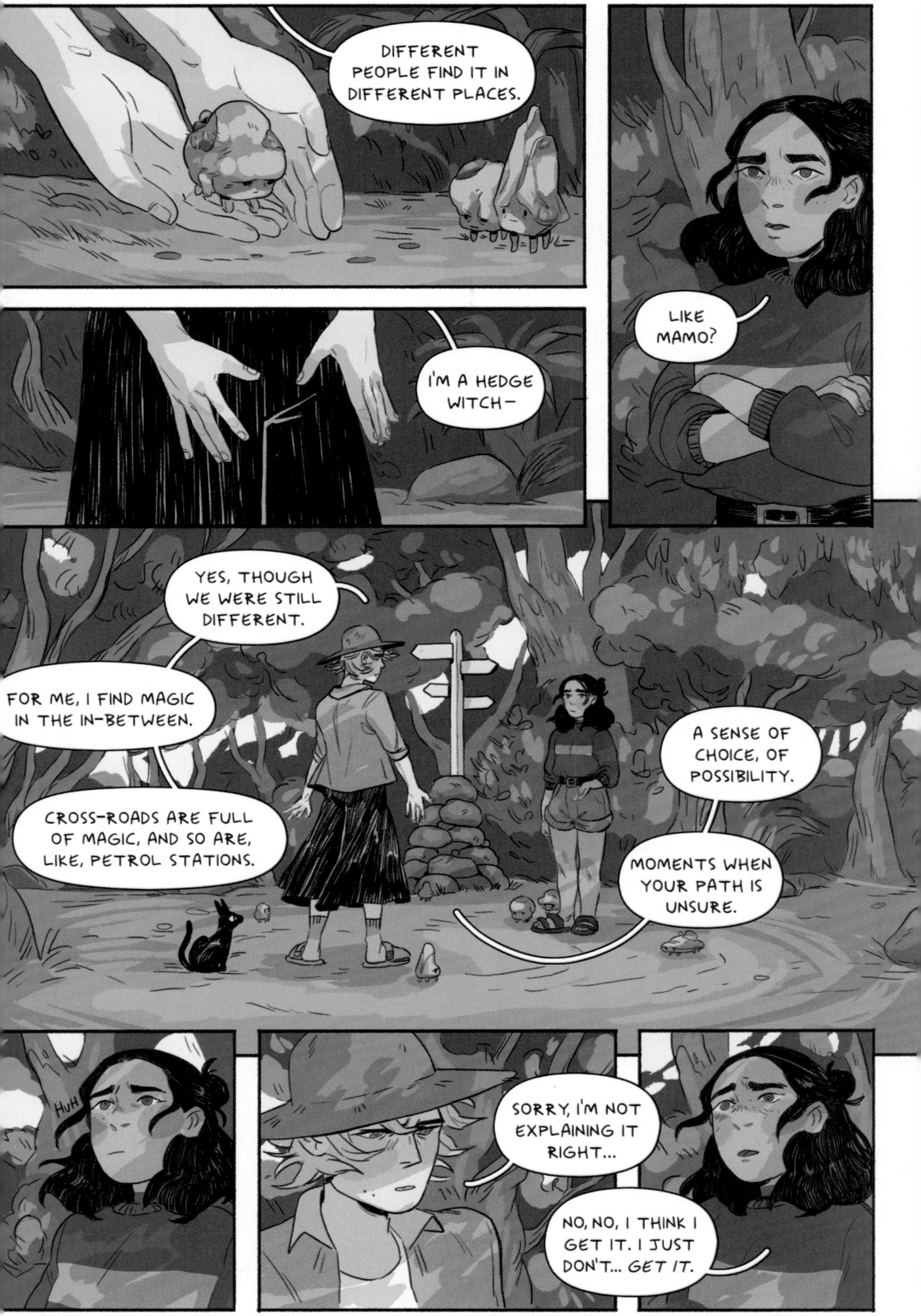
DIFFERENT PEOPLE FIND IT IN DIFFERENT PLACES.
I'M A HEDGE WITCH—
LIKE MAMO?
YES, THOUGH WE WERE STILL DIFFERENT.
FOR ME, I FIND MAGIC IN THE IN-BETWEEN.
CROSS-ROADS ARE FULL OF MAGIC, AND SO ARE, LIKE, PETROL STATIONS.
A SENSE OF CHOICE, OF POSSIBILITY.
MOMENTS WHEN YOUR PATH IS UNSURE.
HUH
SORRY, I'M NOT EXPLAINING IT RIGHT...
NO, NO, I THINK I GET IT. I JUST DON'T... *GET IT*.

IT'S LIKE... YOU KNOW WHEN YOU WALK DOWN THE MIDDLE OF A ROAD, OR WHEN YOU LIE THE WRONG WAY UP IN BED?
LIKE WHEN YOU'RE AT AN INTERSECTION THAT YOU NORMALLY TURN LEFT AT, BUT REALIZE THAT THERE'S ABSOLUTELY NOTHING STOPPING YOU FROM TURNING RIGHT?
THAT AWARENESS, THAT POTENTIAL, THERE'S POWER IN *THAT.*

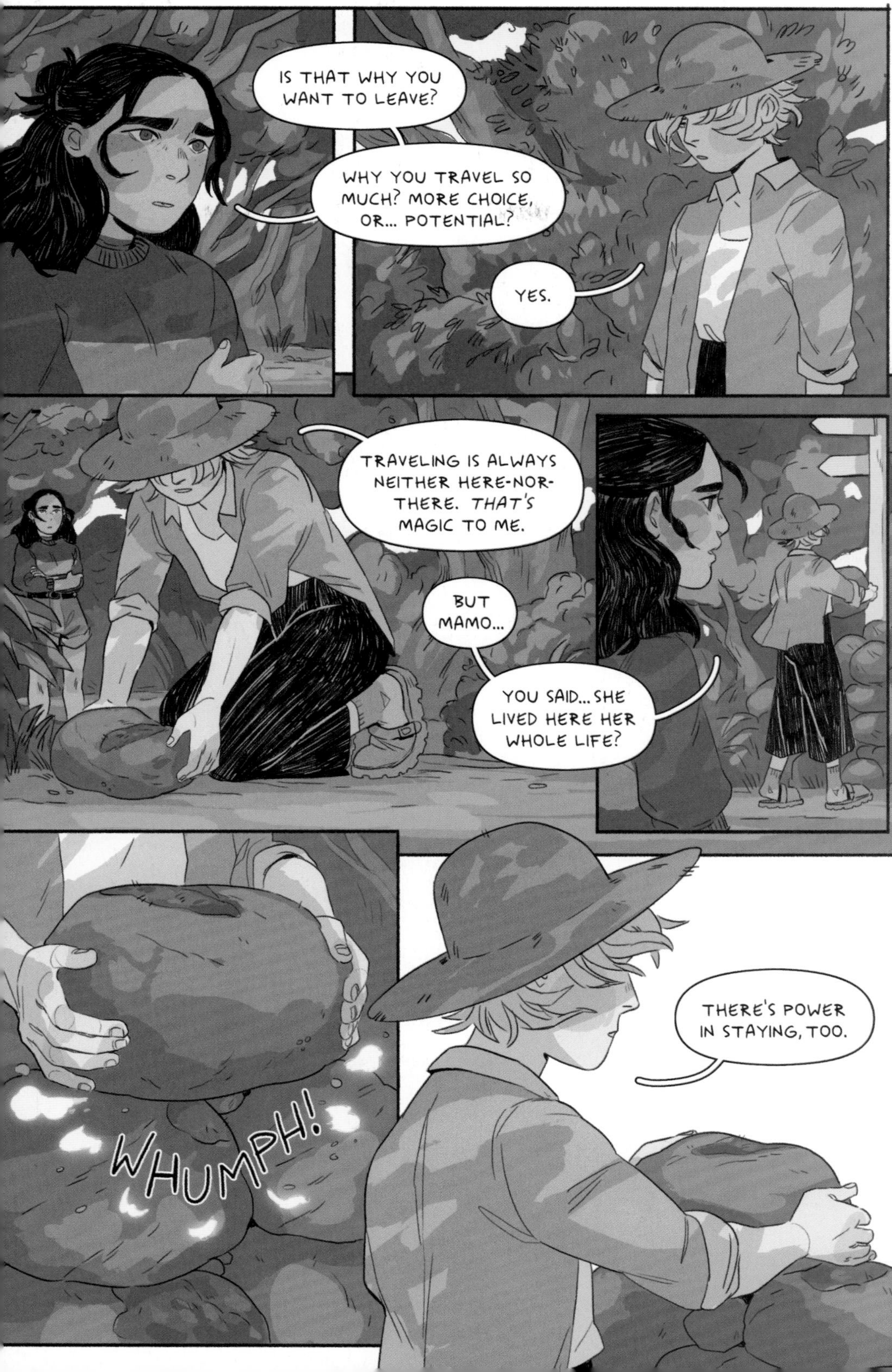
IS THAT WHY YOU WANT TO LEAVE?
WHY YOU TRAVEL SO MUCH? MORE CHOICE, OR... POTENTIAL?
YES.
TRAVELING IS ALWAYS NEITHER HERE-NOR-THERE. *THAT'S* MAGIC TO ME.
BUT MAMO...
YOU SAID... SHE LIVED HERE HER WHOLE LIFE?
WHUMPH!
THERE'S POWER IN STAYING, TOO.

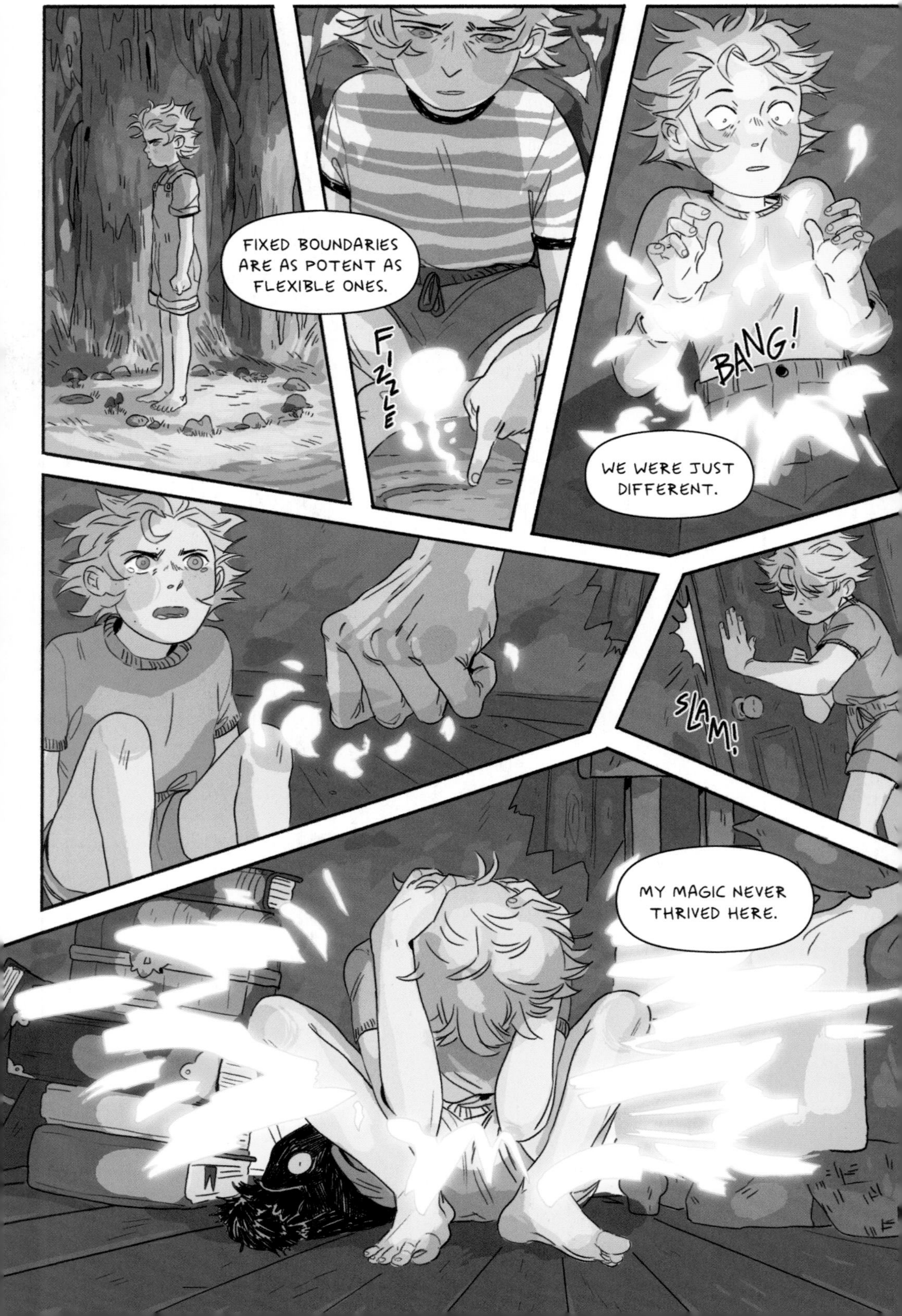
FIXED BOUNDARIES ARE AS POTENT AS FLEXIBLE ONES.
FIZZLE
BANG!
WE WERE JUST DIFFERENT.
SLAM!
MY MAGIC NEVER THRIVED HERE.

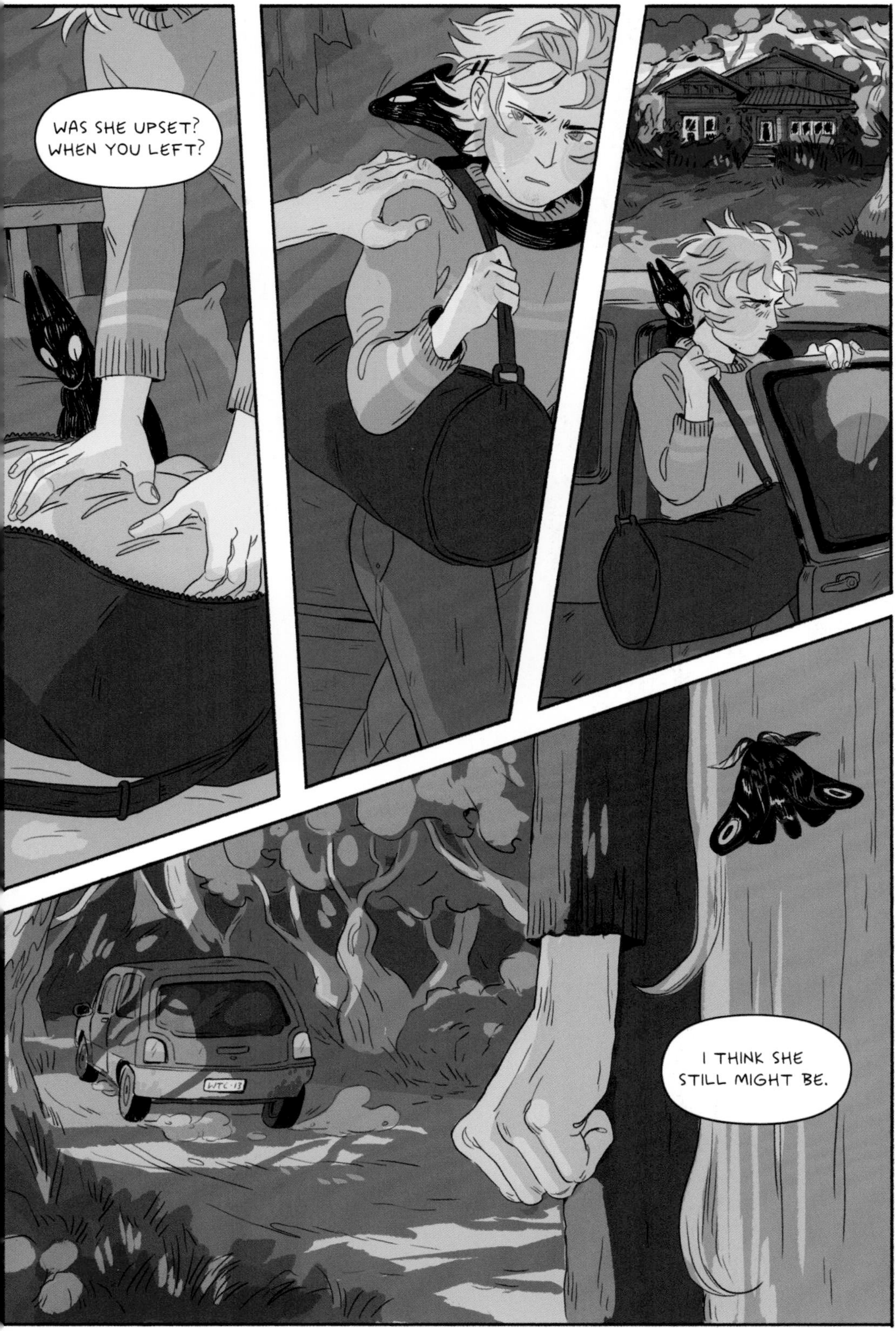
WAS SHE UPSET? WHEN YOU LEFT?
I THINK SHE STILL MIGHT BE.

Chapter
3

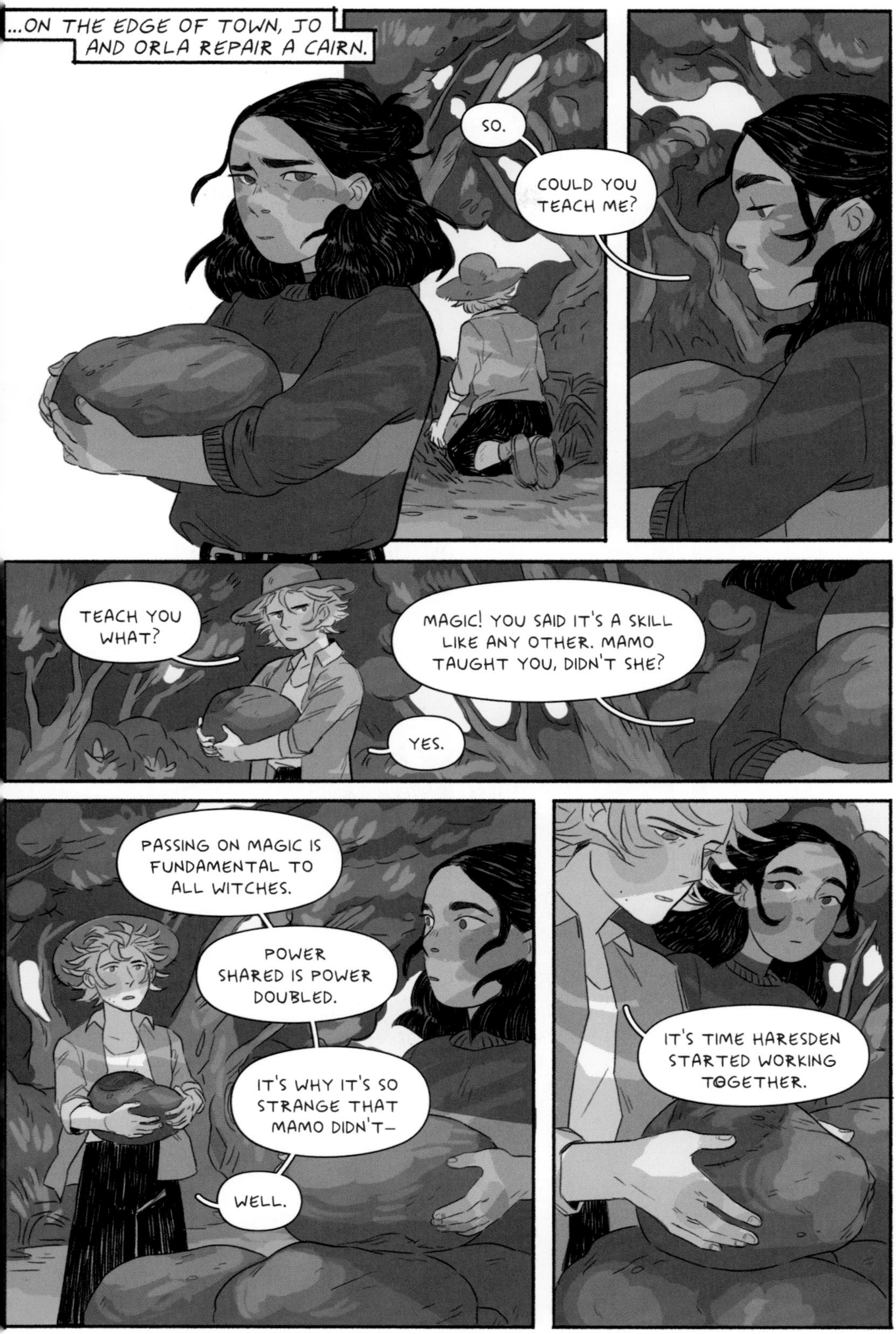
...ON THE EDGE OF TOWN, JO AND ORLA REPAIR A CAIRN.
SO.
COULD YOU TEACH ME?
TEACH YOU WHAT?
MAGIC! YOU SAID IT'S A SKILL LIKE ANY OTHER. MAMO TAUGHT YOU, DIDN'T SHE?
YES.
PASSING ON MAGIC IS FUNDAMENTAL TO ALL WITCHES.
POWER SHARED IS POWER DOUBLED.
IT'S WHY IT'S SO STRANGE THAT MAMO DIDN'T–
WELL.
IT'S TIME HARESDEN STARTED WORKING TOGETHER.

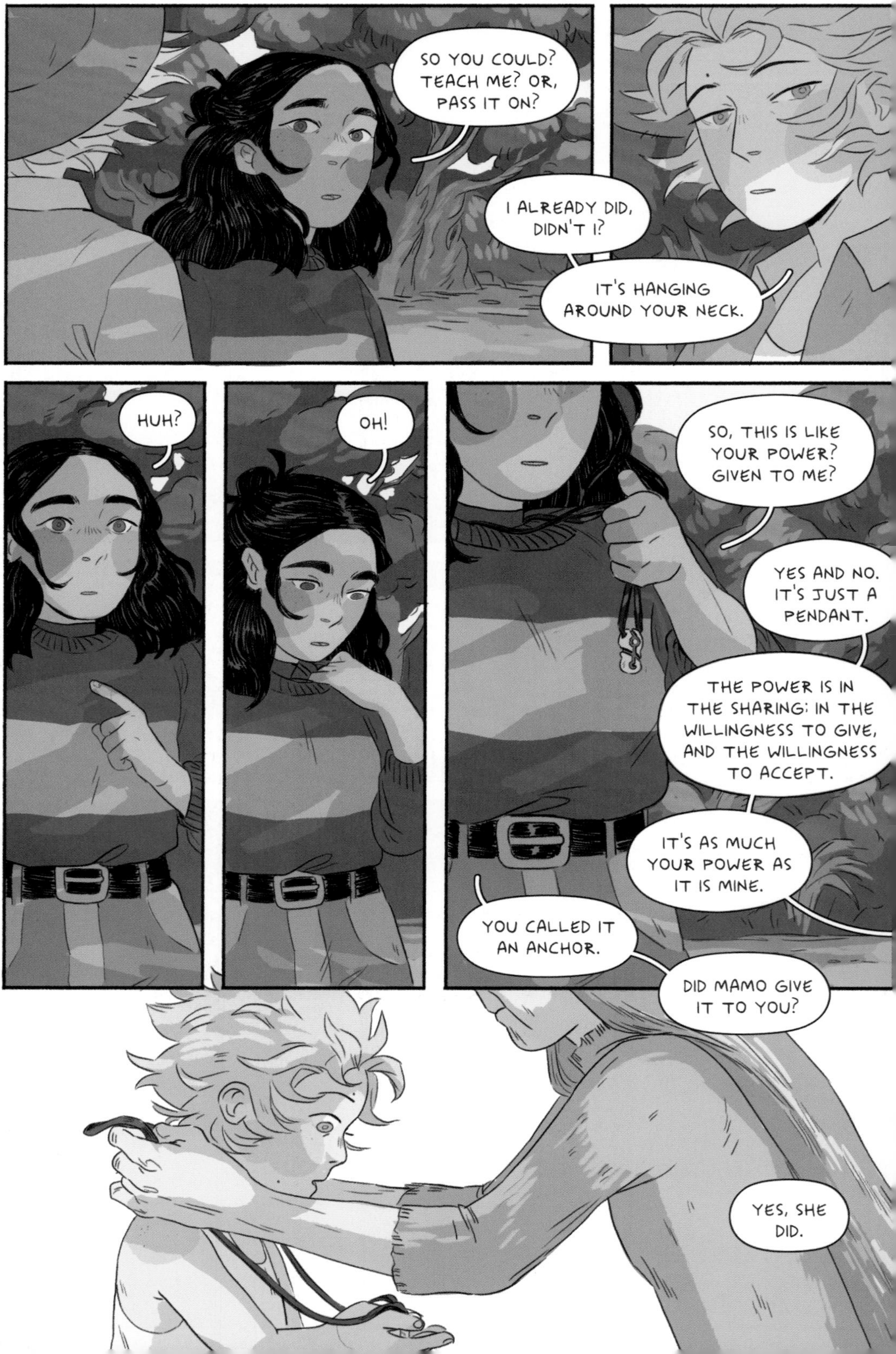
SO YOU COULD? TEACH ME? OR, PASS IT ON?
I ALREADY DID, DIDN'T I?
IT'S HANGING AROUND YOUR NECK.
HUH?
OH!
SO, THIS IS LIKE YOUR POWER? GIVEN TO ME?
YES AND NO. IT'S JUST A PENDANT.
THE POWER IS IN THE SHARING; IN THE WILLINGNESS TO GIVE, AND THE WILLINGNESS TO ACCEPT.
IT'S AS MUCH YOUR POWER AS IT IS MINE.
YOU CALLED IT AN ANCHOR.
DID MAMO GIVE IT TO YOU?
YES, SHE DID.

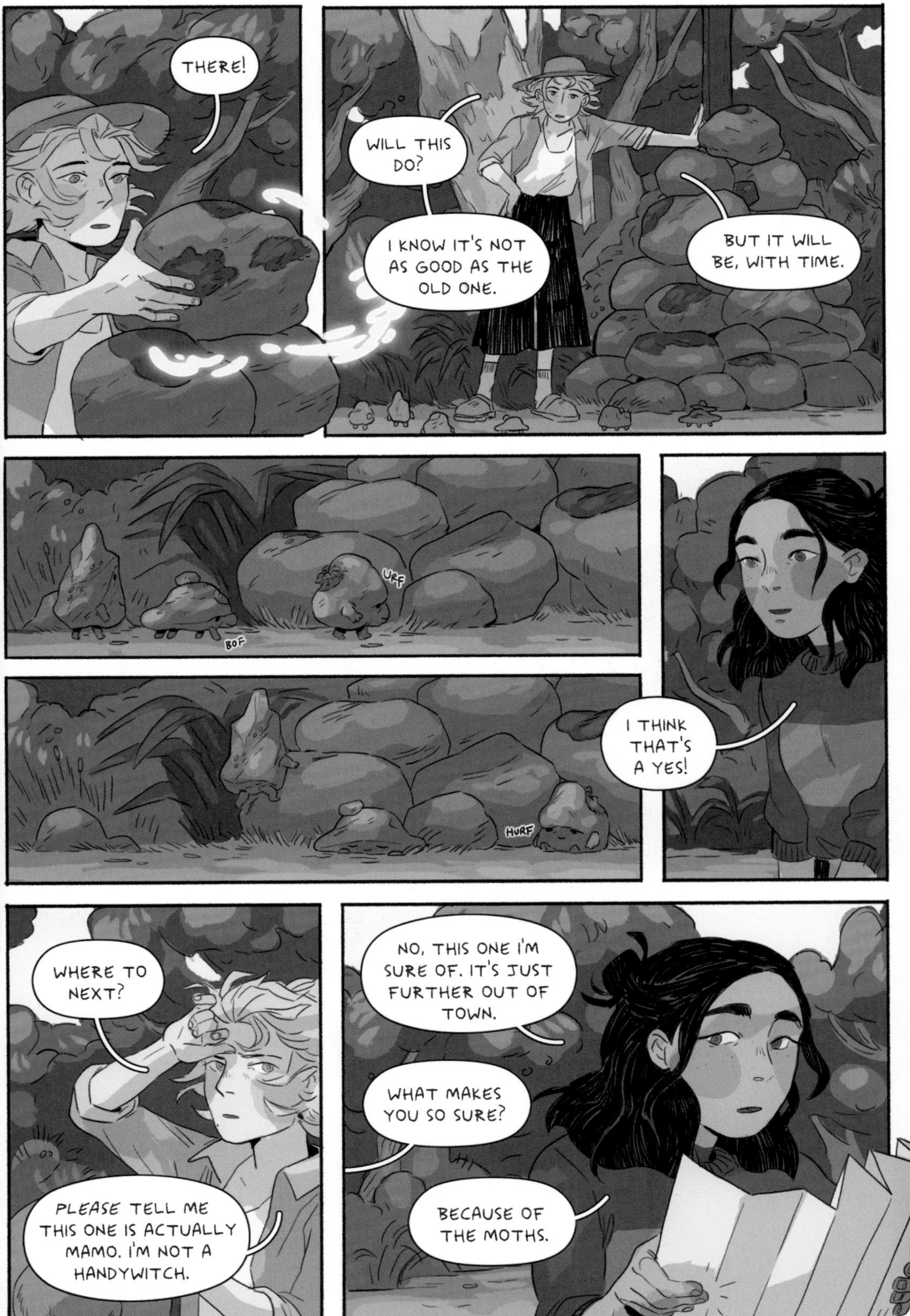
THERE!
WILL THIS DO?
I KNOW IT'S NOT AS GOOD AS THE OLD ONE.
BUT IT WILL BE, WITH TIME.
URF
BOF
I THINK THAT'S A YES!
HURF
WHERE TO NEXT?
PLEASE TELL ME THIS ONE IS ACTUALLY MAMO. I'M NOT A HANDYWITCH.
NO, THIS ONE I'M SURE OF. IT'S JUST FURTHER OUT OF TOWN.
WHAT MAKES YOU SO SURE?
BECAUSE OF THE MOTHS.

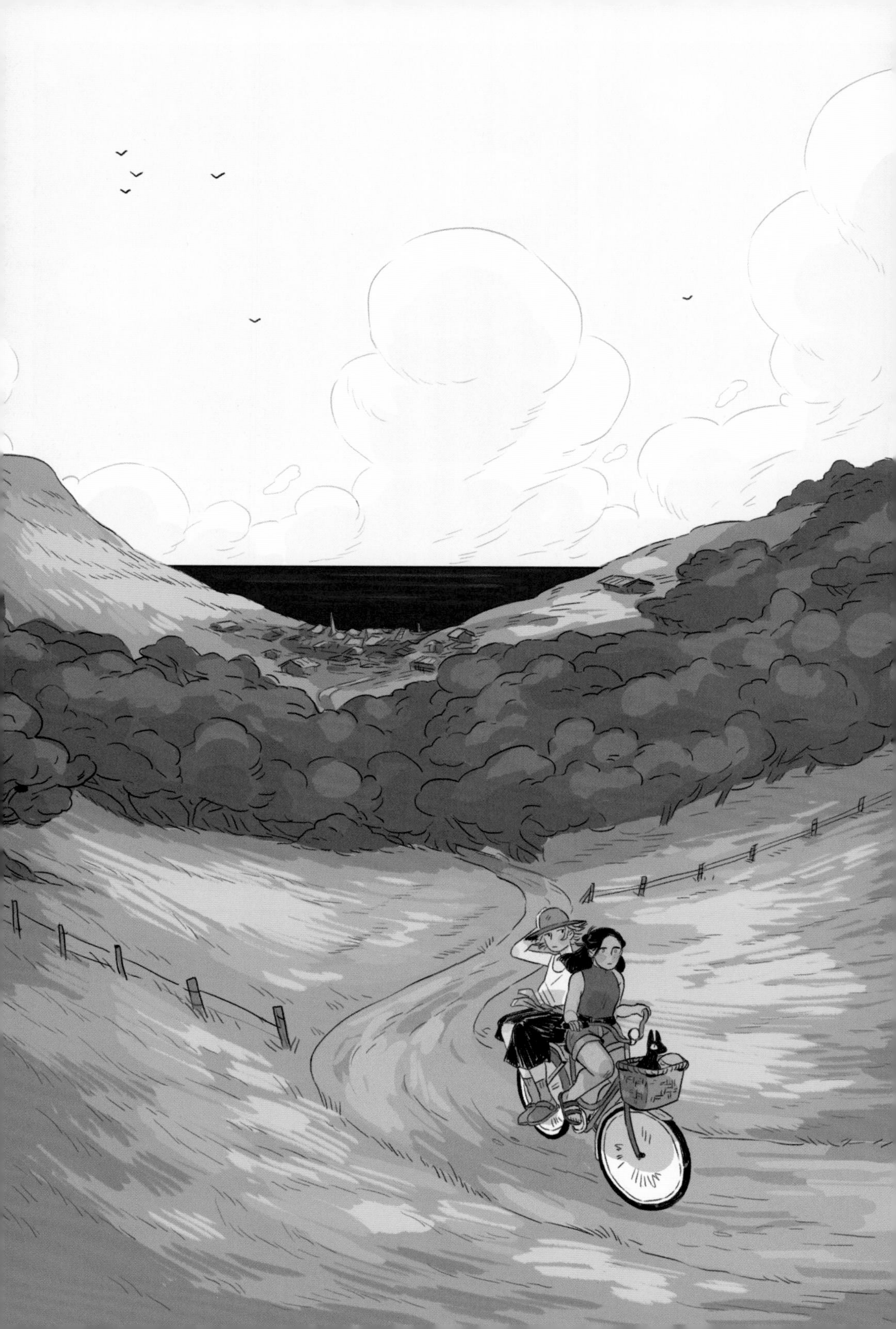

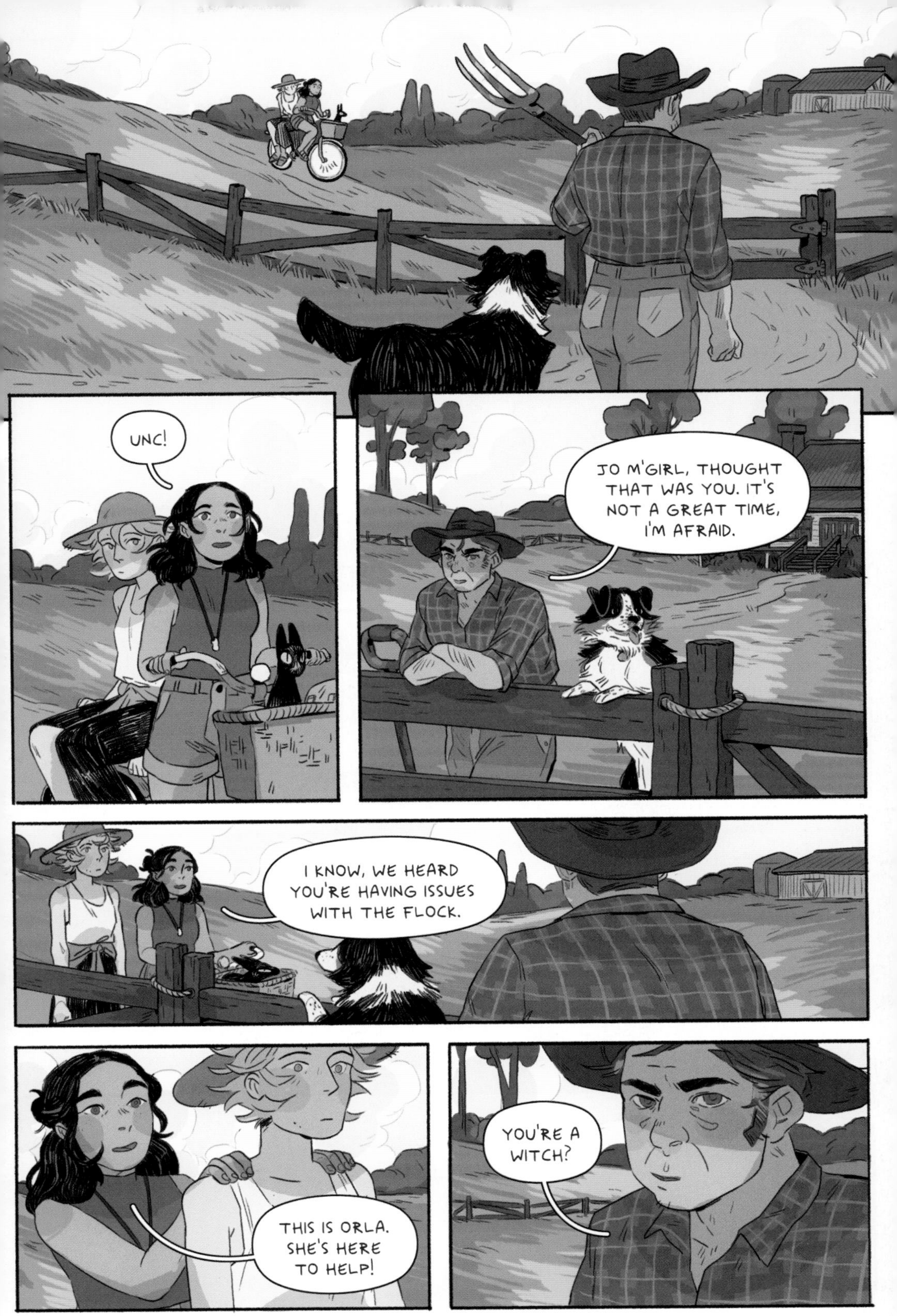
UNC!
JO M'GIRL, THOUGHT THAT WAS YOU. IT'S NOT A GREAT TIME, I'M AFRAID.
I KNOW, WE HEARD YOU'RE HAVING ISSUES WITH THE FLOCK.
THIS IS ORLA. SHE'S HERE TO HELP!
YOU'RE A WITCH?

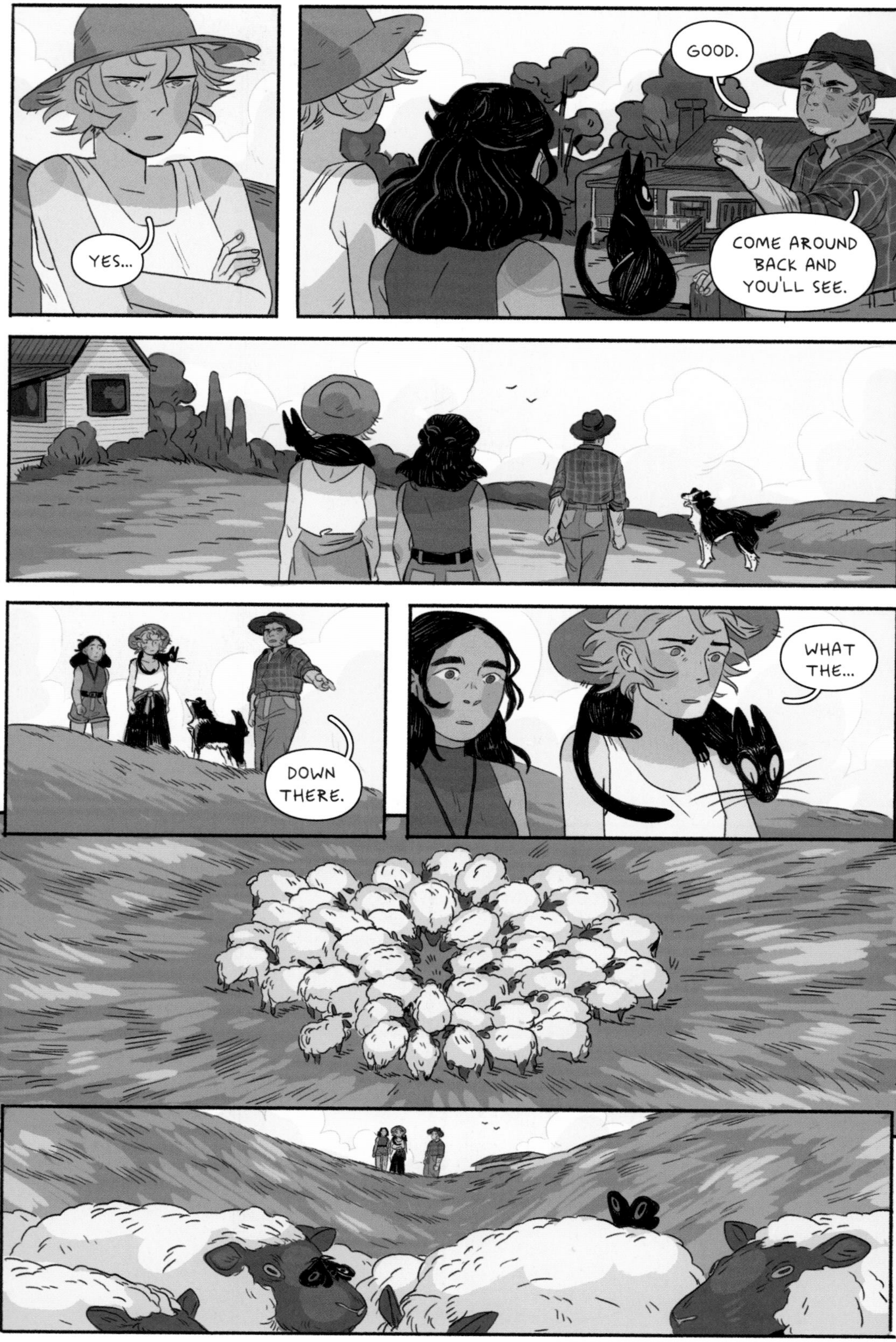
YES...
GOOD.
COME AROUND BACK AND YOU'LL SEE.
DOWN THERE.
WHAT THE...

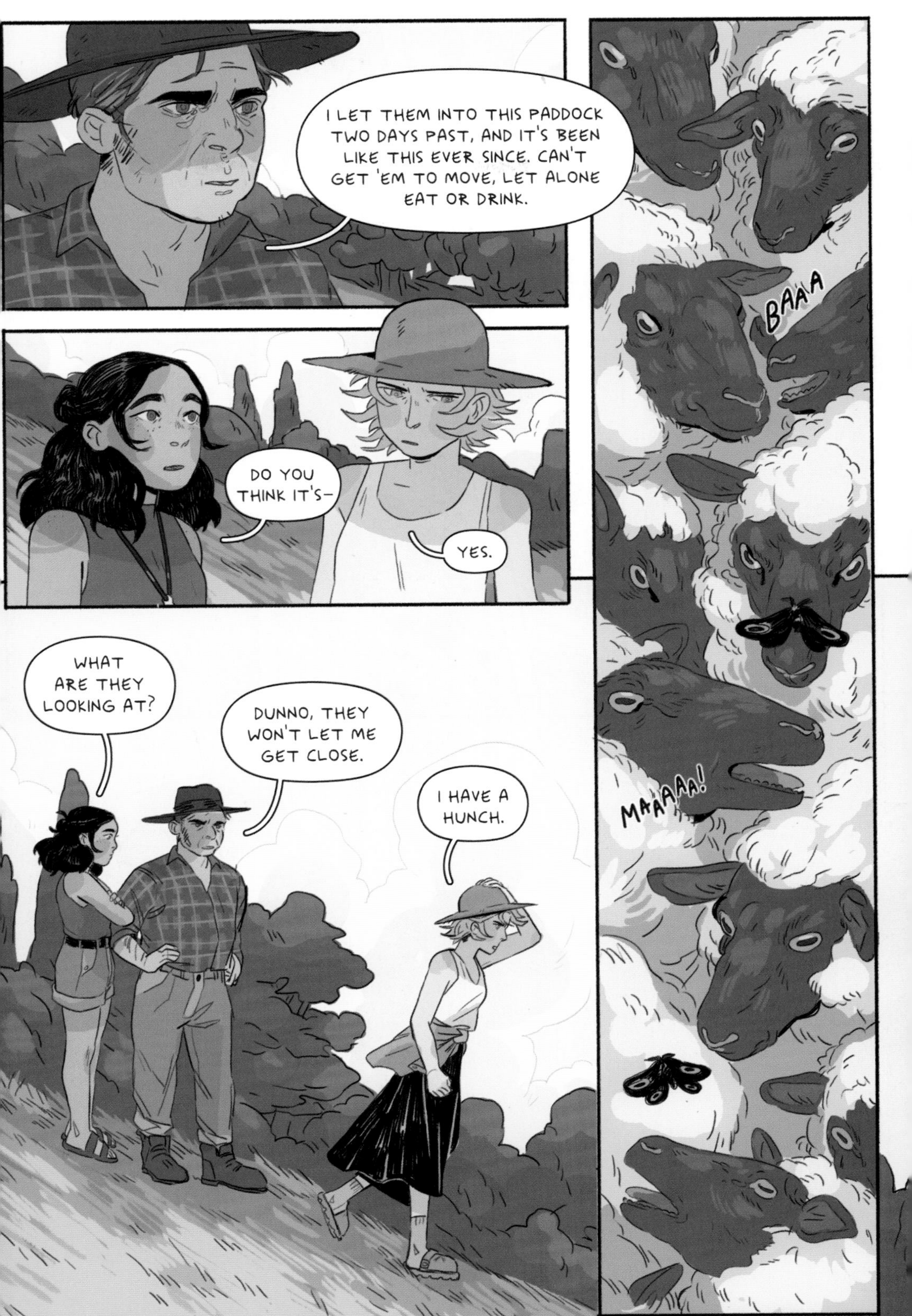
I LET THEM INTO THIS PADDOCK TWO DAYS PAST, AND IT'S BEEN LIKE THIS EVER SINCE. CAN'T GET 'EM TO MOVE, LET ALONE EAT OR DRINK.
BAAA
DO YOU THINK IT'S—
YES.
WHAT ARE THEY LOOKING AT?
DUNNO, THEY WON'T LET ME GET CLOSE.
I HAVE A HUNCH.
MAAAAA!

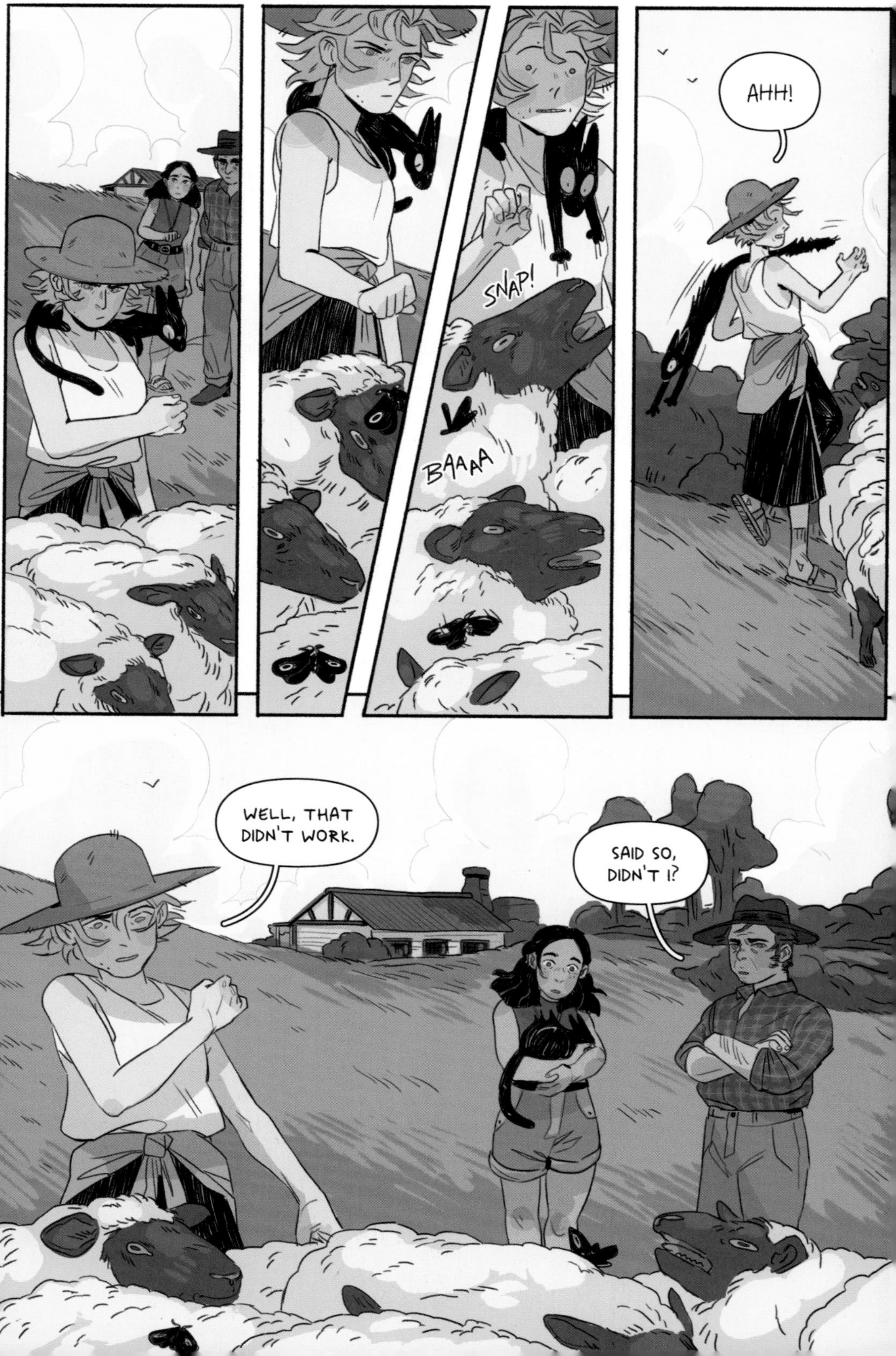
SNAP!
BAAAA
AHH!
WELL, THAT DIDN'T WORK.
SAID SO, DIDN'T I?

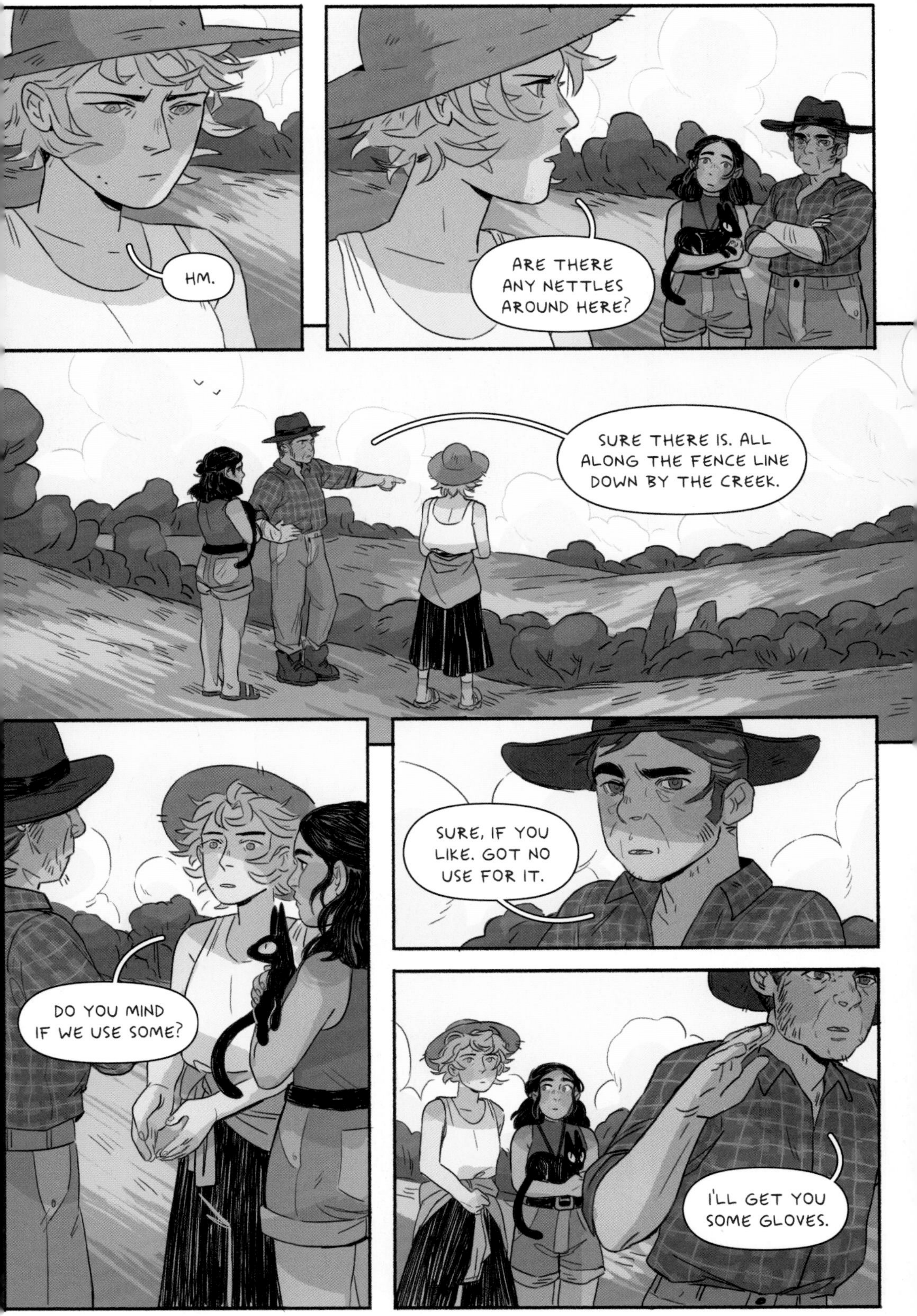
HM.
ARE THERE ANY NETTLES AROUND HERE?
SURE THERE IS. ALL ALONG THE FENCE LINE DOWN BY THE CREEK.
DO YOU MIND IF WE USE SOME?
SURE, IF YOU LIKE. GOT NO USE FOR IT.
I'LL GET YOU SOME GLOVES.

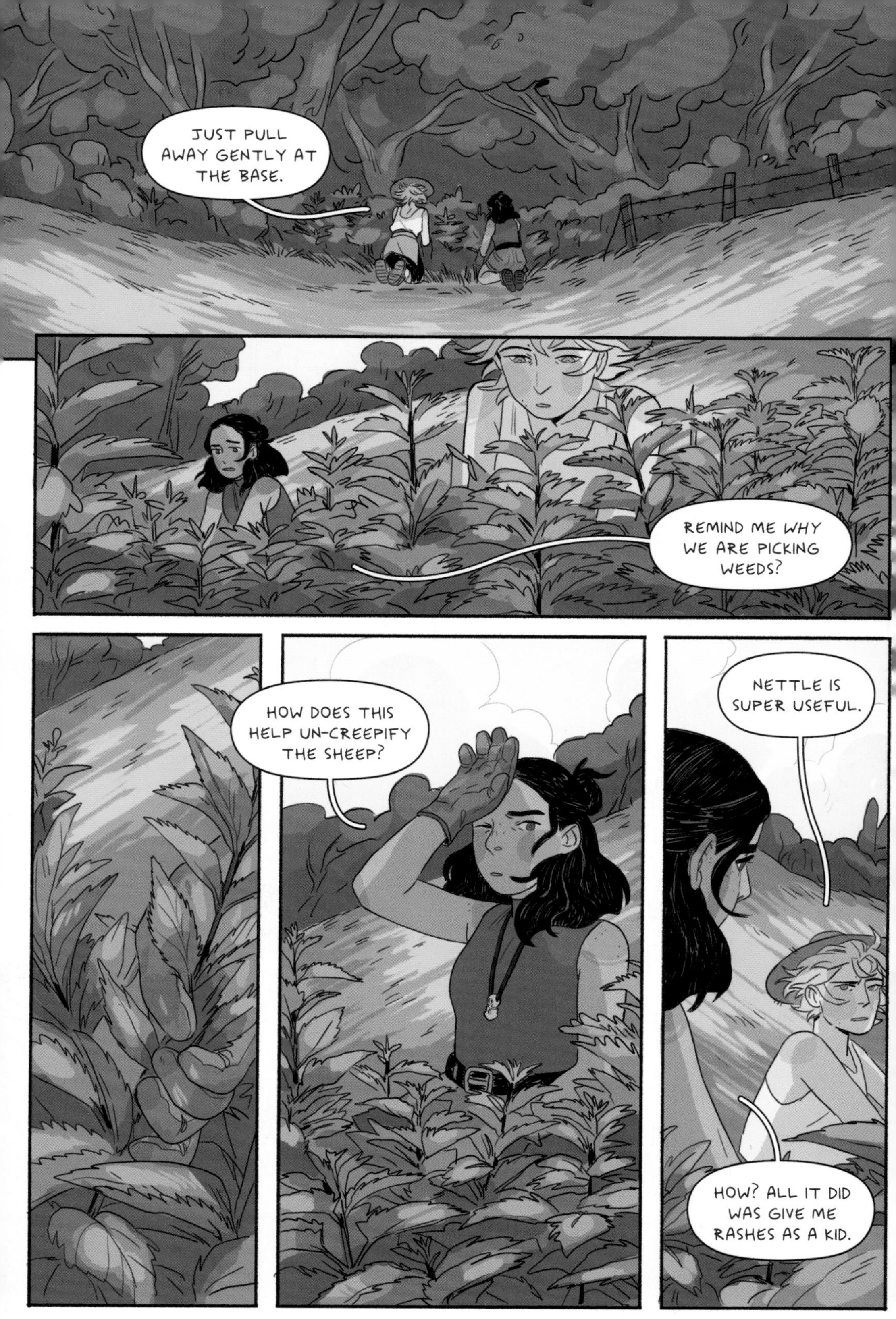
JUST PULL AWAY GENTLY AT THE BASE.
REMIND ME WHY WE ARE PICKING WEEDS?
HOW DOES THIS HELP UN-CREEPIFY THE SHEEP?
NETTLE IS SUPER USEFUL.
HOW? ALL IT DID WAS GIVE ME RASHES AS A KID.

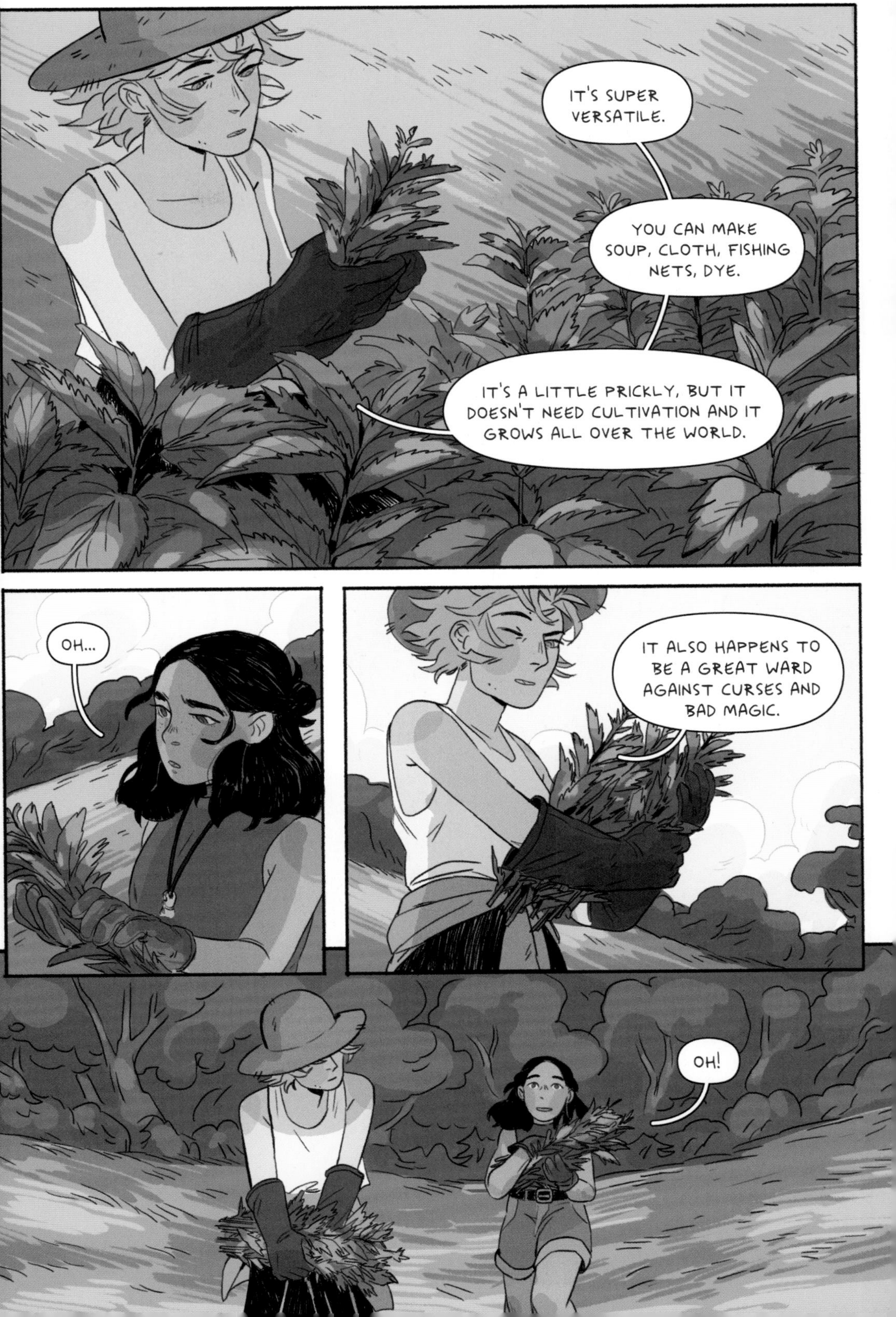
IT'S SUPER VERSATILE.
YOU CAN MAKE SOUP, CLOTH, FISHING NETS, DYE.
IT'S A LITTLE PRICKLY, BUT IT DOESN'T NEED CULTIVATION AND IT GROWS ALL OVER THE WORLD.
OH...
IT ALSO HAPPENS TO BE A GREAT WARD AGAINST CURSES AND BAD MAGIC.
OH!

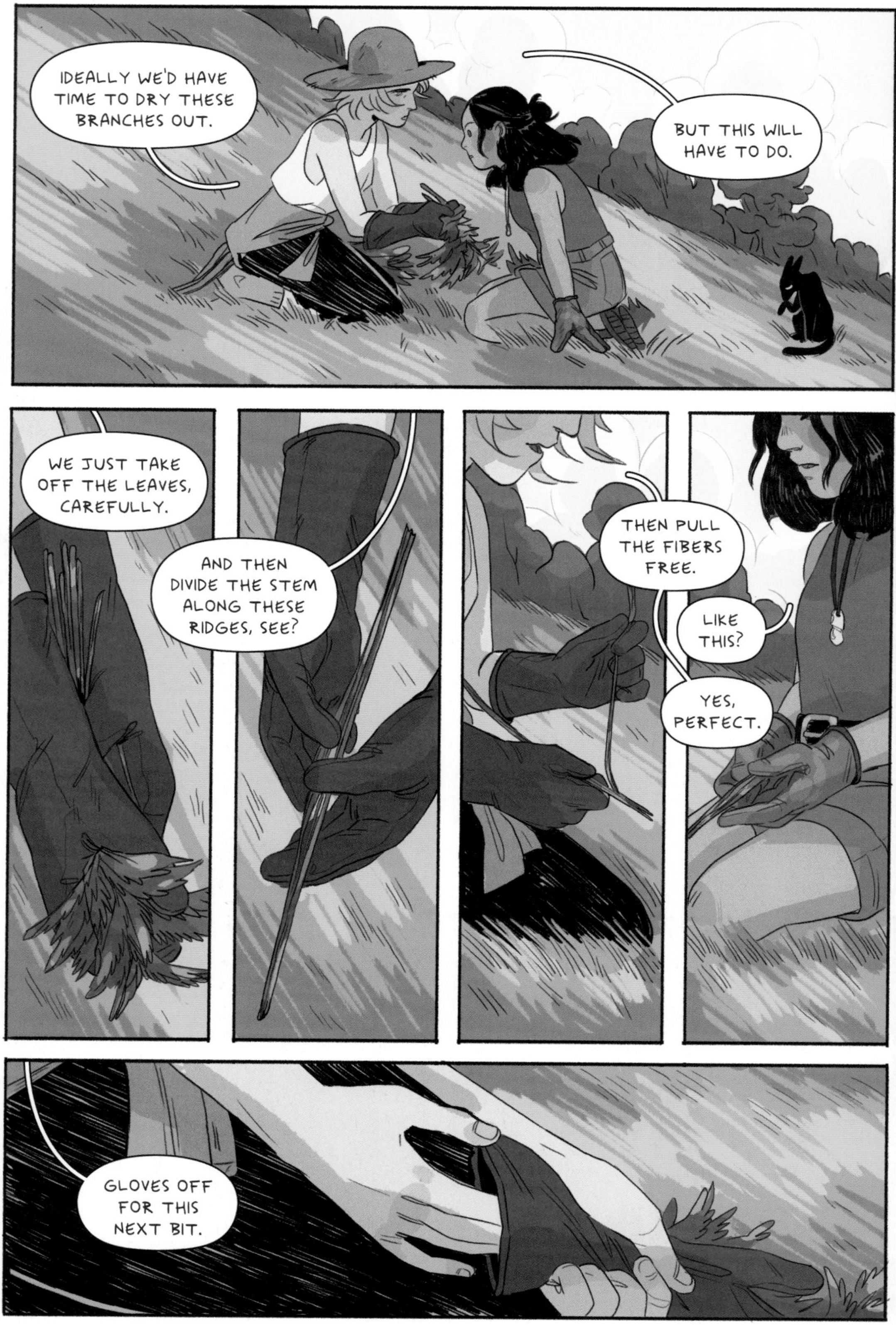
IDEALLY WE'D HAVE TIME TO DRY THESE BRANCHES OUT.
BUT THIS WILL HAVE TO DO.
WE JUST TAKE OFF THE LEAVES, CAREFULLY.
AND THEN DIVIDE THE STEM ALONG THESE RIDGES, SEE?
THEN PULL THE FIBERS FREE.
LIKE THIS?
YES, PERFECT.
GLOVES OFF FOR THIS NEXT BIT.

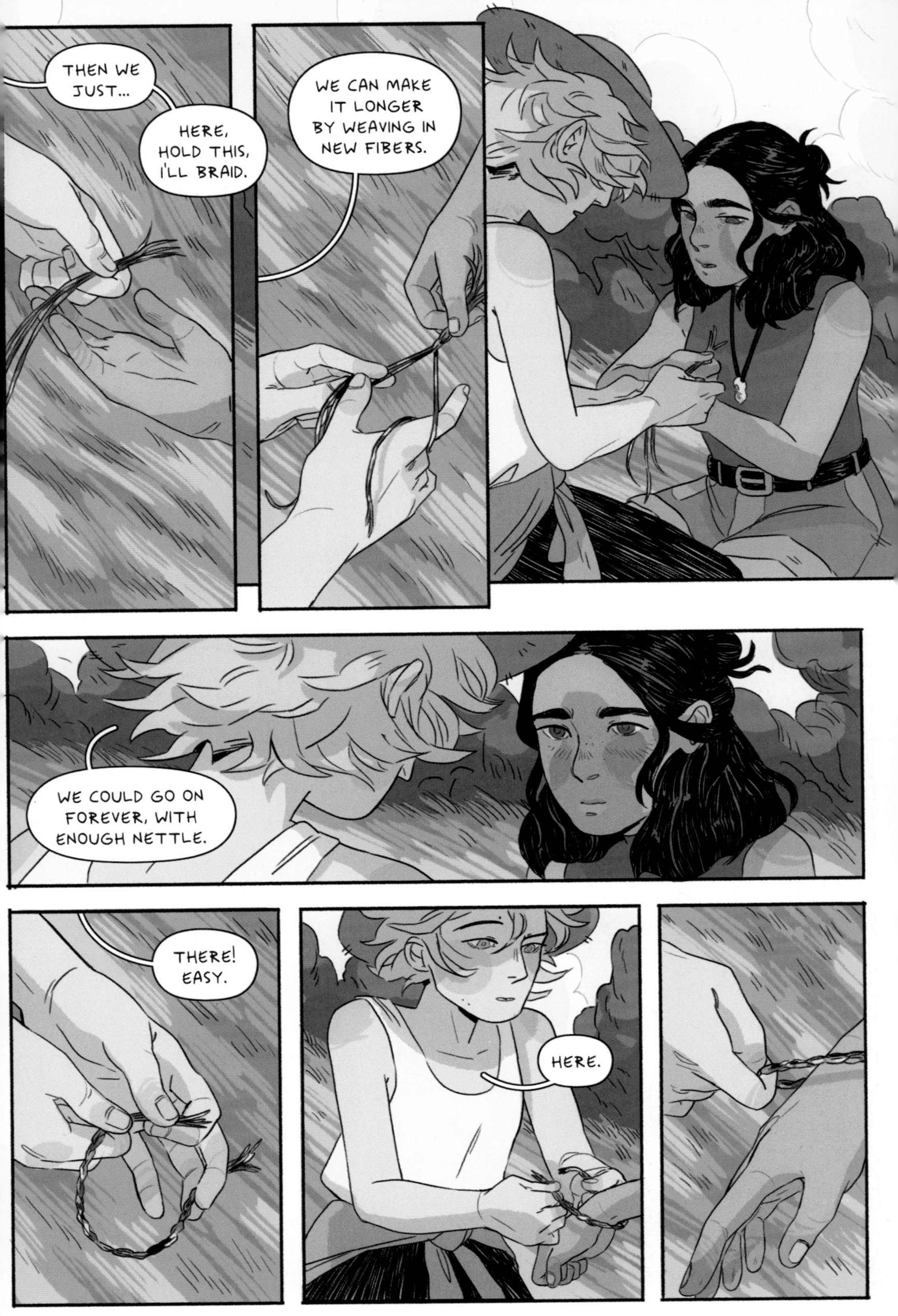
THEN WE JUST...
HERE, HOLD THIS, I'LL BRAID.
WE CAN MAKE IT LONGER BY WEAVING IN NEW FIBERS.
WE COULD GO ON FOREVER, WITH ENOUGH NETTLE.
THERE! EASY.
HERE.

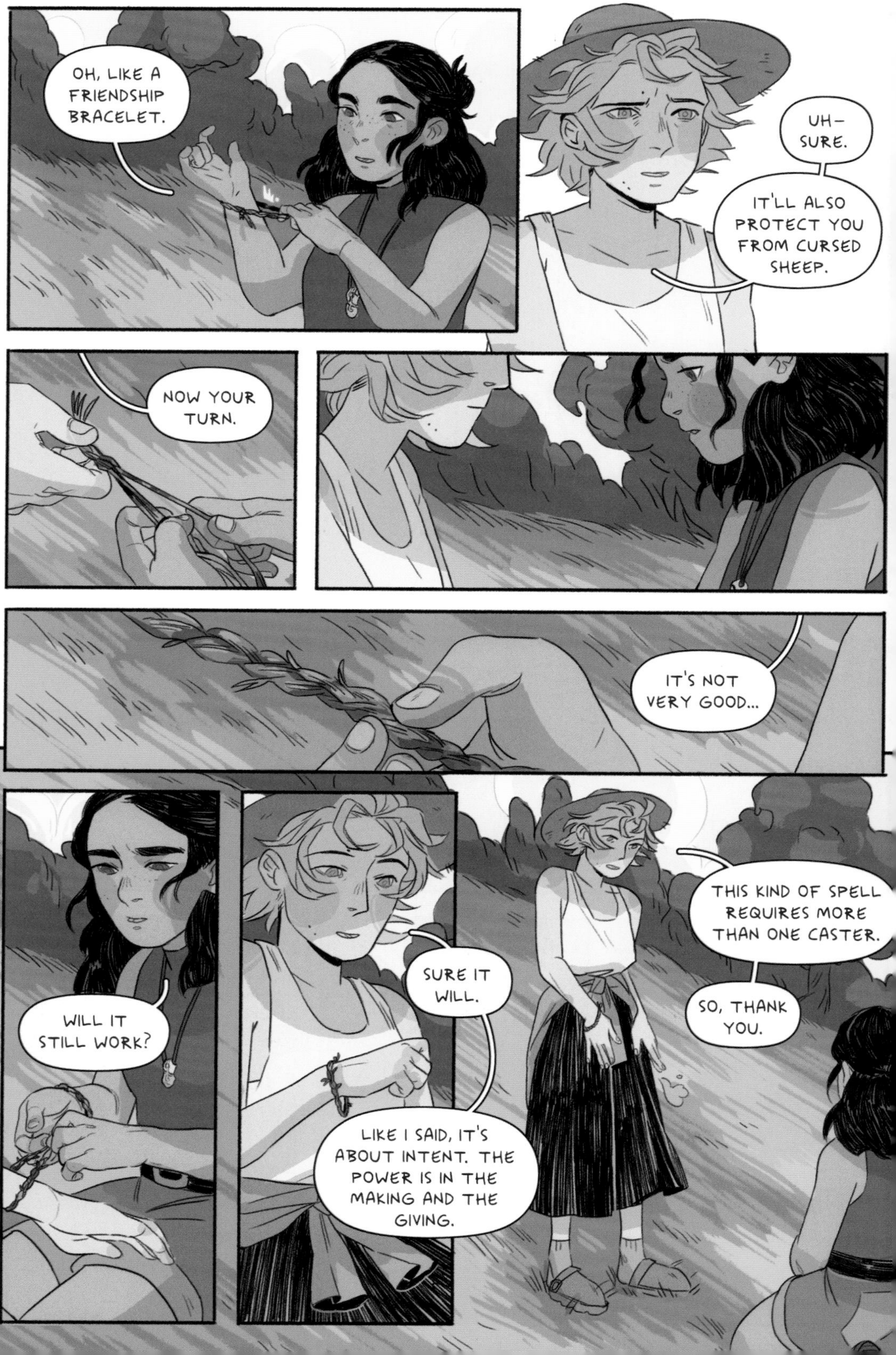
OH, LIKE A FRIENDSHIP BRACELET.
UH— SURE.
IT'LL ALSO PROTECT YOU FROM CURSED SHEEP.
NOW YOUR TURN.
IT'S NOT VERY GOOD...
WILL IT STILL WORK?
SURE IT WILL.
LIKE I SAID, IT'S ABOUT INTENT. THE POWER IS IN THE MAKING AND THE GIVING.
THIS KIND OF SPELL REQUIRES MORE THAN ONE CASTER.
SO, THANK YOU.

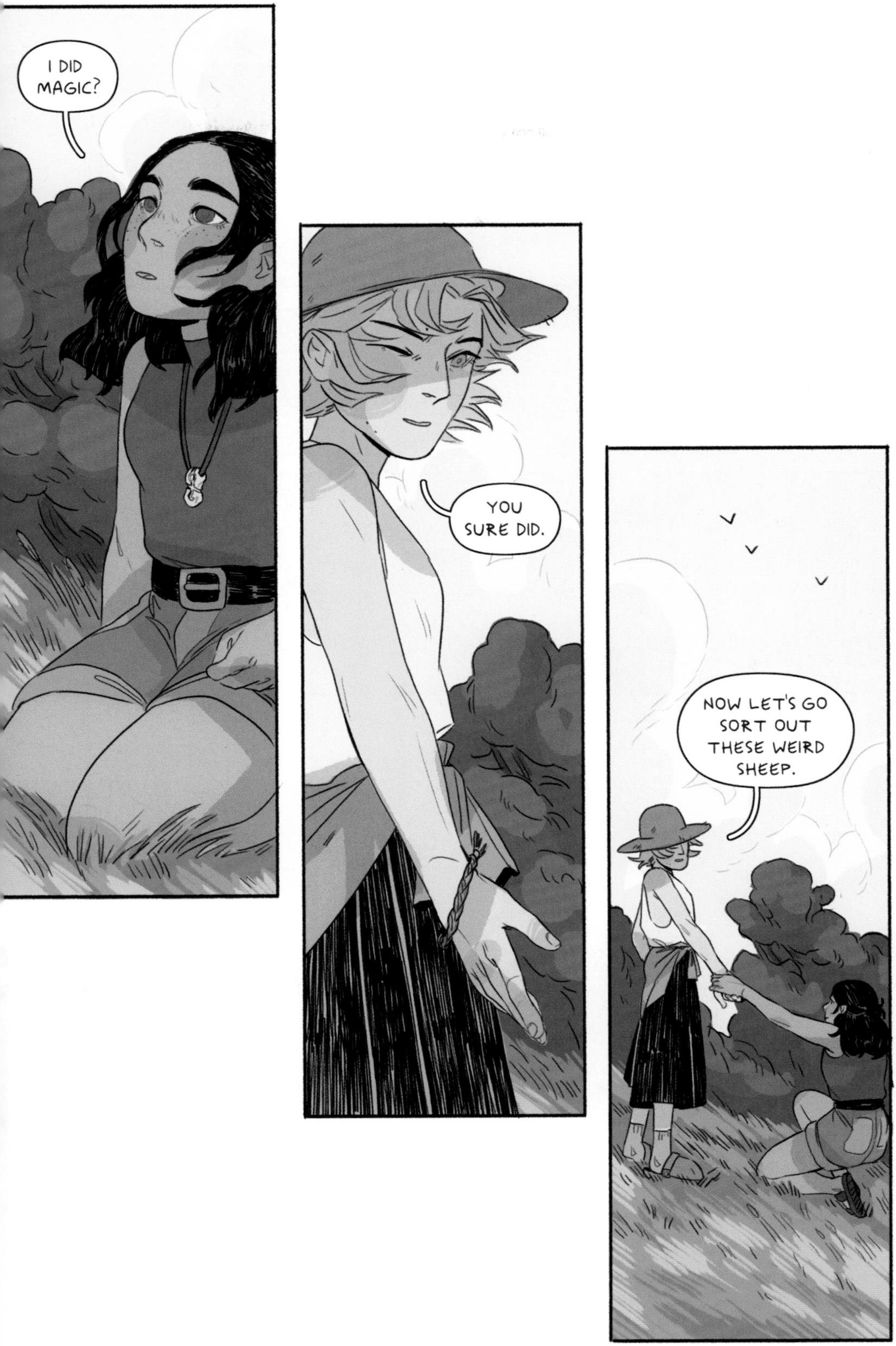
I DID MAGIC?
YOU SURE DID.
NOW LET'S GO SORT OUT THESE WEIRD SHEEP.

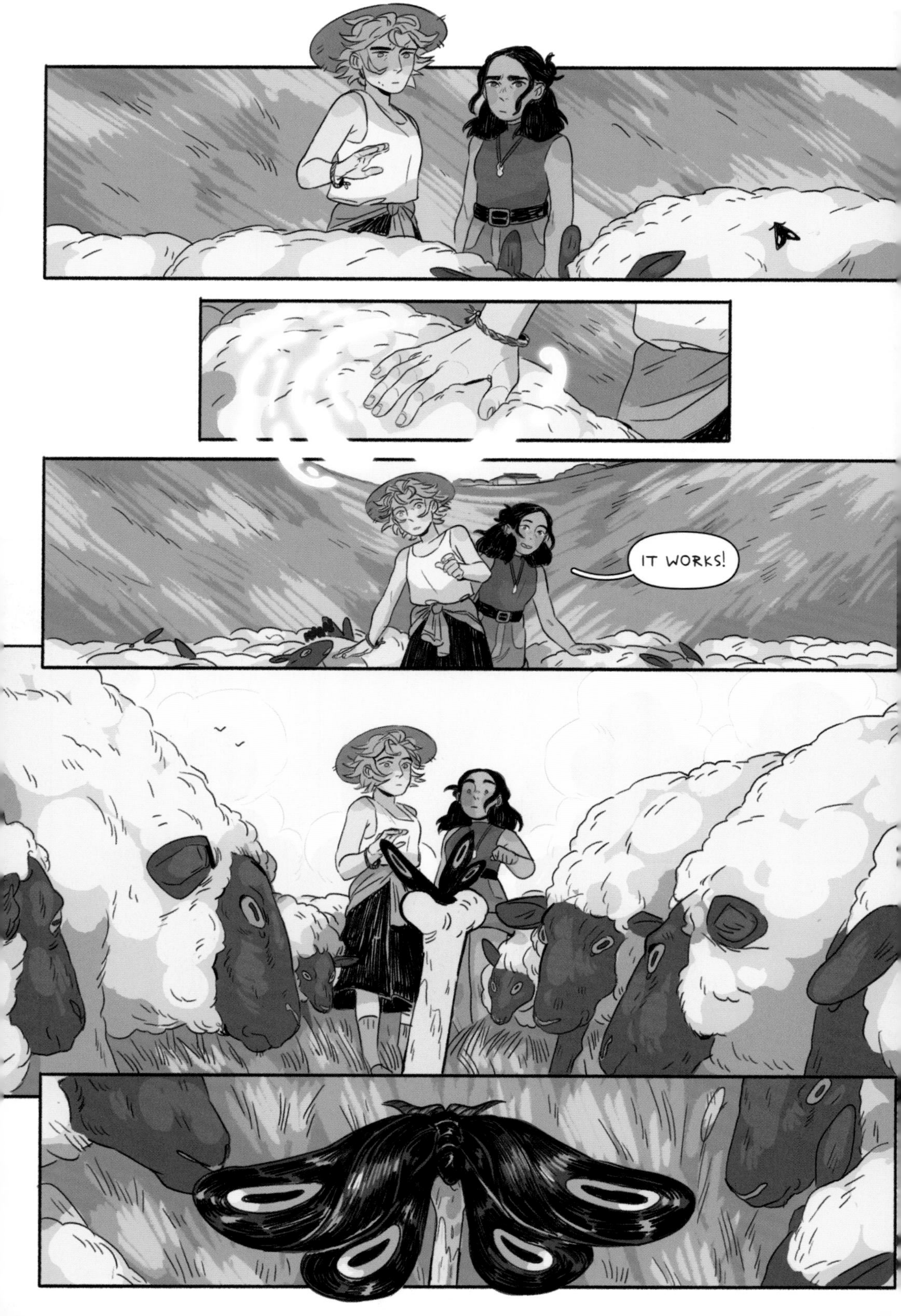
IT WORKS!

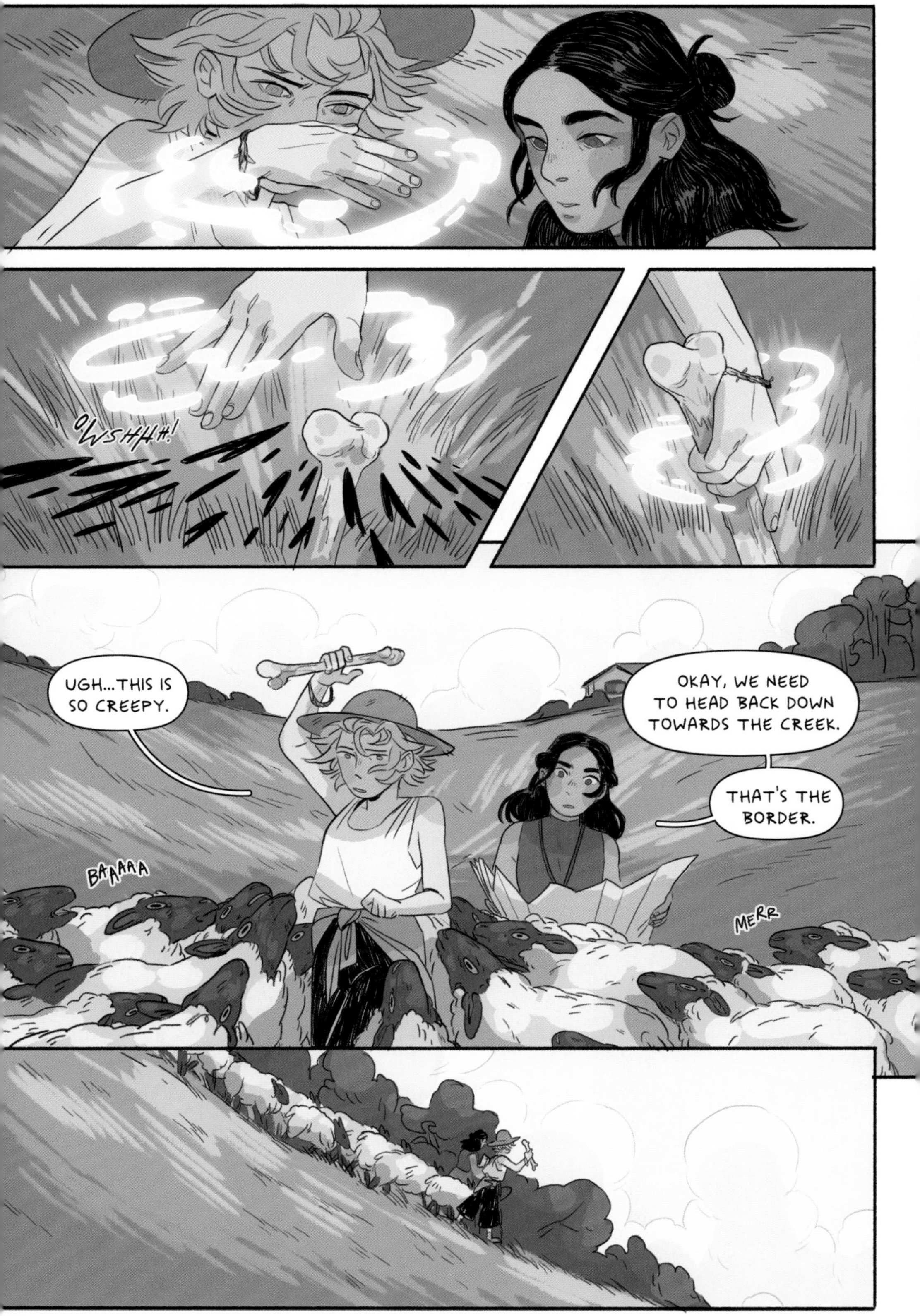

OWSHHH!
UGH...THIS IS SO CREEPY.
OKAY, WE NEED TO HEAD BACK DOWN TOWARDS THE CREEK.
THAT'S THE BORDER.
BAAAAA
MERR

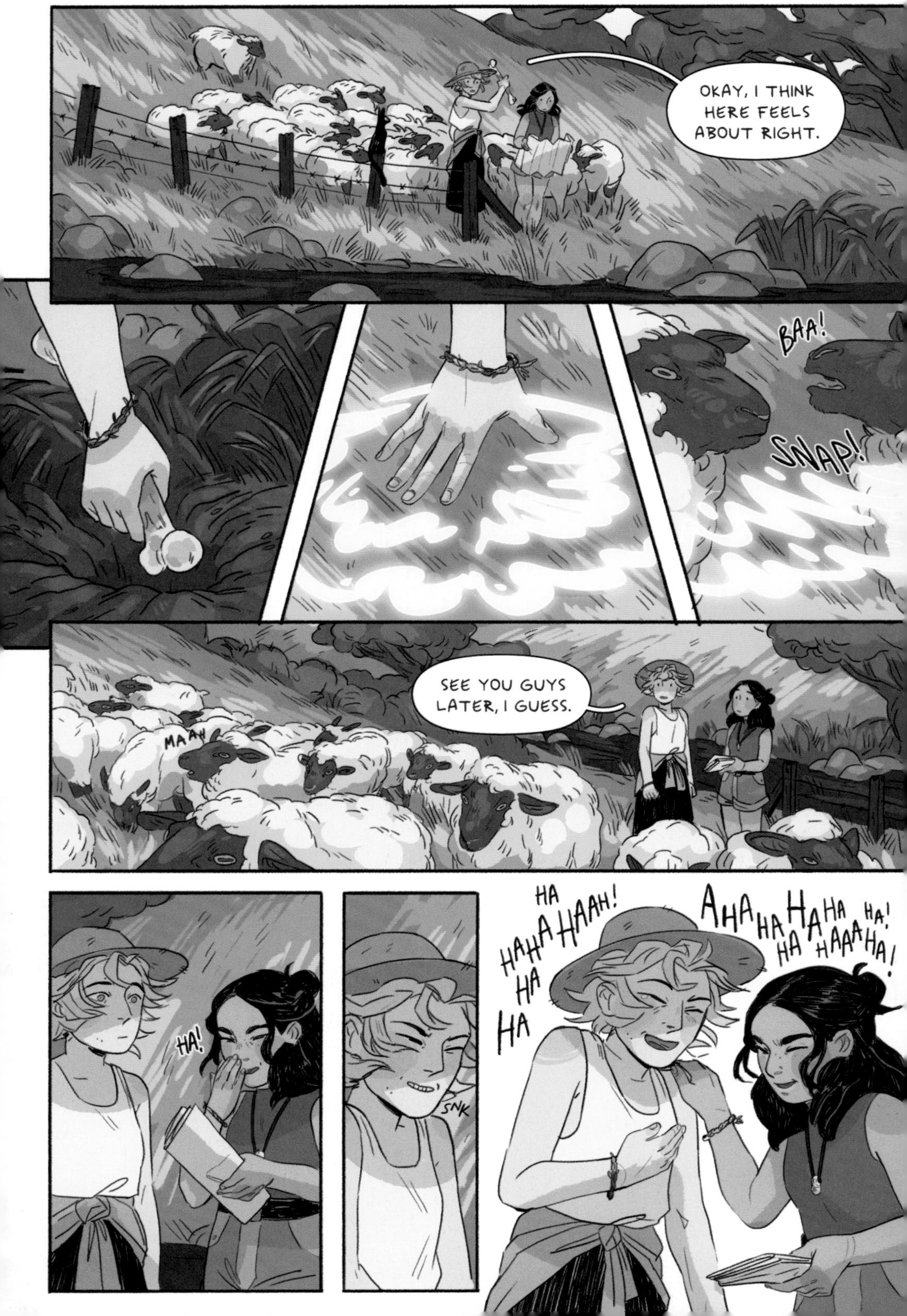
OKAY, I THINK HERE FEELS ABOUT RIGHT.
BAA!
SNAP!
MAAH
SEE YOU GUYS LATER, I GUESS.
HA!
SNK
HA HAHAHAAAH! HA HA HA
AHAHAHAHAHA HA! HA HAAAHA!

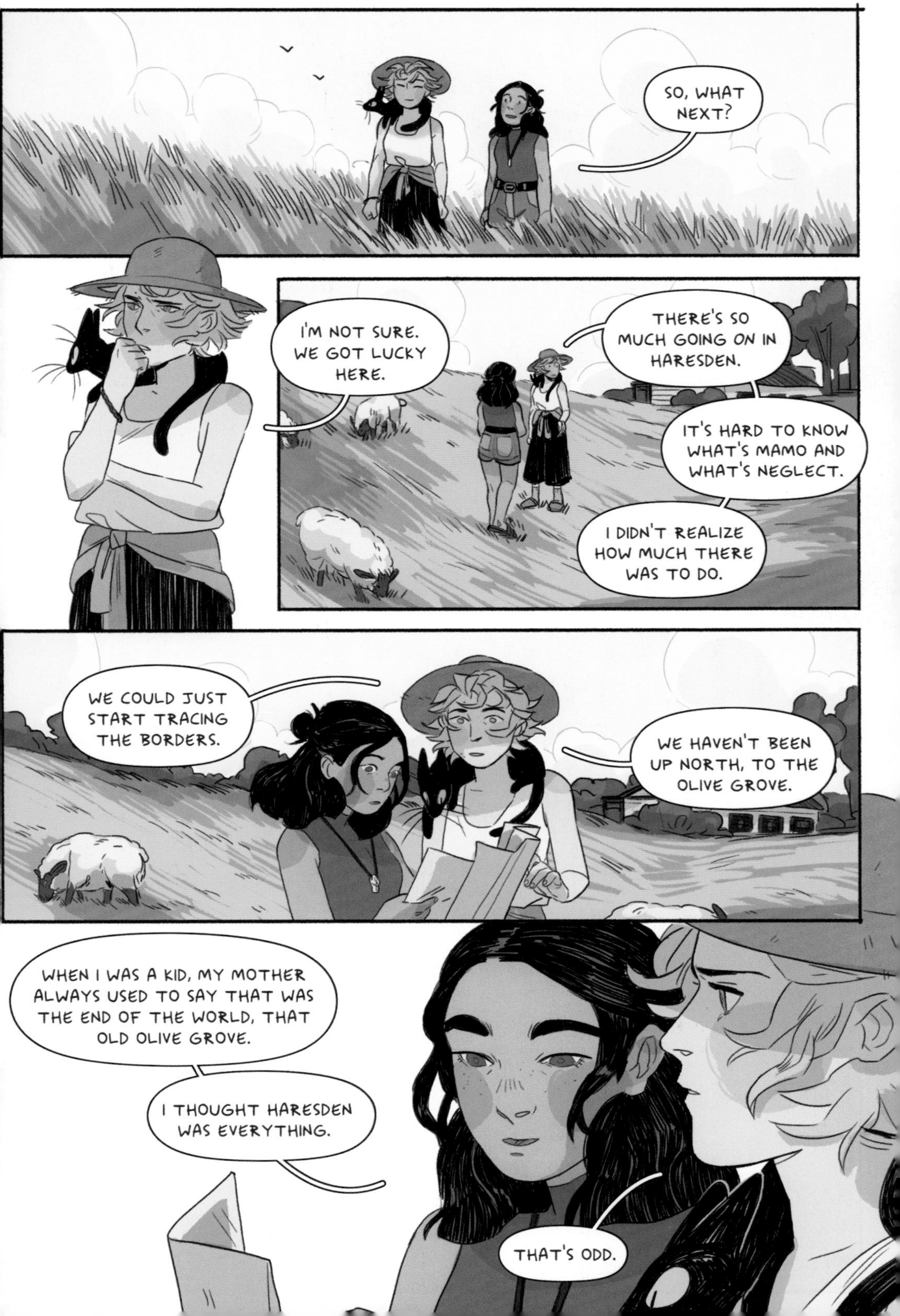
SO, WHAT NEXT?
I'M NOT SURE. WE GOT LUCKY HERE.
THERE'S SO MUCH GOING ON IN HARESDEN.
IT'S HARD TO KNOW WHAT'S MAMO AND WHAT'S NEGLECT.
I DIDN'T REALIZE HOW MUCH THERE WAS TO DO.
WE COULD JUST START TRACING THE BORDERS.
WE HAVEN'T BEEN UP NORTH, TO THE OLIVE GROVE.
WHEN I WAS A KID, MY MOTHER ALWAYS USED TO SAY THAT WAS THE END OF THE WORLD, THAT OLD OLIVE GROVE.
I THOUGHT HARESDEN WAS EVERYTHING.
THAT'S ODD.

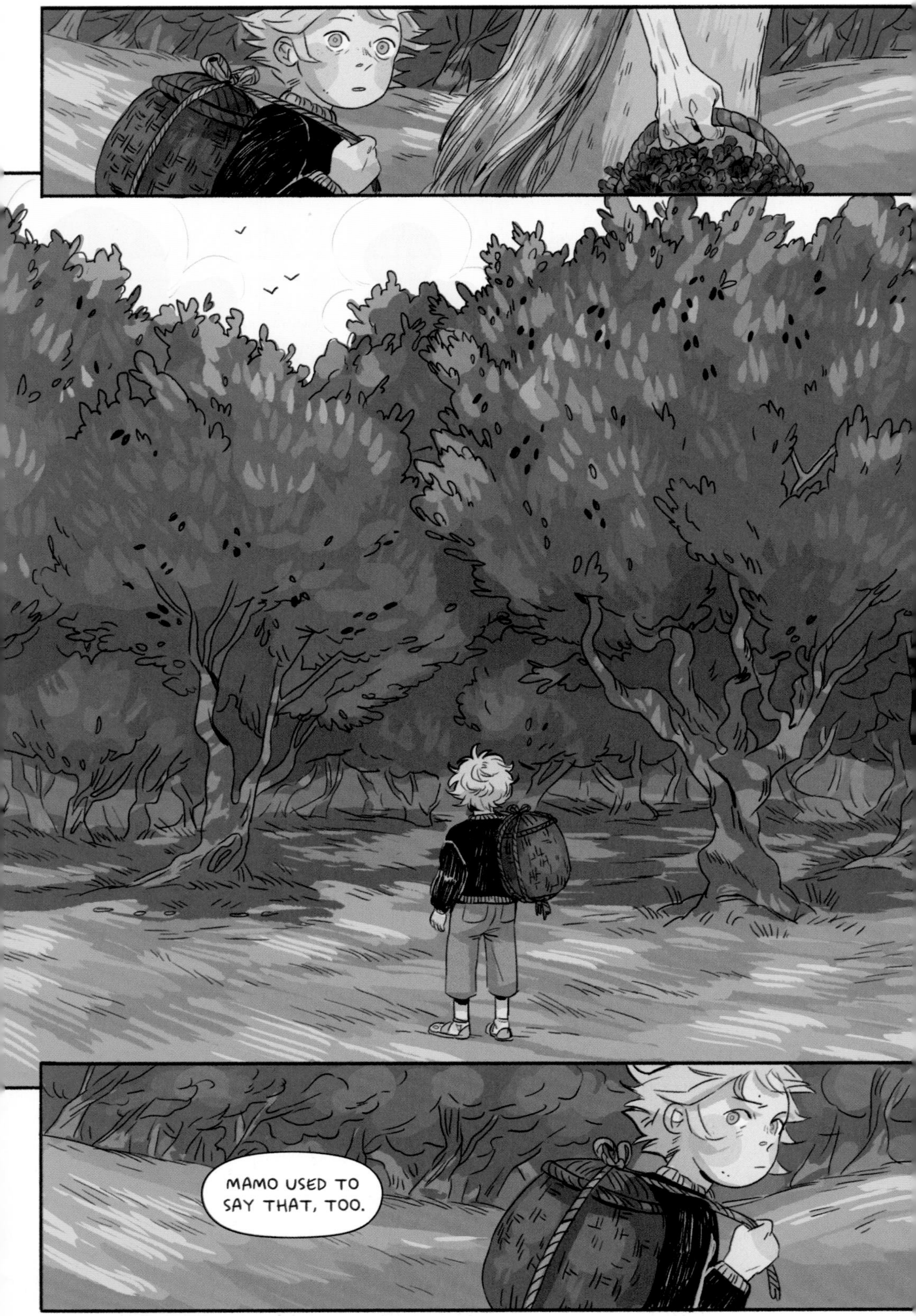
MAMO USED TO
SAY THAT, TOO.

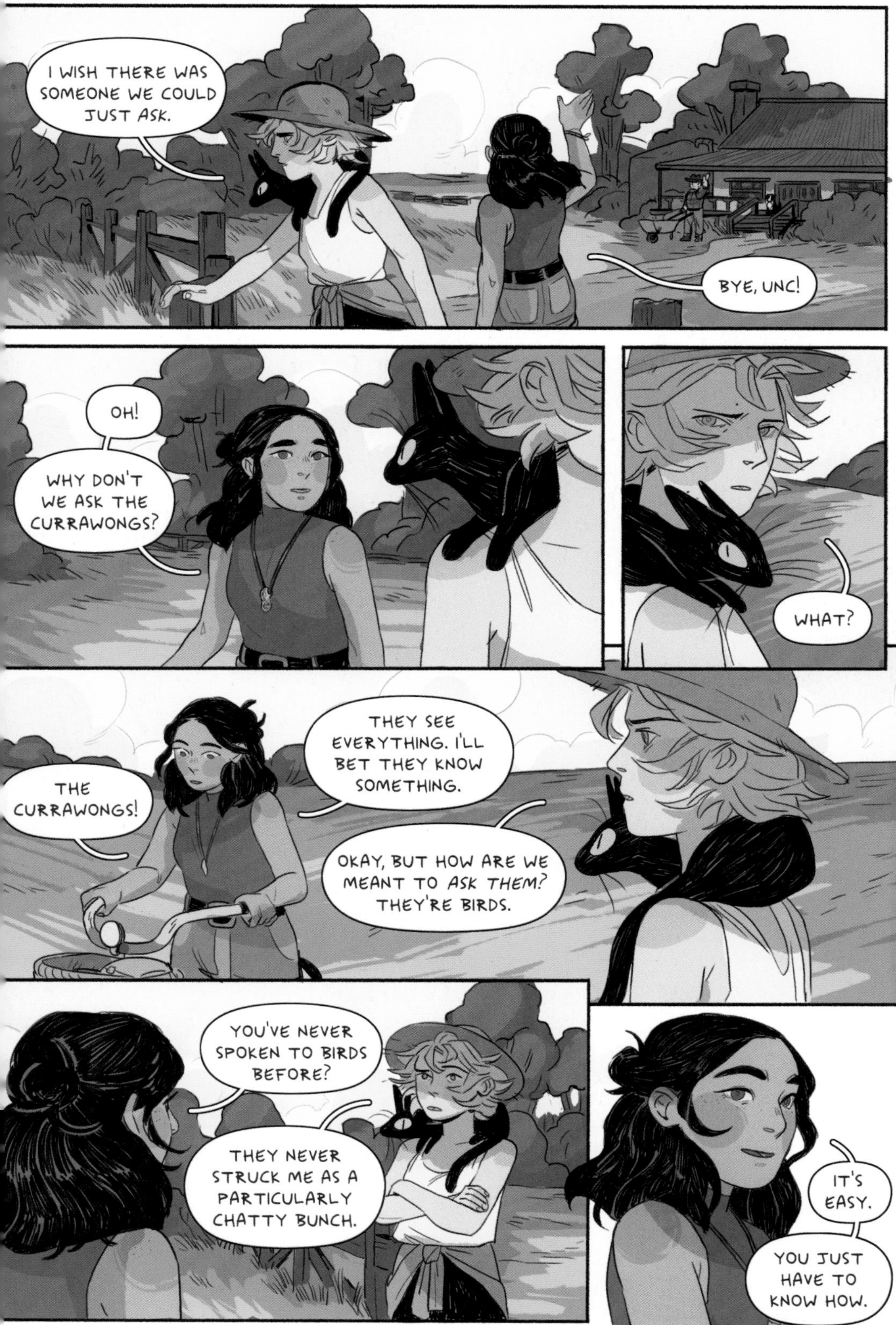
I WISH THERE WAS SOMEONE WE COULD JUST ASK.
BYE, UNC!
OH!
WHY DON'T WE ASK THE CURRAWONGS?
WHAT?
THE CURRAWONGS!
THEY SEE EVERYTHING. I'LL BET THEY KNOW SOMETHING.
OKAY, BUT HOW ARE WE MEANT TO ASK THEM? THEY'RE BIRDS.
YOU'VE NEVER SPOKEN TO BIRDS BEFORE?
THEY NEVER STRUCK ME AS A PARTICULARLY CHATTY BUNCH.
IT'S EASY.
YOU JUST HAVE TO KNOW HOW.

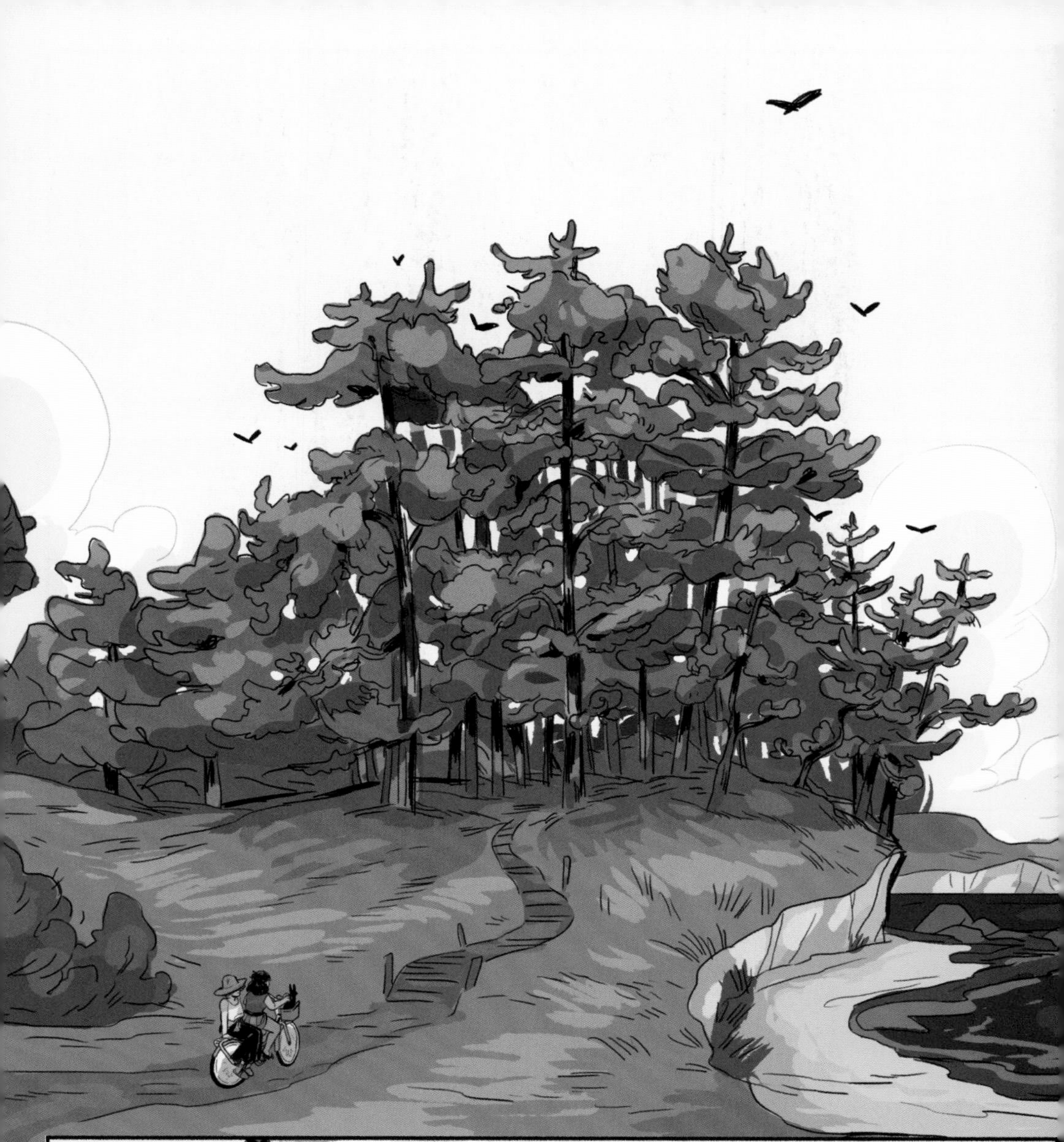
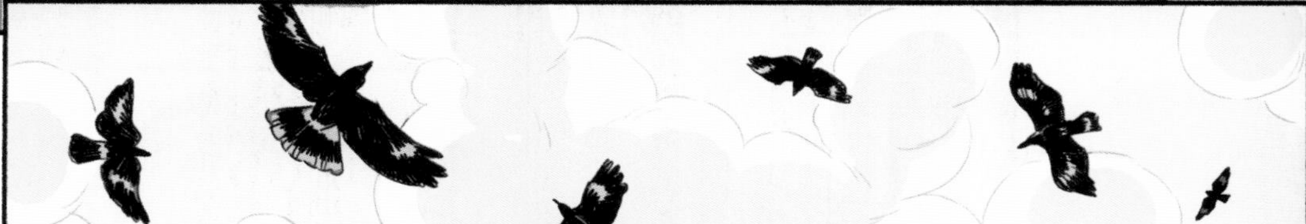
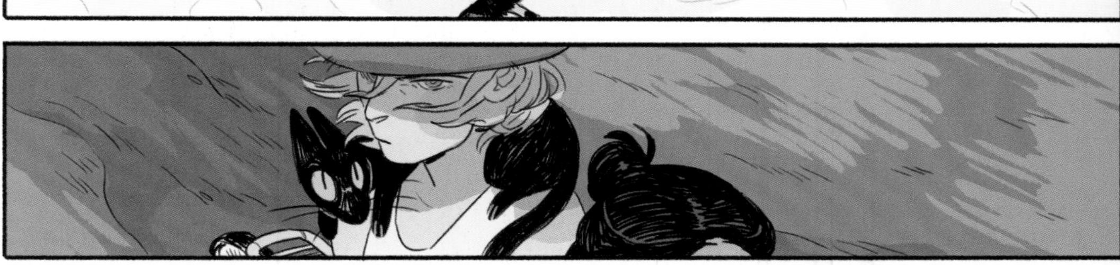

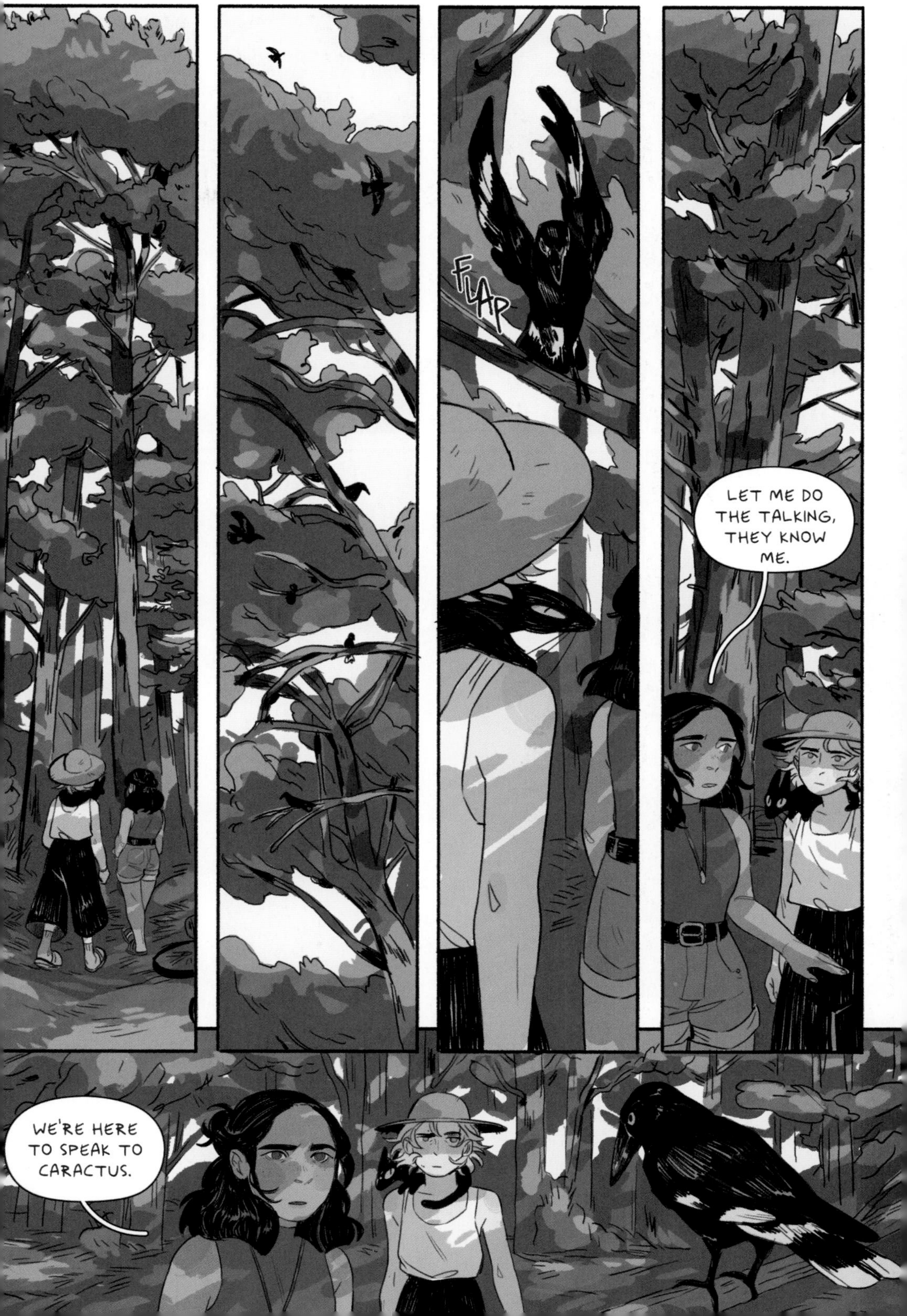
FLAP
LET ME DO THE TALKING, THEY KNOW ME.
WE'RE HERE TO SPEAK TO CARACTUS.

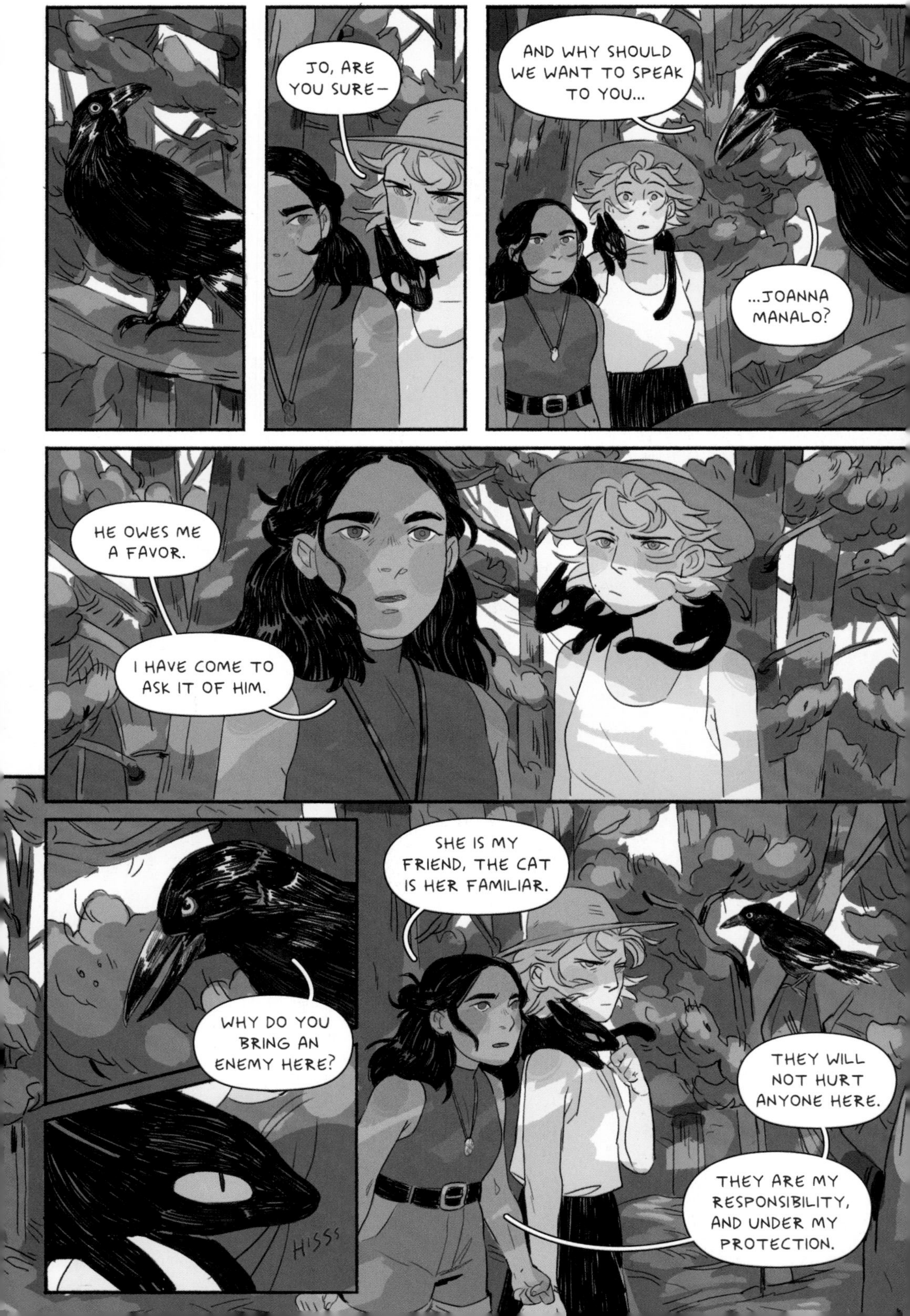
JO, ARE YOU SURE—
AND WHY SHOULD WE WANT TO SPEAK TO YOU...
...JOANNA MANALO?
HE OWES ME A FAVOR.
I HAVE COME TO ASK IT OF HIM.
WHY DO YOU BRING AN ENEMY HERE?
HISSS
SHE IS MY FRIEND, THE CAT IS HER FAMILIAR.
THEY WILL NOT HURT ANYONE HERE.
THEY ARE MY RESPONSIBILITY, AND UNDER MY PROTECTION.

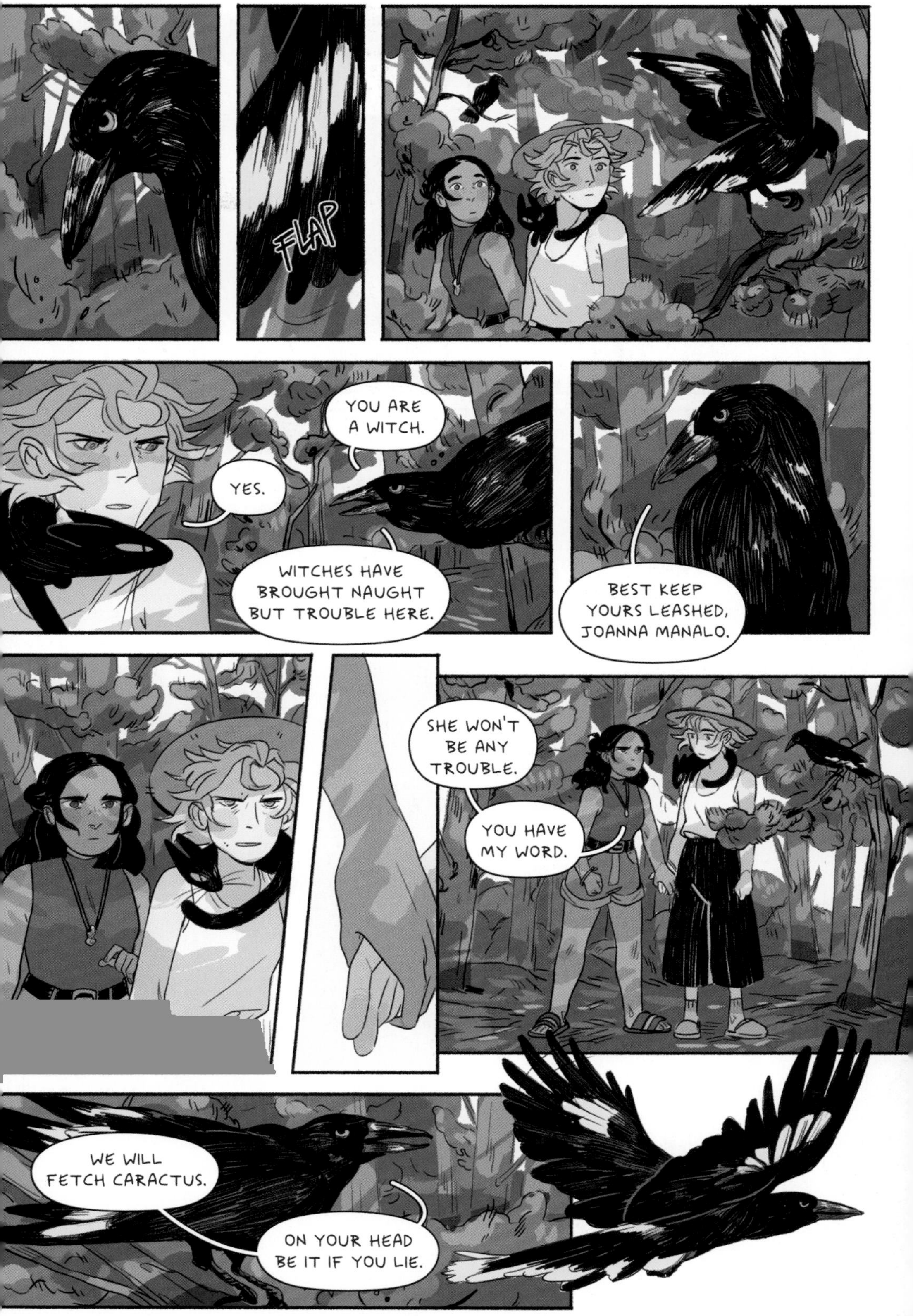
FLAP
YOU ARE A WITCH.
YES.
WITCHES HAVE BROUGHT NAUGHT BUT TROUBLE HERE.
BEST KEEP YOURS LEASHED, JOANNA MANALO.
SHE WON'T BE ANY TROUBLE.
YOU HAVE MY WORD.
WE WILL FETCH CARACTUS.
ON YOUR HEAD BE IT IF YOU LIE.

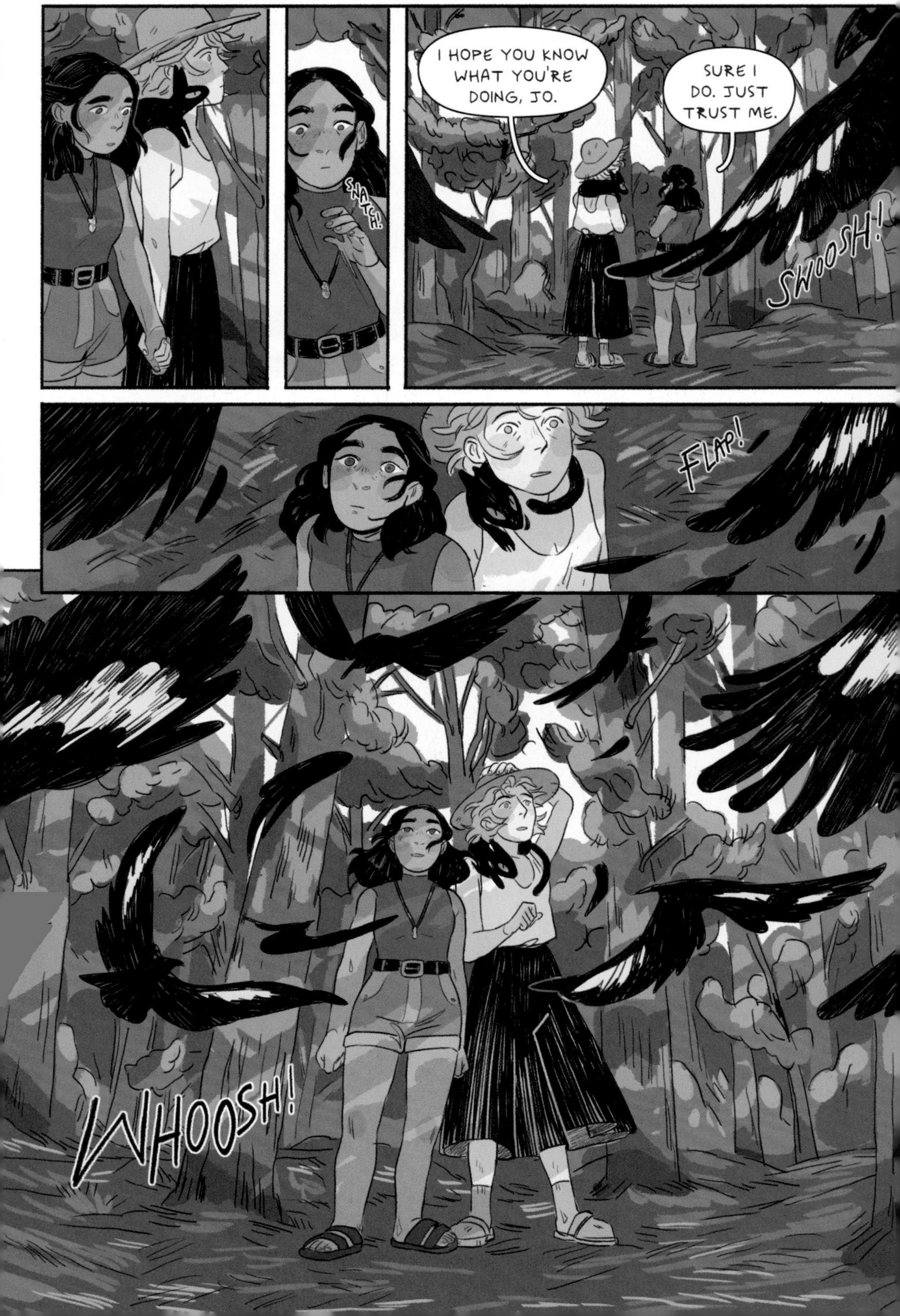
SNATCH!
I HOPE YOU KNOW WHAT YOU'RE DOING, JO.
SURE I DO. JUST TRUST ME.
SWOOSH!
FLAP!
WHOOSH!

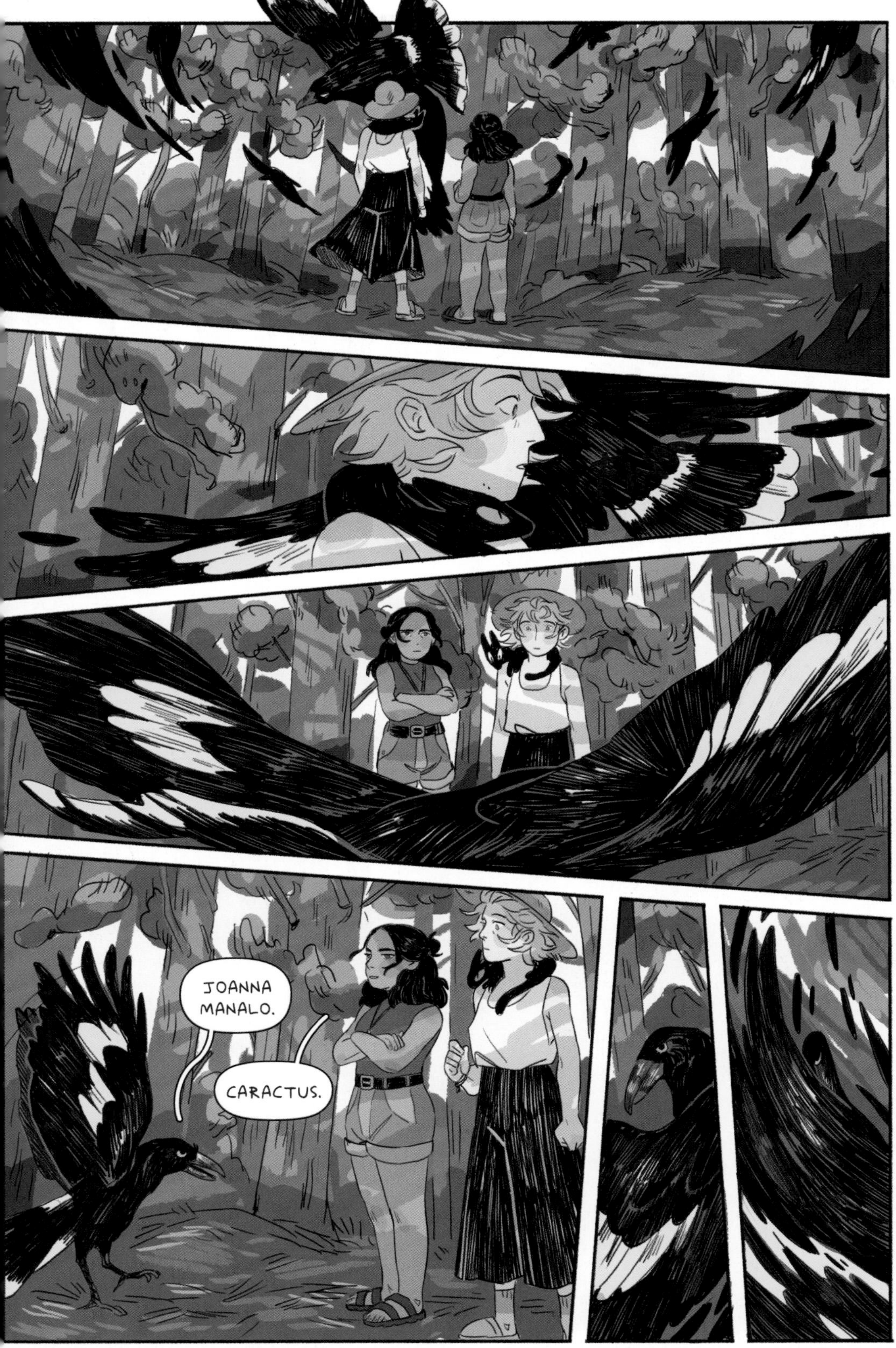
JOANNA MANALO.
CARACTUS.

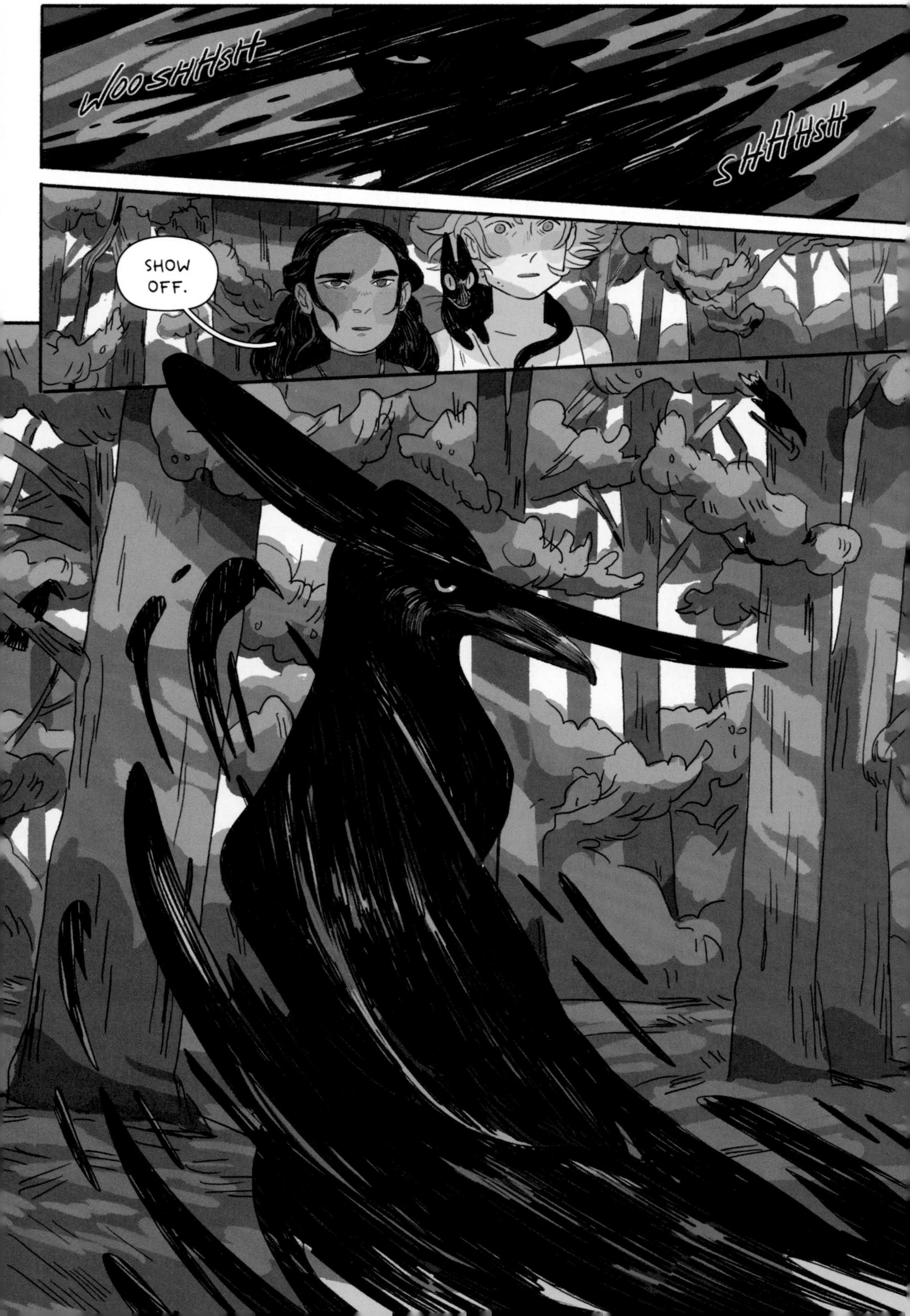
WOOSHHHSH
SHHHSH
SHOW OFF.

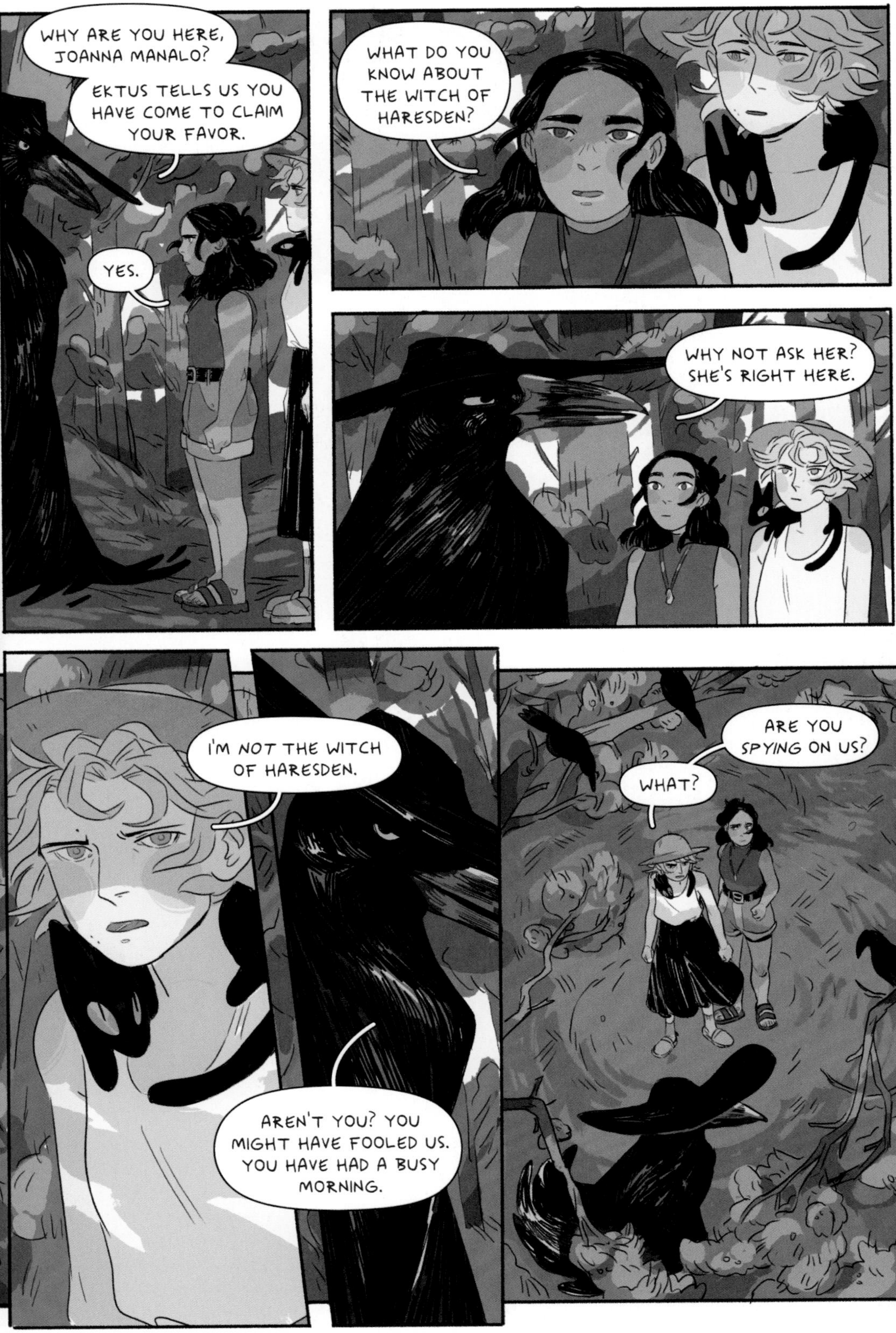
WHY ARE YOU HERE, JOANNA MANALO?
EKTUS TELLS US YOU HAVE COME TO CLAIM YOUR FAVOR.
YES.
WHAT DO YOU KNOW ABOUT THE WITCH OF HARESDEN?
WHY NOT ASK HER? SHE'S RIGHT HERE.
I'M *NOT* THE WITCH OF HARESDEN.
AREN'T YOU? YOU MIGHT HAVE FOOLED US. YOU HAVE HAD A BUSY MORNING.
WHAT?
ARE YOU *SPYING* ON US?

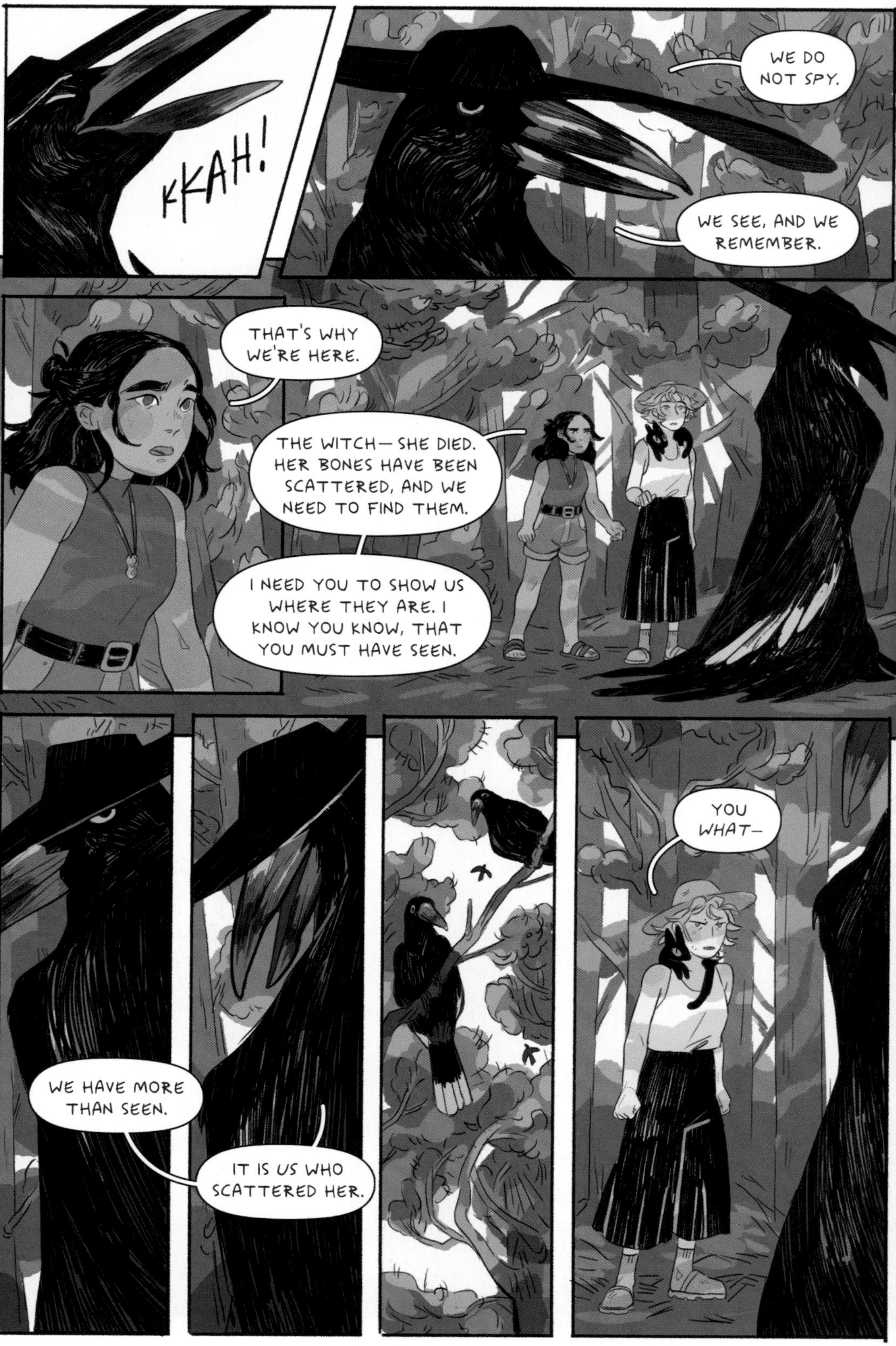
KKAH!
WE DO NOT SPY.
WE SEE, AND WE REMEMBER.
THAT'S WHY WE'RE HERE.
THE WITCH— SHE DIED. HER BONES HAVE BEEN SCATTERED, AND WE NEED TO FIND THEM.
I NEED YOU TO SHOW US WHERE THEY ARE. I KNOW YOU KNOW, THAT YOU MUST HAVE SEEN.
WE HAVE MORE THAN SEEN.
IT IS US WHO SCATTERED HER.
YOU WHAT—

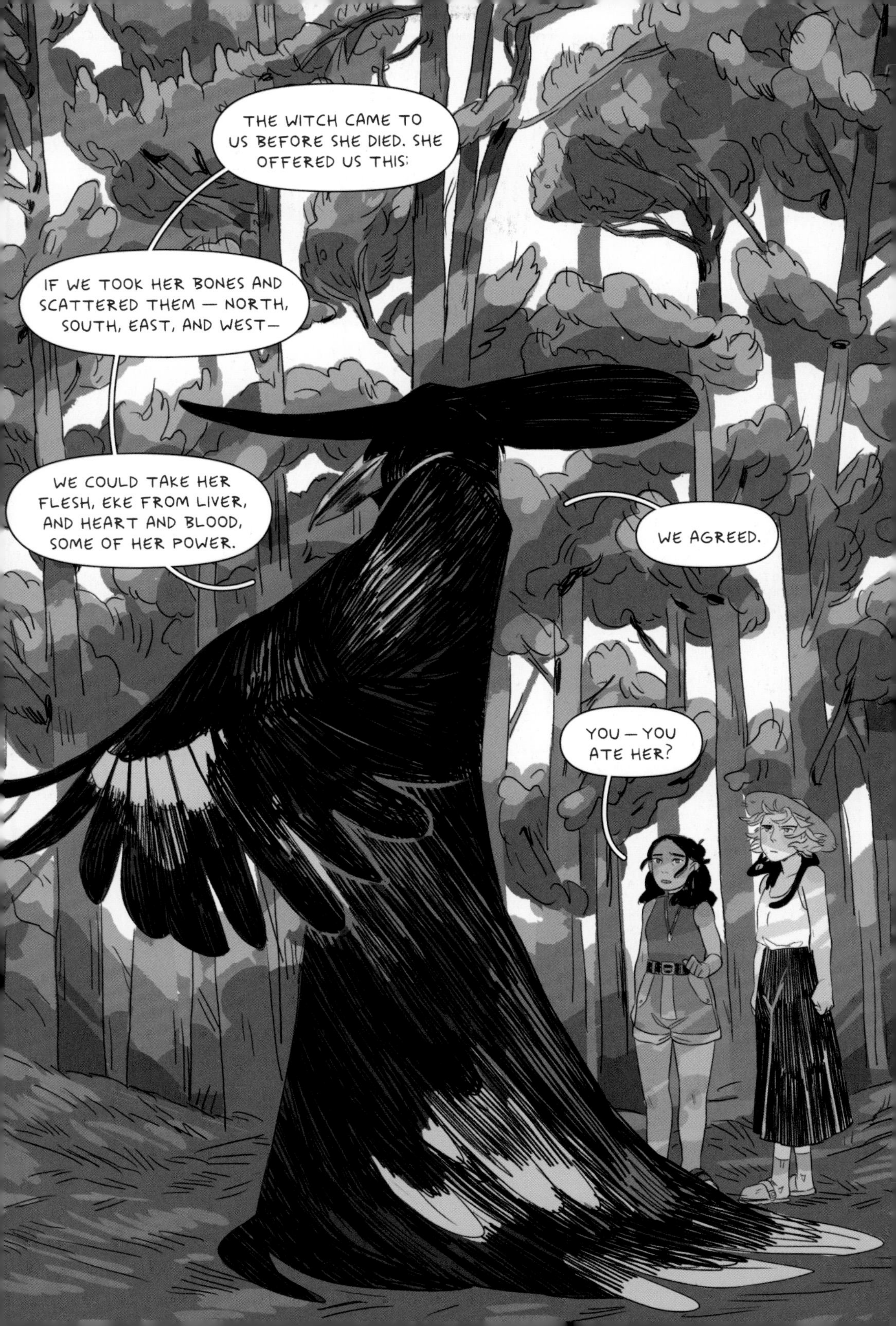
THE WITCH CAME TO US BEFORE SHE DIED. SHE OFFERED US THIS:
IF WE TOOK HER BONES AND SCATTERED THEM — NORTH, SOUTH, EAST, AND WEST—
WE COULD TAKE HER FLESH, EKE FROM LIVER, AND HEART AND BLOOD, SOME OF HER POWER.
WE AGREED.
YOU — YOU ATE HER?

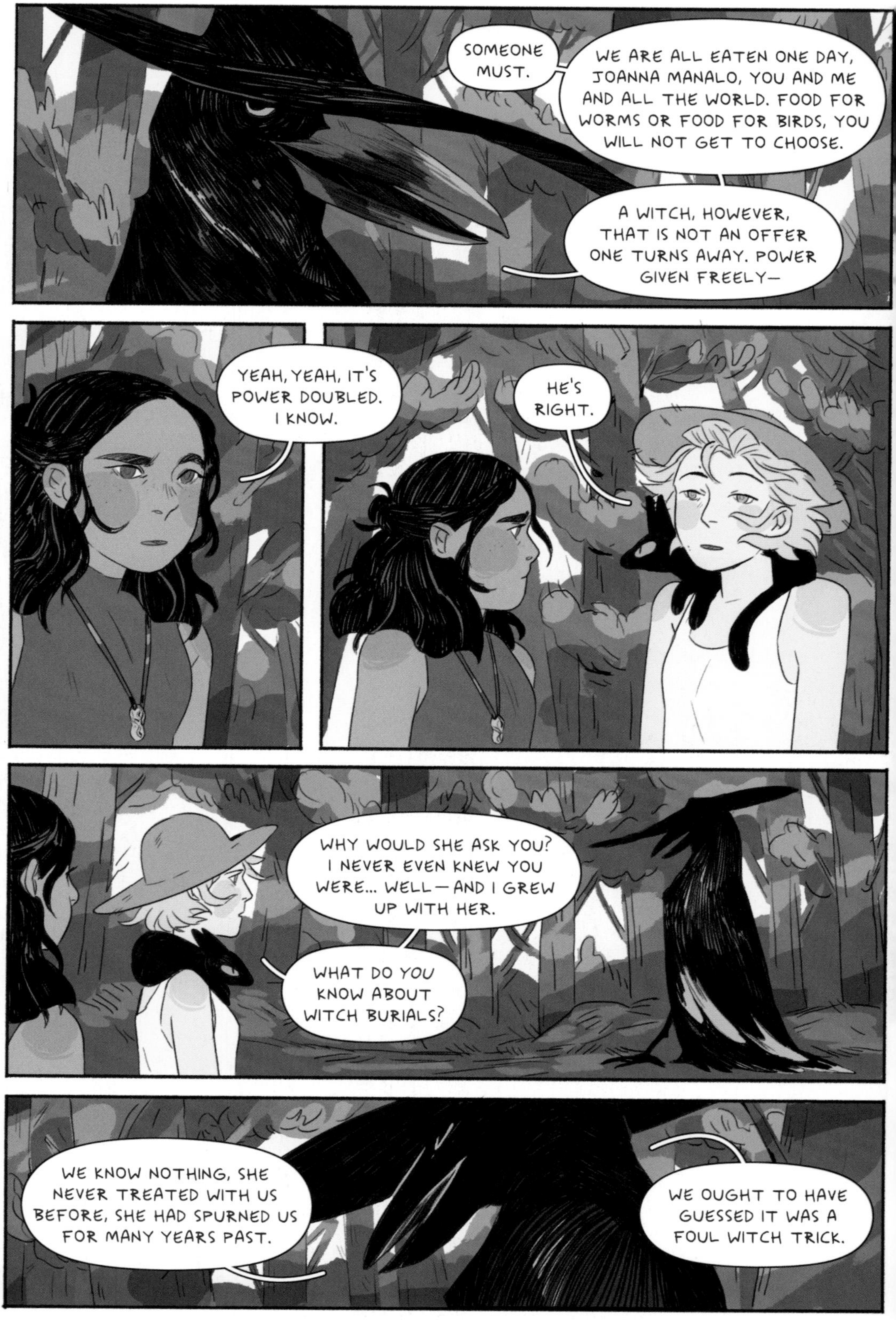
SOMEONE MUST.
WE ARE ALL EATEN ONE DAY, JOANNA MANALO, YOU AND ME AND ALL THE WORLD. FOOD FOR WORMS OR FOOD FOR BIRDS, YOU WILL NOT GET TO CHOOSE.
A WITCH, HOWEVER, THAT IS NOT AN OFFER ONE TURNS AWAY. POWER GIVEN FREELY—
YEAH, YEAH, IT'S POWER DOUBLED. I KNOW.
HE'S RIGHT.
WHY WOULD SHE ASK YOU? I NEVER EVEN KNEW YOU WERE... WELL—AND I GREW UP WITH HER.
WHAT DO YOU KNOW ABOUT WITCH BURIALS?
WE KNOW NOTHING, SHE NEVER TREATED WITH US BEFORE, SHE HAD SPURNED US FOR MANY YEARS PAST.
WE OUGHT TO HAVE GUESSED IT WAS A FOUL WITCH TRICK.

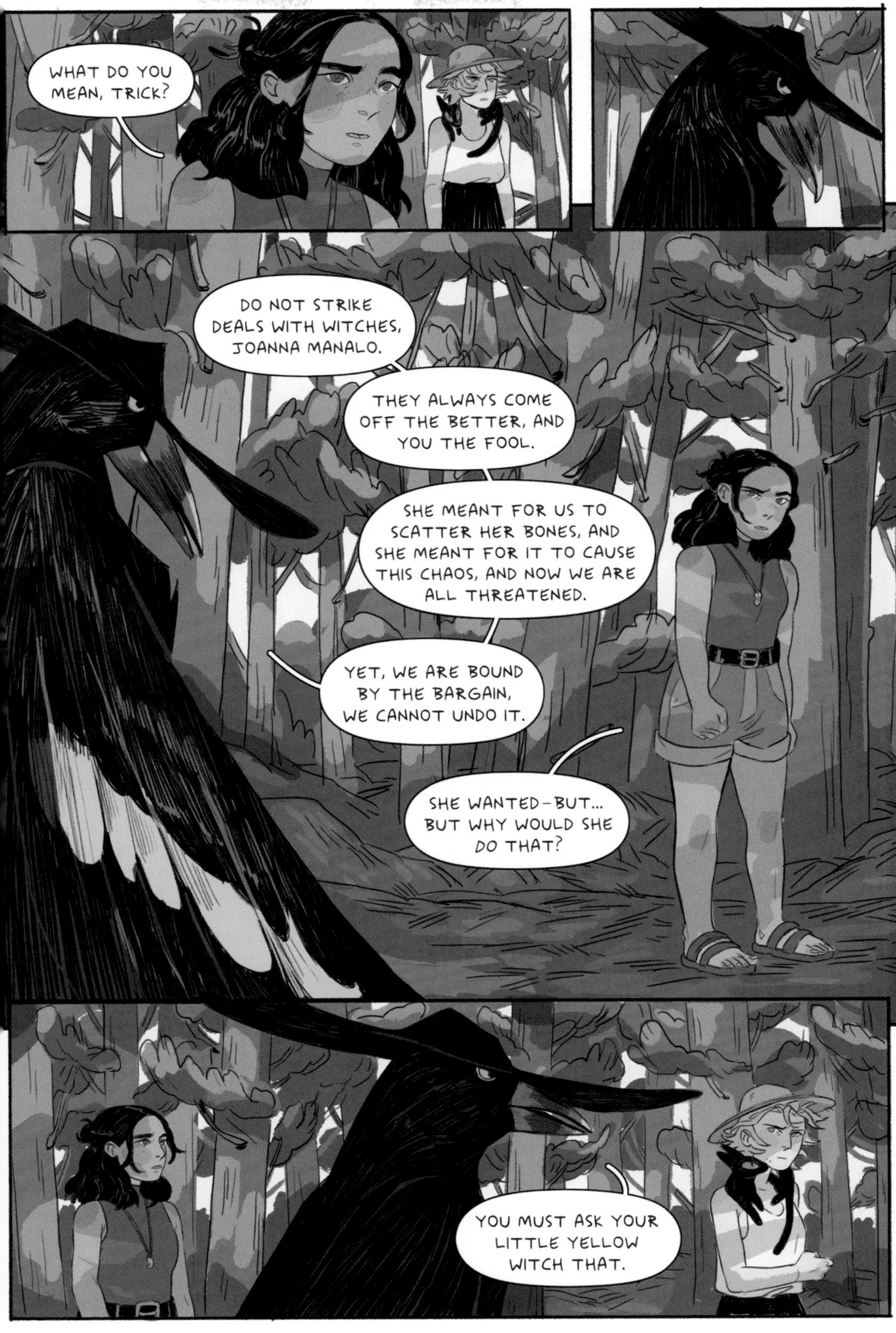
WHAT DO YOU MEAN, TRICK?
DO NOT STRIKE DEALS WITH WITCHES, JOANNA MANALO.
THEY ALWAYS COME OFF THE BETTER, AND YOU THE FOOL.
SHE MEANT FOR US TO SCATTER HER BONES, AND SHE MEANT FOR IT TO CAUSE THIS CHAOS, AND NOW WE ARE ALL THREATENED.
YET, WE ARE BOUND BY THE BARGAIN, WE CANNOT UNDO IT.
SHE WANTED—BUT... BUT WHY WOULD SHE DO THAT?
YOU MUST ASK YOUR LITTLE YELLOW WITCH THAT.

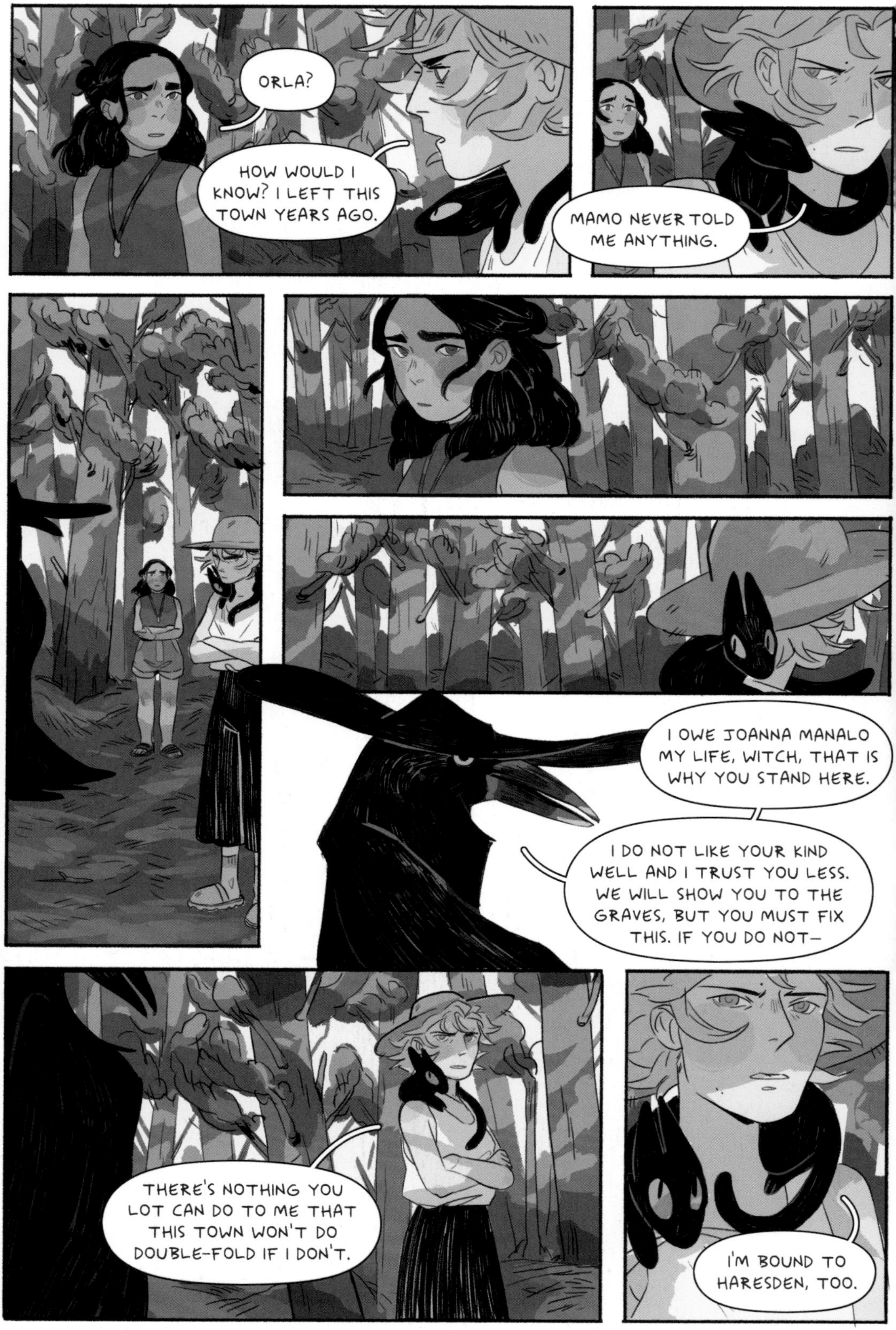
ORLA?
HOW WOULD I KNOW? I LEFT THIS TOWN YEARS AGO.
MAMO NEVER TOLD ME ANYTHING.
I OWE JOANNA MANALO MY LIFE, WITCH, THAT IS WHY YOU STAND HERE.
I DO NOT LIKE YOUR KIND WELL AND I TRUST YOU LESS. WE WILL SHOW YOU TO THE GRAVES, BUT YOU MUST FIX THIS. IF YOU DO NOT—
THERE'S NOTHING YOU LOT CAN DO TO ME THAT THIS TOWN WON'T DO DOUBLE-FOLD IF I DON'T.
I'M BOUND TO HARESDEN, TOO.

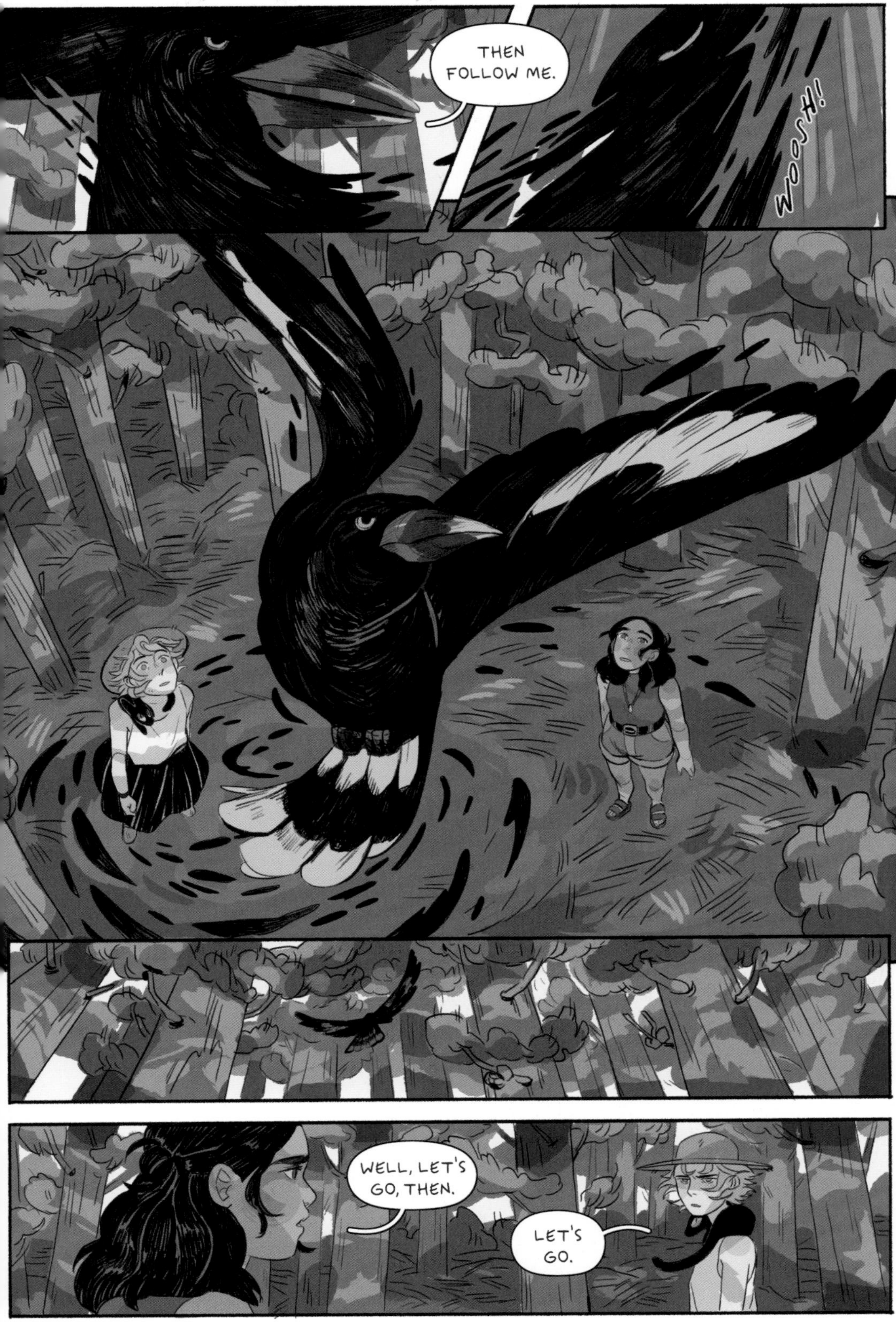
THEN FOLLOW ME.
WOOSH!
WELL, LET'S GO, THEN.
LET'S GO.

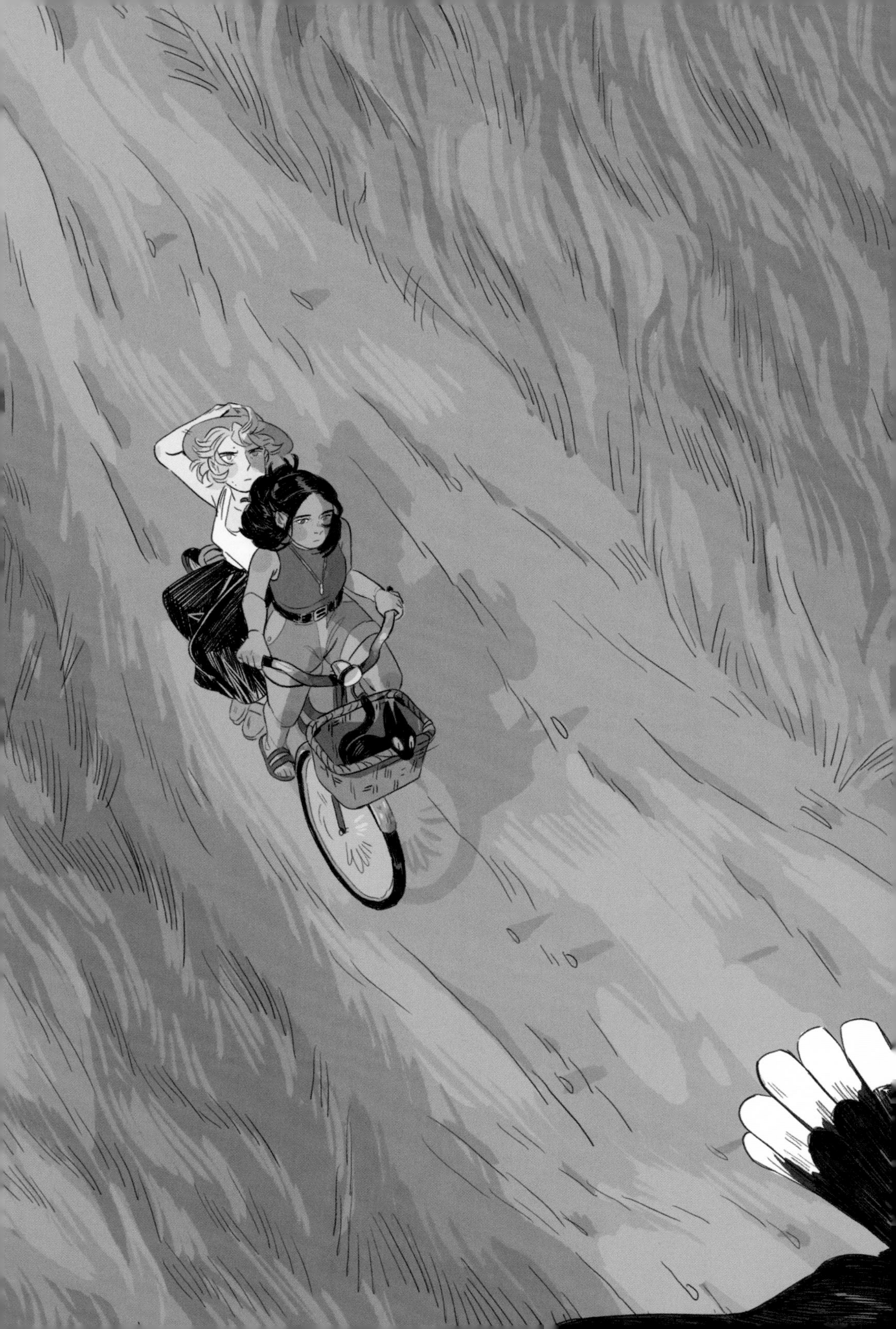

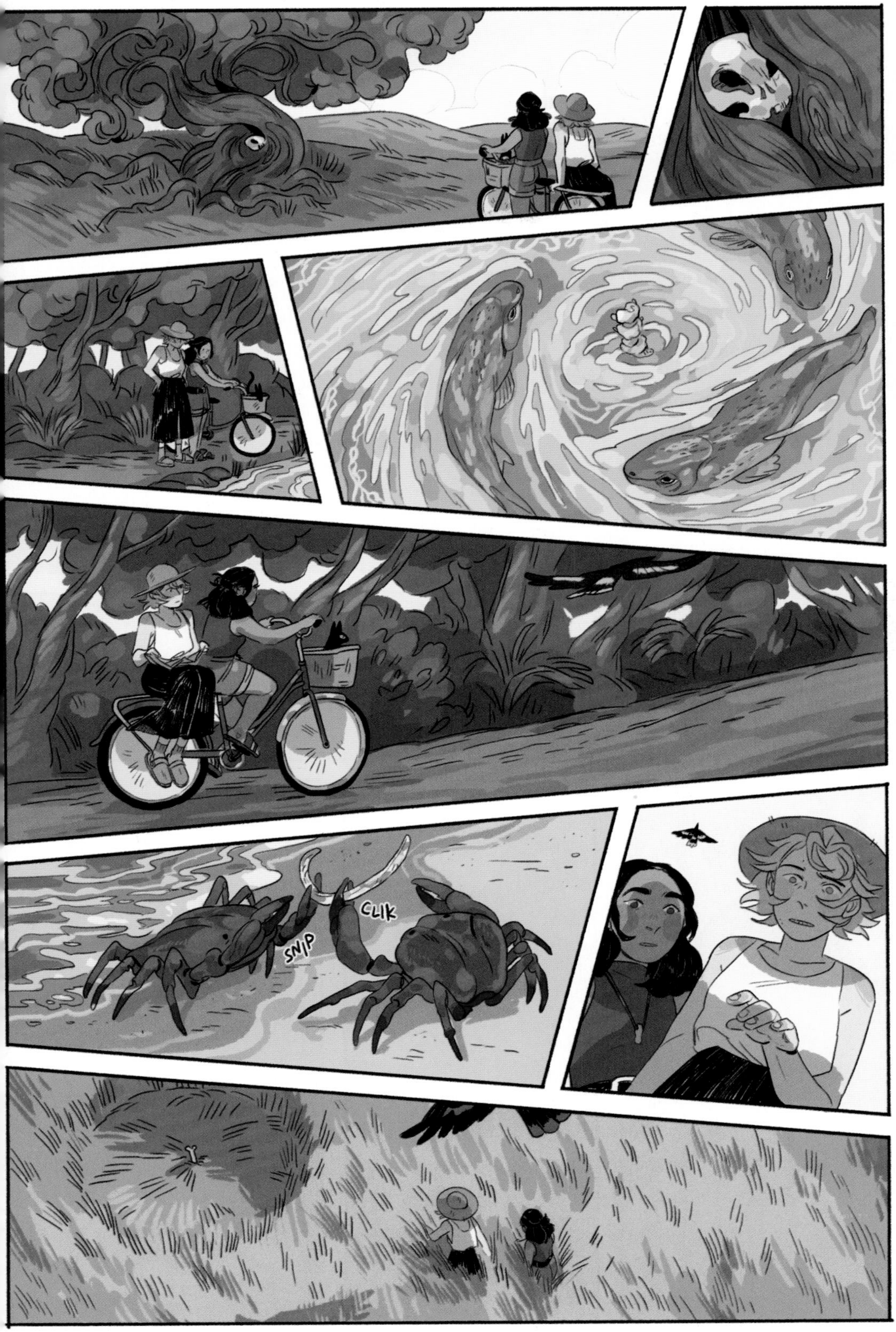
CLIK
SNIP

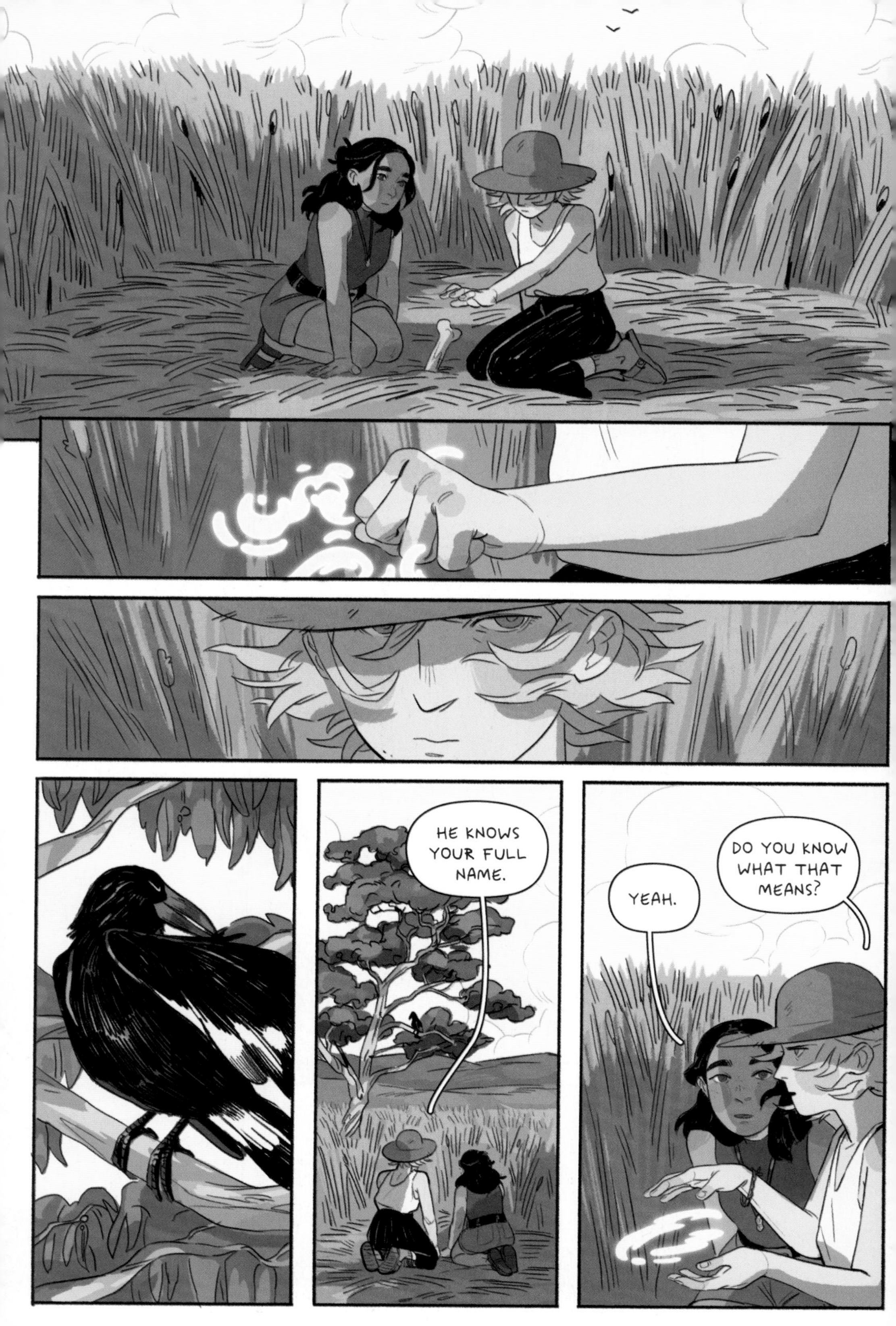
HE KNOWS YOUR FULL NAME.
DO YOU KNOW WHAT THAT MEANS?
YEAH.

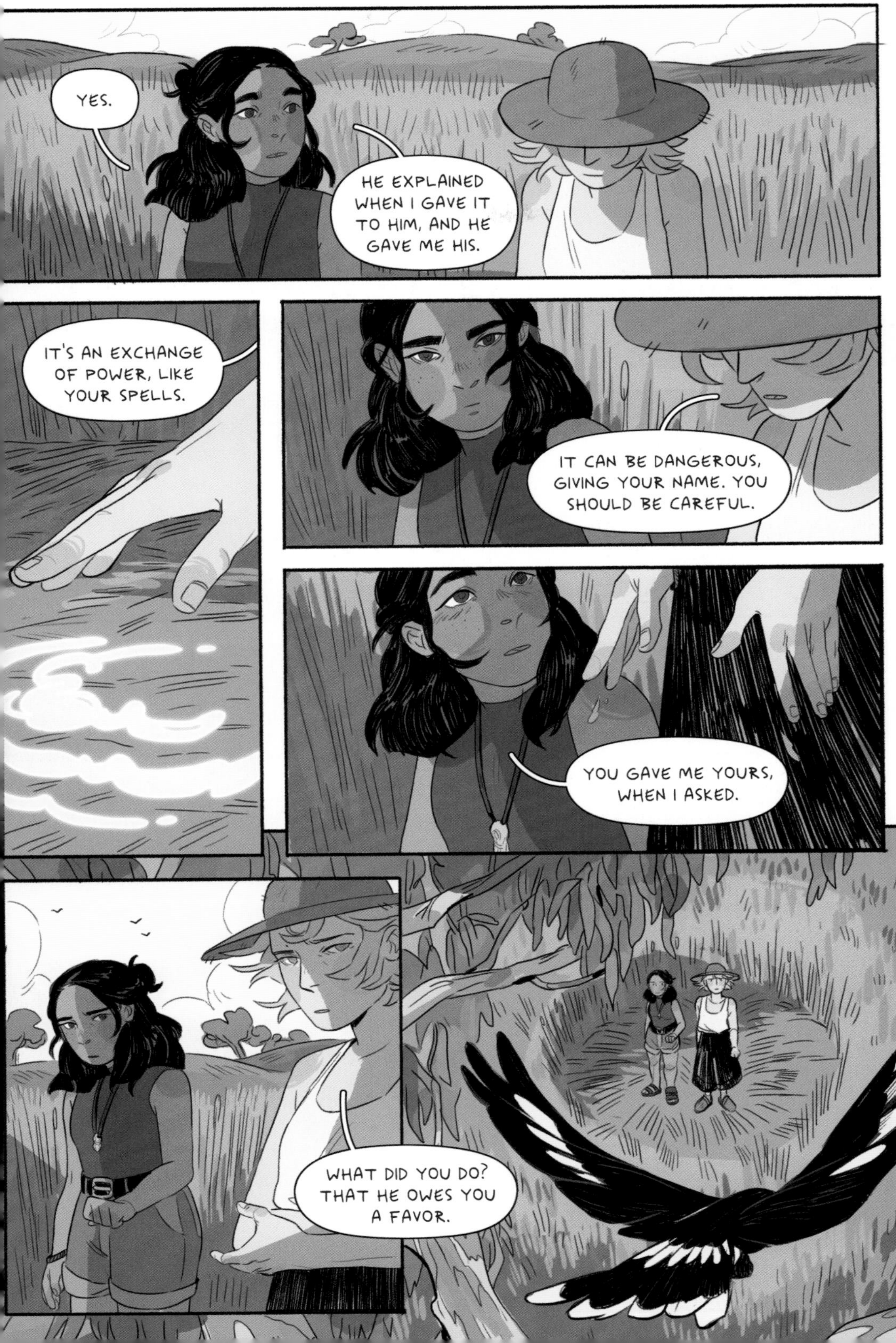
YES.
HE EXPLAINED WHEN I GAVE IT TO HIM, AND HE GAVE ME HIS.
IT'S AN EXCHANGE OF POWER, LIKE YOUR SPELLS.
IT CAN BE DANGEROUS, GIVING YOUR NAME. YOU SHOULD BE CAREFUL.
YOU GAVE ME YOURS, WHEN I ASKED.
WHAT DID YOU DO? THAT HE OWES YOU A FAVOR.

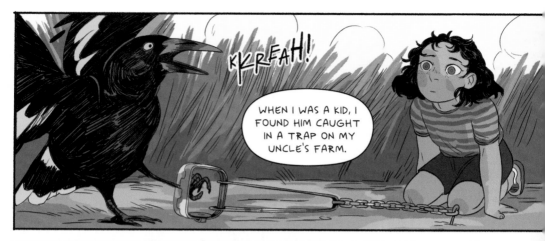

KKREAH!

WHEN I WAS A KID, I FOUND HIM CAUGHT IN A TRAP ON MY UNCLE'S FARM.

HE WOULDN'T LET ME GET NEAR HIM AT FIRST.

I SAT WITH HIM.

EVENTUALLY HE CAME AROUND.

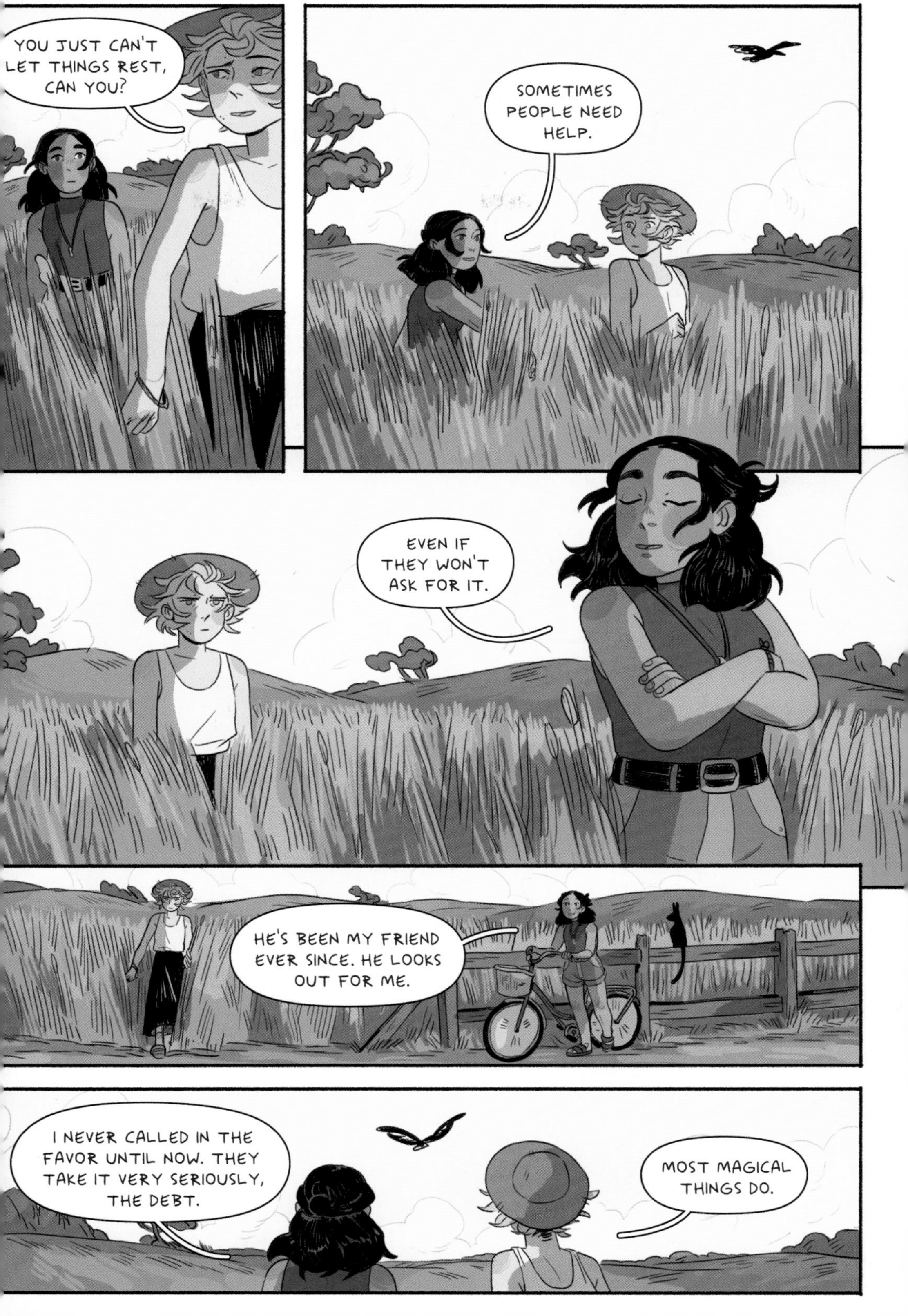
YOU JUST CAN'T LET THINGS REST, CAN YOU?
SOMETIMES PEOPLE NEED HELP.
EVEN IF THEY WON'T ASK FOR IT.
HE'S BEEN MY FRIEND EVER SINCE. HE LOOKS OUT FOR ME.
I NEVER CALLED IN THE FAVOR UNTIL NOW. THEY TAKE IT VERY SERIOUSLY, THE DEBT.
MOST MAGICAL THINGS DO.

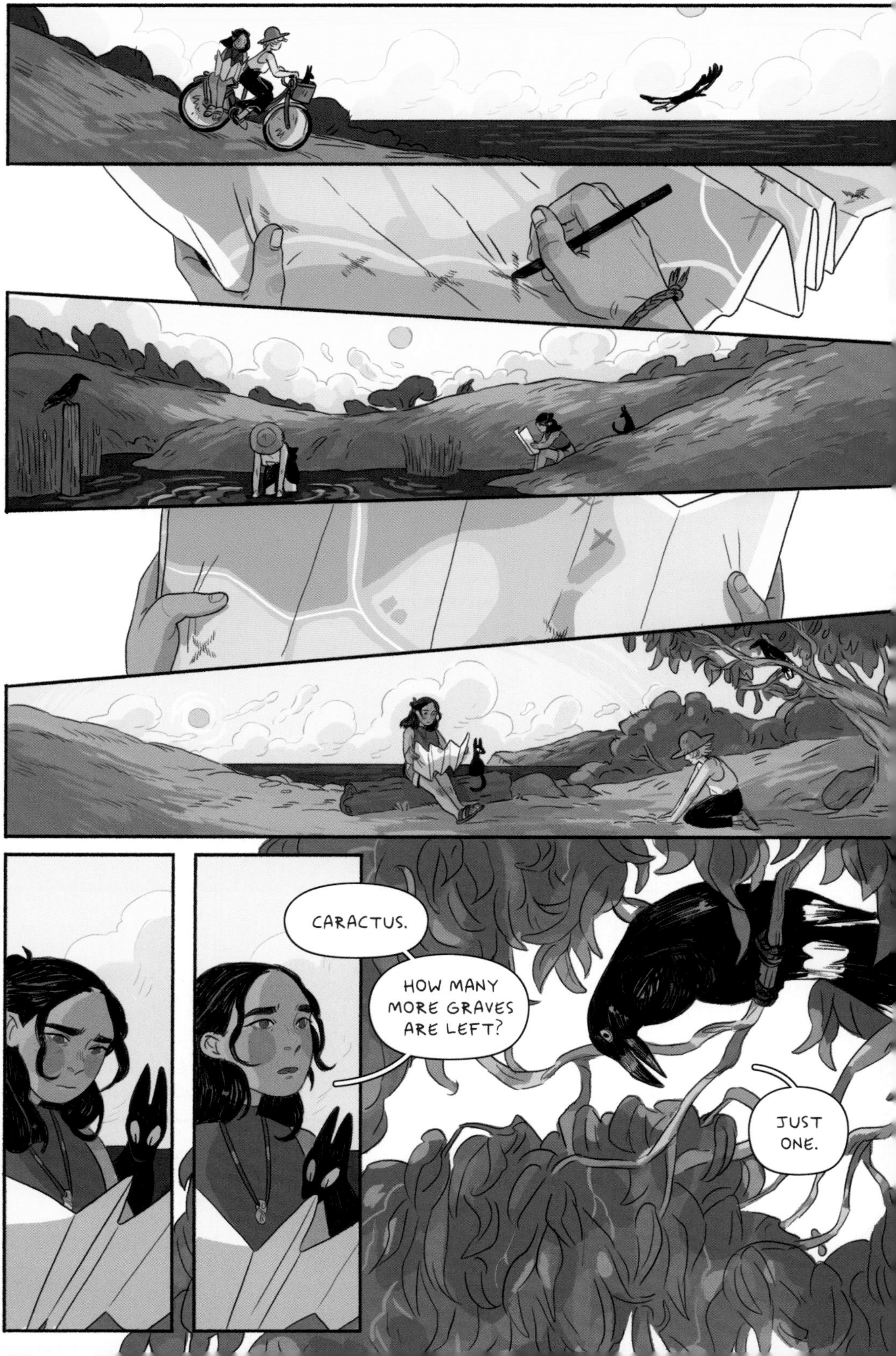
CARACTUS.
HOW MANY MORE GRAVES ARE LEFT?
JUST ONE.

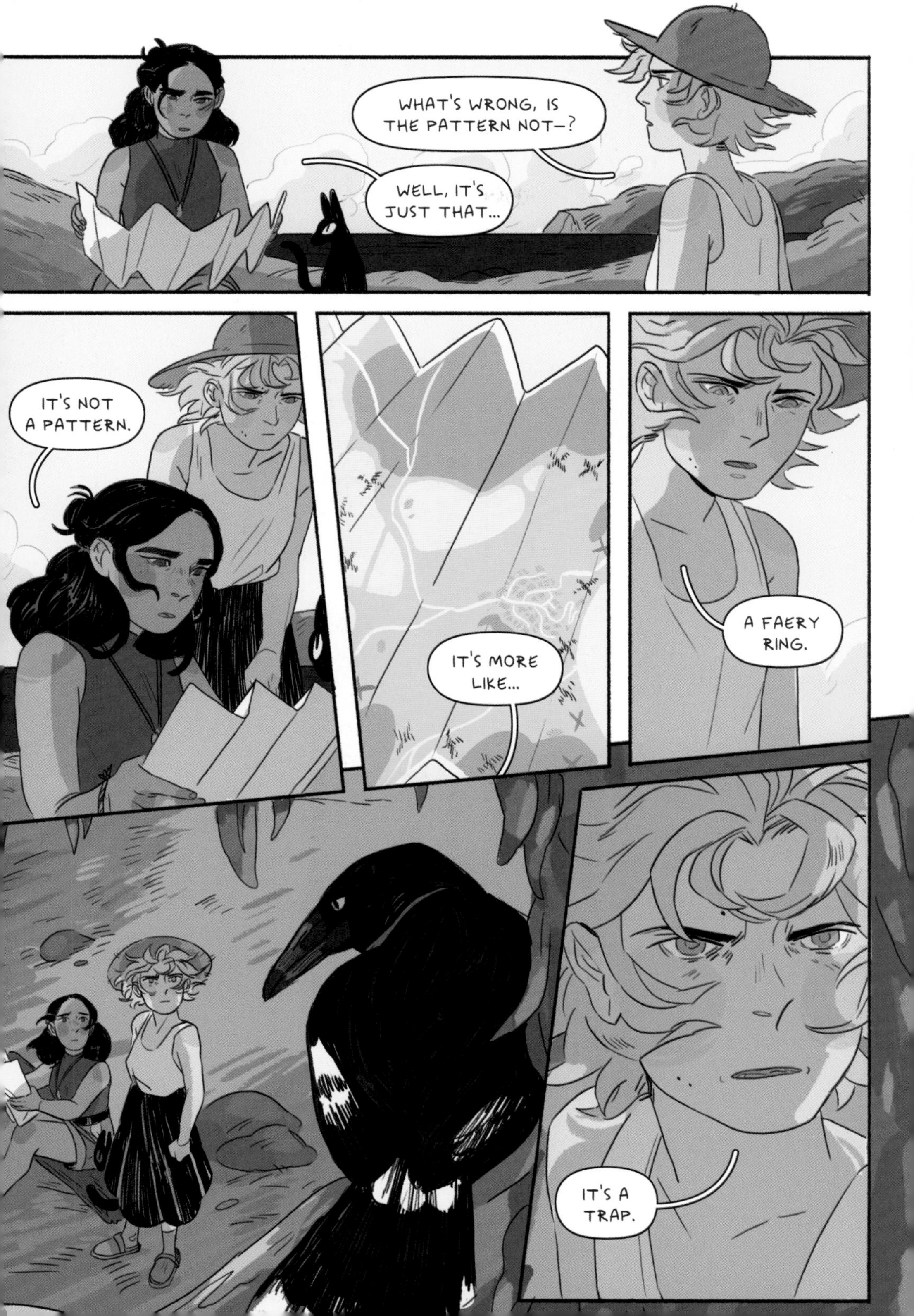
WHAT'S WRONG, IS THE PATTERN NOT–?
WELL, IT'S JUST THAT...
IT'S NOT A PATTERN.
IT'S MORE LIKE...
A FAERY RING.
IT'S A TRAP.

Chapter 4

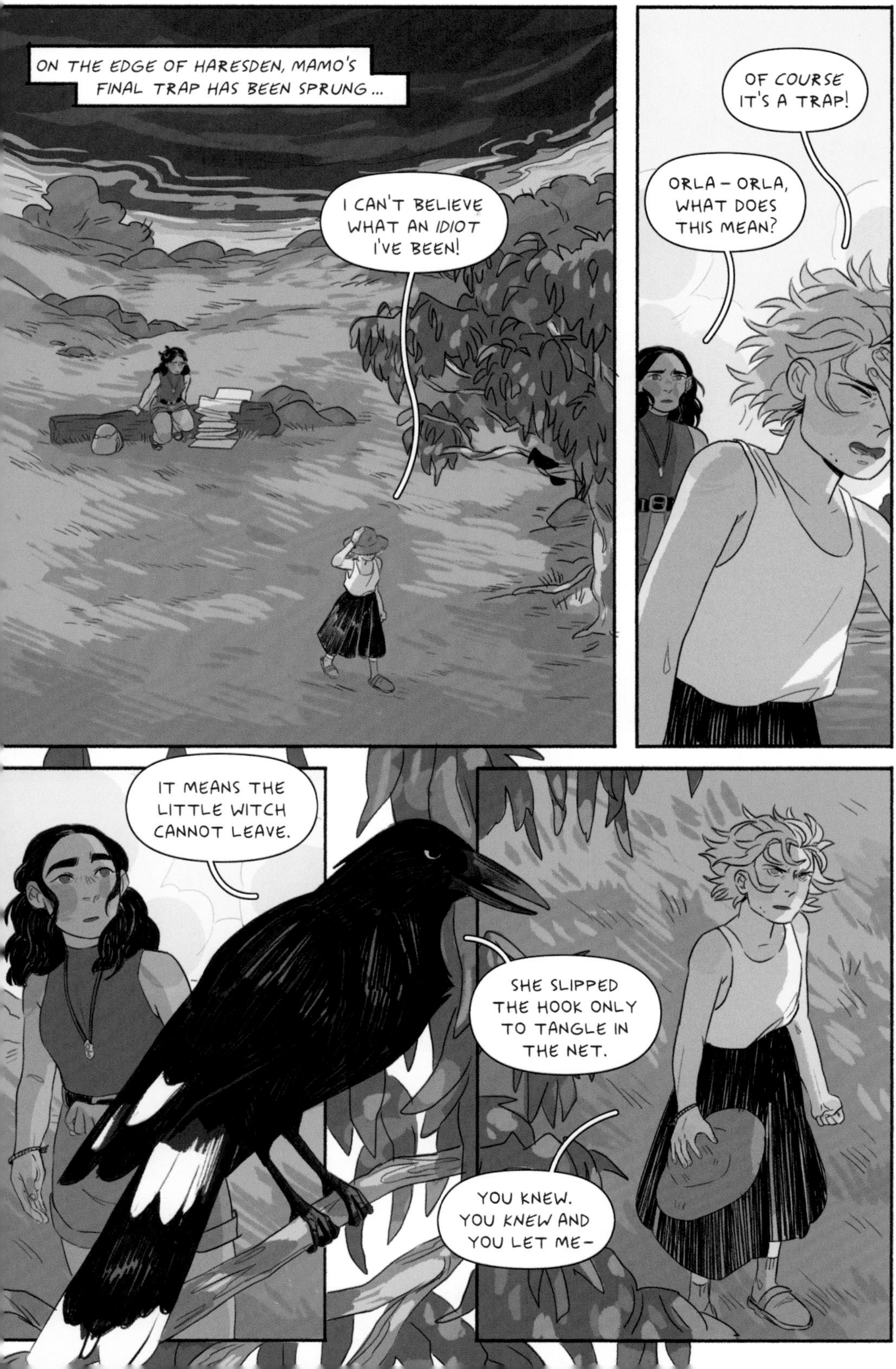
ON THE EDGE OF HARESDEN, MAMO'S FINAL TRAP HAS BEEN SPRUNG...
I CAN'T BELIEVE WHAT AN *IDIOT* I'VE BEEN!
OF COURSE IT'S A TRAP!
ORLA – ORLA, WHAT DOES THIS MEAN?
IT MEANS THE LITTLE WITCH CANNOT LEAVE.
SHE SLIPPED THE HOOK ONLY TO TANGLE IN THE NET.
YOU KNEW. YOU *KNEW* AND YOU LET ME–

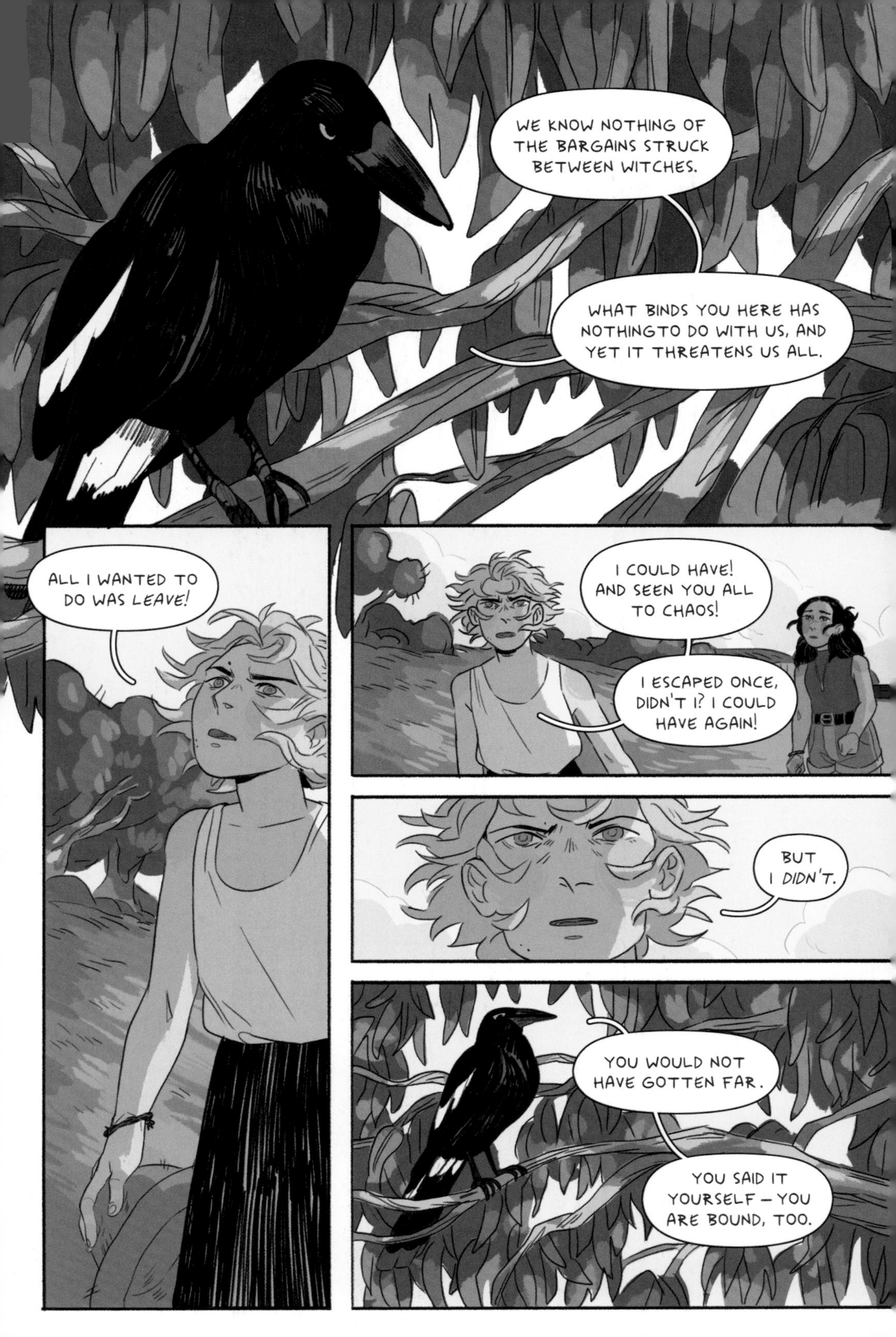
WE KNOW NOTHING OF THE BARGAINS STRUCK BETWEEN WITCHES.
WHAT BINDS YOU HERE HAS NOTHINGTO DO WITH US, AND YET IT THREATENS US ALL.
ALL I WANTED TO DO WAS *LEAVE*!
I COULD HAVE! AND SEEN YOU ALL TO CHAOS!
I ESCAPED ONCE, DIDN'T I? I COULD HAVE AGAIN!
BUT I *DIDN'T*.
YOU WOULD NOT HAVE GOTTEN FAR.
YOU SAID IT YOURSELF — YOU ARE BOUND, TOO.

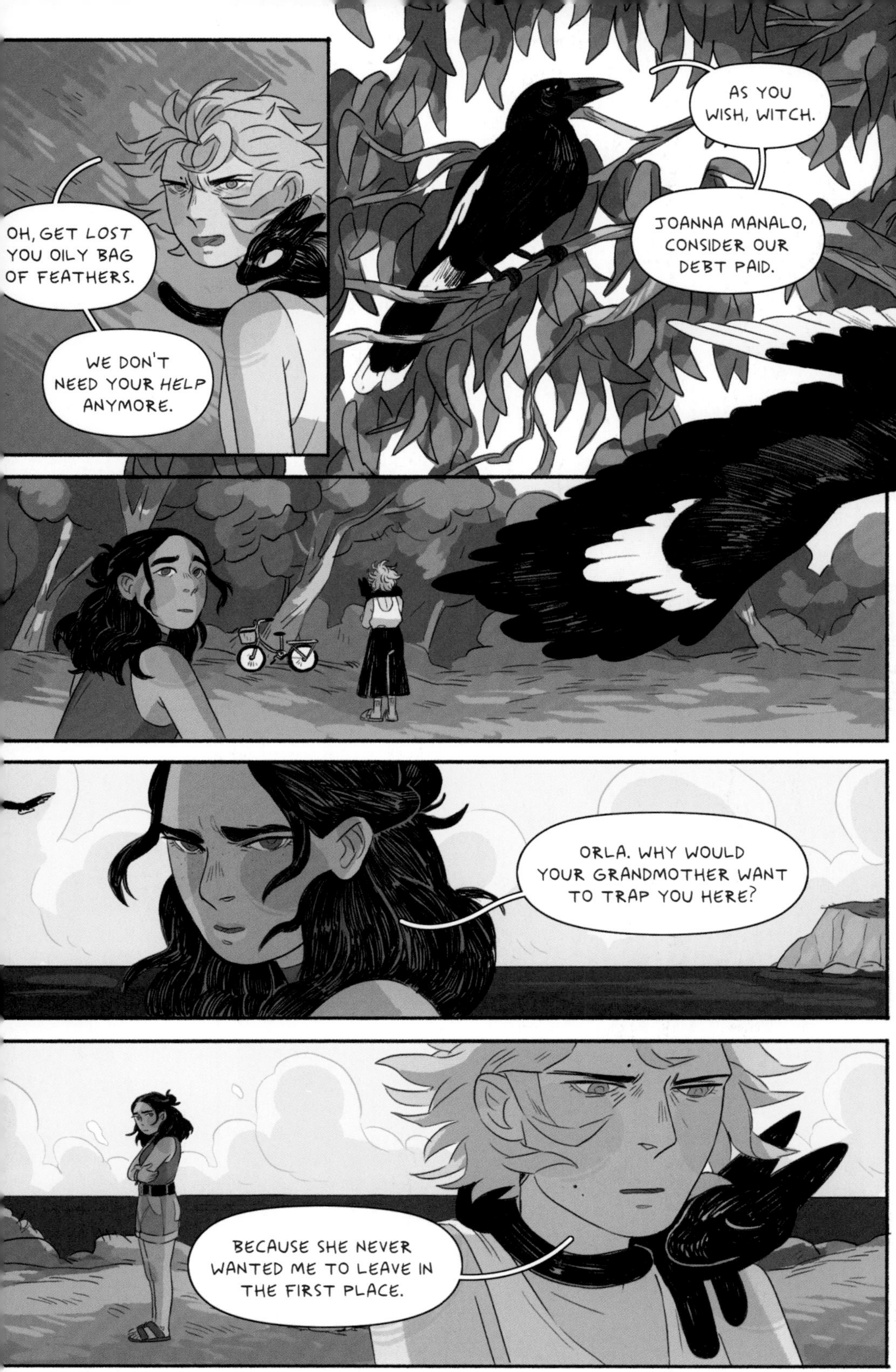
OH, GET LOST YOU OILY BAG OF FEATHERS.
WE DON'T NEED YOUR HELP ANYMORE.
AS YOU WISH, WITCH.
JOANNA MANALO, CONSIDER OUR DEBT PAID.
ORLA. WHY WOULD YOUR GRANDMOTHER WANT TO TRAP YOU HERE?
BECAUSE SHE NEVER WANTED ME TO LEAVE IN THE FIRST PLACE.

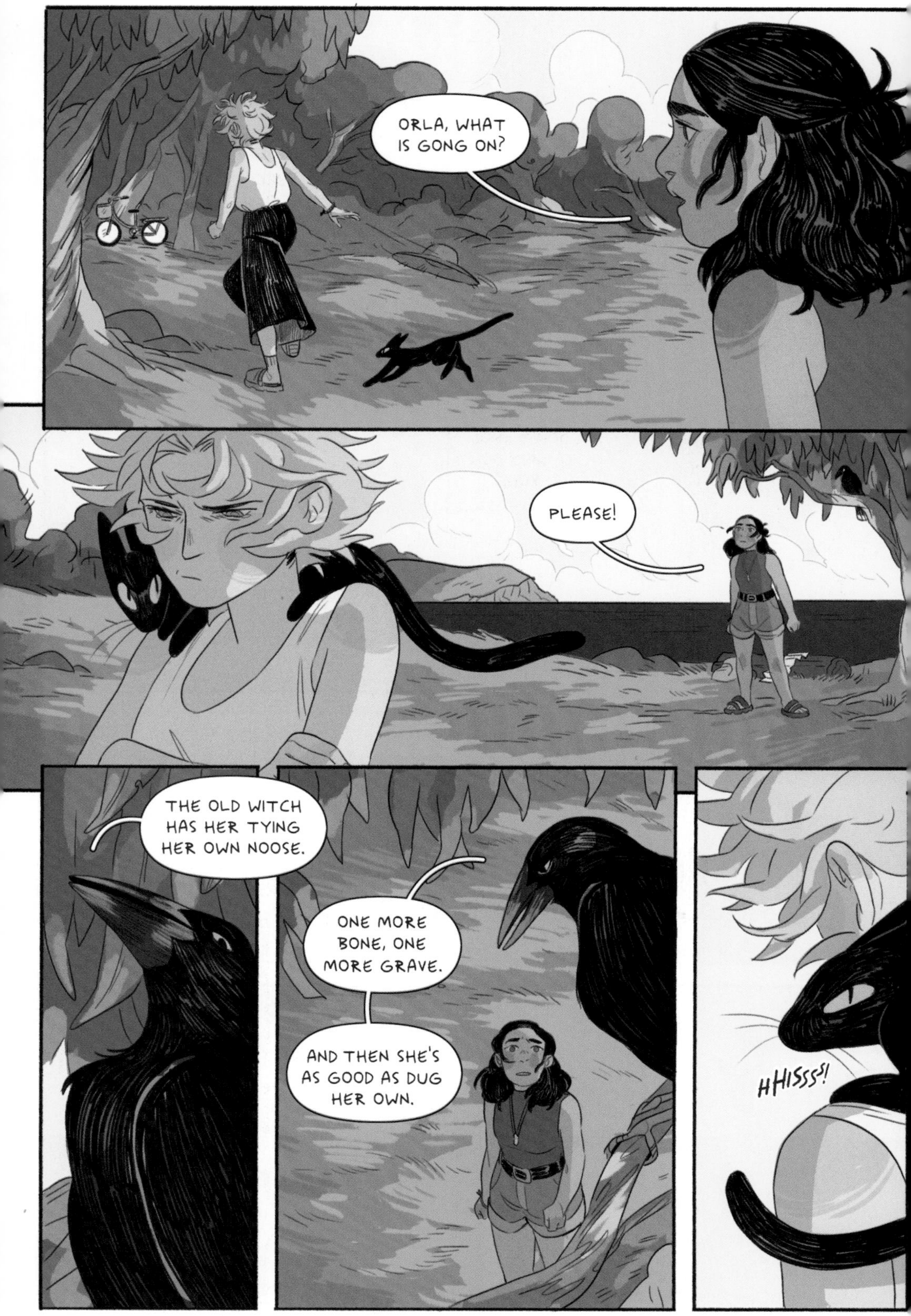
ORLA, WHAT IS GONG ON?
PLEASE!
THE OLD WITCH HAS HER TYING HER OWN NOOSE.
ONE MORE BONE, ONE MORE GRAVE.
AND THEN SHE'S AS GOOD AS DUG HER OWN.
HHISSS-S!

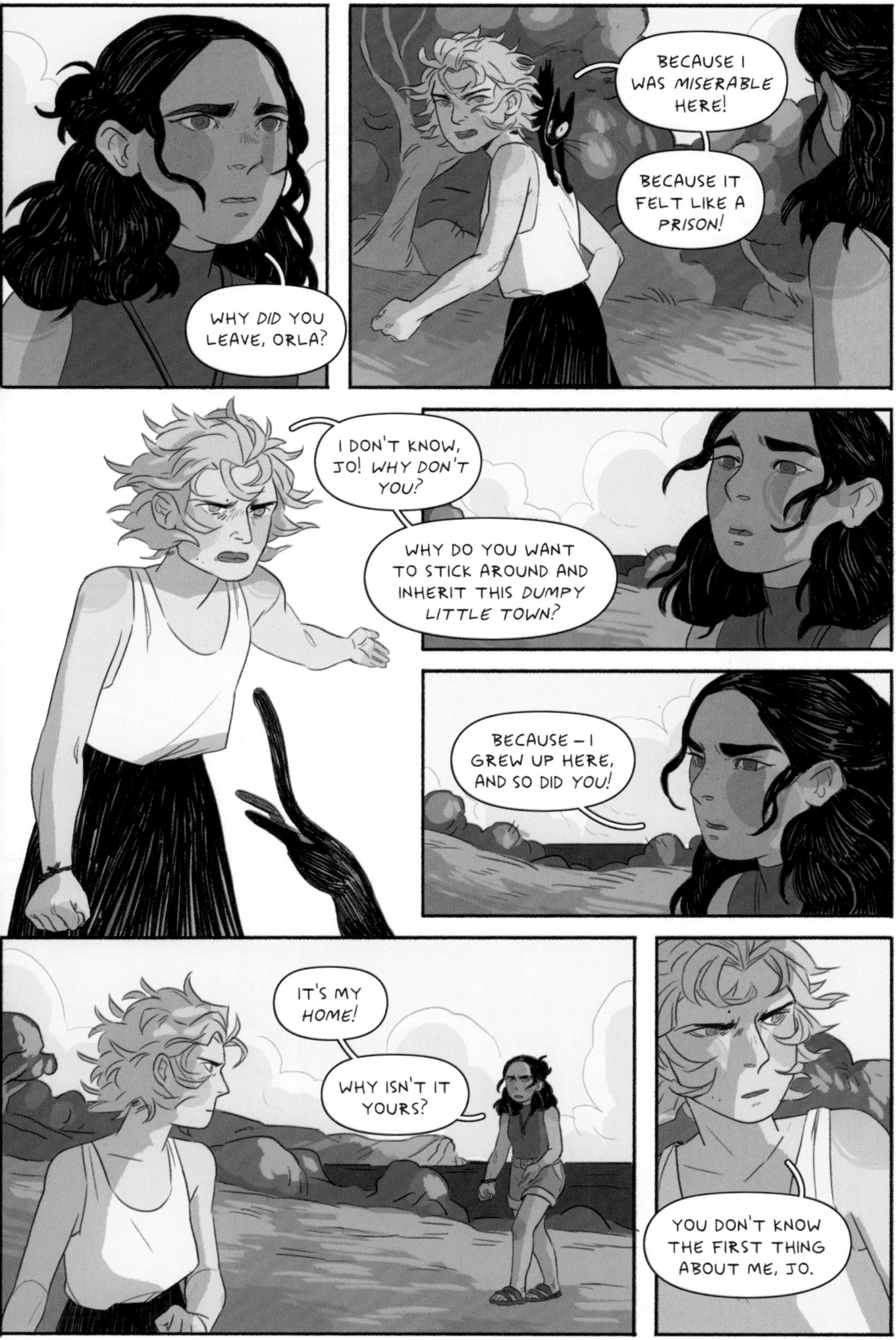
WHY DID YOU LEAVE, ORLA?
BECAUSE I WAS MISERABLE HERE!
BECAUSE IT FELT LIKE A PRISON!
I DON'T KNOW, JO! WHY DON'T YOU?
WHY DO YOU WANT TO STICK AROUND AND INHERIT THIS DUMPY LITTLE TOWN?
BECAUSE – I GREW UP HERE, AND SO DID YOU!
IT'S MY HOME!
WHY ISN'T IT YOURS?
YOU DON'T KNOW THE FIRST THING ABOUT ME, JO.

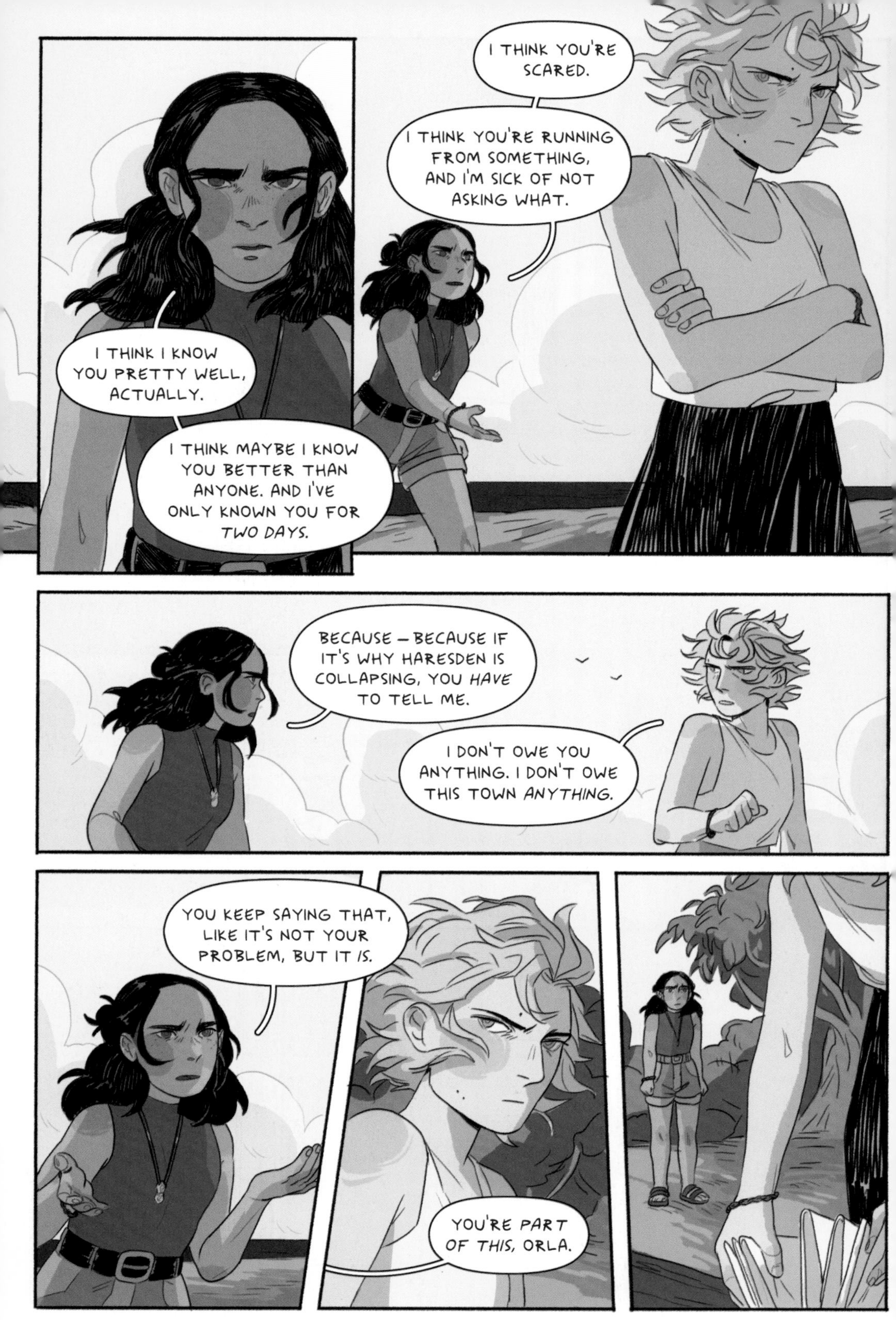
I THINK I KNOW YOU PRETTY WELL, ACTUALLY.
I THINK MAYBE I KNOW YOU BETTER THAN ANYONE. AND I'VE ONLY KNOWN YOU FOR *TWO DAYS*.
I THINK YOU'RE SCARED.
I THINK YOU'RE RUNNING FROM SOMETHING, AND I'M SICK OF NOT ASKING WHAT.
BECAUSE — BECAUSE IF IT'S WHY HARESDEN IS COLLAPSING, YOU *HAVE* TO TELL ME.
I DON'T OWE YOU ANYTHING. I DON'T OWE THIS TOWN *ANYTHING*.
YOU KEEP SAYING THAT, LIKE IT'S NOT YOUR PROBLEM, BUT IT *IS*.
YOU'RE PART OF THIS, ORLA.

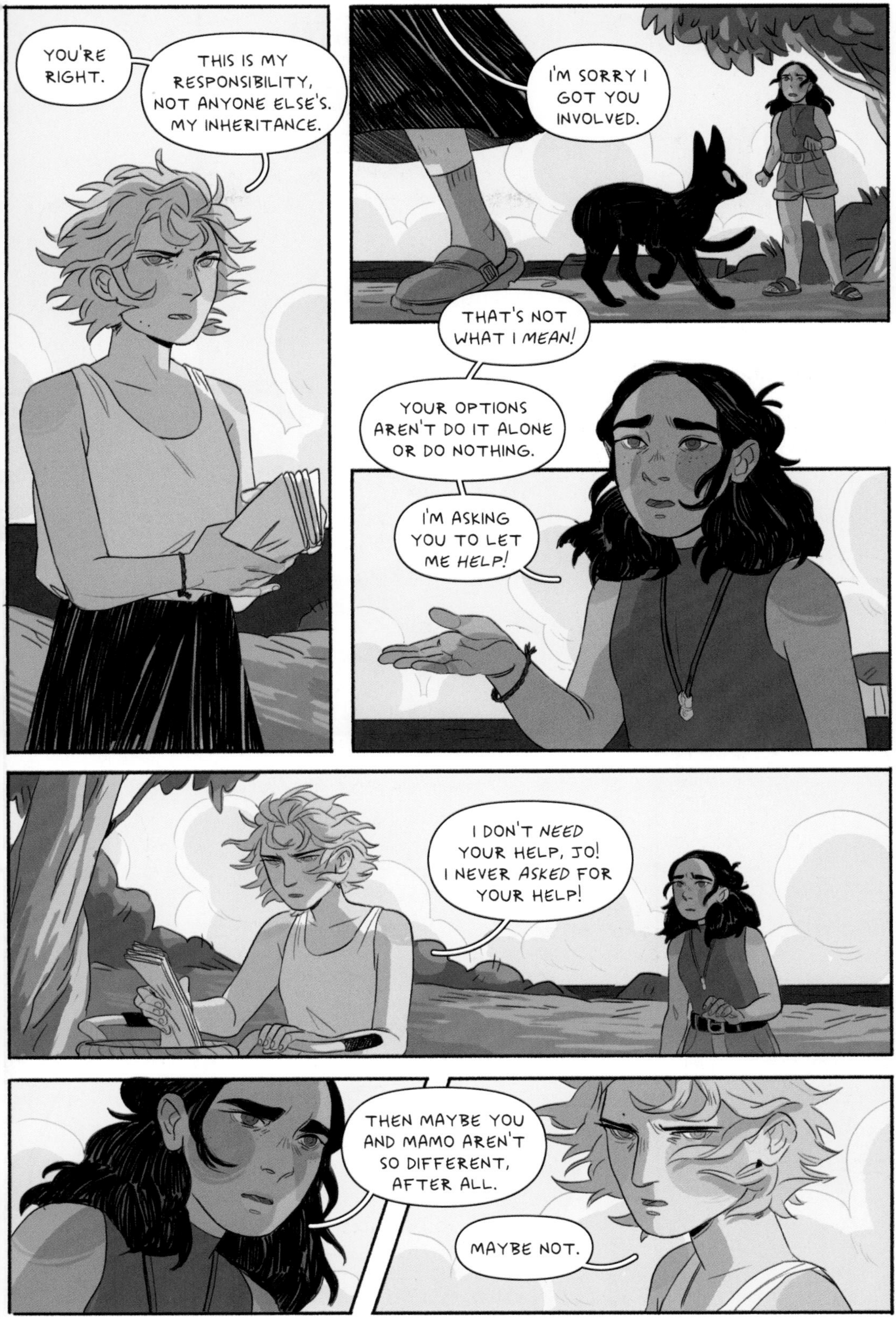
YOU'RE RIGHT.
THIS IS MY RESPONSIBILITY, NOT ANYONE ELSE'S. MY INHERITANCE.
I'M SORRY I GOT YOU INVOLVED.
THAT'S NOT WHAT I MEAN!
YOUR OPTIONS AREN'T DO IT ALONE OR DO NOTHING.
I'M ASKING YOU TO LET ME HELP!
I DON'T NEED YOUR HELP, JO! I NEVER ASKED FOR YOUR HELP!
THEN MAYBE YOU AND MAMO AREN'T SO DIFFERENT, AFTER ALL.
MAYBE NOT.

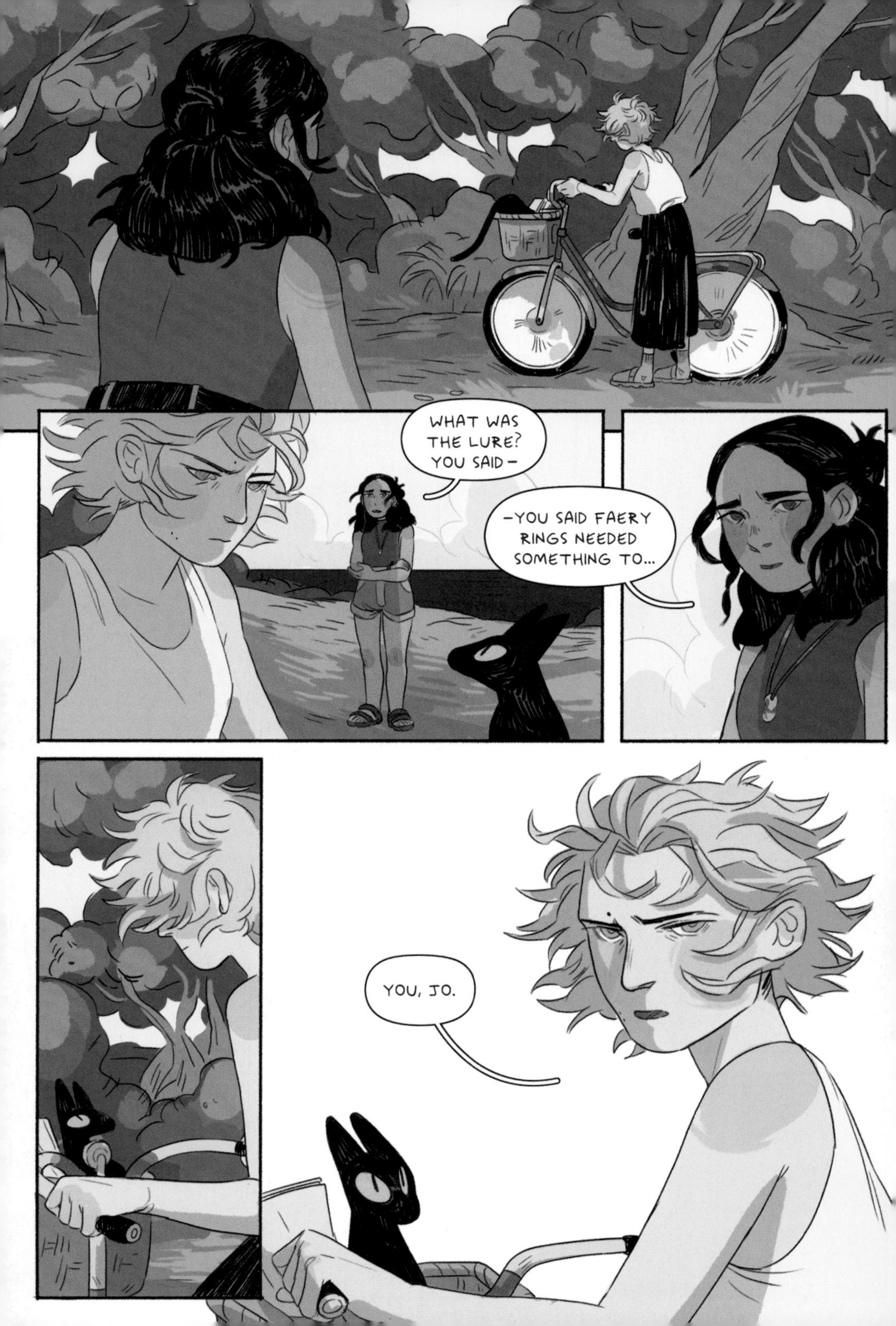
WHAT WAS THE LURE? YOU SAID—
—YOU SAID FAERY RINGS NEEDED SOMETHING TO...
YOU, JO.

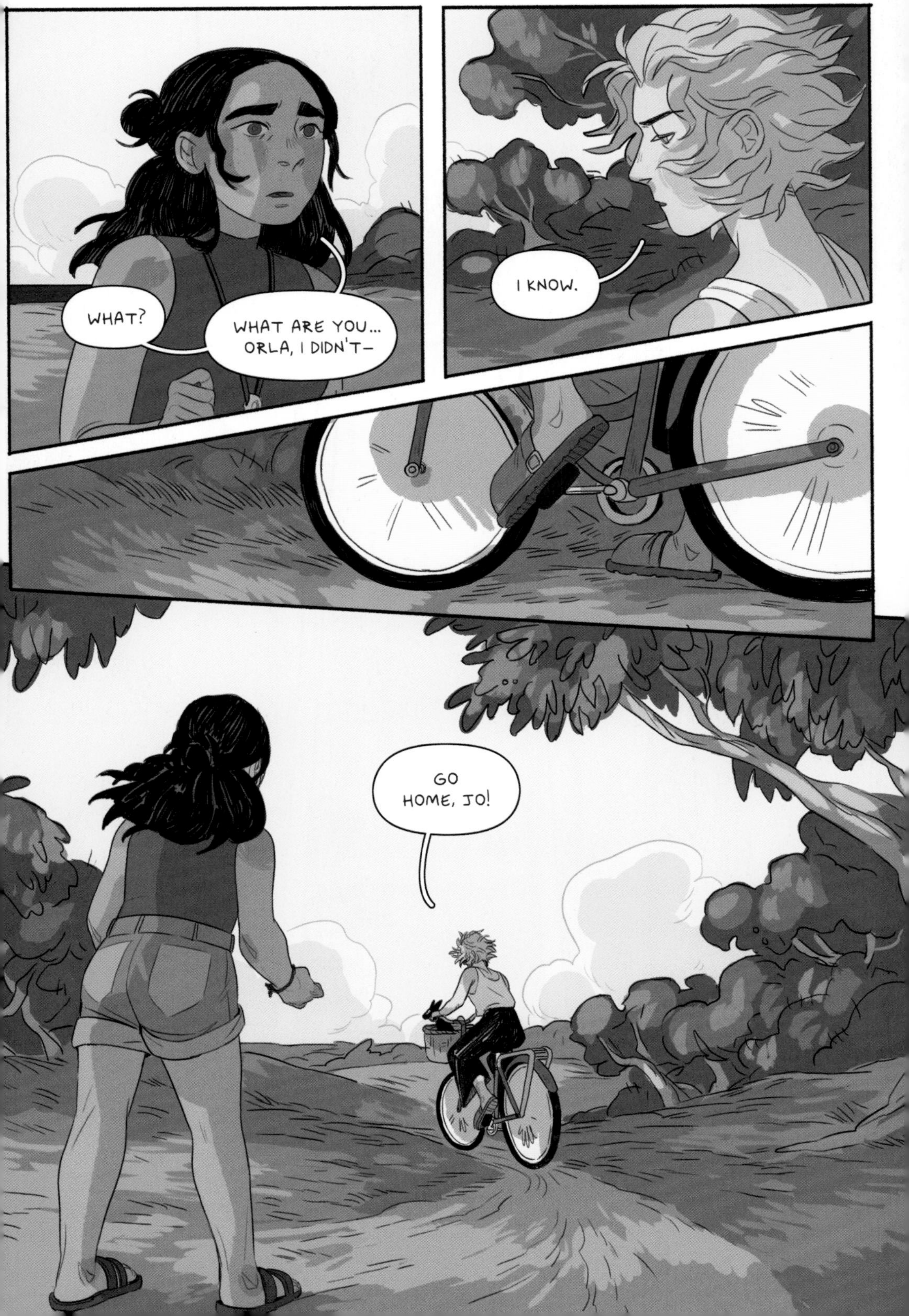
WHAT?
WHAT ARE YOU... ORLA, I DIDN'T—
I KNOW.
GO HOME, JO!

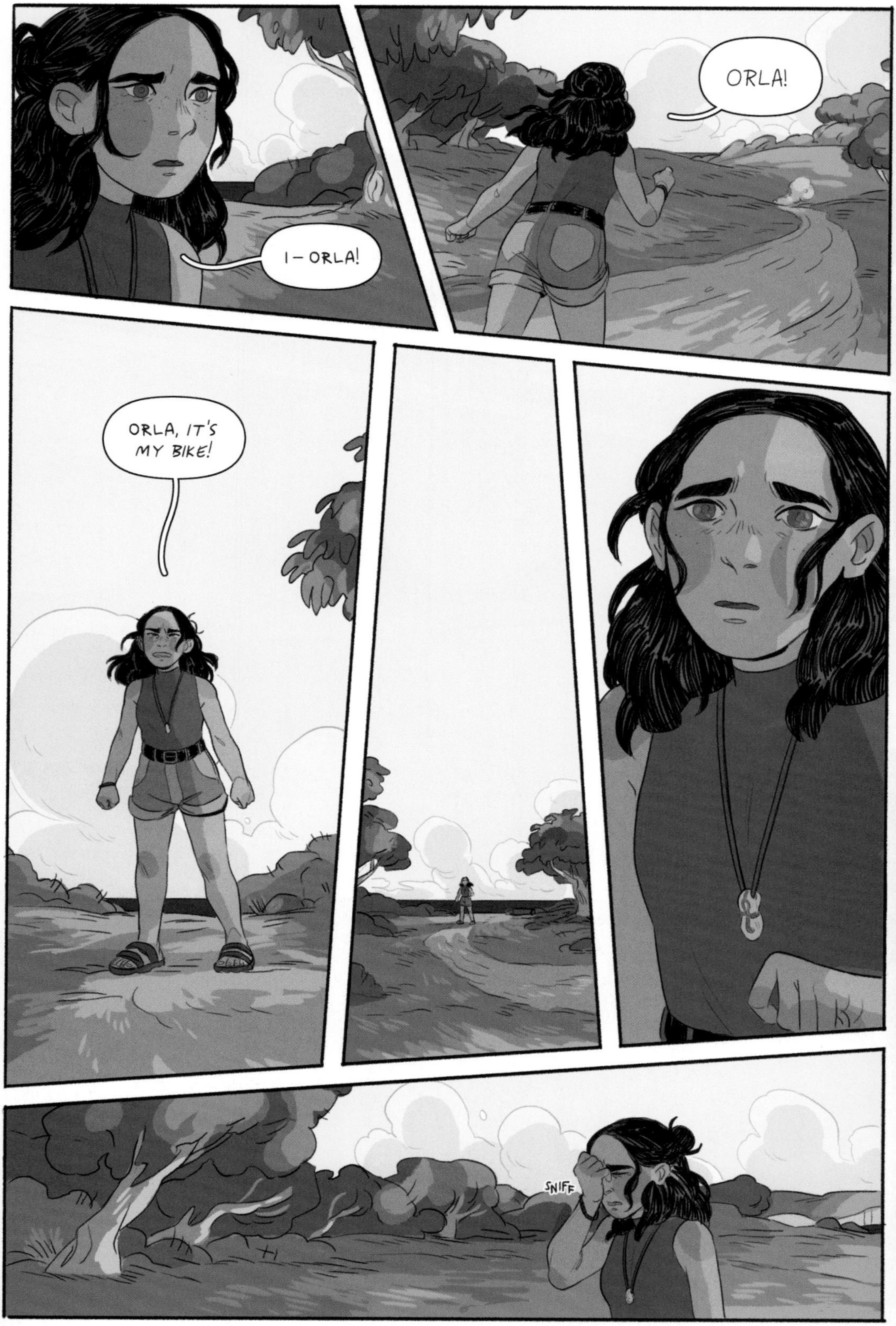
I— ORLA!
ORLA!
ORLA, IT'S MY BIKE!
SNIFF

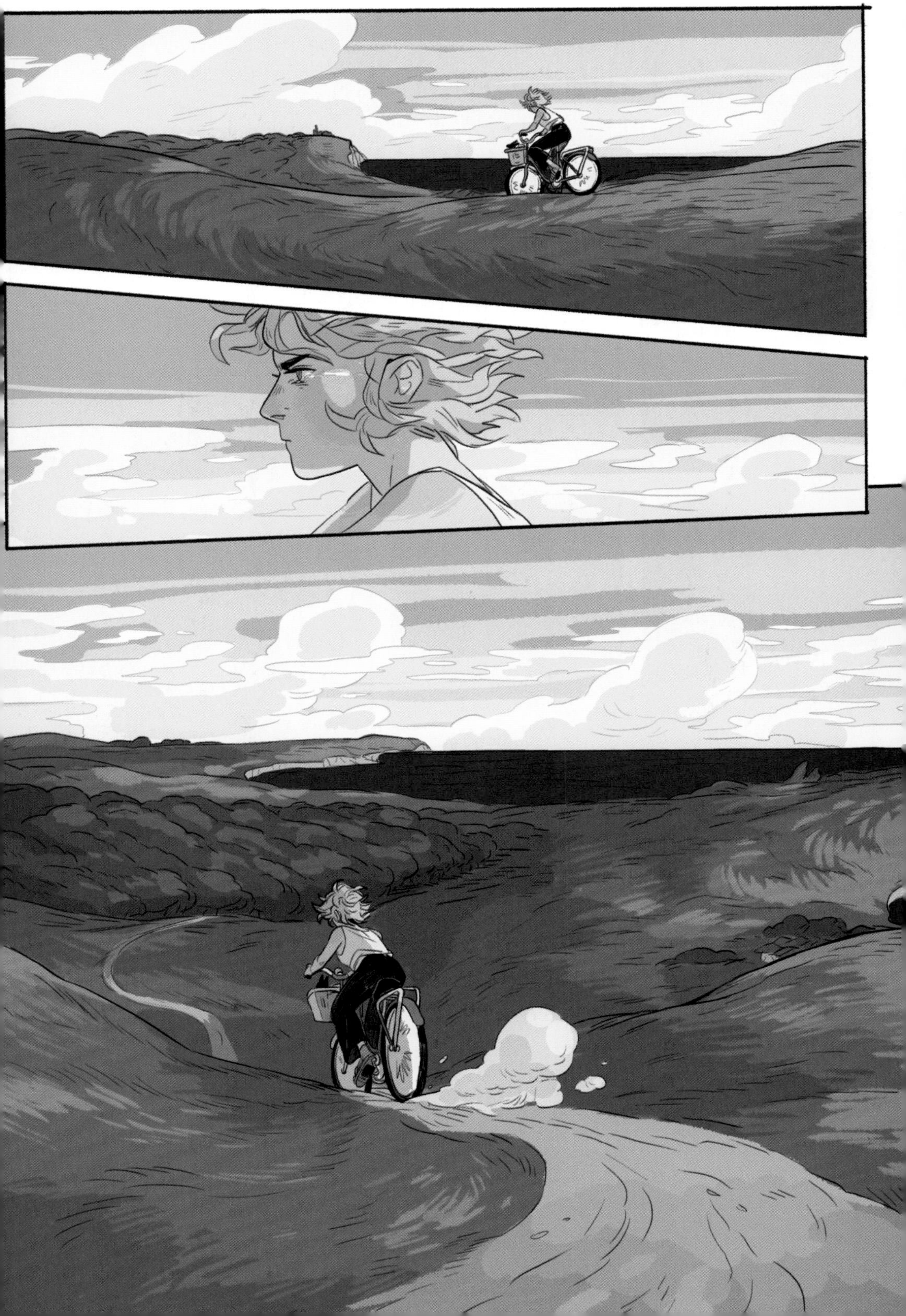

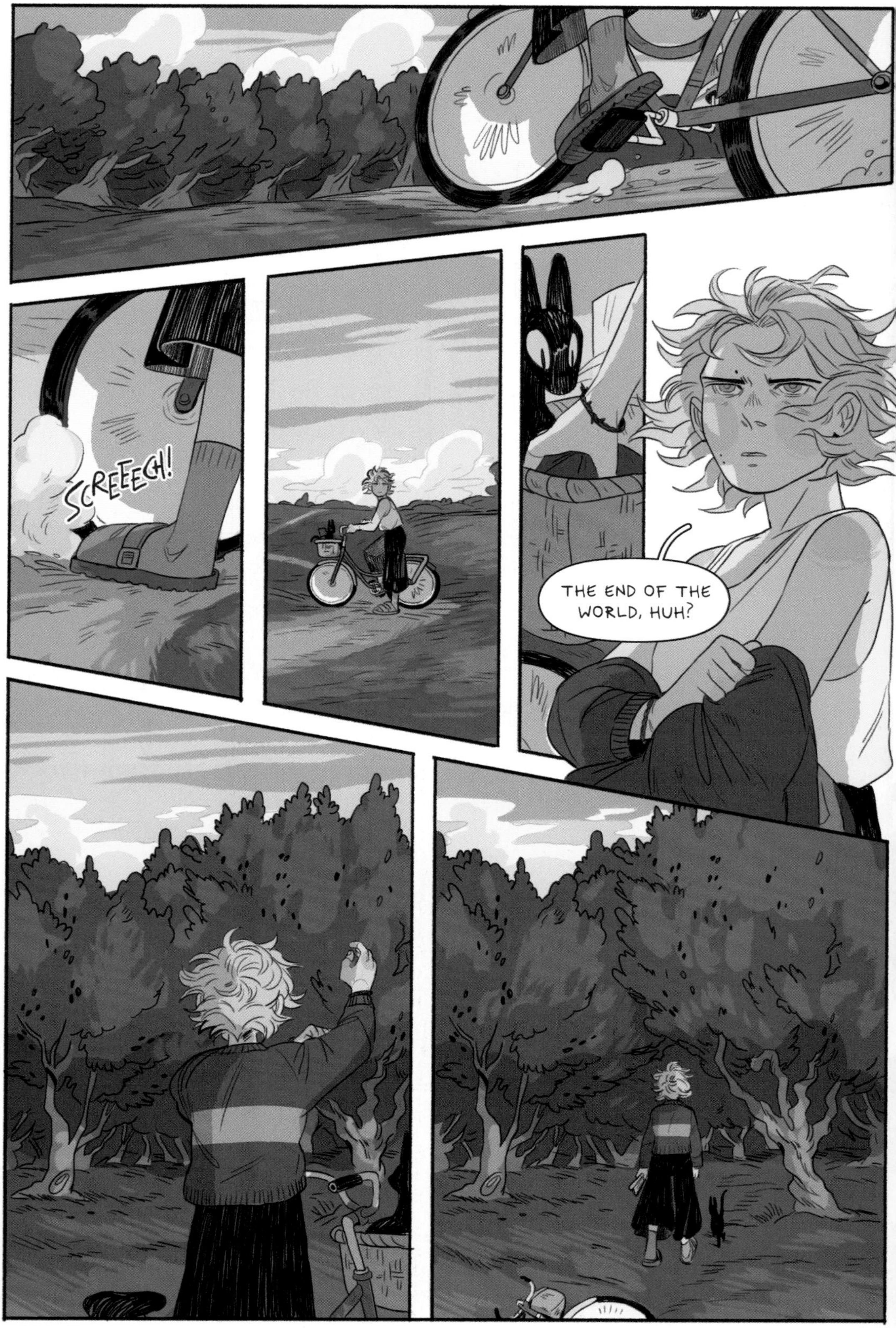
SCREEECH!
THE END OF THE WORLD, HUH?

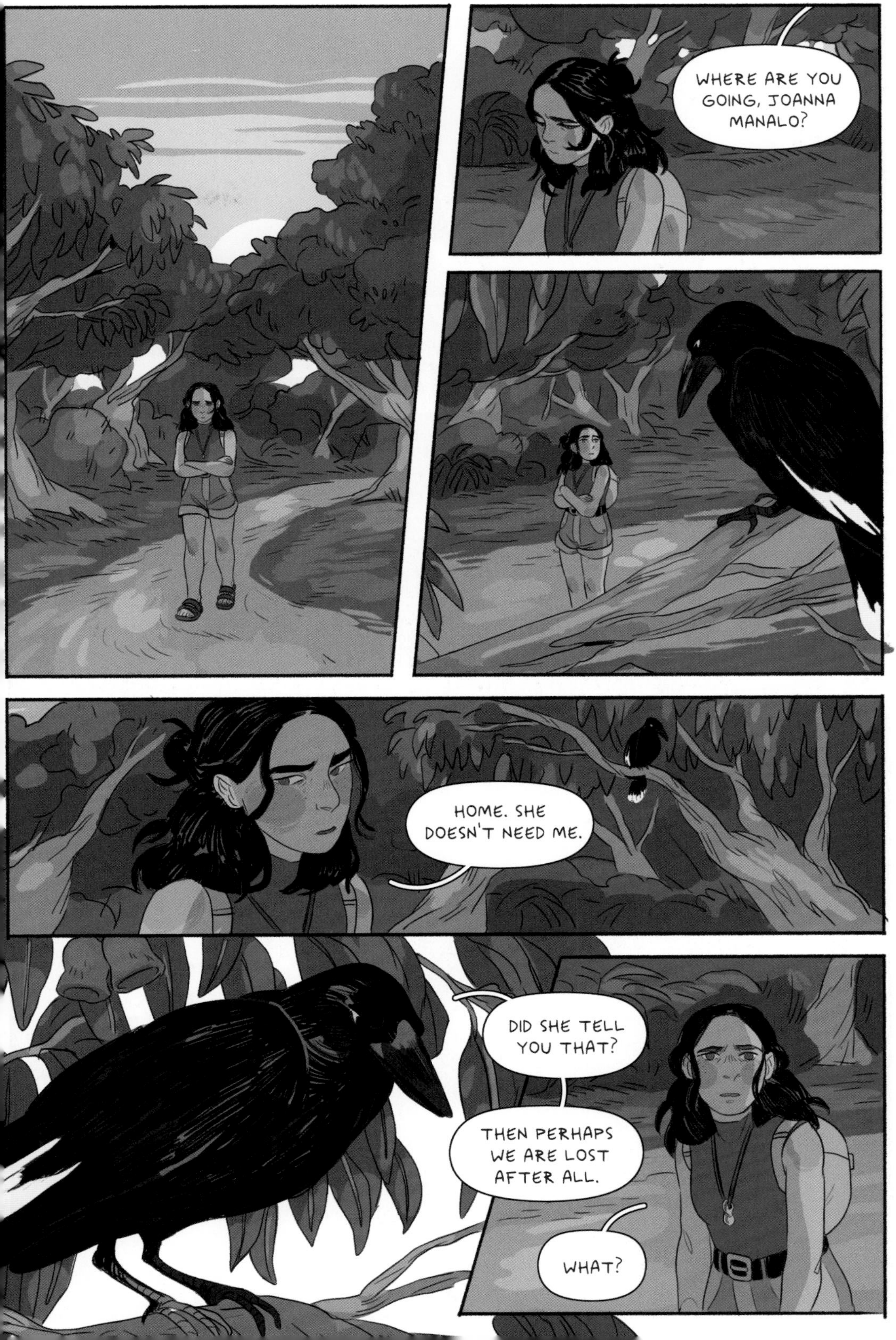

WHERE ARE YOU GOING, JOANNA MANALO?
HOME. SHE DOESN'T NEED ME.
DID SHE TELL YOU THAT?
THEN PERHAPS WE ARE LOST AFTER ALL.
WHAT?

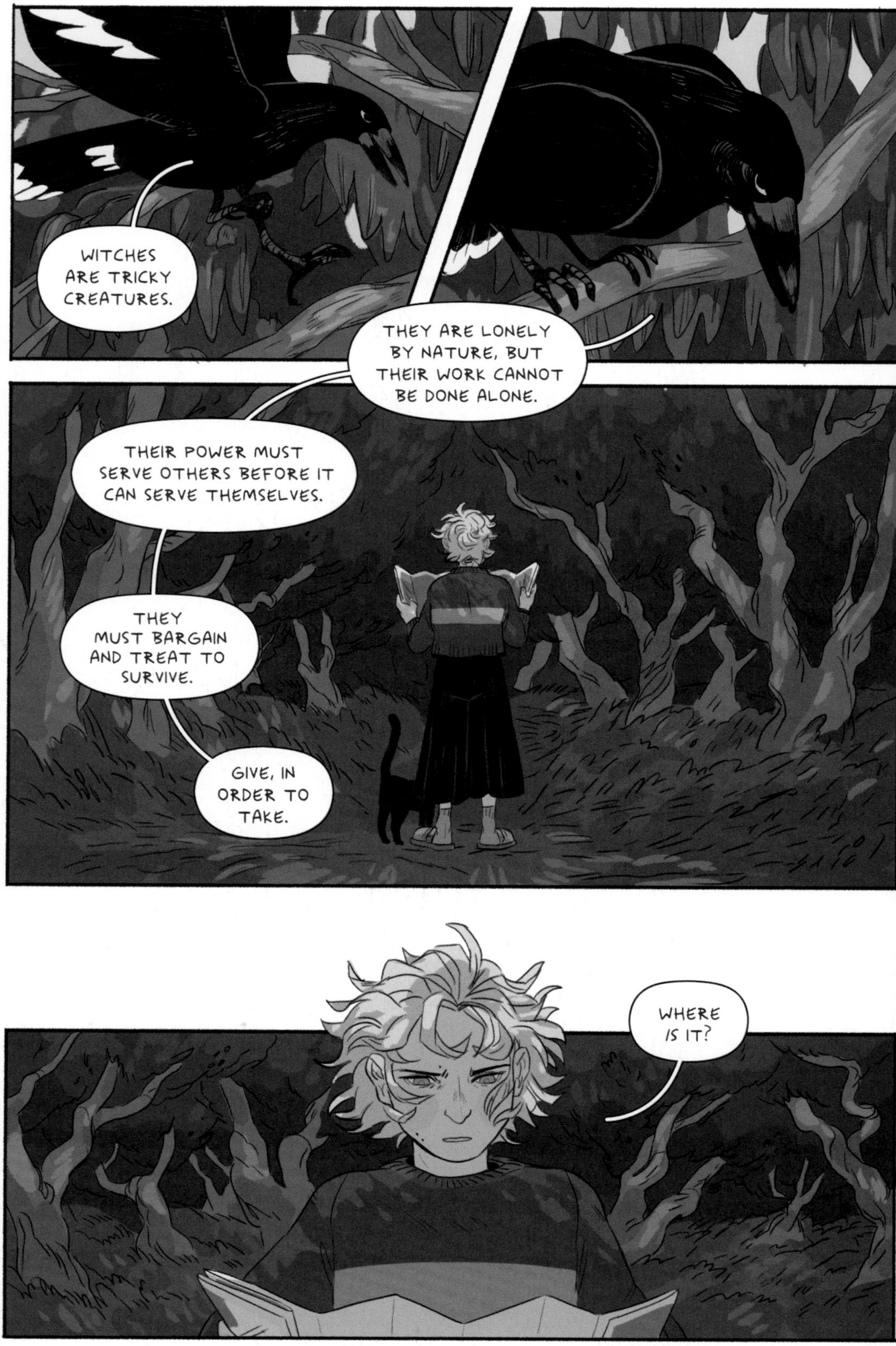
WITCHES ARE TRICKY CREATURES.
THEY ARE LONELY BY NATURE, BUT THEIR WORK CANNOT BE DONE ALONE.
THEIR POWER MUST SERVE OTHERS BEFORE IT CAN SERVE THEMSELVES.
THEY MUST BARGAIN AND TREAT TO SURVIVE.
GIVE, IN ORDER TO TAKE.
WHERE IS IT?

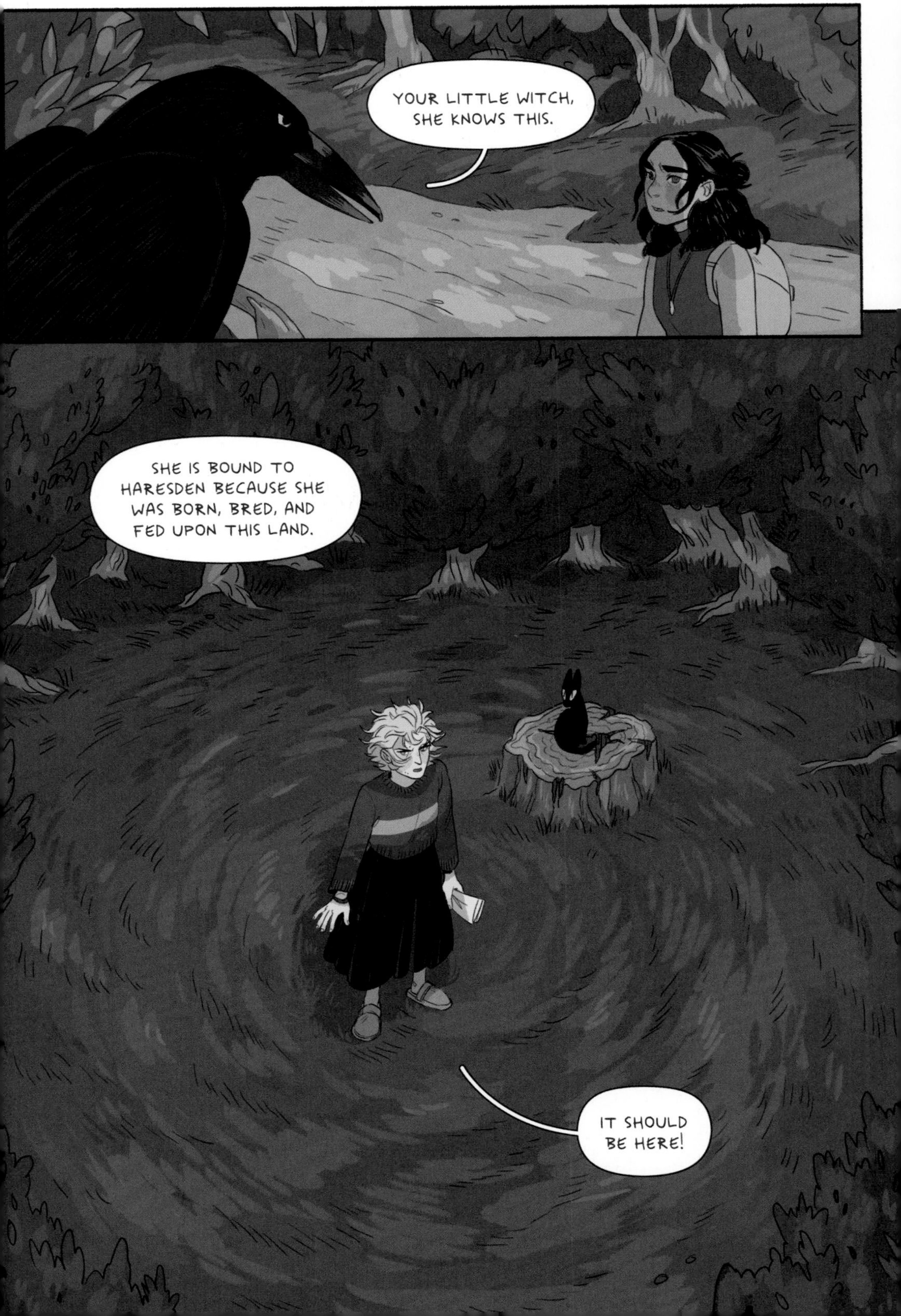
YOUR LITTLE WITCH, SHE KNOWS THIS.
SHE IS BOUND TO HARESDEN BECAUSE SHE WAS BORN, BRED, AND FED UPON THIS LAND.
IT SHOULD BE HERE!

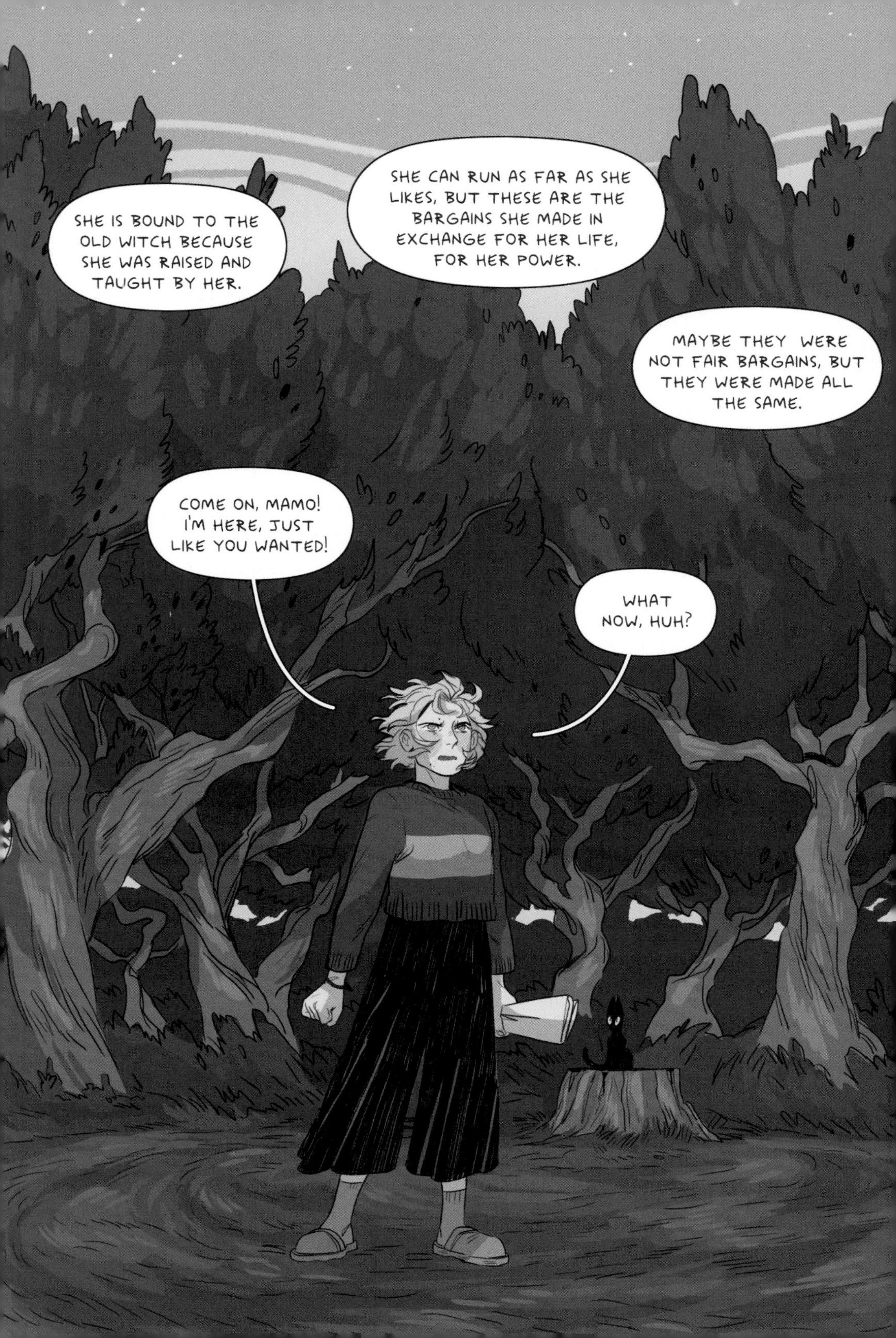
SHE IS BOUND TO THE OLD WITCH BECAUSE SHE WAS RAISED AND TAUGHT BY HER.
SHE CAN RUN AS FAR AS SHE LIKES, BUT THESE ARE THE BARGAINS SHE MADE IN EXCHANGE FOR HER LIFE, FOR HER POWER.
MAYBE THEY WERE NOT FAIR BARGAINS, BUT THEY WERE MADE ALL THE SAME.
COME ON, MAMO! I'M HERE, JUST LIKE YOU WANTED!
WHAT NOW, HUH?

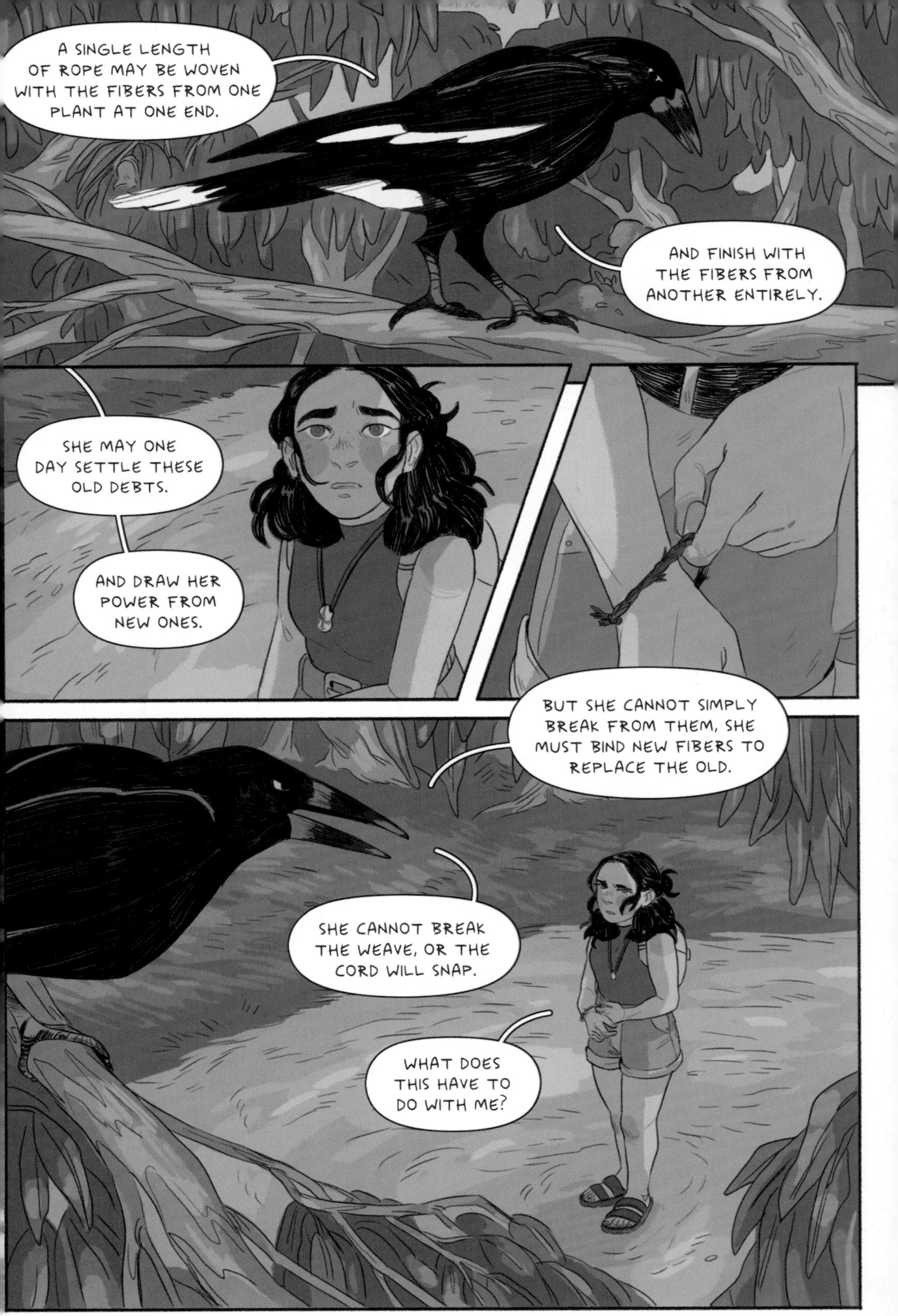
A SINGLE LENGTH OF ROPE MAY BE WOVEN WITH THE FIBERS FROM ONE PLANT AT ONE END.
AND FINISH WITH THE FIBERS FROM ANOTHER ENTIRELY.
SHE MAY ONE DAY SETTLE THESE OLD DEBTS.
AND DRAW HER POWER FROM NEW ONES.
BUT SHE CANNOT SIMPLY BREAK FROM THEM, SHE MUST BIND NEW FIBERS TO REPLACE THE OLD.
SHE CANNOT BREAK THE WEAVE, OR THE CORD WILL SNAP.
WHAT DOES THIS HAVE TO DO WITH ME?

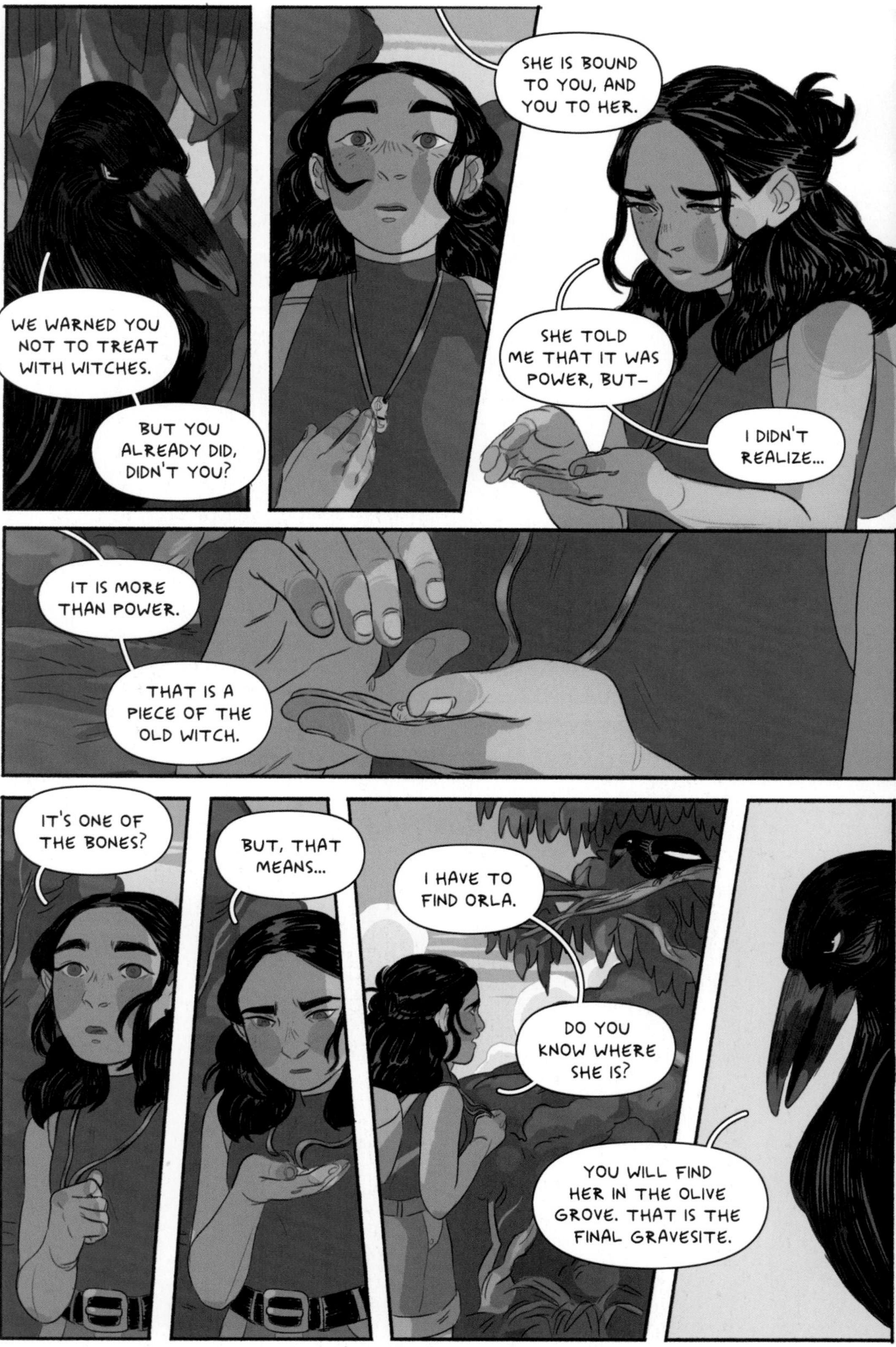
WE WARNED YOU NOT TO TREAT WITH WITCHES.
BUT YOU ALREADY DID, DIDN'T YOU?
SHE IS BOUND TO YOU, AND YOU TO HER.
SHE TOLD ME THAT IT WAS POWER, BUT–
I DIDN'T REALIZE...
IT IS MORE THAN POWER.
THAT IS A PIECE OF THE OLD WITCH.
IT'S ONE OF THE BONES?
BUT, THAT MEANS...
I HAVE TO FIND ORLA.
DO YOU KNOW WHERE SHE IS?
YOU WILL FIND HER IN THE OLIVE GROVE. THAT IS THE FINAL GRAVESITE.

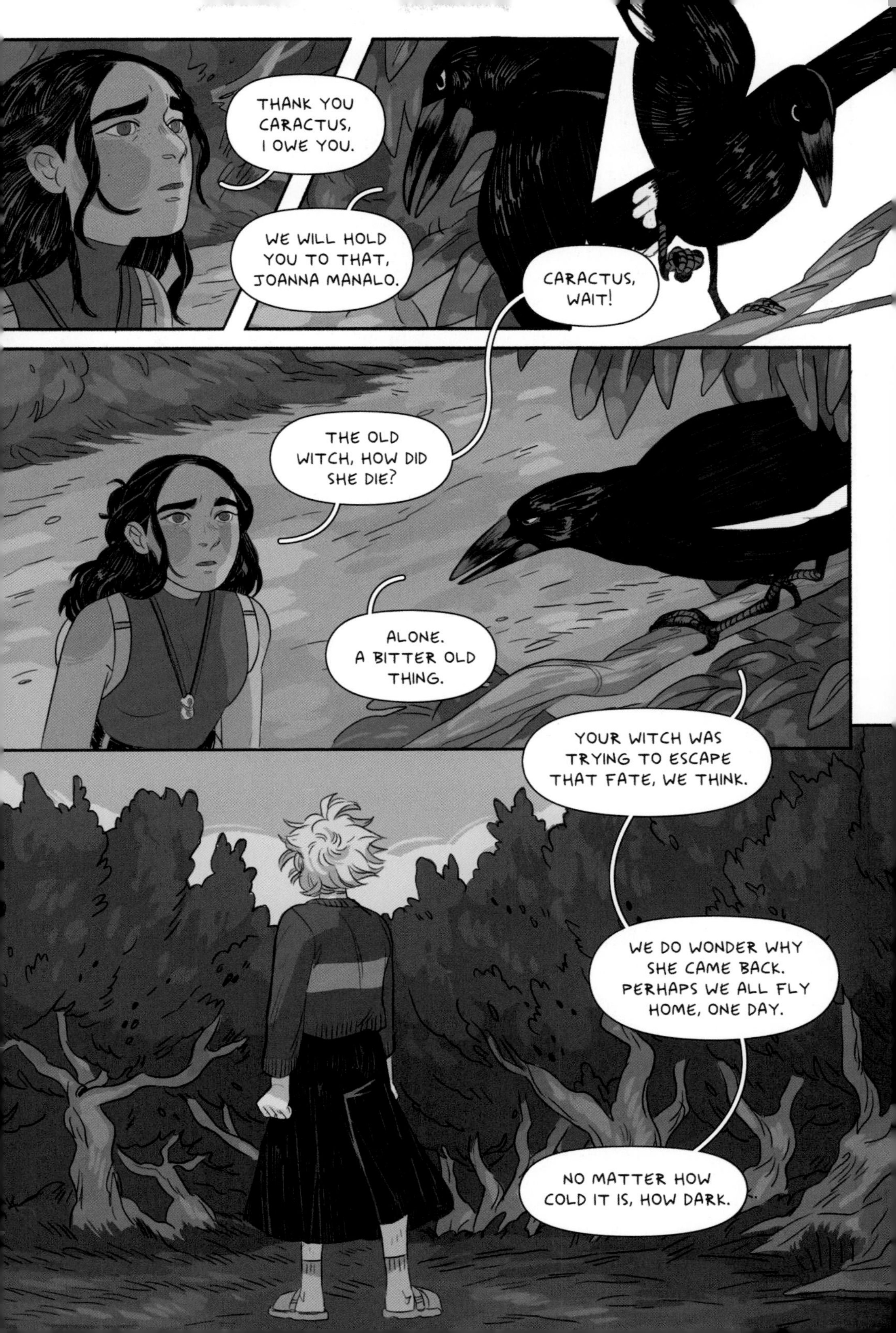
THANK YOU CARACTUS, I OWE YOU.
WE WILL HOLD YOU TO THAT, JOANNA MANALO.
CARACTUS, WAIT!
THE OLD WITCH, HOW DID SHE DIE?
ALONE. A BITTER OLD THING.
YOUR WITCH WAS TRYING TO ESCAPE THAT FATE, WE THINK.
WE DO WONDER WHY SHE CAME BACK. PERHAPS WE ALL FLY HOME, ONE DAY.
NO MATTER HOW COLD IT IS, HOW DARK.

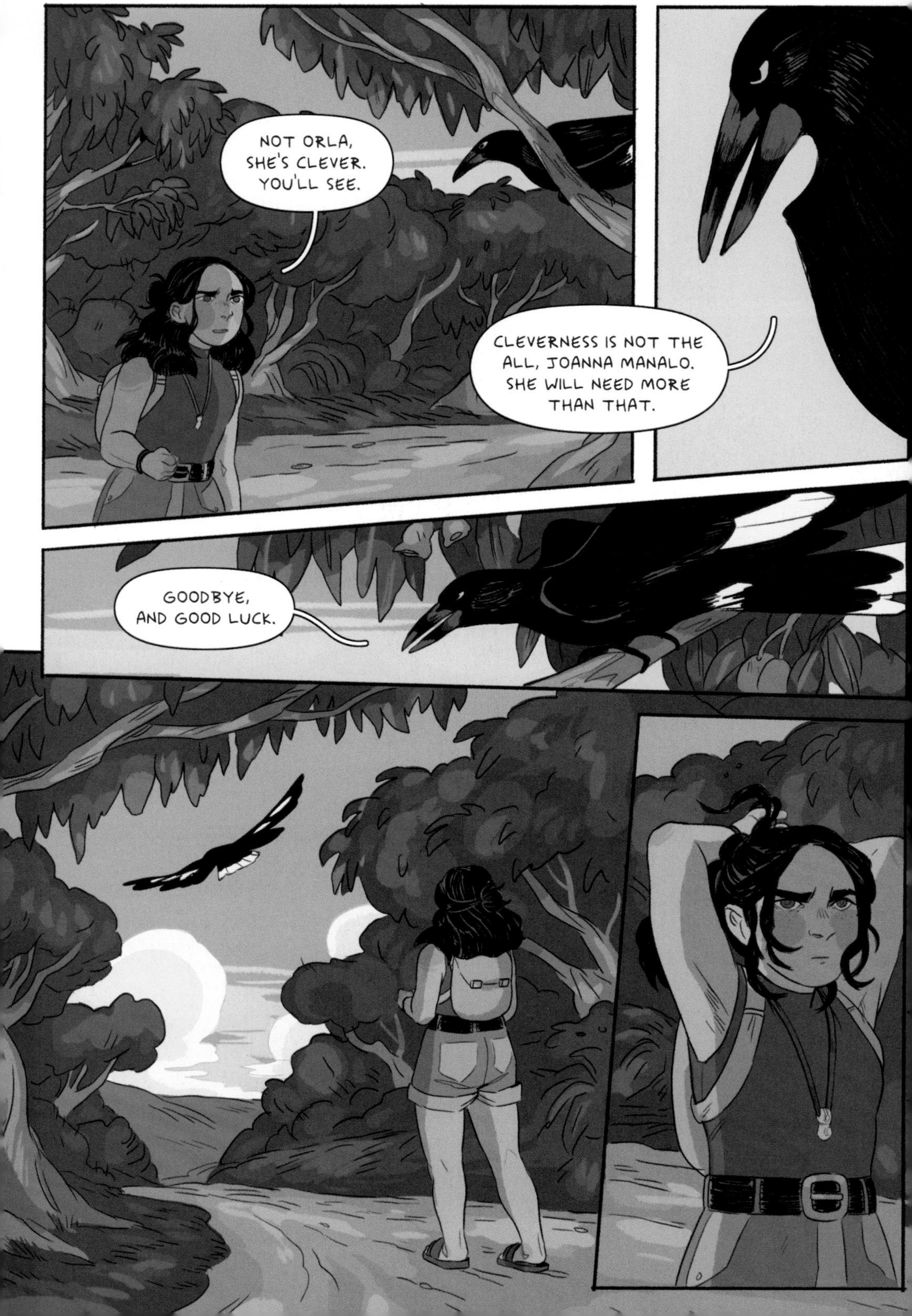
NOT ORLA, SHE'S CLEVER. YOU'LL SEE.
CLEVERNESS IS NOT THE ALL, JOANNA MANALO. SHE WILL NEED MORE THAN THAT.
GOODBYE, AND GOOD LUCK.

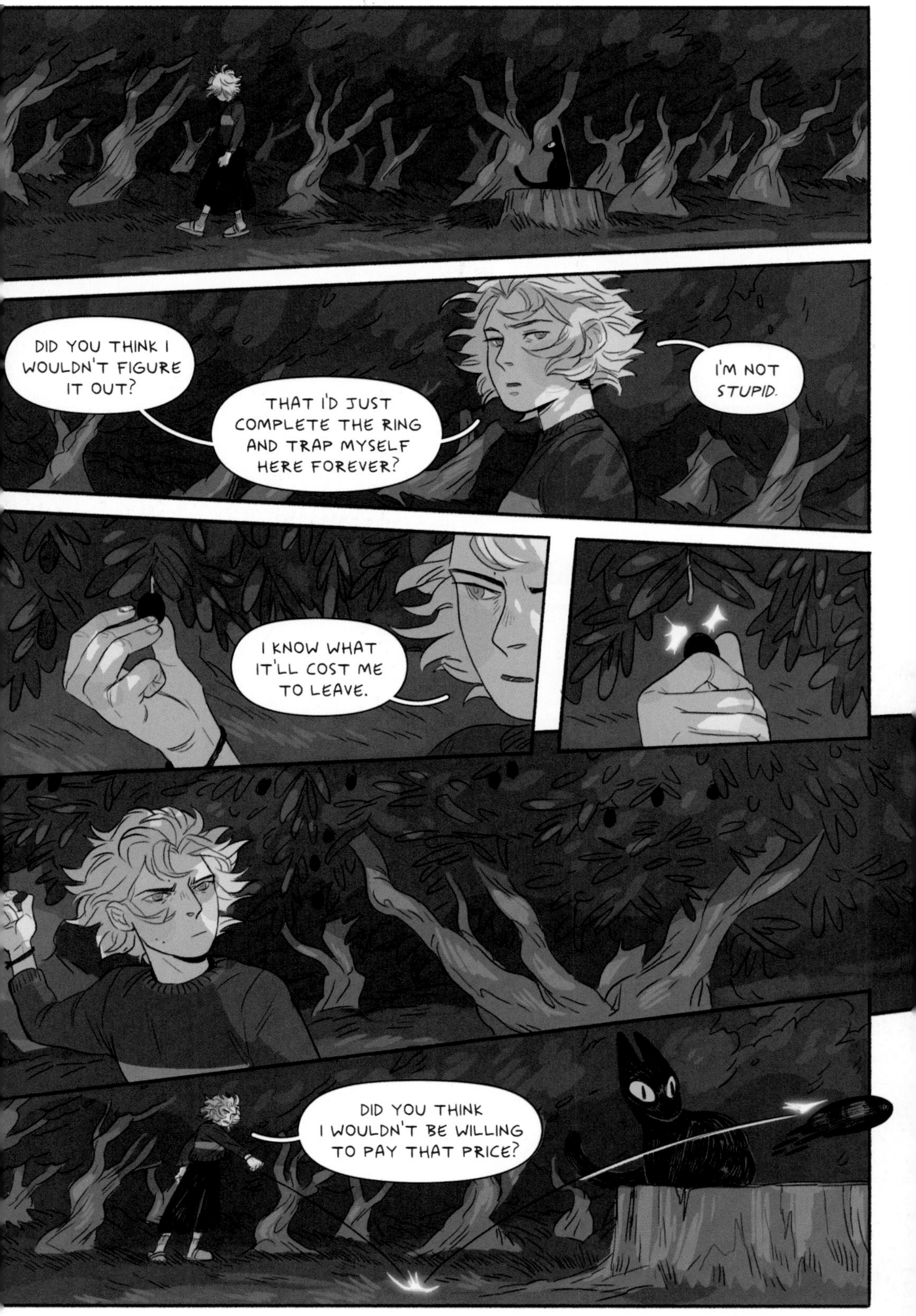
DID YOU THINK I WOULDN'T FIGURE IT OUT?
THAT I'D JUST COMPLETE THE RING AND TRAP MYSELF HERE FOREVER?
I'M NOT *STUPID*.
I KNOW WHAT IT'LL COST ME TO LEAVE.
DID YOU THINK I WOULDN'T BE WILLING TO PAY THAT PRICE?

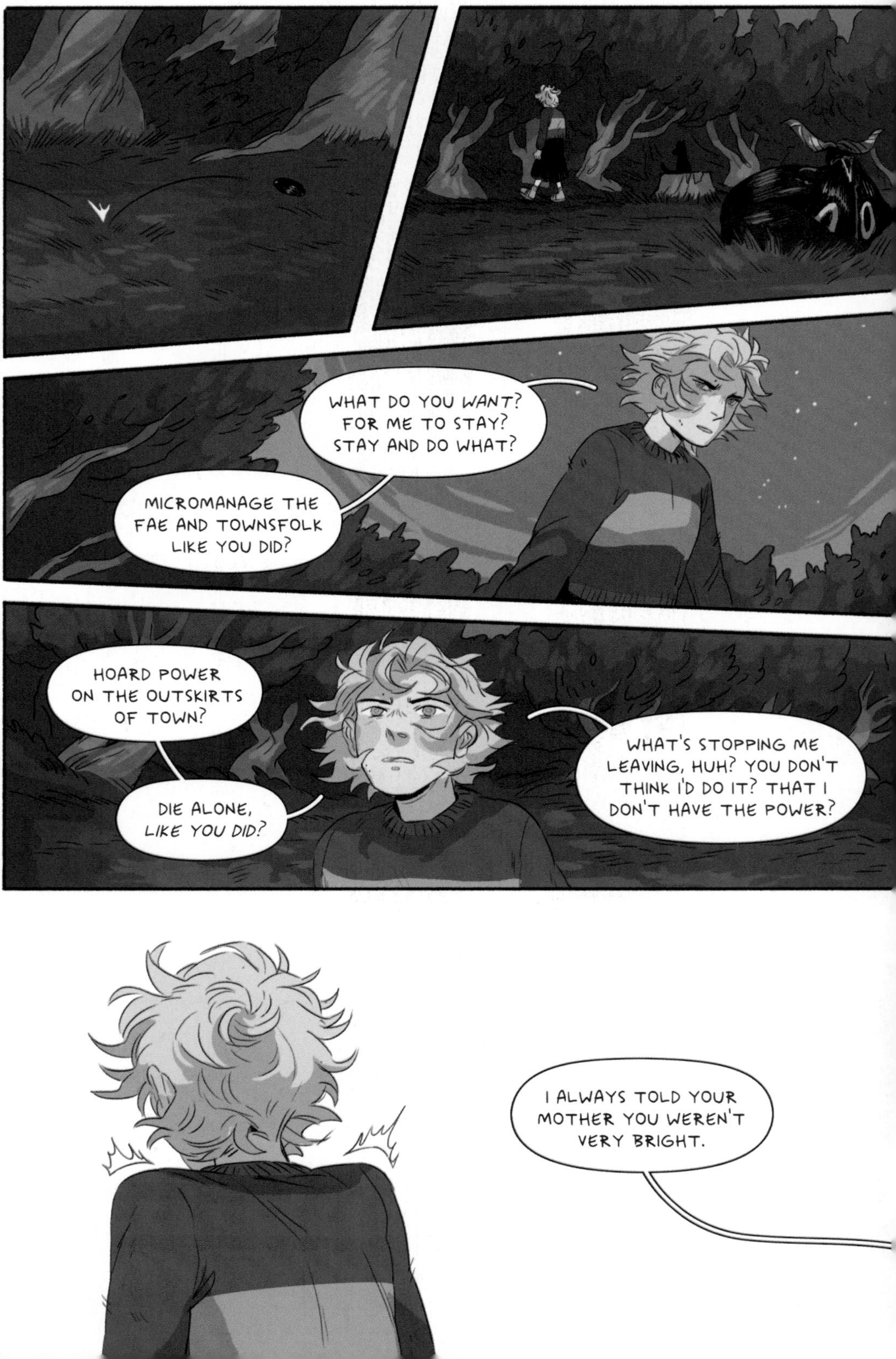
WHAT DO YOU WANT? FOR ME TO STAY? STAY AND DO WHAT?
MICROMANAGE THE FAE AND TOWNSFOLK LIKE YOU DID?
HOARD POWER ON THE OUTSKIRTS OF TOWN?
DIE ALONE, LIKE YOU DID?
WHAT'S STOPPING ME LEAVING, HUH? YOU DON'T THINK I'D DO IT? THAT I DON'T HAVE THE POWER?
I ALWAYS TOLD YOUR MOTHER YOU WEREN'T VERY BRIGHT.

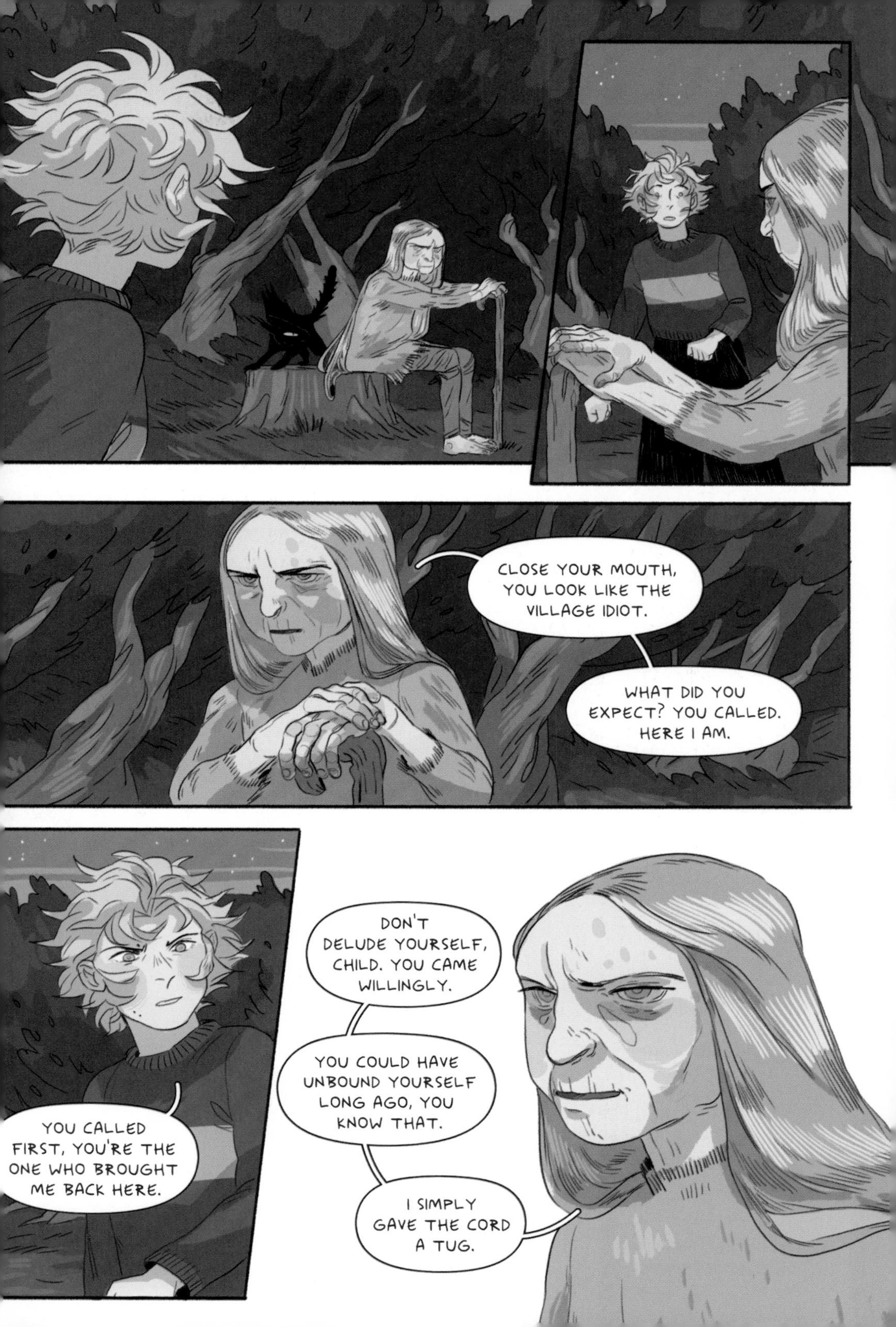
CLOSE YOUR MOUTH, YOU LOOK LIKE THE VILLAGE IDIOT.
WHAT DID YOU EXPECT? YOU CALLED. HERE I AM.
YOU CALLED FIRST, YOU'RE THE ONE WHO BROUGHT ME BACK HERE.
DON'T DELUDE YOURSELF, CHILD. YOU CAME WILLINGLY.
YOU COULD HAVE UNBOUND YOURSELF LONG AGO, YOU KNOW THAT.
I SIMPLY GAVE THE CORD A TUG.

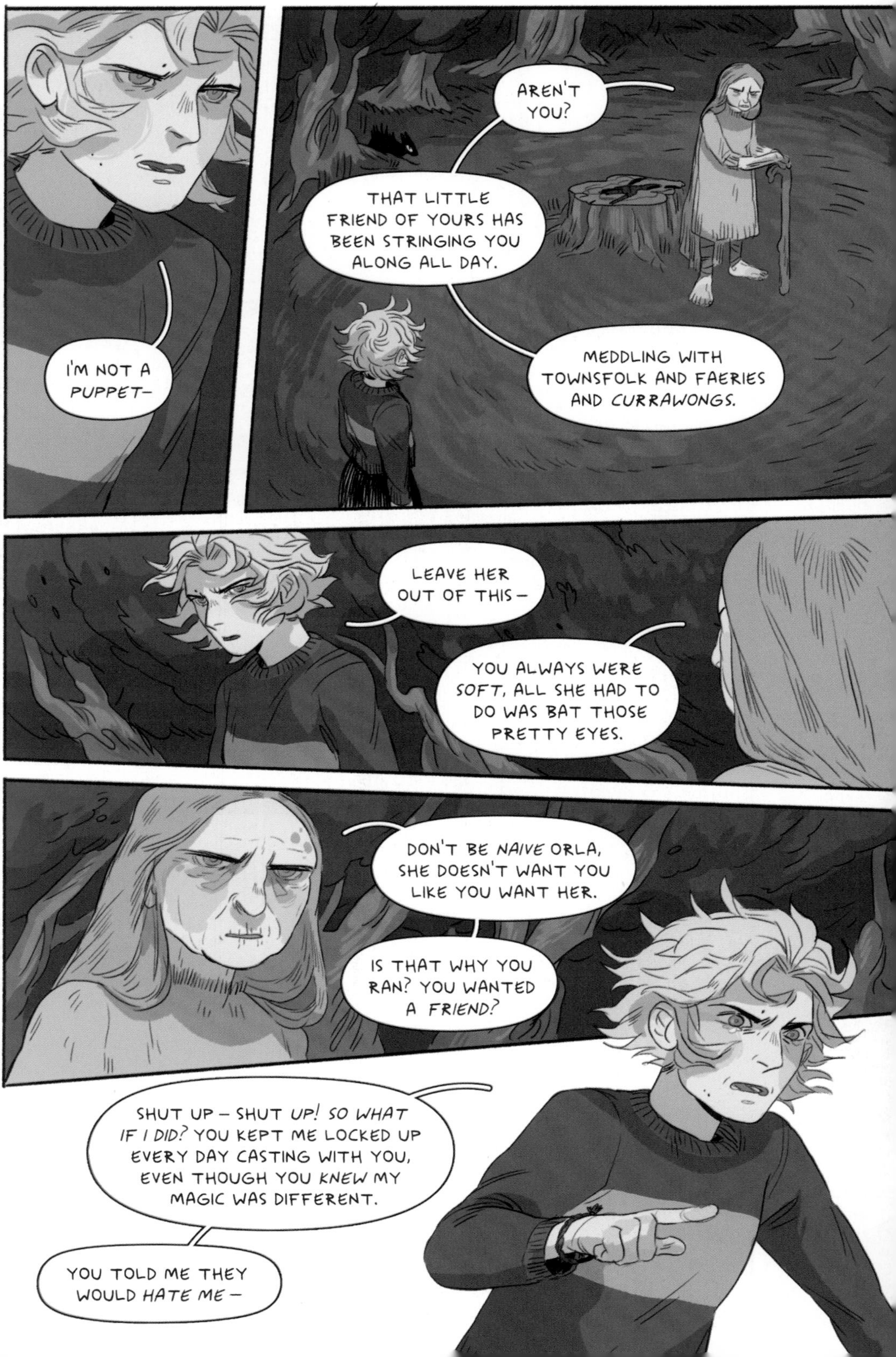
I'M NOT A PUPPET–
AREN'T YOU?
THAT LITTLE FRIEND OF YOURS HAS BEEN STRINGING YOU ALONG ALL DAY.
MEDDLING WITH TOWNSFOLK AND FAERIES AND CURRAWONGS.
LEAVE HER OUT OF THIS–
YOU ALWAYS WERE SOFT, ALL SHE HAD TO DO WAS BAT THOSE PRETTY EYES.
DON'T BE NAIVE ORLA, SHE DOESN'T WANT YOU LIKE YOU WANT HER.
IS THAT WHY YOU RAN? YOU WANTED A FRIEND?
SHUT UP – SHUT UP! SO WHAT IF I DID? YOU KEPT ME LOCKED UP EVERY DAY CASTING WITH YOU, EVEN THOUGH YOU KNEW MY MAGIC WAS DIFFERENT.
YOU TOLD ME THEY WOULD HATE ME –

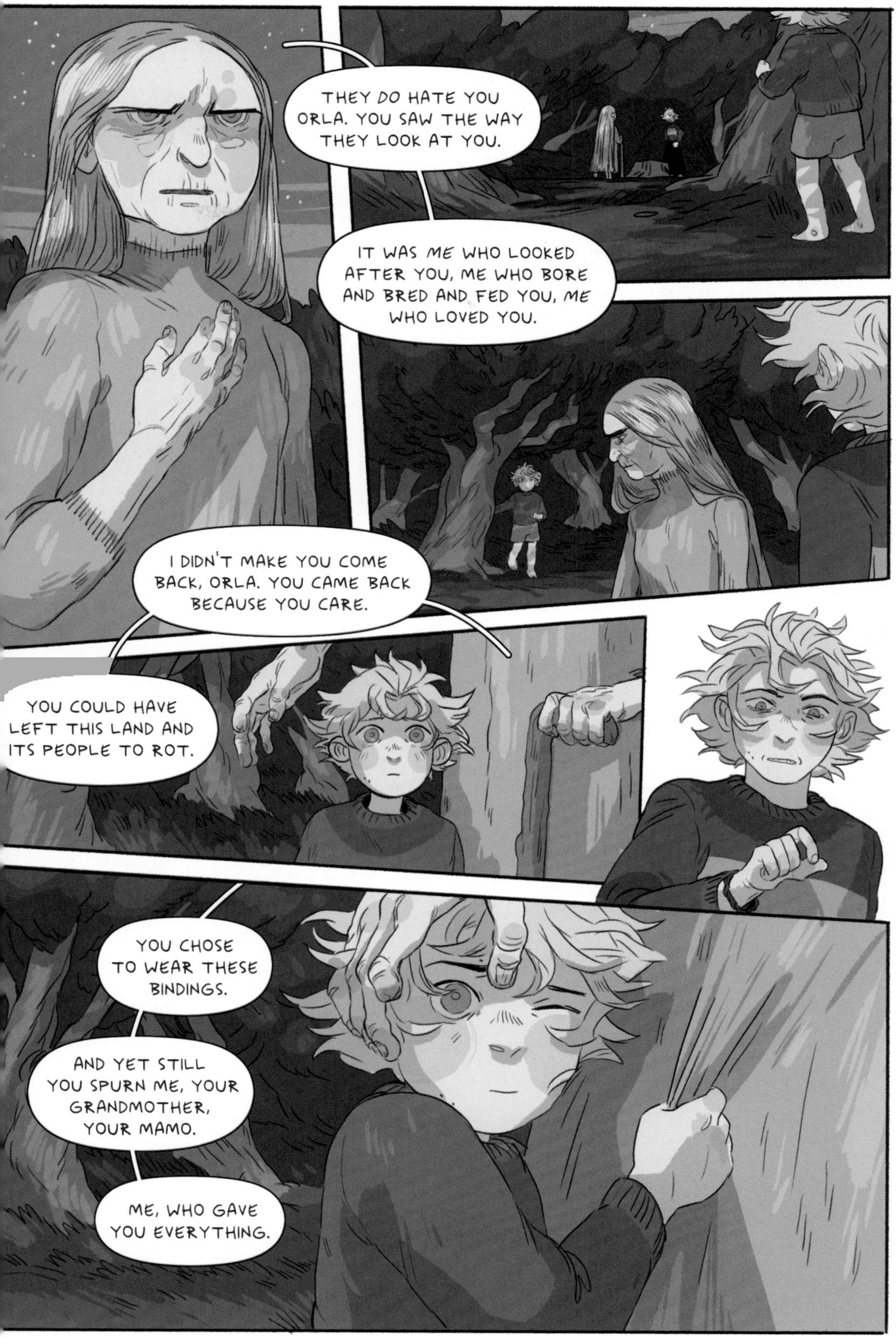
THEY DO HATE YOU ORLA. YOU SAW THE WAY THEY LOOK AT YOU.
IT WAS ME WHO LOOKED AFTER YOU, ME WHO BORE AND BRED AND FED YOU, ME WHO LOVED YOU.
I DIDN'T MAKE YOU COME BACK, ORLA. YOU CAME BACK BECAUSE YOU CARE.
YOU COULD HAVE LEFT THIS LAND AND ITS PEOPLE TO ROT.
YOU CHOSE TO WEAR THESE BINDINGS.
AND YET STILL YOU SPURN ME, YOUR GRANDMOTHER, YOUR MAMO.
ME, WHO GAVE YOU EVERYTHING.

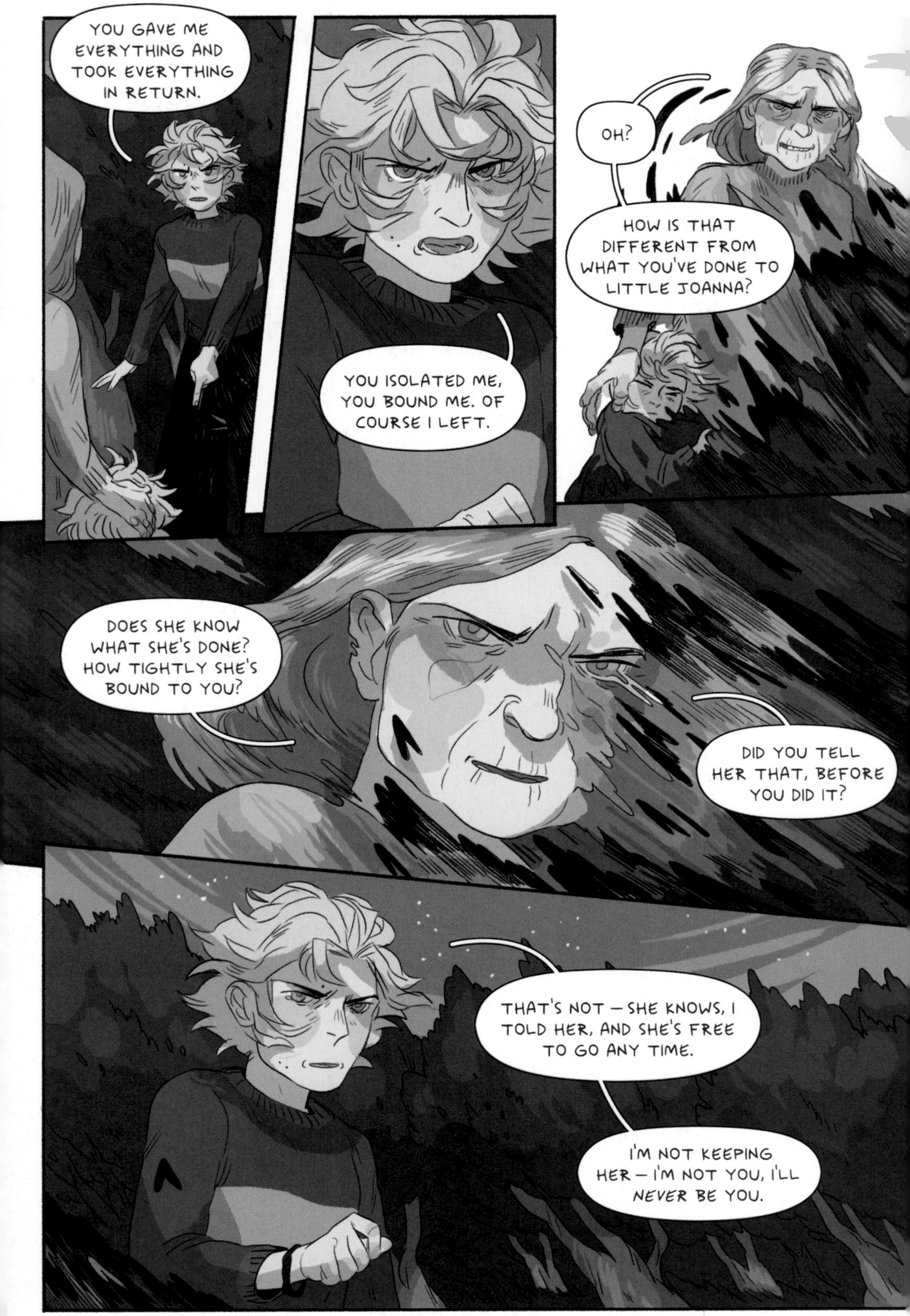
YOU GAVE ME EVERYTHING AND TOOK EVERYTHING IN RETURN.
YOU ISOLATED ME, YOU BOUND ME. OF COURSE I LEFT.
OH?
HOW IS THAT DIFFERENT FROM WHAT YOU'VE DONE TO LITTLE JOANNA?
DOES SHE KNOW WHAT SHE'S DONE? HOW TIGHTLY SHE'S BOUND TO YOU?
DID YOU TELL HER THAT, BEFORE YOU DID IT?
THAT'S NOT — SHE KNOWS, I TOLD HER, AND SHE'S FREE TO GO ANY TIME.
I'M NOT KEEPING HER — I'M NOT YOU, I'LL *NEVER* BE YOU.

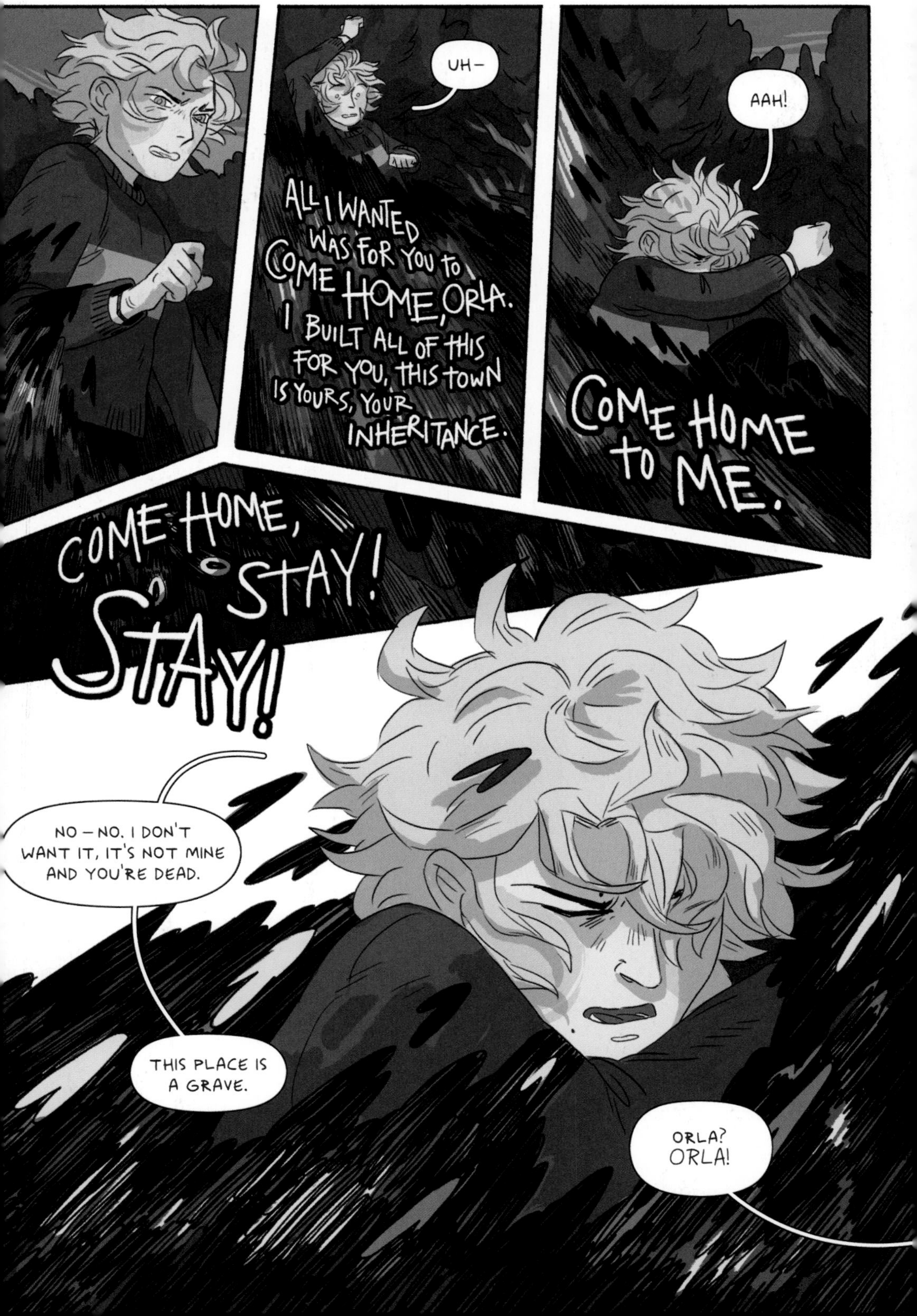
UH–
ALL I WANTED WAS FOR YOU TO COME HOME, ORLA. I BUILT ALL OF THIS FOR YOU, THIS TOWN IS YOURS, YOUR INHERITANCE.
AAH!
COME HOME TO ME.
COME HOME, STAY!
STAY!
NO – NO. I DON'T WANT IT, IT'S NOT MINE AND YOU'RE DEAD.
THIS PLACE IS A GRAVE.
ORLA? ORLA!

Chapter 5

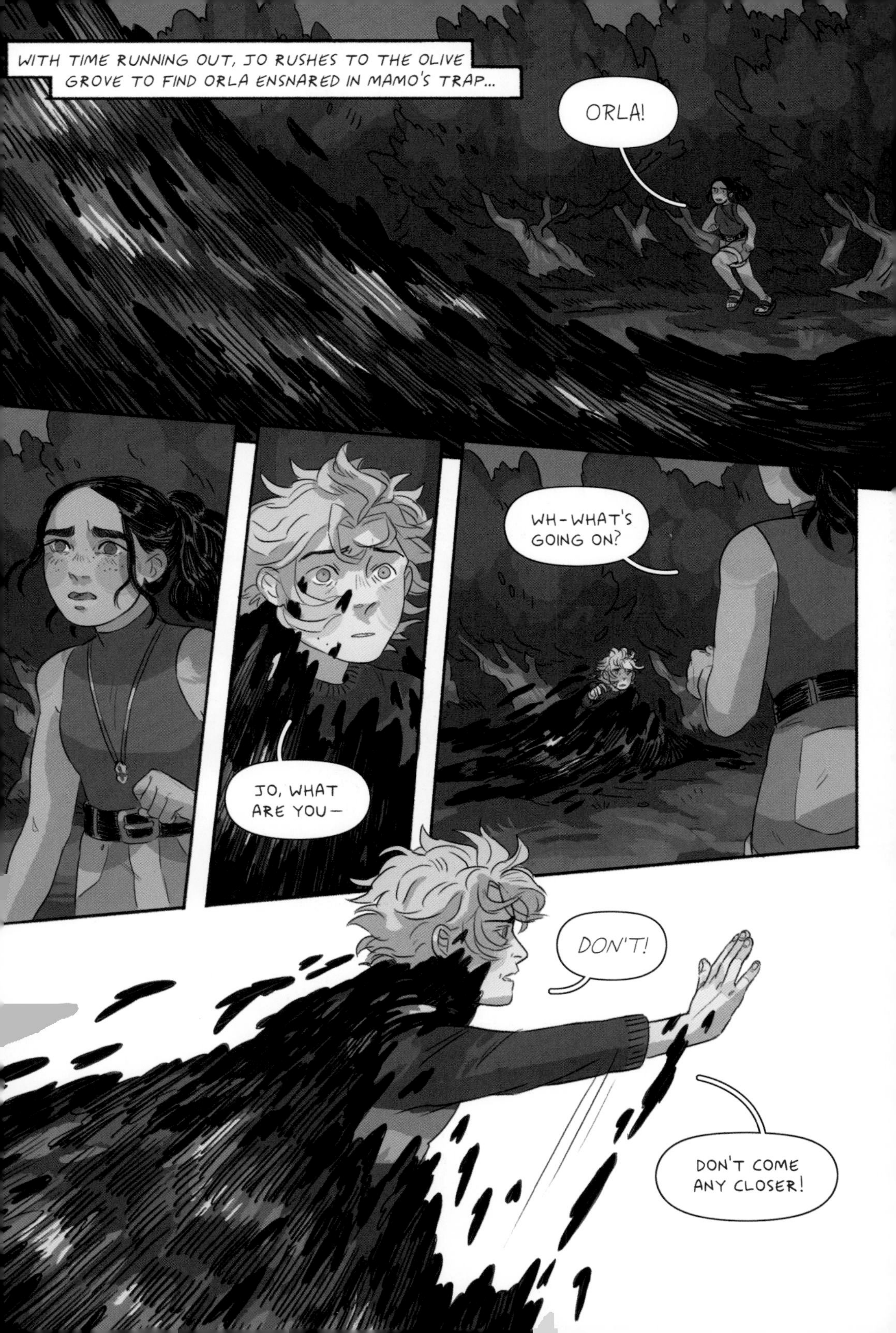
WITH TIME RUNNING OUT, JO RUSHES TO THE OLIVE GROVE TO FIND ORLA ENSNARED IN MAMO'S TRAP...
ORLA!
JO, WHAT ARE YOU—
WH-WHAT'S GOING ON?
DON'T!
DON'T COME ANY CLOSER!

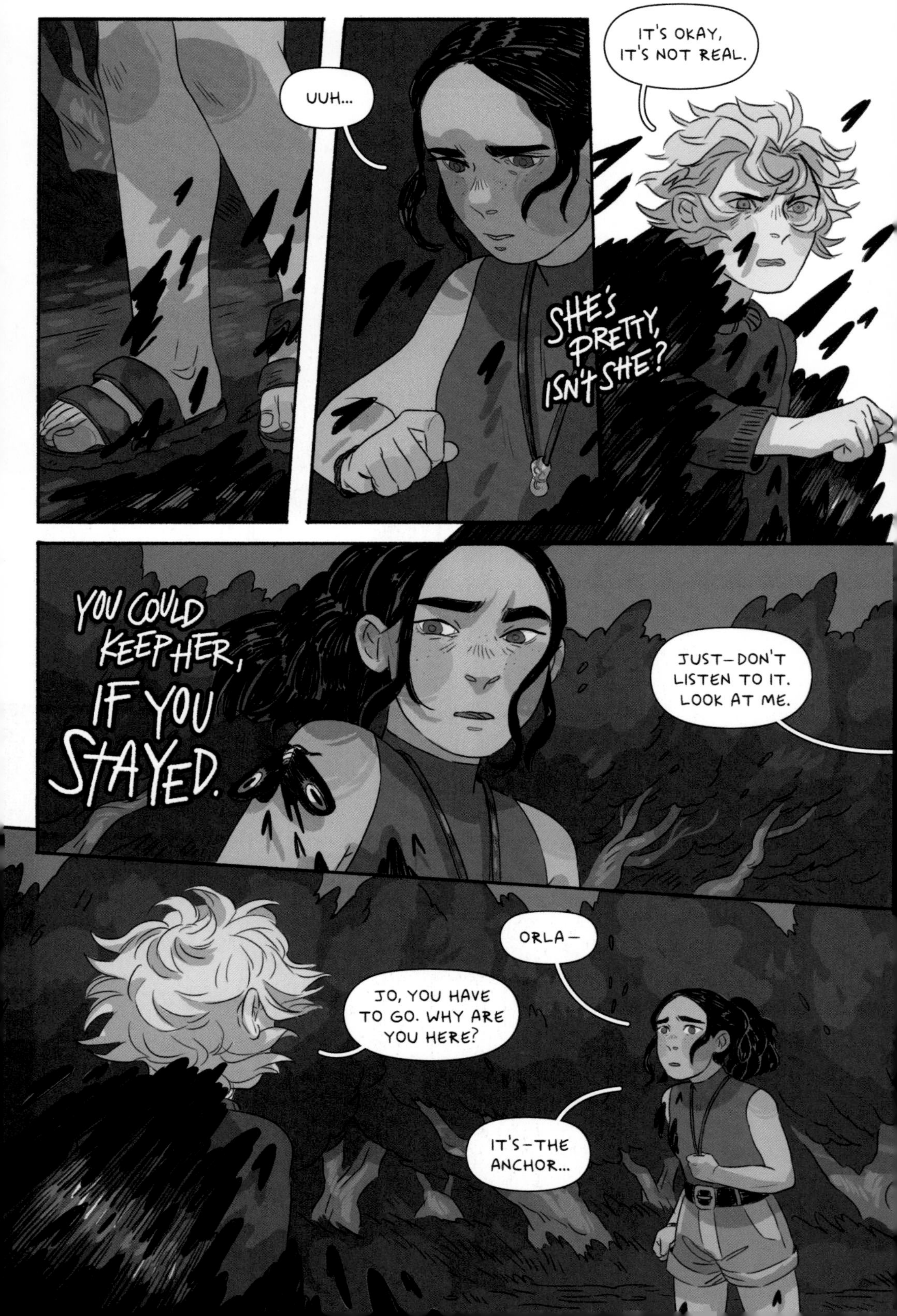
UUH...
IT'S OKAY, IT'S NOT REAL.
SHE'S PRETTY, ISN'T SHE?
YOU COULD KEEP HER, IF YOU STAYED.
JUST—DON'T LISTEN TO IT. LOOK AT ME.
ORLA—
JO, YOU HAVE TO GO. WHY ARE YOU HERE?
IT'S—THE ANCHOR...

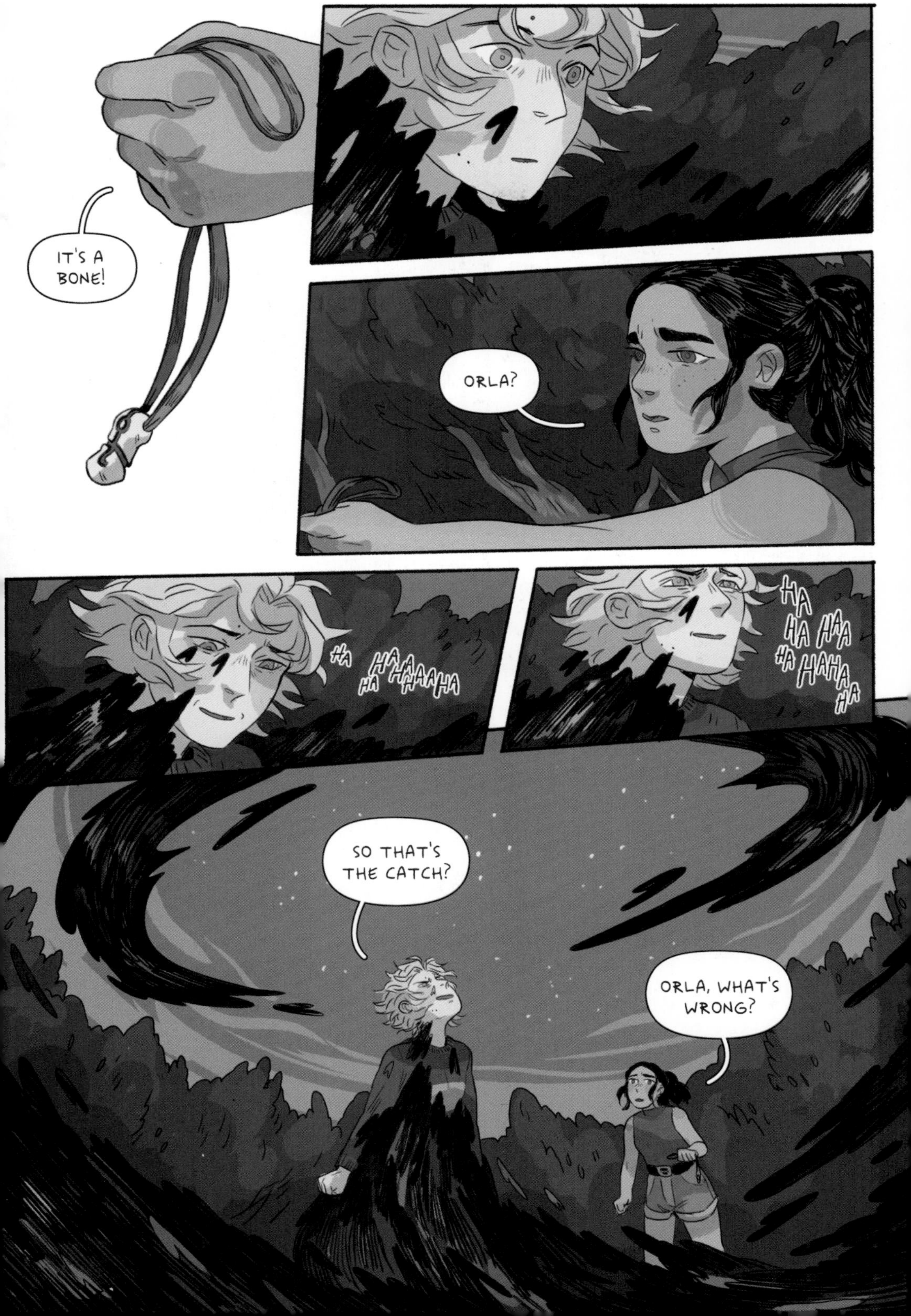
IT'S A BONE!
ORLA?
HA HAHAHA HAHAHAAAHA
HA HA HAA HA HAHAHA HA
SO THAT'S THE CATCH?
ORLA, WHAT'S WRONG?

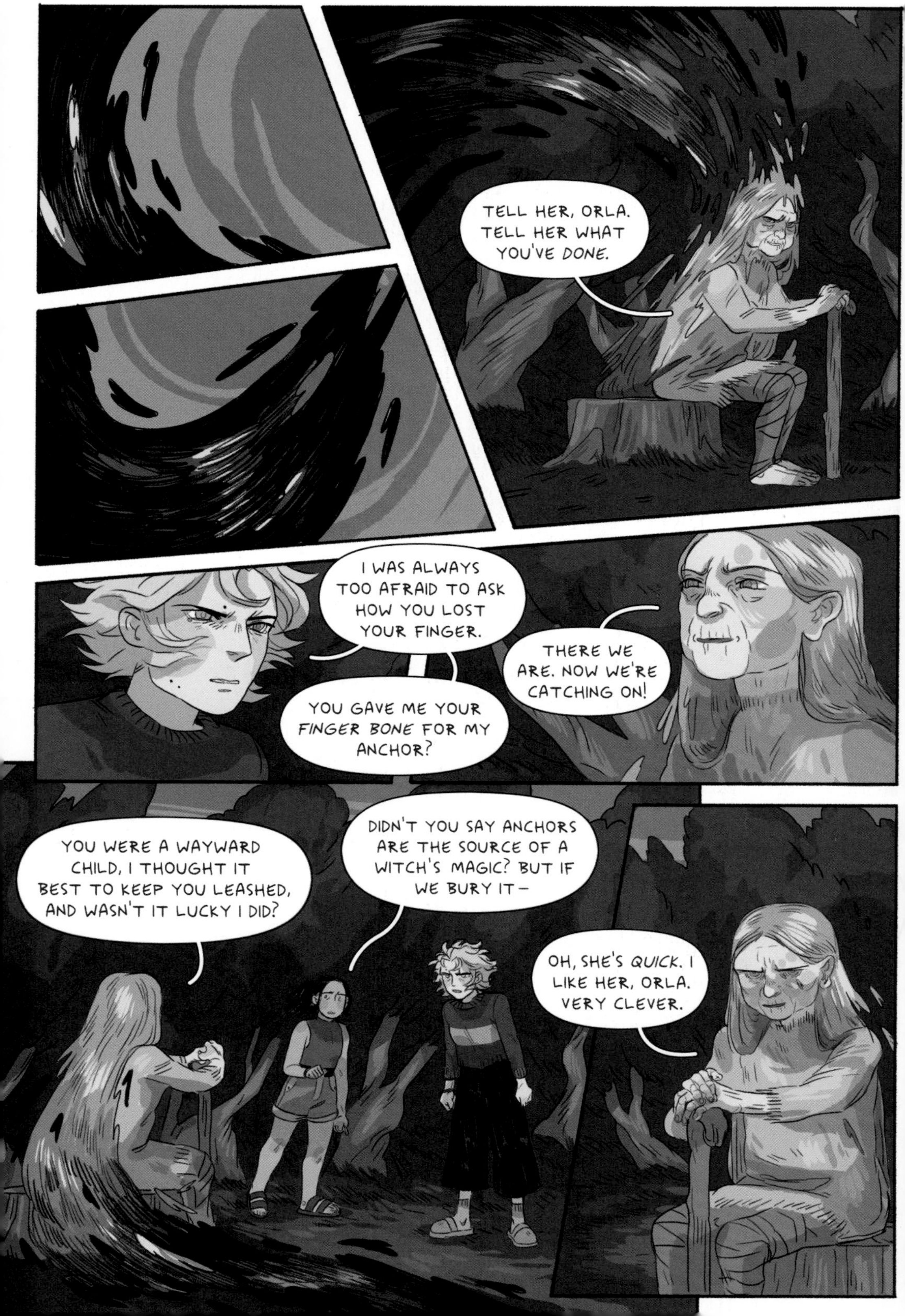
TELL HER, ORLA. TELL HER WHAT YOU'VE *DONE*.
I WAS ALWAYS TOO AFRAID TO ASK HOW YOU LOST YOUR FINGER.
YOU GAVE ME YOUR *FINGER BONE* FOR MY ANCHOR?
THERE WE ARE. NOW WE'RE CATCHING ON!
YOU WERE A WAYWARD CHILD. I THOUGHT IT BEST TO KEEP YOU LEASHED. AND WASN'T IT LUCKY I DID?
DIDN'T YOU SAY ANCHORS ARE THE SOURCE OF A WITCH'S MAGIC? BUT IF WE BURY IT—
OH, SHE'S *QUICK*. I LIKE HER, ORLA. VERY CLEVER.

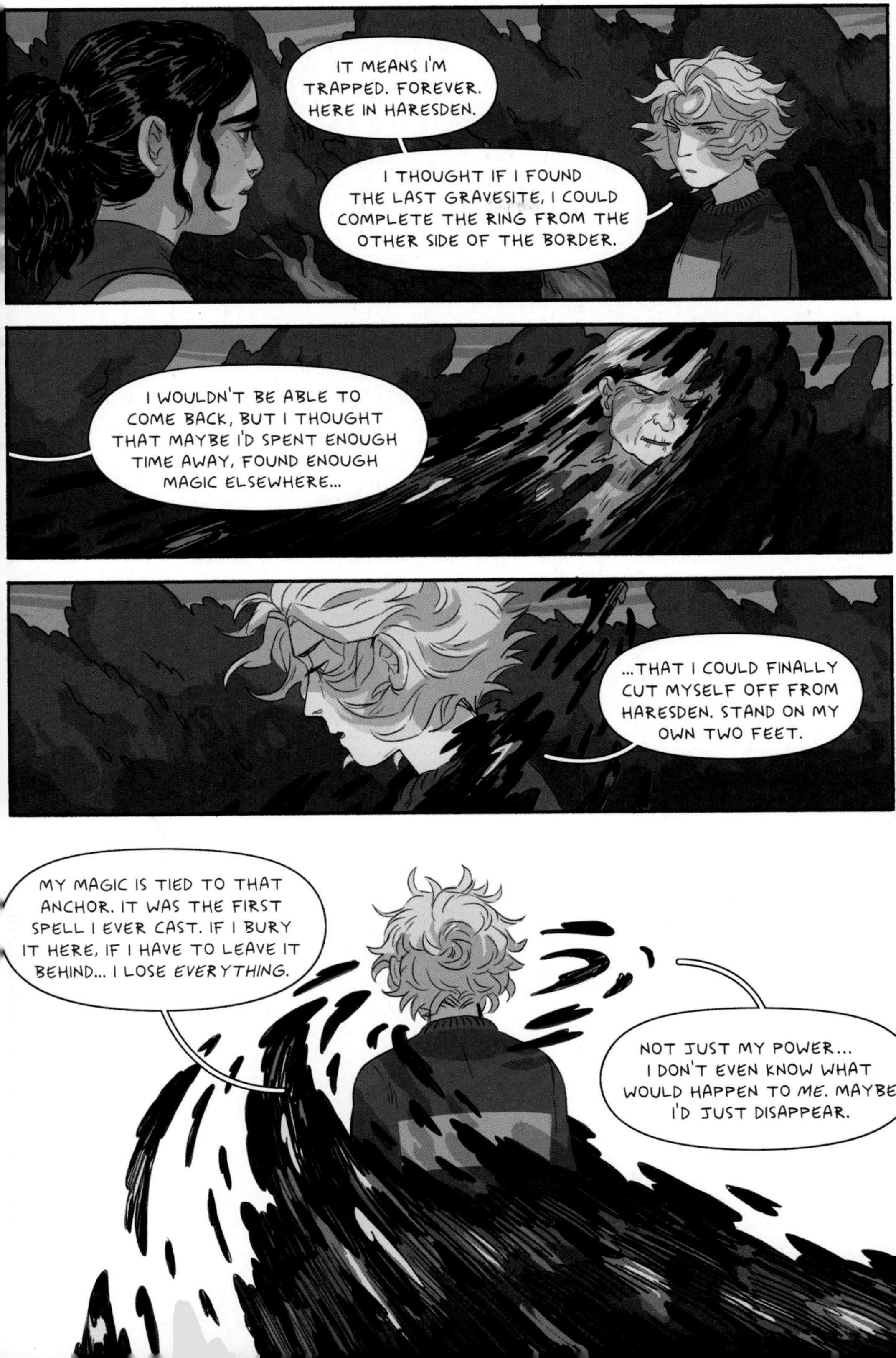
IT MEANS I'M TRAPPED. FOREVER. HERE IN HARESDEN.
I THOUGHT IF I FOUND THE LAST GRAVESITE, I COULD COMPLETE THE RING FROM THE OTHER SIDE OF THE BORDER.
I WOULDN'T BE ABLE TO COME BACK, BUT I THOUGHT THAT MAYBE I'D SPENT ENOUGH TIME AWAY, FOUND ENOUGH MAGIC ELSEWHERE...
...THAT I COULD FINALLY CUT MYSELF OFF FROM HARESDEN. STAND ON MY OWN TWO FEET.
MY MAGIC IS TIED TO THAT ANCHOR. IT WAS THE FIRST SPELL I EVER CAST. IF I BURY IT HERE, IF I HAVE TO LEAVE IT BEHIND... I LOSE *EVERYTHING*.
NOT JUST MY POWER... I DON'T EVEN KNOW WHAT WOULD HAPPEN TO ME. MAYBE I'D JUST DISAPPEAR.

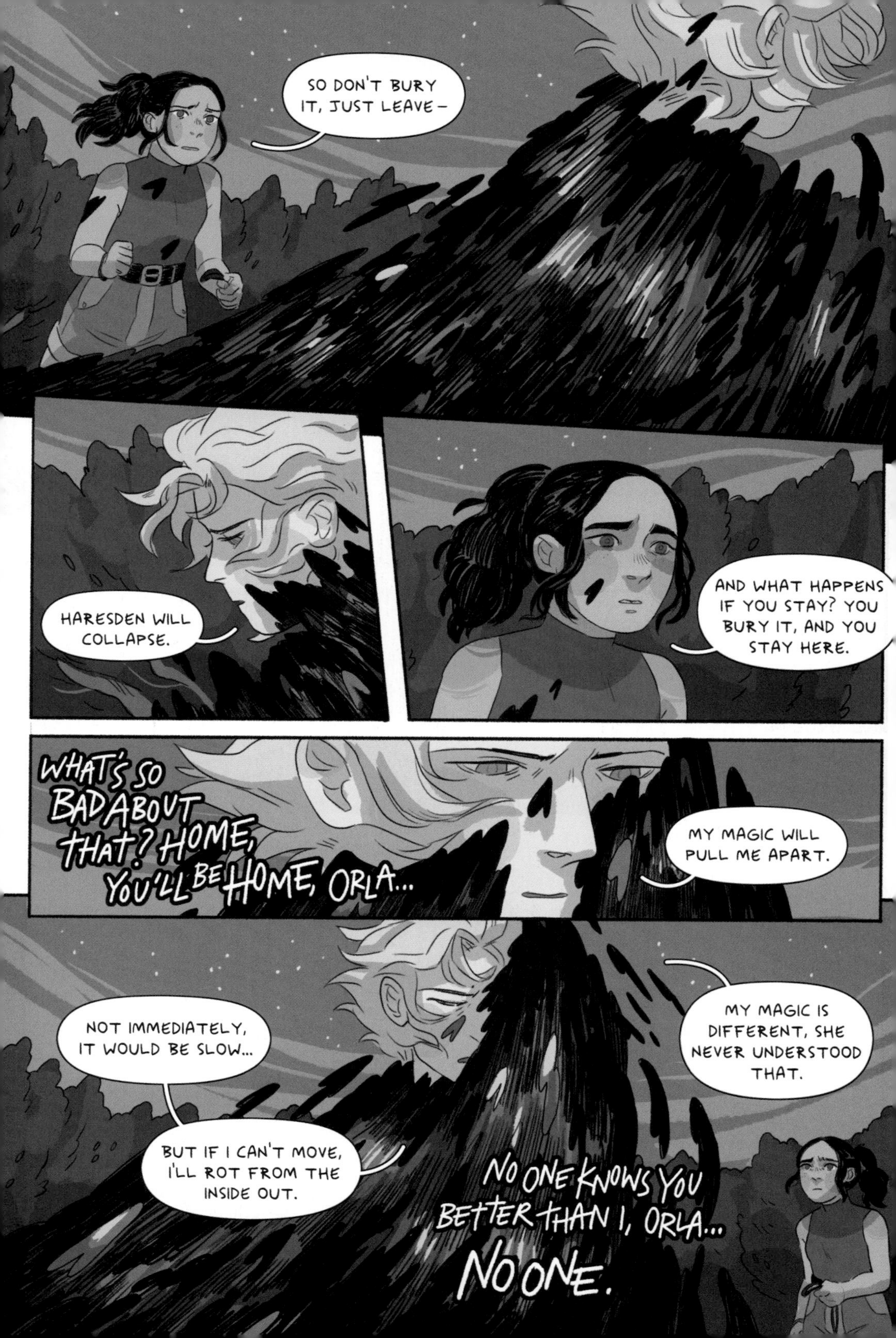
SO DON'T BURY IT, JUST LEAVE –
HARESDEN WILL COLLAPSE.
AND WHAT HAPPENS IF YOU STAY? YOU BURY IT, AND YOU STAY HERE.
WHAT'S SO BAD ABOUT THAT? HOME, YOU'LL BE HOME, ORLA...
MY MAGIC WILL PULL ME APART.
NOT IMMEDIATELY, IT WOULD BE SLOW...
BUT IF I CAN'T MOVE, I'LL ROT FROM THE INSIDE OUT.
MY MAGIC IS DIFFERENT, SHE NEVER UNDERSTOOD THAT.
NO ONE KNOWS YOU BETTER THAN I, ORLA... NO ONE.

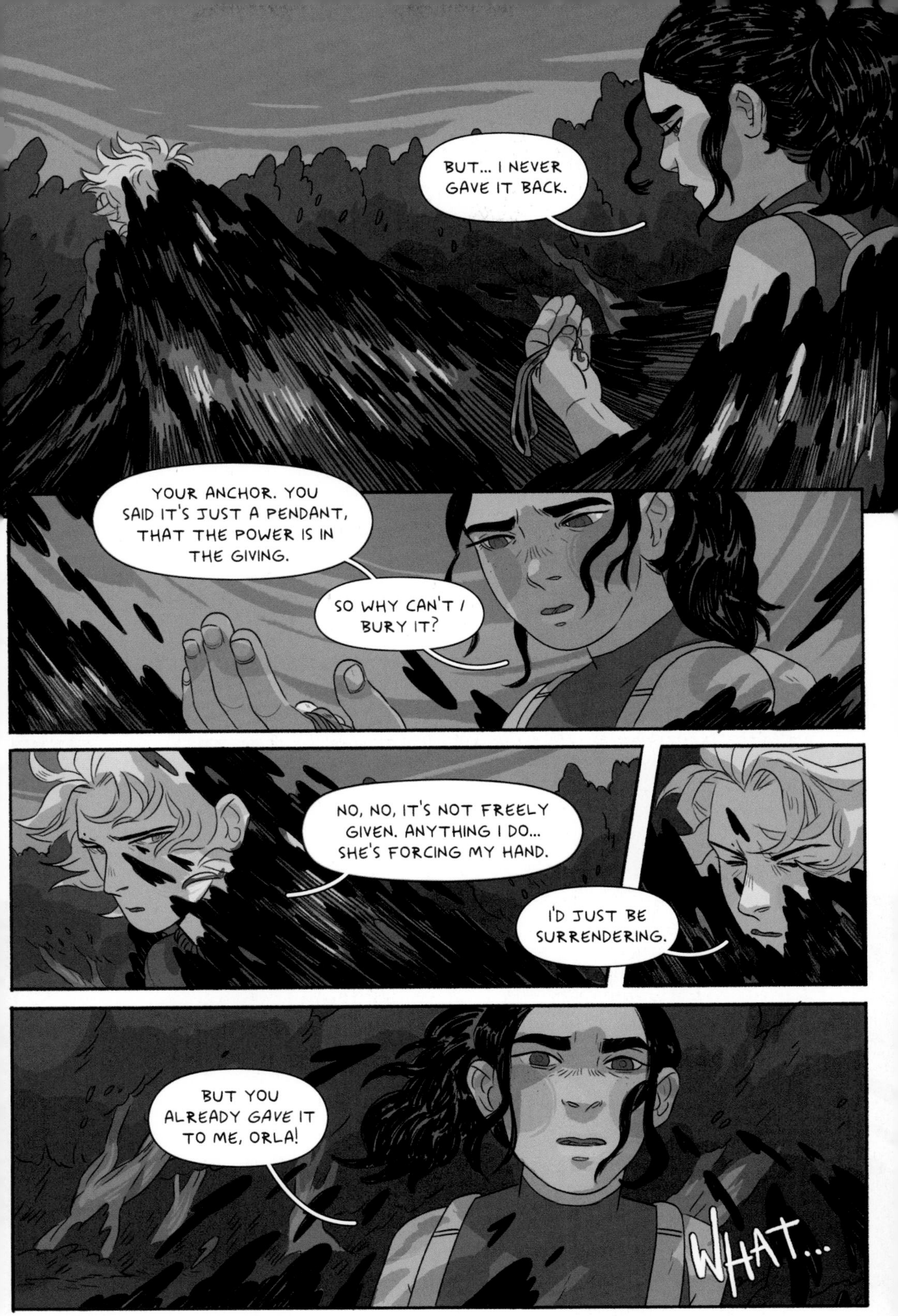
BUT... I NEVER GAVE IT BACK.
YOUR ANCHOR. YOU SAID IT'S JUST A PENDANT, THAT THE POWER IS IN THE GIVING.
SO WHY CAN'T I BURY IT?
NO, NO, IT'S NOT FREELY GIVEN. ANYTHING I DO... SHE'S FORCING MY HAND.
I'D JUST BE SURRENDERING.
BUT YOU ALREADY GAVE IT TO ME, ORLA!
WHAT...

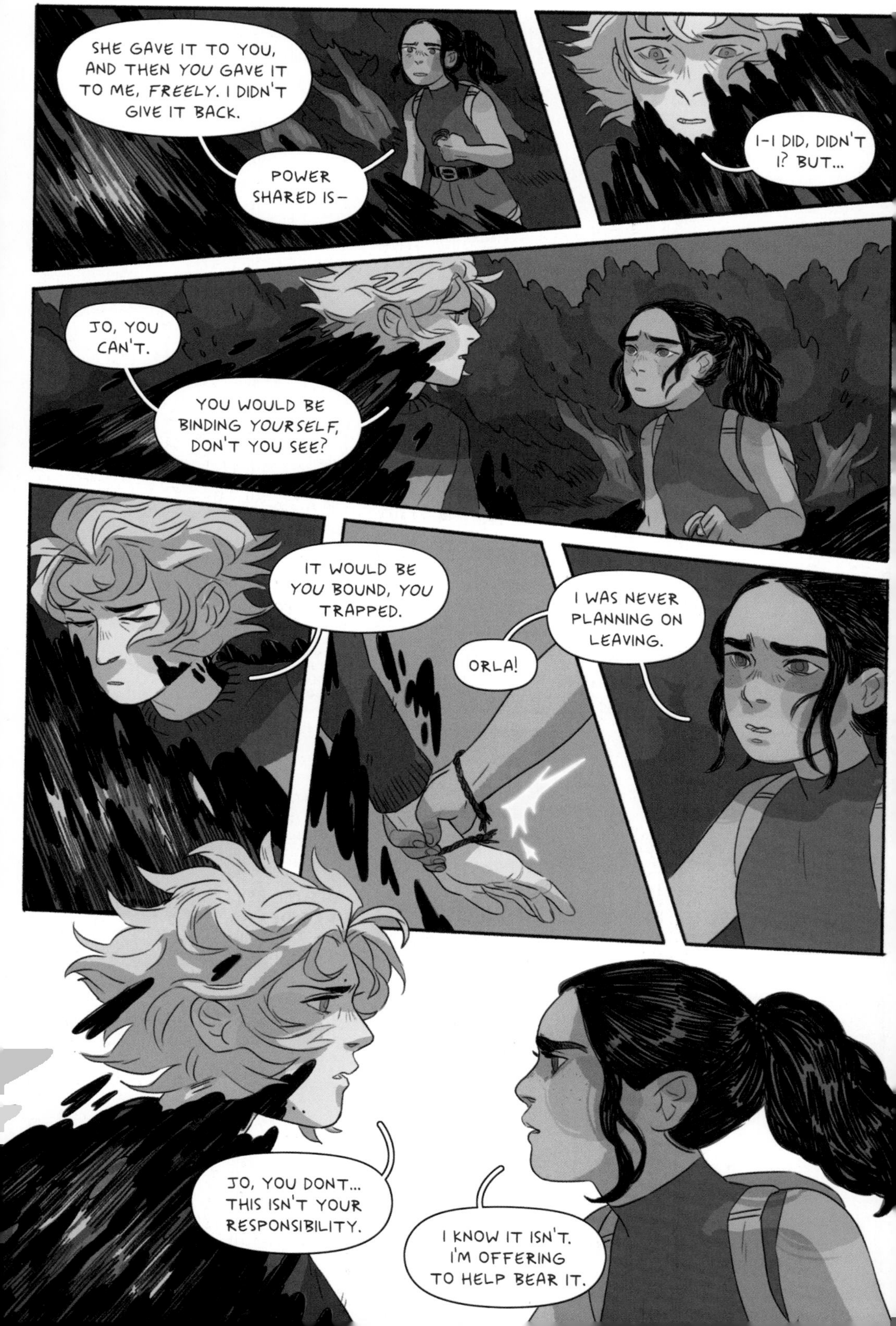
SHE GAVE IT TO YOU, AND THEN YOU GAVE IT TO ME, FREELY. I DIDN'T GIVE IT BACK.
POWER SHARED IS—
I-I DID, DIDN'T I? BUT...
JO, YOU CAN'T.
YOU WOULD BE BINDING YOURSELF, DON'T YOU SEE?
IT WOULD BE YOU BOUND, YOU TRAPPED.
ORLA!
I WAS NEVER PLANNING ON LEAVING.
JO, YOU DONT... THIS ISN'T YOUR RESPONSIBILITY.
I KNOW IT ISN'T. I'M OFFERING TO HELP BEAR IT.

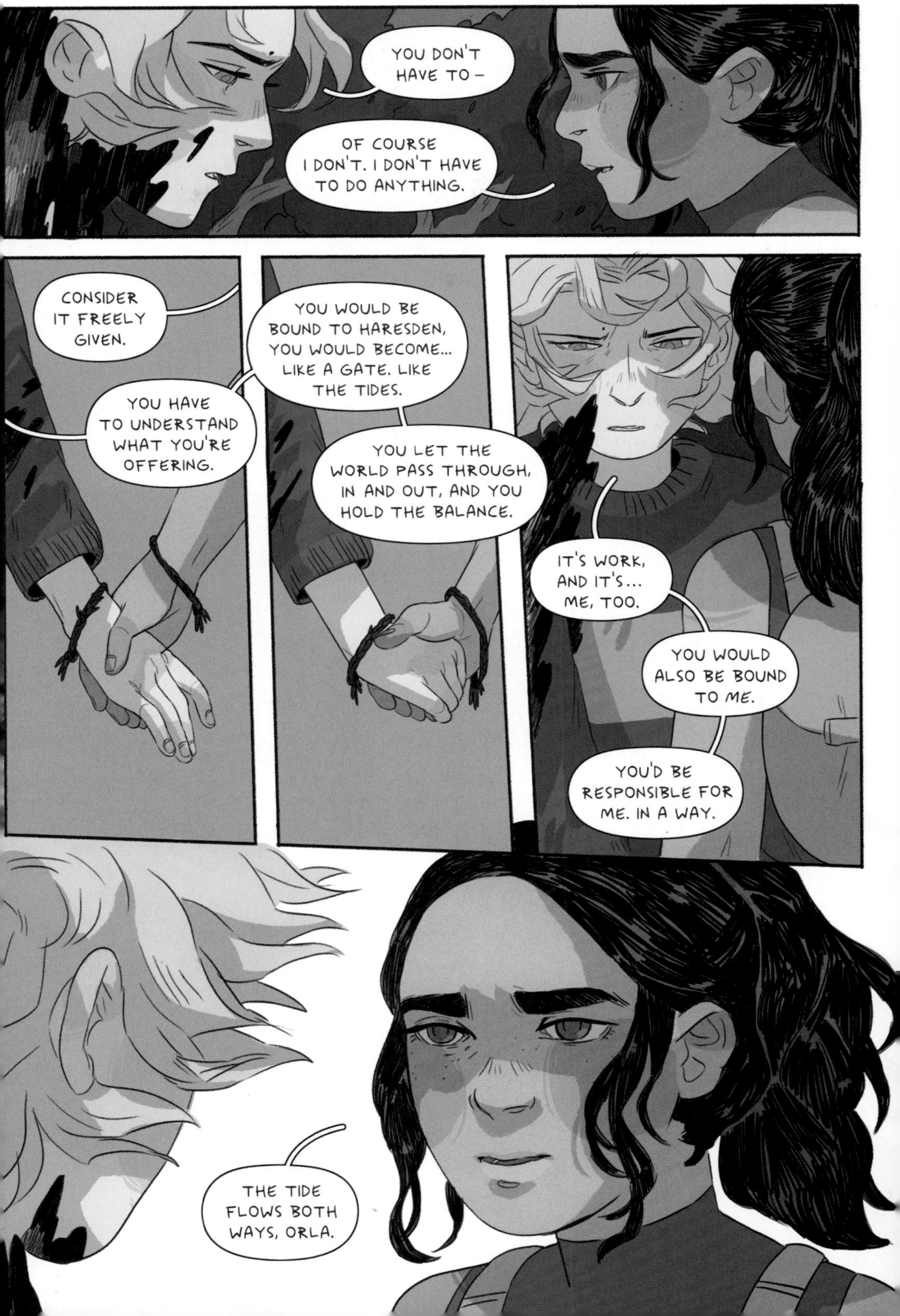
YOU DON'T HAVE TO –
OF COURSE I DON'T. I DON'T HAVE TO DO ANYTHING.
CONSIDER IT FREELY GIVEN.
YOU HAVE TO UNDERSTAND WHAT YOU'RE OFFERING.
YOU WOULD BE BOUND TO HARESDEN, YOU WOULD BECOME... LIKE A GATE. LIKE THE TIDES.
YOU LET THE WORLD PASS THROUGH, IN AND OUT, AND YOU HOLD THE BALANCE.
IT'S WORK, AND IT'S... ME, TOO.
YOU WOULD ALSO BE BOUND TO ME.
YOU'D BE RESPONSIBLE FOR ME. IN A WAY.
THE TIDE FLOWS BOTH WAYS, ORLA.

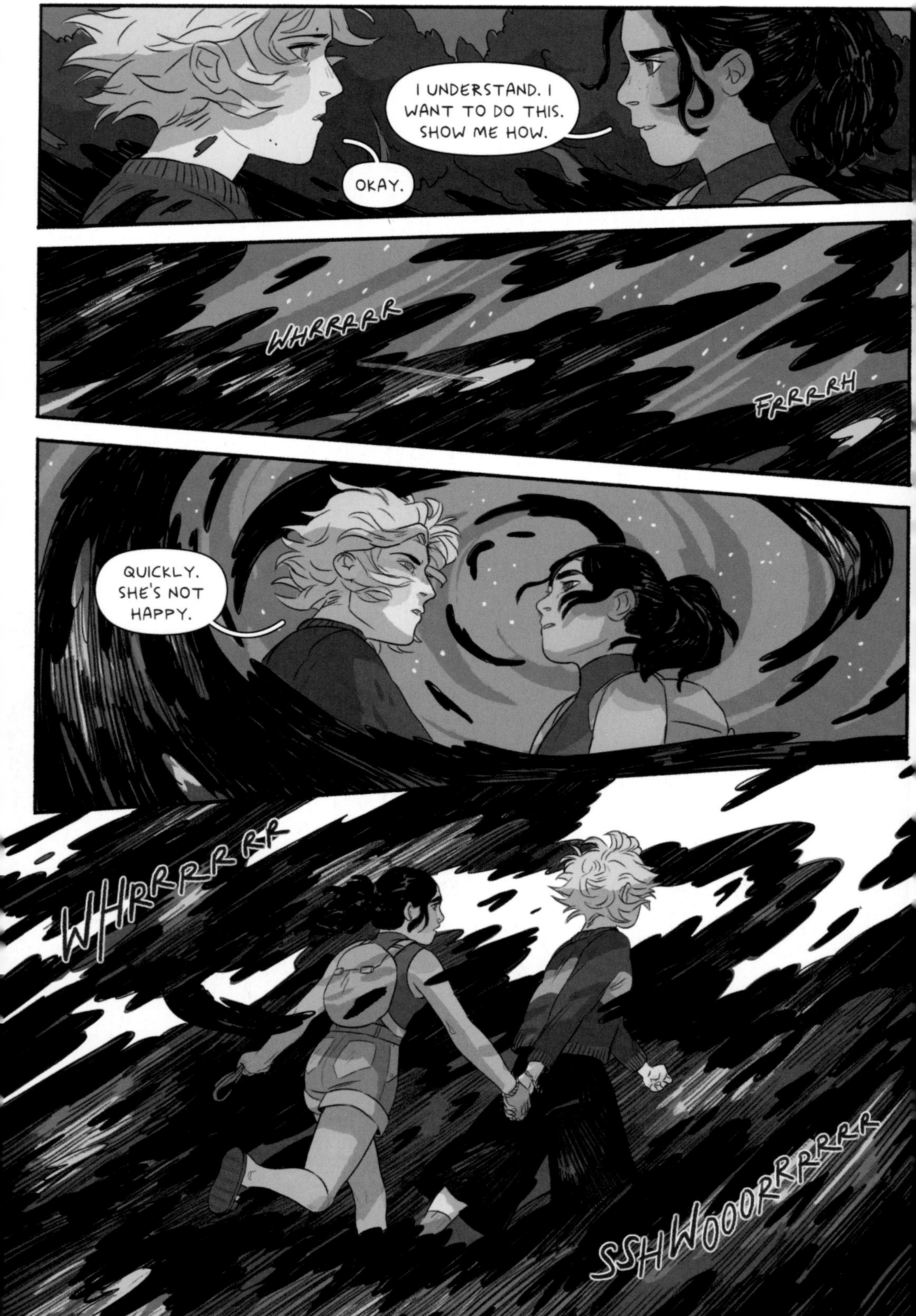
I UNDERSTAND. I WANT TO DO THIS. SHOW ME HOW.
OKAY.
WHRRRRR
FRRRRH
QUICKLY. SHE'S NOT HAPPY.
WHRRRRRR
SSHWOOORRRRRR

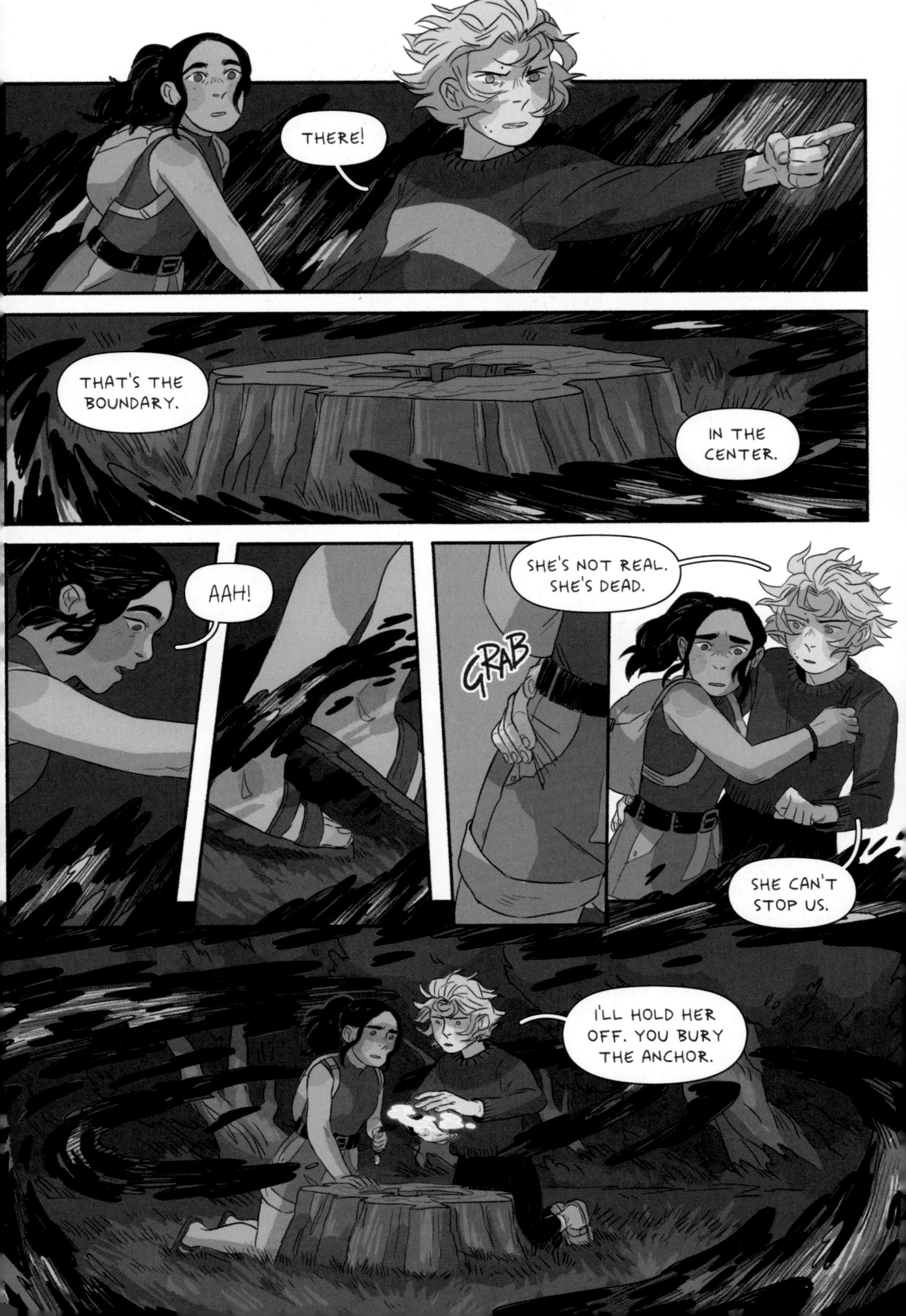
THERE!
THAT'S THE BOUNDARY.
IN THE CENTER.
AAH!
GRAB
SHE'S NOT REAL. SHE'S DEAD.
SHE CAN'T STOP US.
I'LL HOLD HER OFF. YOU BURY THE ANCHOR.

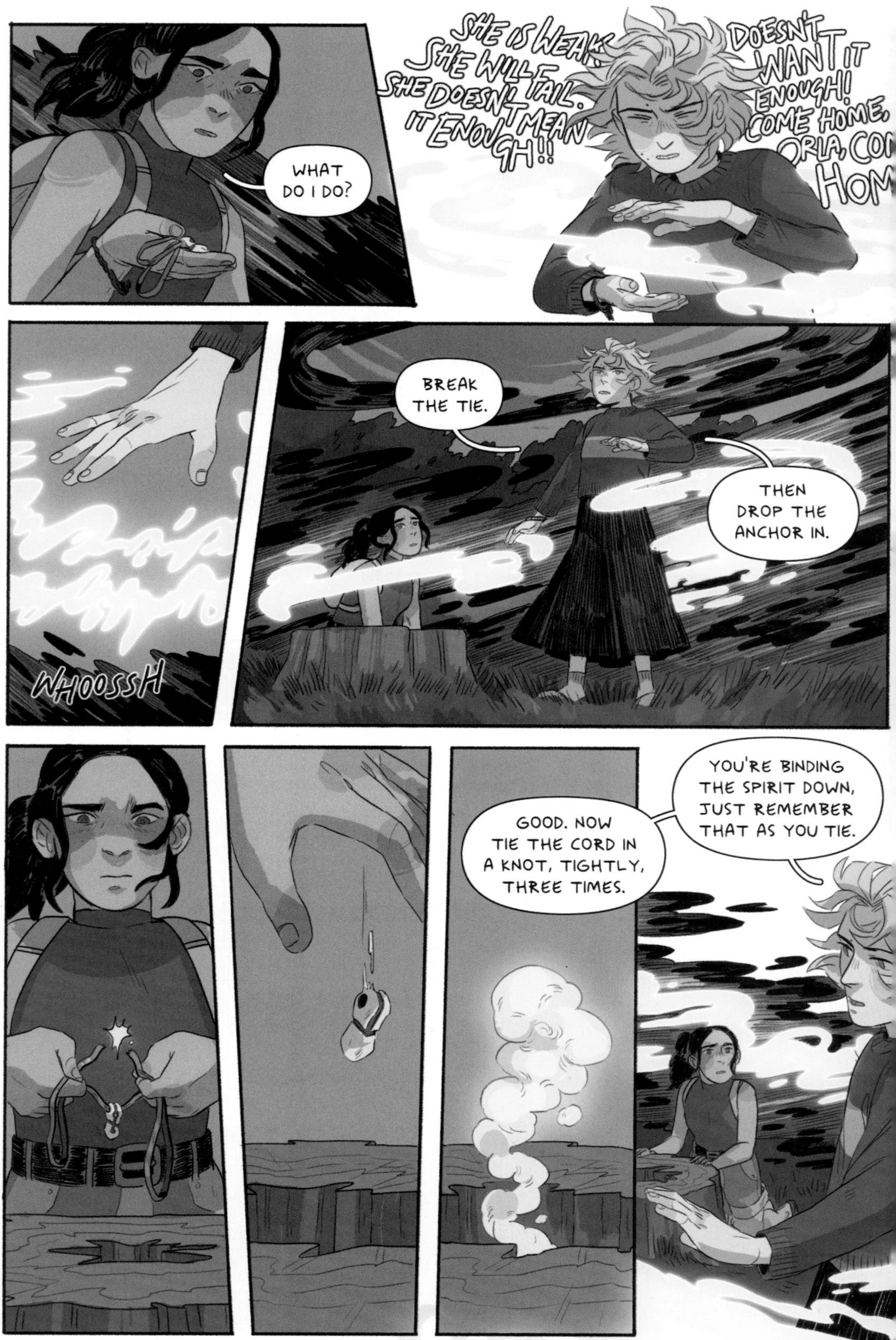
SHE IS WEAK.
SHE WILL FAIL.
SHE DOESN'T MEAN IT ENOUGH!!
DOESN'T WANT IT ENOUGH!
COME HOME.
ORLA, COM
HOM
WHAT DO I DO?
WHOOSSH
BREAK THE TIE.
THEN DROP THE ANCHOR IN.
GOOD. NOW TIE THE CORD IN A KNOT, TIGHTLY, THREE TIMES.
YOU'RE BINDING THE SPIRIT DOWN, JUST REMEMBER THAT AS YOU TIE.

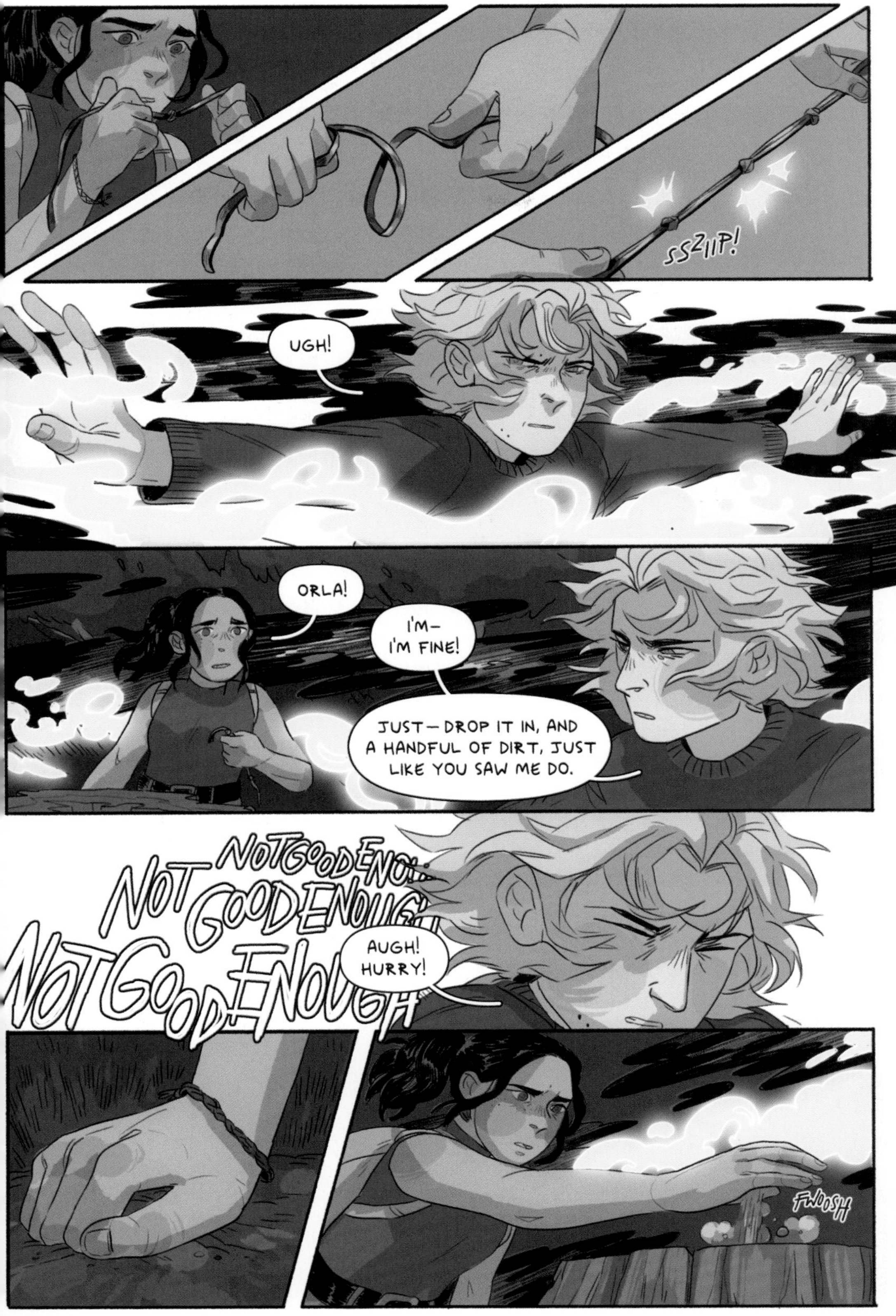
SSZIIP!
UGH!
ORLA!
I'M— I'M FINE!
JUST—DROP IT IN, AND A HANDFUL OF DIRT, JUST LIKE YOU SAW ME DO.
NOT GOOD ENOUGH
NOT GOOD ENOUGH
AUGH! HURRY!
FWOOSH

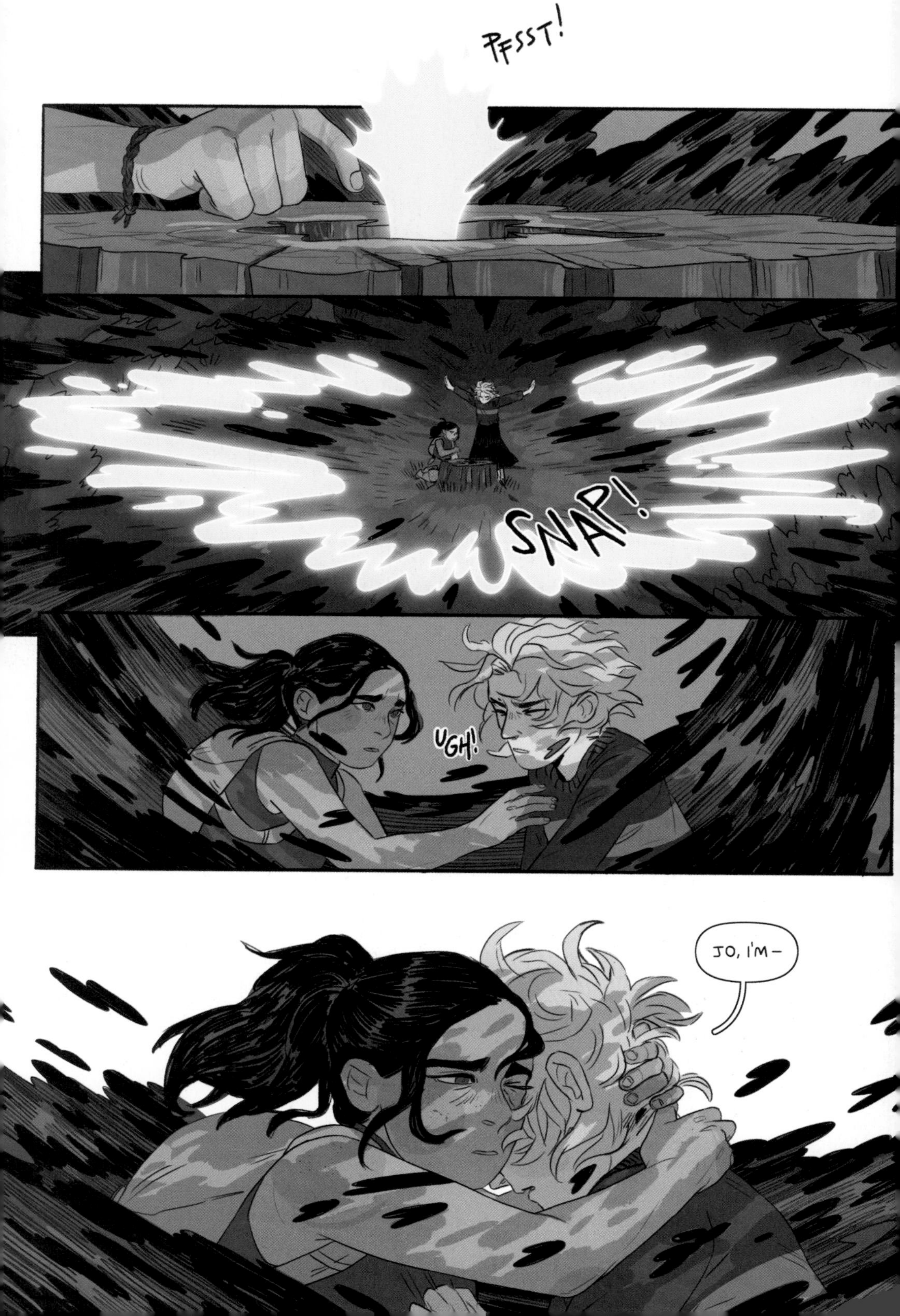
PFSST!
SNAP!
UGH!
JO, I'M—

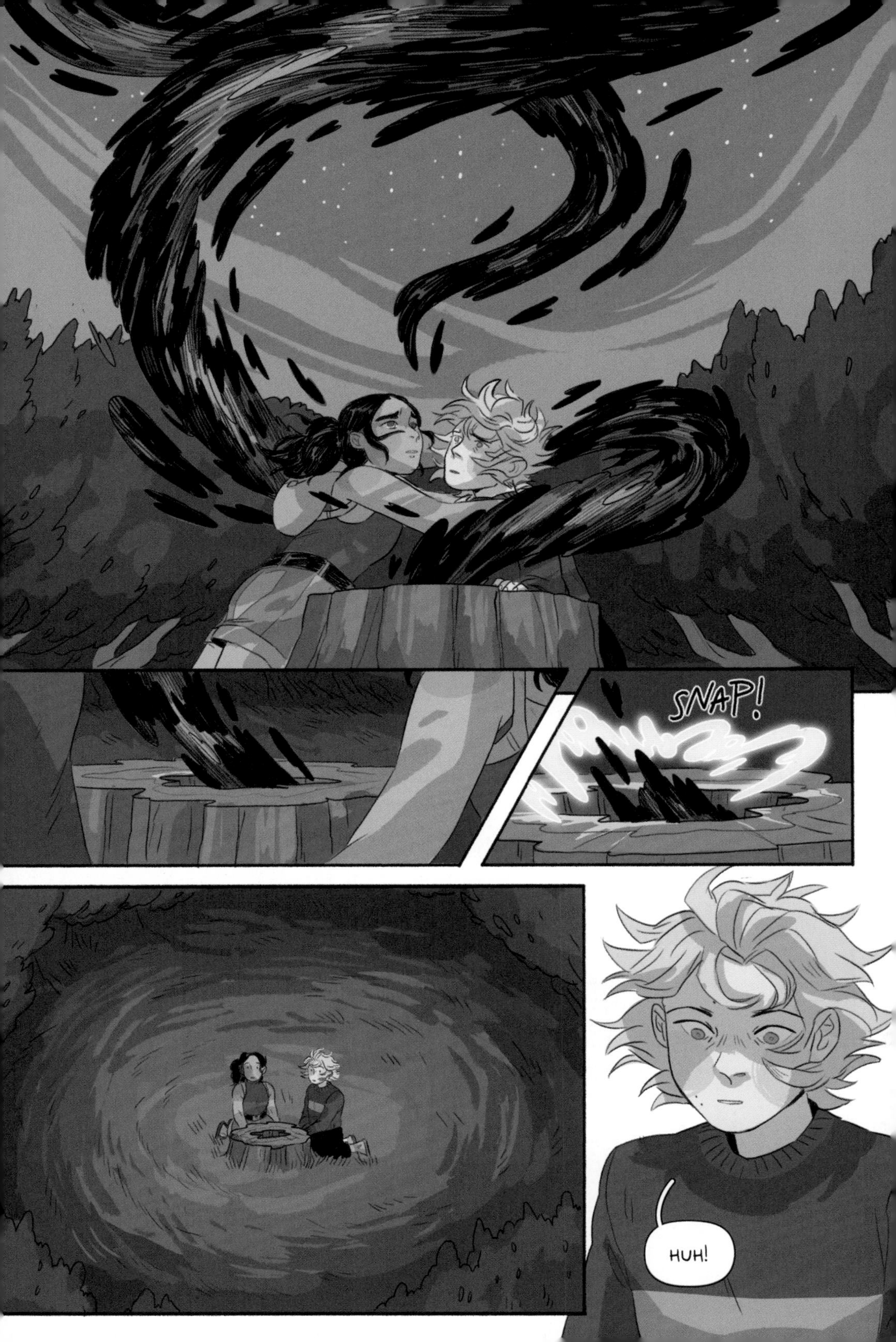
SNAP!
HUH!

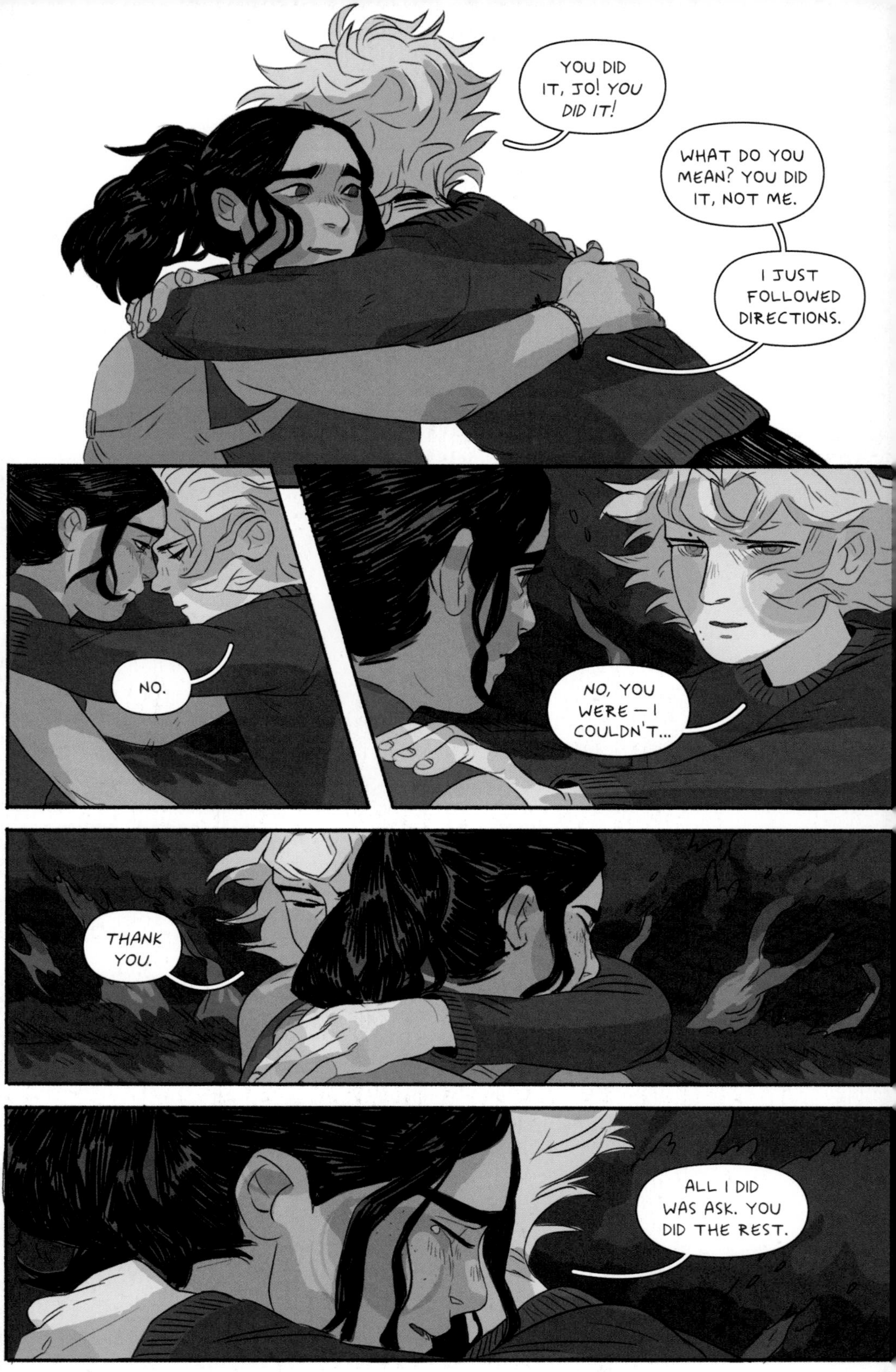
YOU DID IT, JO! YOU DID IT!
WHAT DO YOU MEAN? YOU DID IT, NOT ME.
I JUST FOLLOWED DIRECTIONS.
NO.
NO, YOU WERE — I COULDN'T...
THANK YOU.
ALL I DID WAS ASK. YOU DID THE REST.

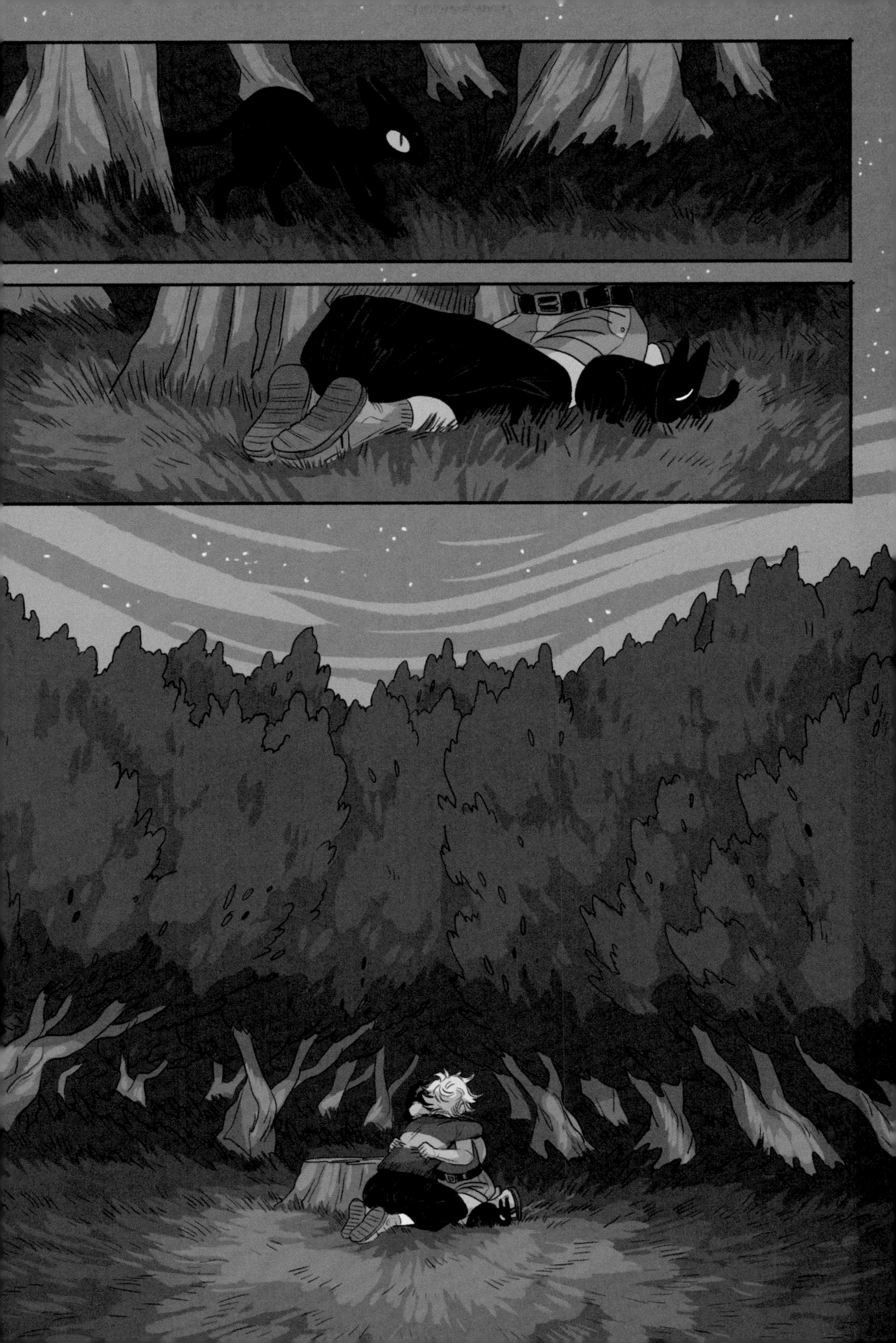

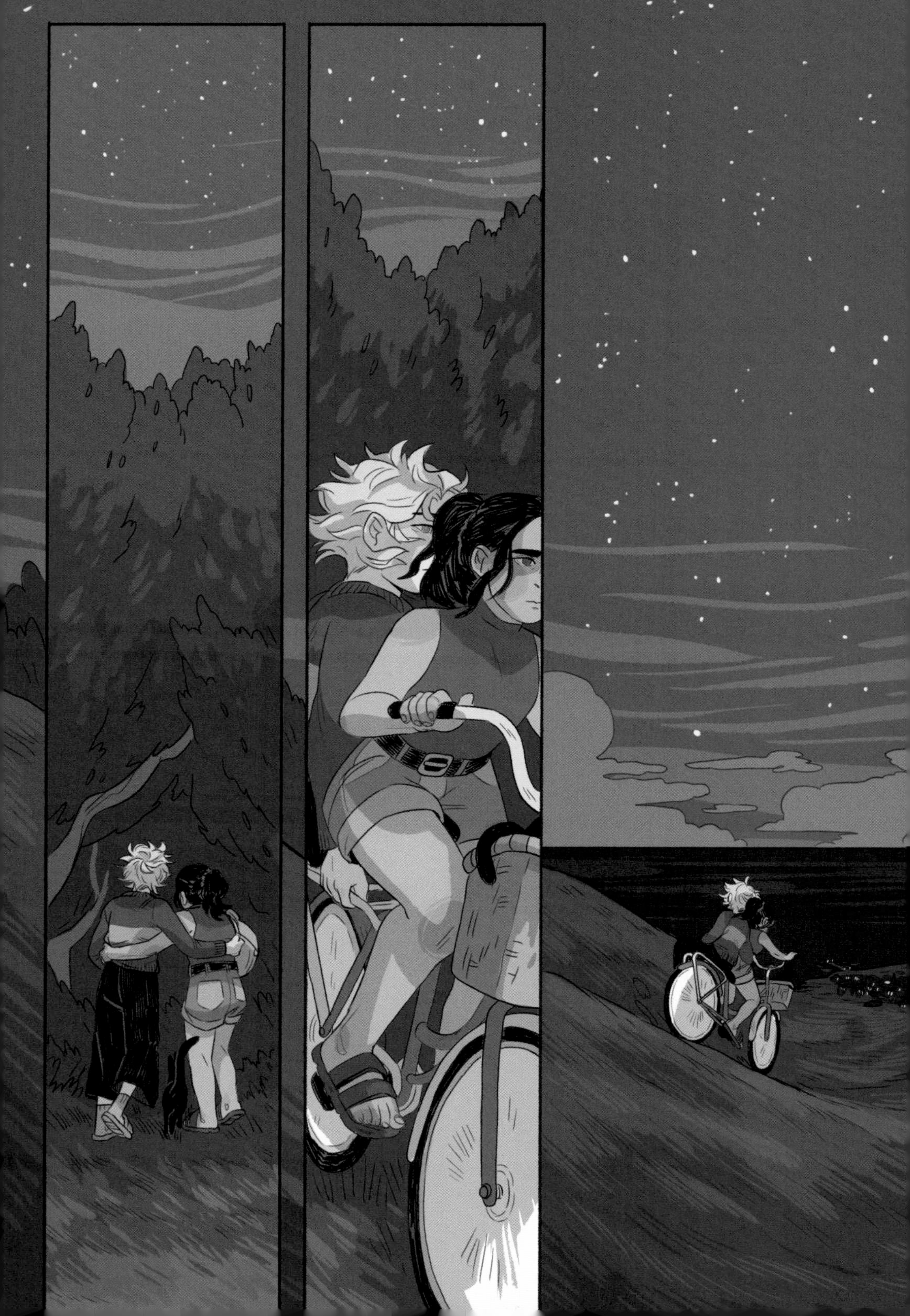

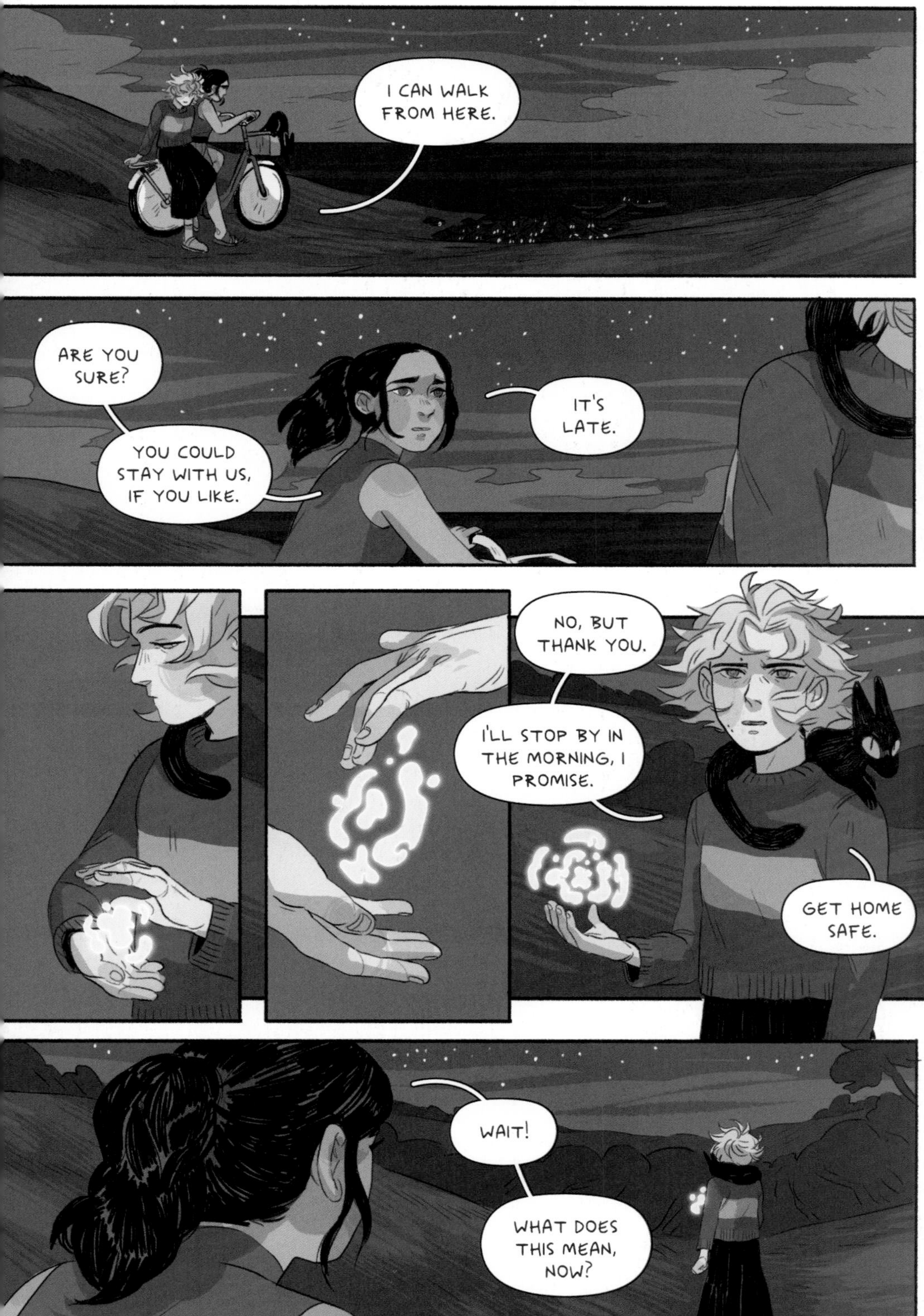
I CAN WALK FROM HERE.
ARE YOU SURE?
YOU COULD STAY WITH US, IF YOU LIKE.
IT'S LATE.
NO, BUT THANK YOU.
I'LL STOP BY IN THE MORNING, I PROMISE.
GET HOME SAFE.
WAIT!
WHAT DOES THIS MEAN, NOW?

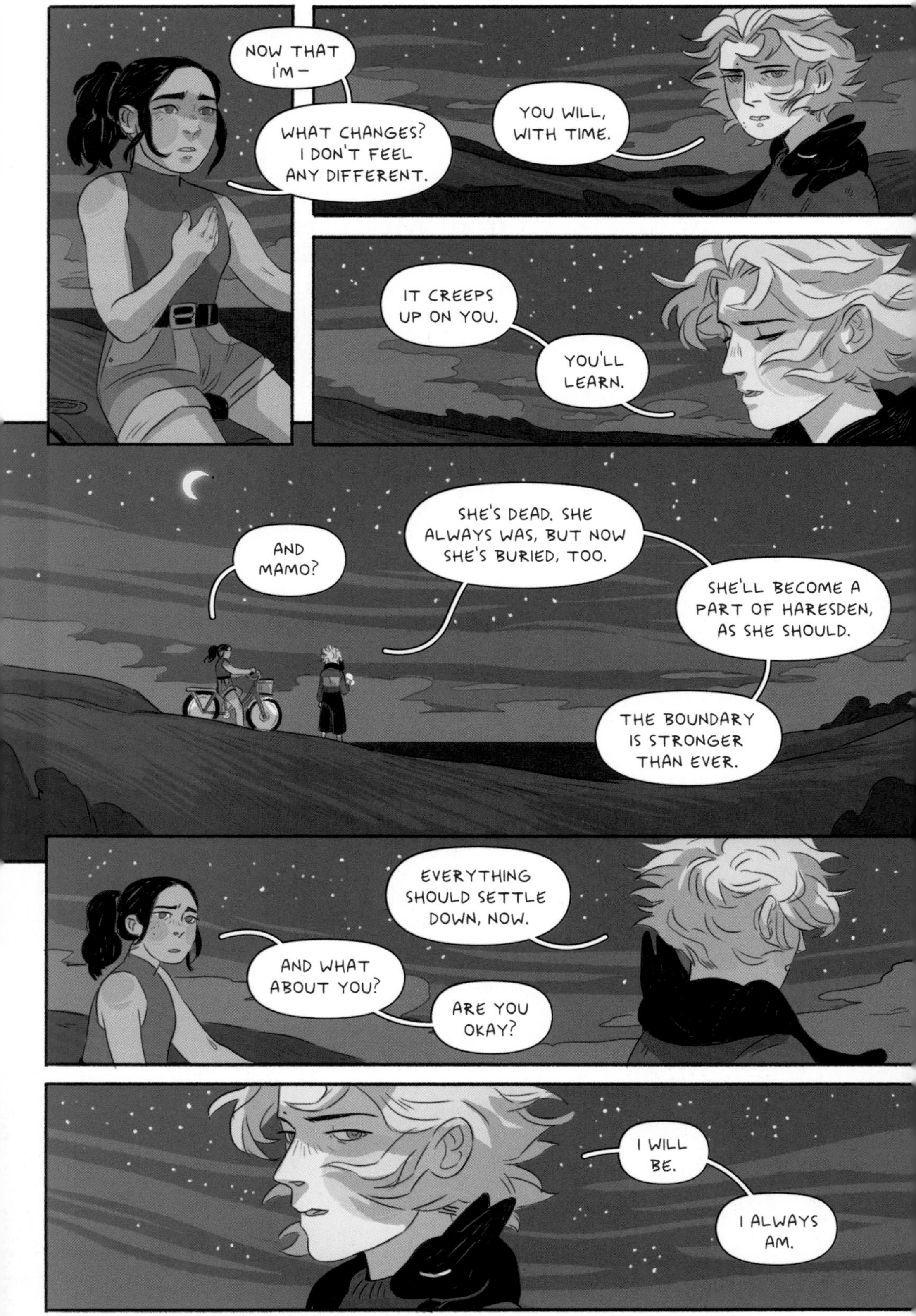
NOW THAT I'M—
WHAT CHANGES? I DON'T FEEL ANY DIFFERENT.
YOU WILL, WITH TIME.
IT CREEPS UP ON YOU.
YOU'LL LEARN.
AND MAMO?
SHE'S DEAD. SHE ALWAYS WAS, BUT NOW SHE'S BURIED, TOO.
SHE'LL BECOME A PART OF HARESDEN, AS SHE SHOULD.
THE BOUNDARY IS STRONGER THAN EVER.
EVERYTHING SHOULD SETTLE DOWN, NOW.
AND WHAT ABOUT YOU?
ARE YOU OKAY?
I WILL BE.
I ALWAYS AM.

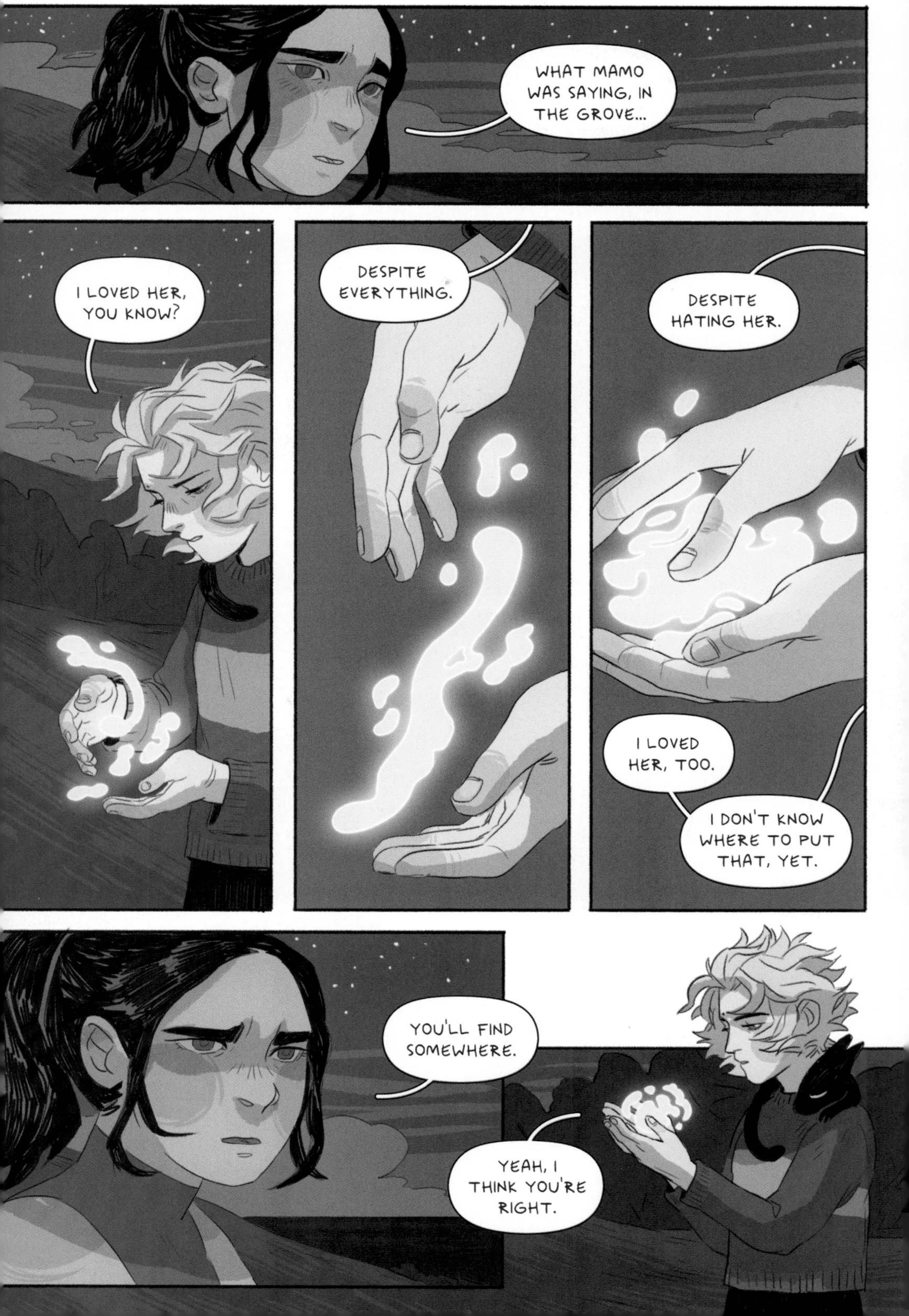
WHAT MAMO WAS SAYING, IN THE GROVE...
I LOVED HER, YOU KNOW?
DESPITE EVERYTHING.
DESPITE HATING HER.
I LOVED HER, TOO.
I DON'T KNOW WHERE TO PUT THAT, YET.
YOU'LL FIND SOMEWHERE.
YEAH, I THINK YOU'RE RIGHT.

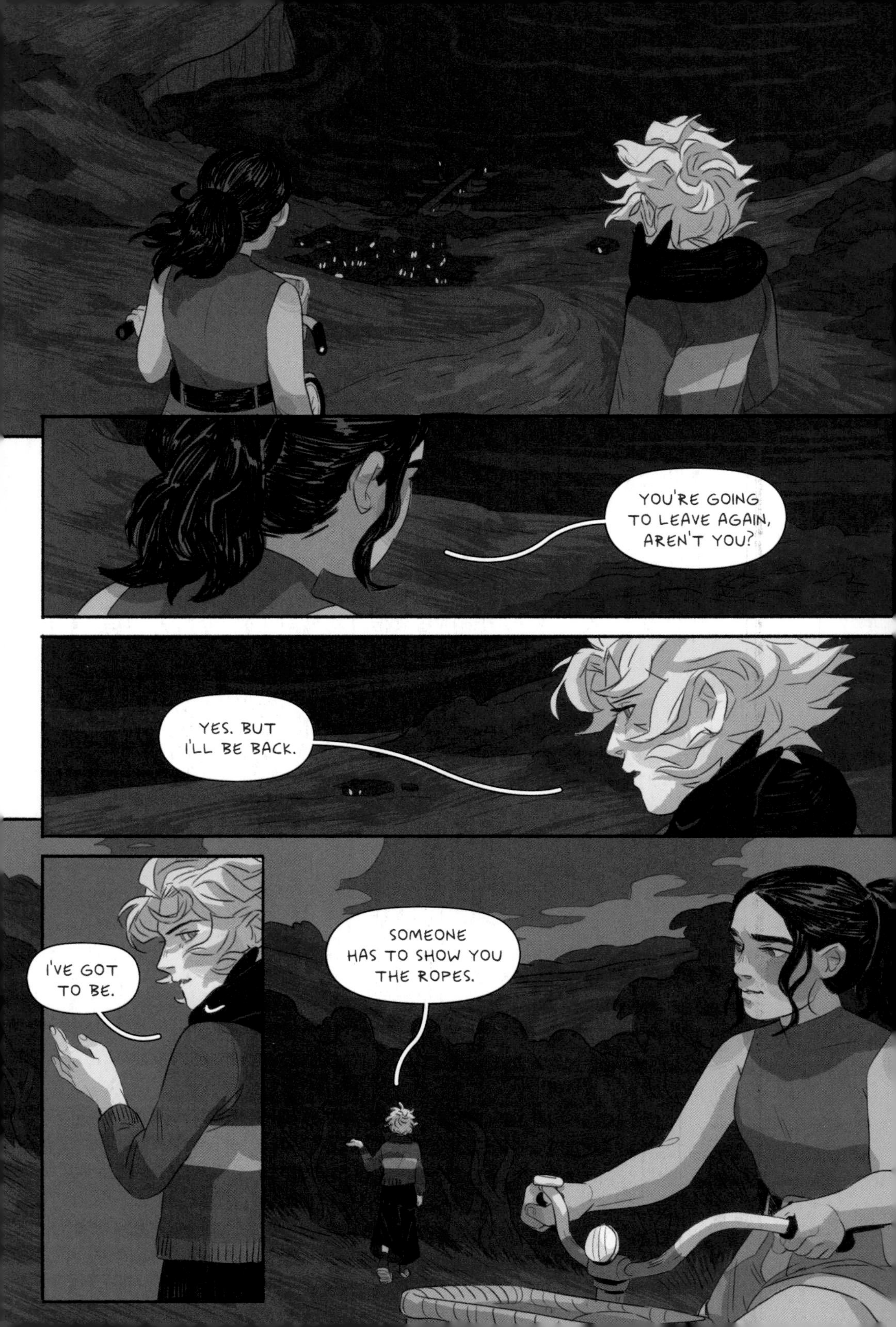
YOU'RE GOING TO LEAVE AGAIN, AREN'T YOU?
YES. BUT I'LL BE BACK.
I'VE GOT TO BE.
SOMEONE HAS TO SHOW YOU THE ROPES.

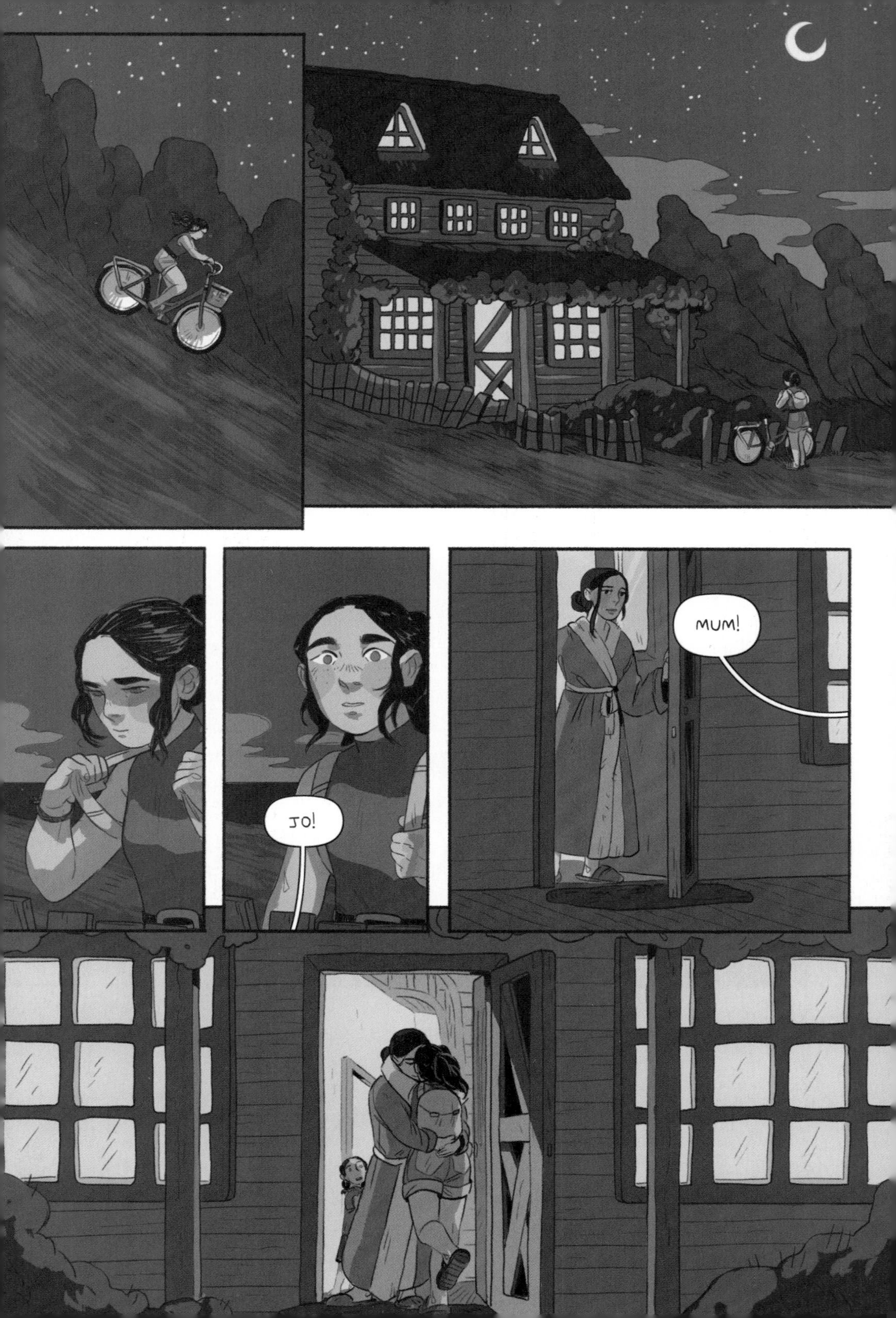
JO!
MUM!

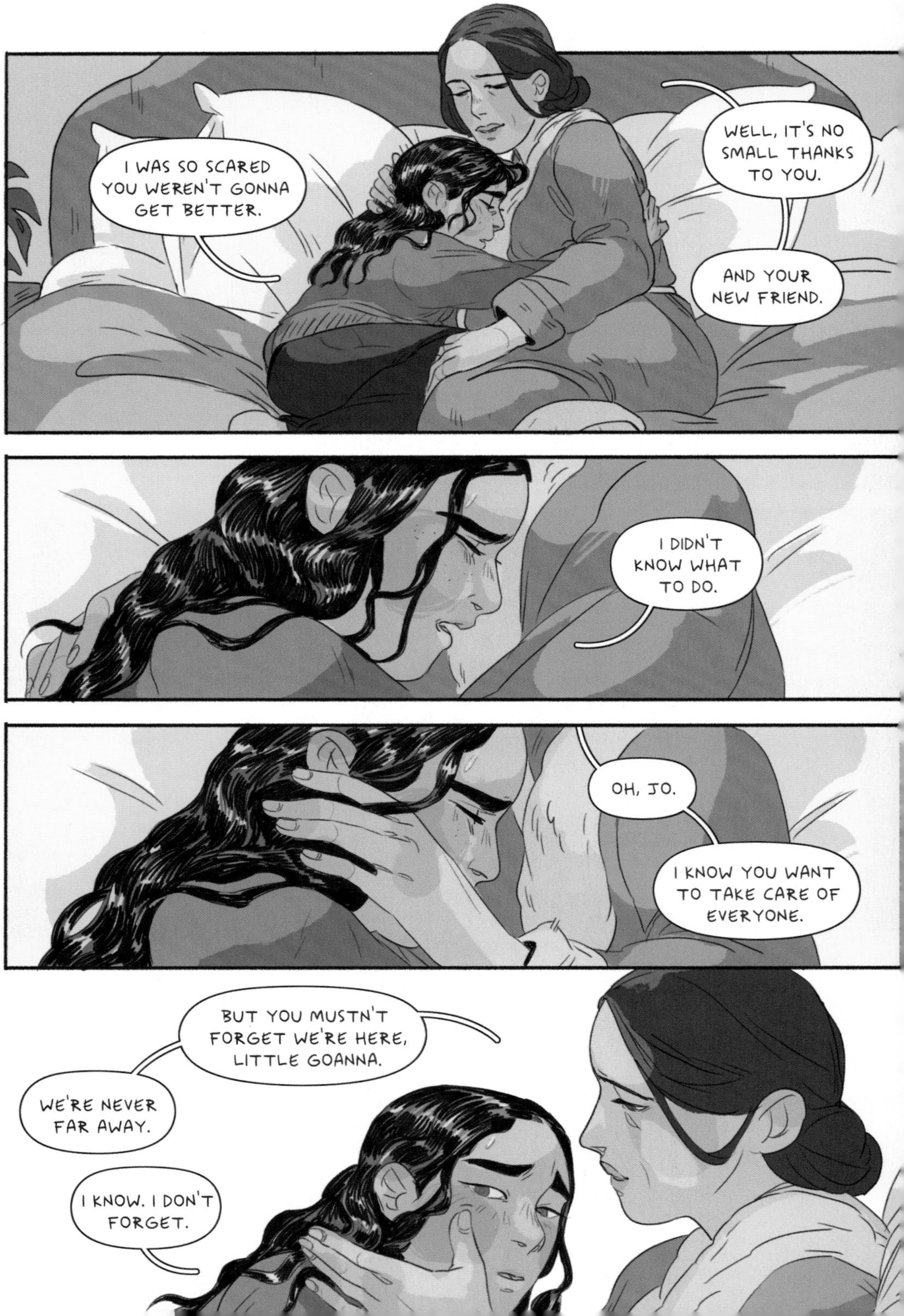
I WAS SO SCARED YOU WEREN'T GONNA GET BETTER.
WELL, IT'S NO SMALL THANKS TO YOU.
AND YOUR NEW FRIEND.
I DIDN'T KNOW WHAT TO DO.
OH, JO.
I KNOW YOU WANT TO TAKE CARE OF EVERYONE.
BUT YOU MUSTN'T FORGET WE'RE HERE, LITTLE GOANNA.
WE'RE NEVER FAR AWAY.
I KNOW. I DON'T FORGET.

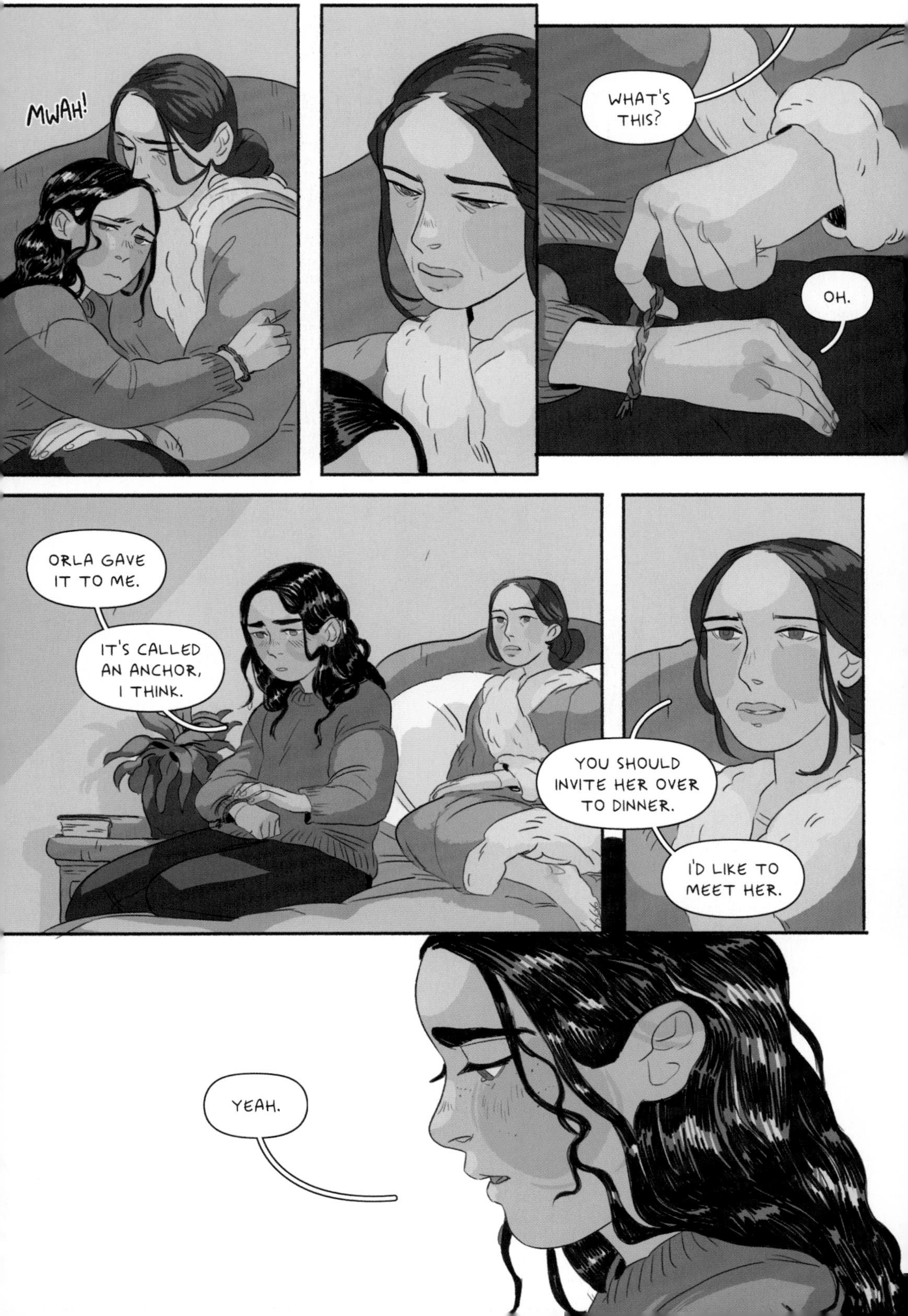
MWAH!
WHAT'S THIS?
OH.
ORLA GAVE IT TO ME.
IT'S CALLED AN ANCHOR, I THINK.
YOU SHOULD INVITE HER OVER TO DINNER.
I'D LIKE TO MEET HER.
YEAH.

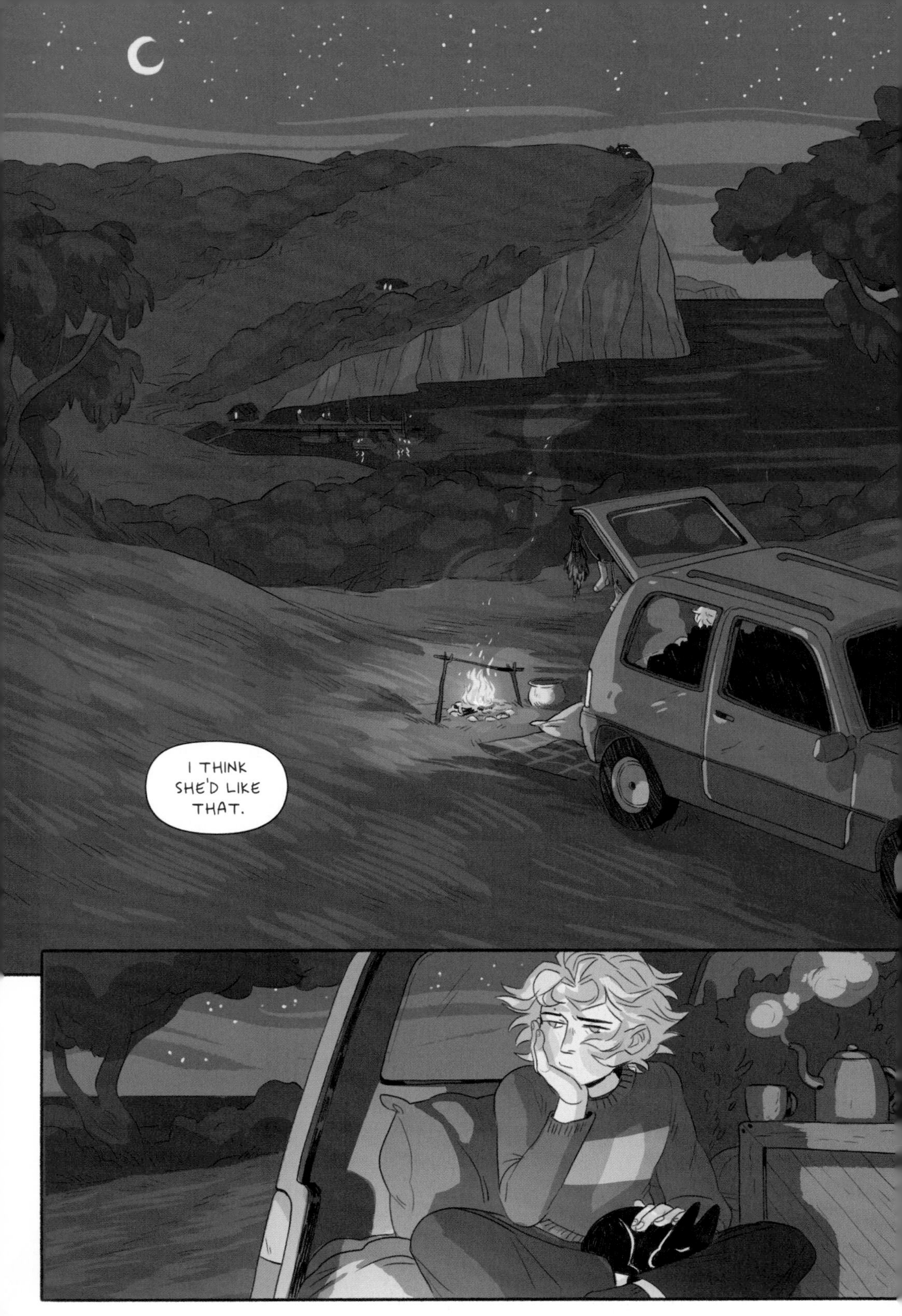
I THINK SHE'D LIKE THAT.

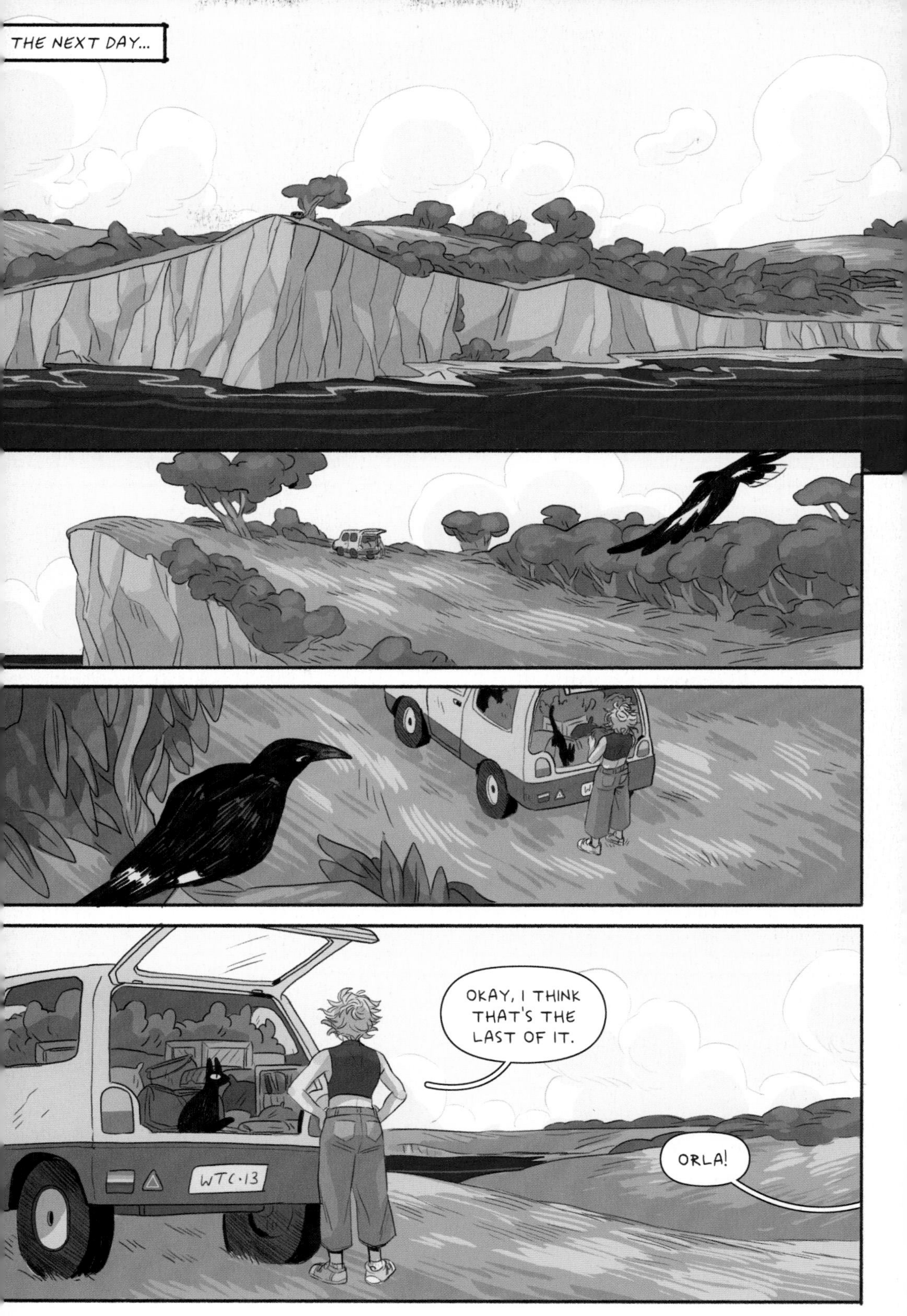
THE NEXT DAY...
OKAY, I THINK THAT'S THE LAST OF IT.
ORLA!
WTC·13

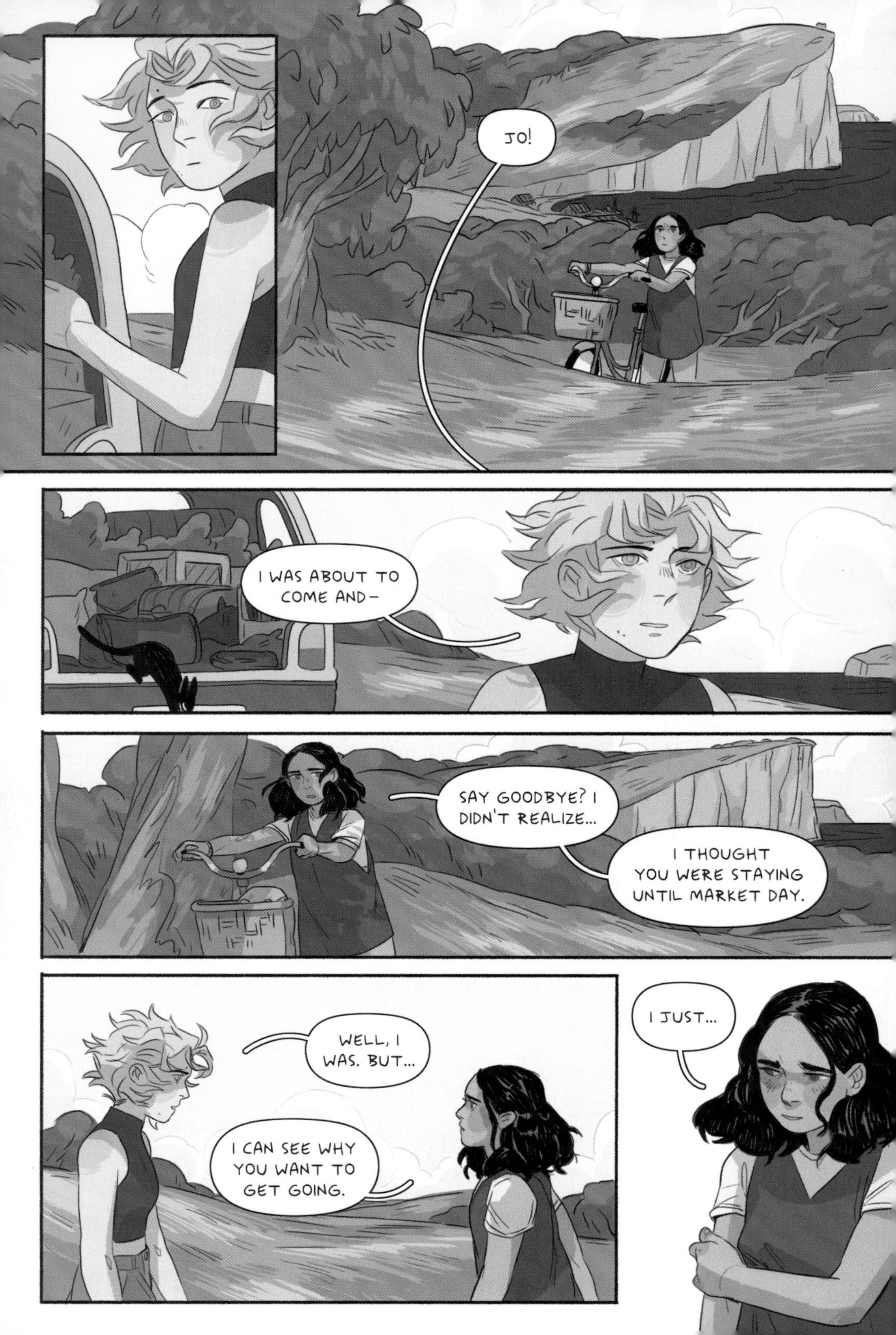
JO!
I WAS ABOUT TO COME AND—
SAY GOODBYE? I DIDN'T REALIZE...
I THOUGHT YOU WERE STAYING UNTIL MARKET DAY.
WELL, I WAS. BUT...
I CAN SEE WHY YOU WANT TO GET GOING.
I JUST...

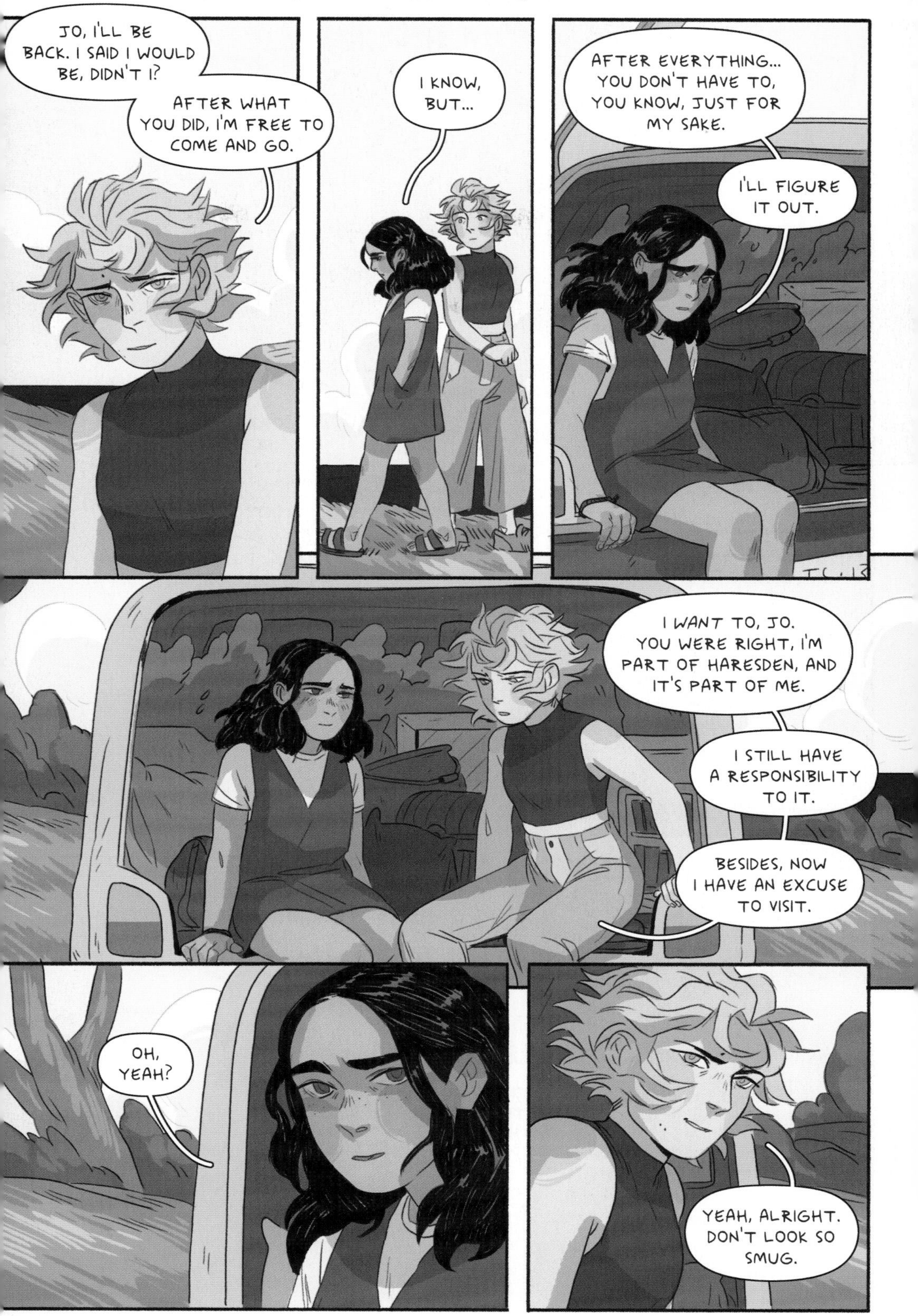
JO, I'LL BE BACK. I SAID I WOULD BE, DIDN'T I?
AFTER WHAT YOU DID, I'M FREE TO COME AND GO.
I KNOW, BUT...
AFTER EVERYTHING... YOU DON'T HAVE TO, YOU KNOW, JUST FOR MY SAKE.
I'LL FIGURE IT OUT.
I WANT TO, JO. YOU WERE RIGHT, I'M PART OF HARESDEN, AND IT'S PART OF ME.
I STILL HAVE A RESPONSIBILITY TO IT.
BESIDES, NOW I HAVE AN EXCUSE TO VISIT.
OH, YEAH?
YEAH, ALRIGHT. DON'T LOOK SO SMUG.

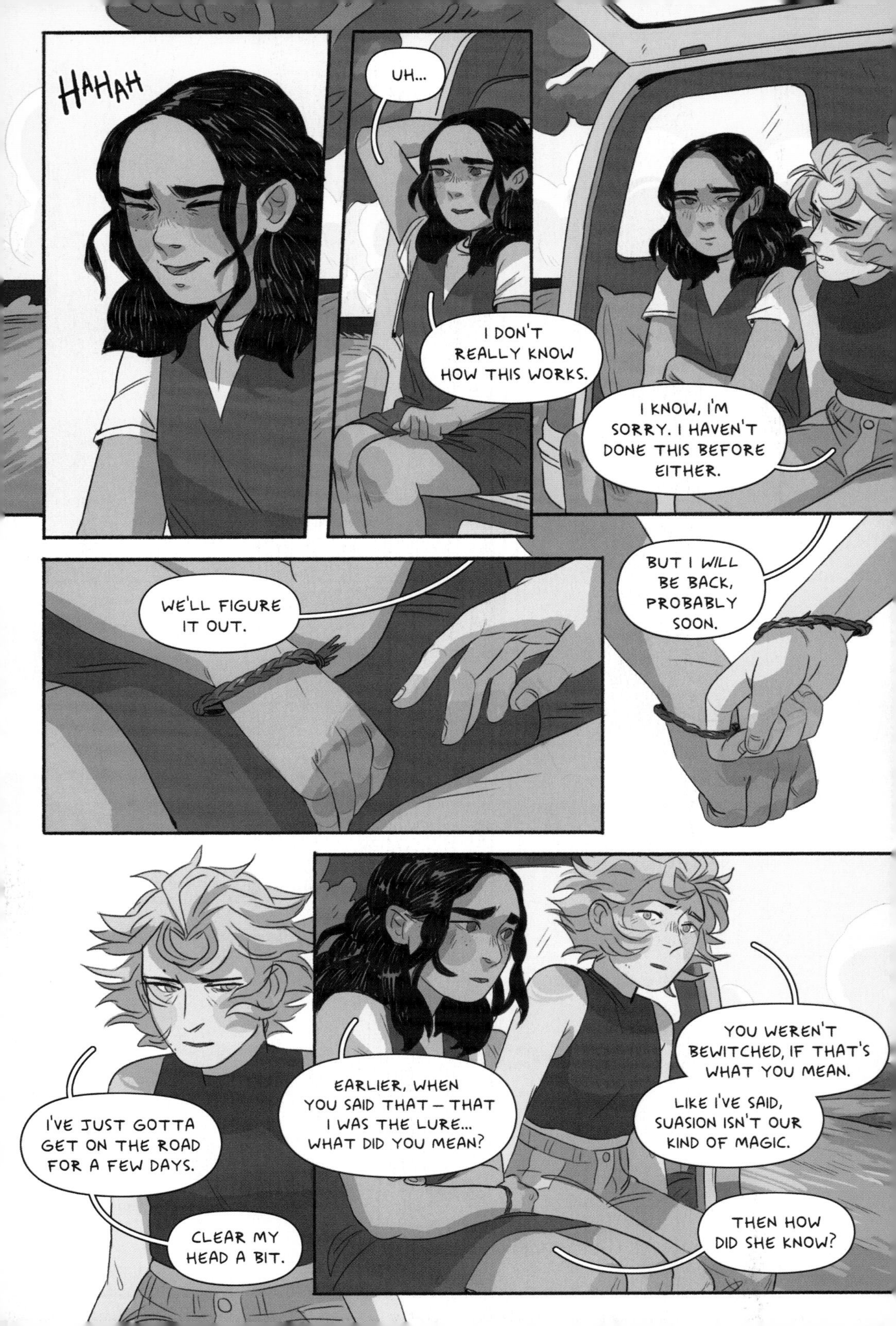
HAHAH
UH...
I DON'T REALLY KNOW HOW THIS WORKS.
I KNOW, I'M SORRY. I HAVEN'T DONE THIS BEFORE EITHER.
WE'LL FIGURE IT OUT.
BUT I *WILL* BE BACK, PROBABLY SOON.
I'VE JUST GOTTA GET ON THE ROAD FOR A FEW DAYS.
CLEAR MY HEAD A BIT.
EARLIER, WHEN YOU SAID THAT — THAT I WAS THE LURE... WHAT DID YOU MEAN?
YOU WEREN'T BEWITCHED, IF THAT'S WHAT YOU MEAN.
LIKE I'VE SAID, SUASION ISN'T OUR KIND OF MAGIC.
THEN HOW DID SHE KNOW?

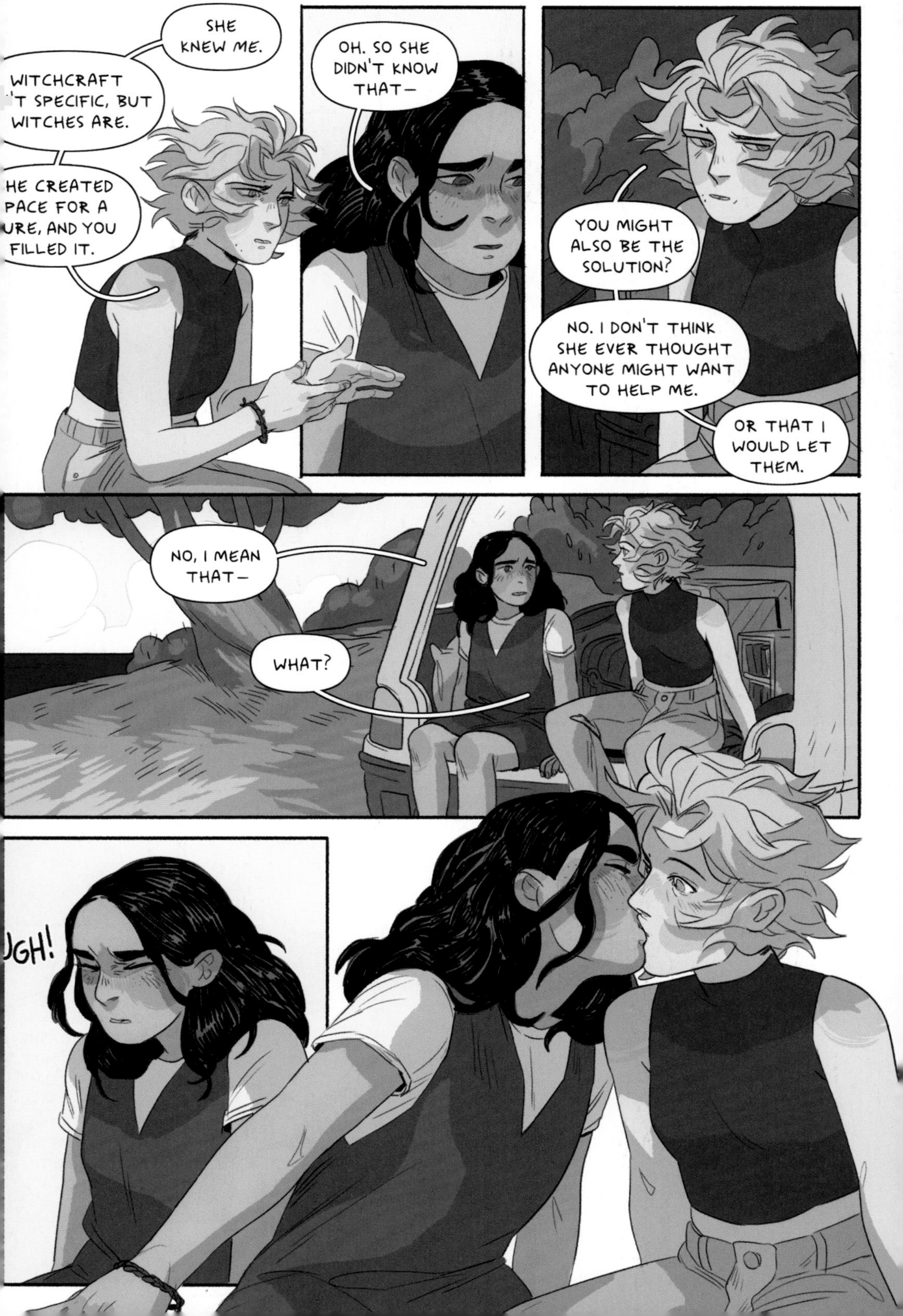

SHE KNEW ME.
WITCHCRAFT 'T SPECIFIC, BUT WITCHES ARE.
HE CREATED PACE FOR A URE, AND YOU FILLED IT.
OH. SO SHE DIDN'T KNOW THAT—
YOU MIGHT ALSO BE THE SOLUTION?
NO. I DON'T THINK SHE EVER THOUGHT ANYONE MIGHT WANT TO HELP ME.
OR THAT I WOULD LET THEM.
NO, I MEAN THAT—
WHAT?
GH!

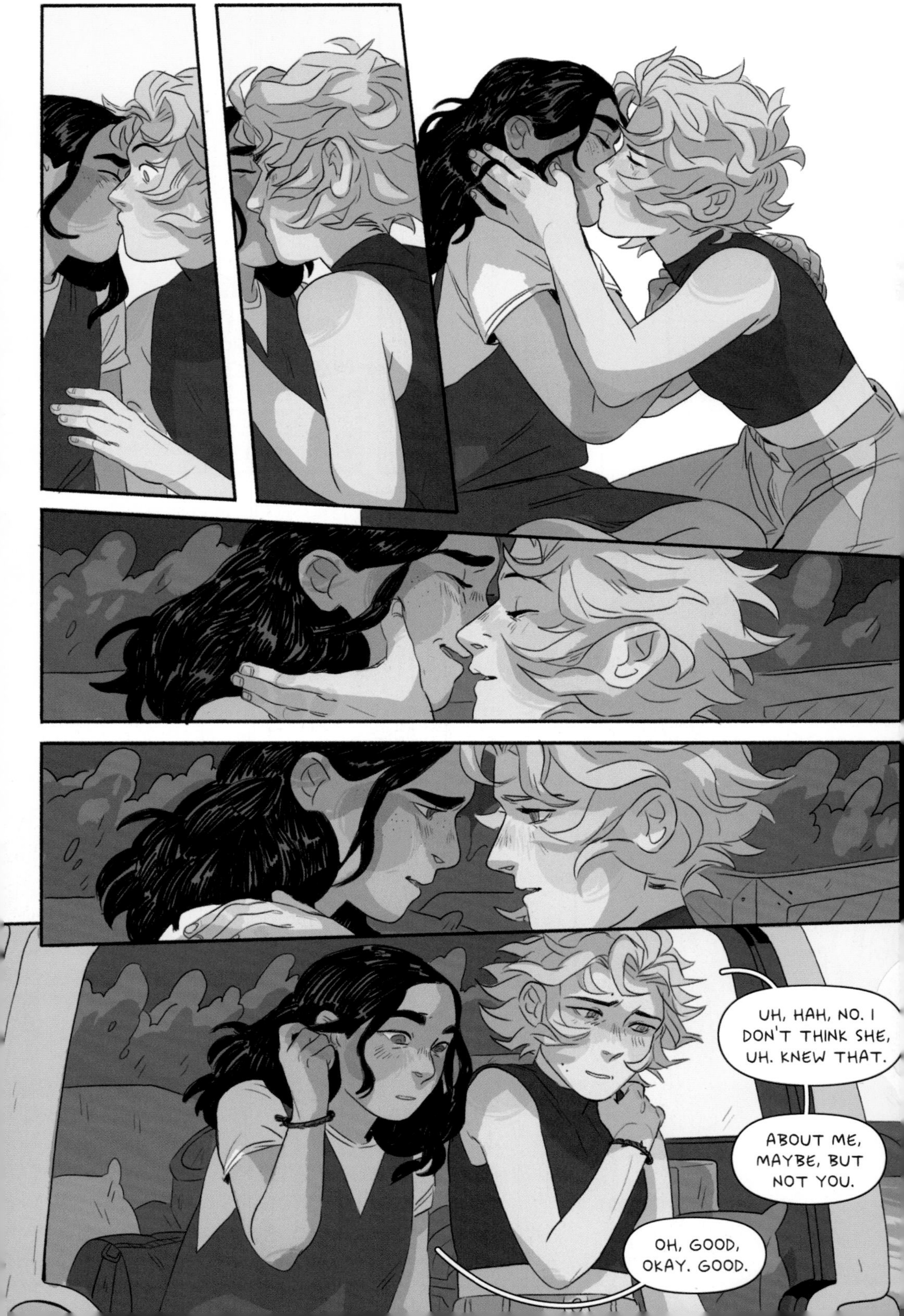
UH, HAH, NO. I DON'T THINK SHE, UH. KNEW THAT.
ABOUT ME, MAYBE, BUT NOT YOU.
OH, GOOD, OKAY. GOOD.

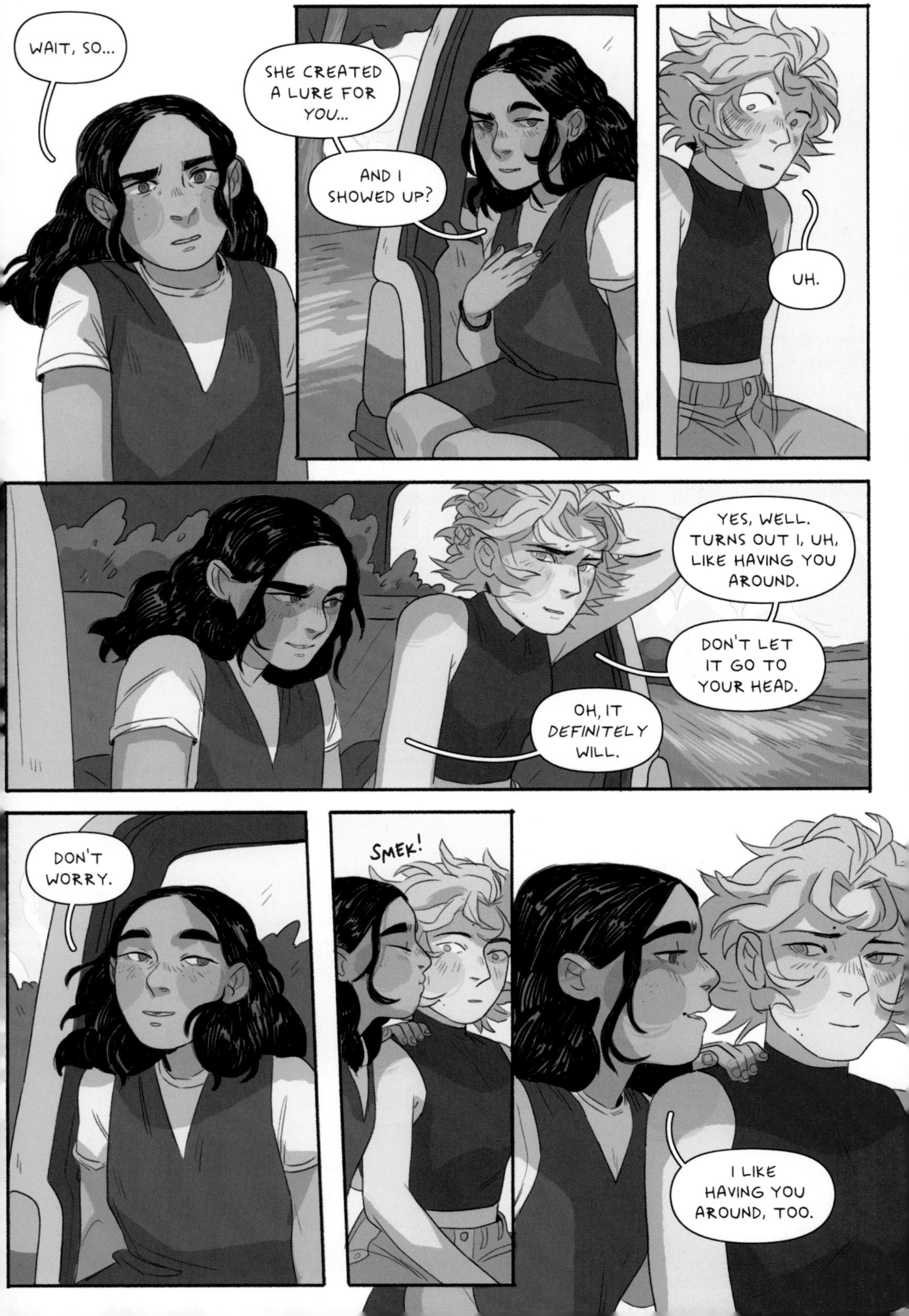
WAIT, SO...
SHE CREATED A LURE FOR YOU...
AND I SHOWED UP?
UH.
YES, WELL. TURNS OUT I, UH, LIKE HAVING YOU AROUND.
DON'T LET IT GO TO YOUR HEAD.
OH, IT DEFINITELY WILL.
DON'T WORRY.
SMEK!
I LIKE HAVING YOU AROUND, TOO.

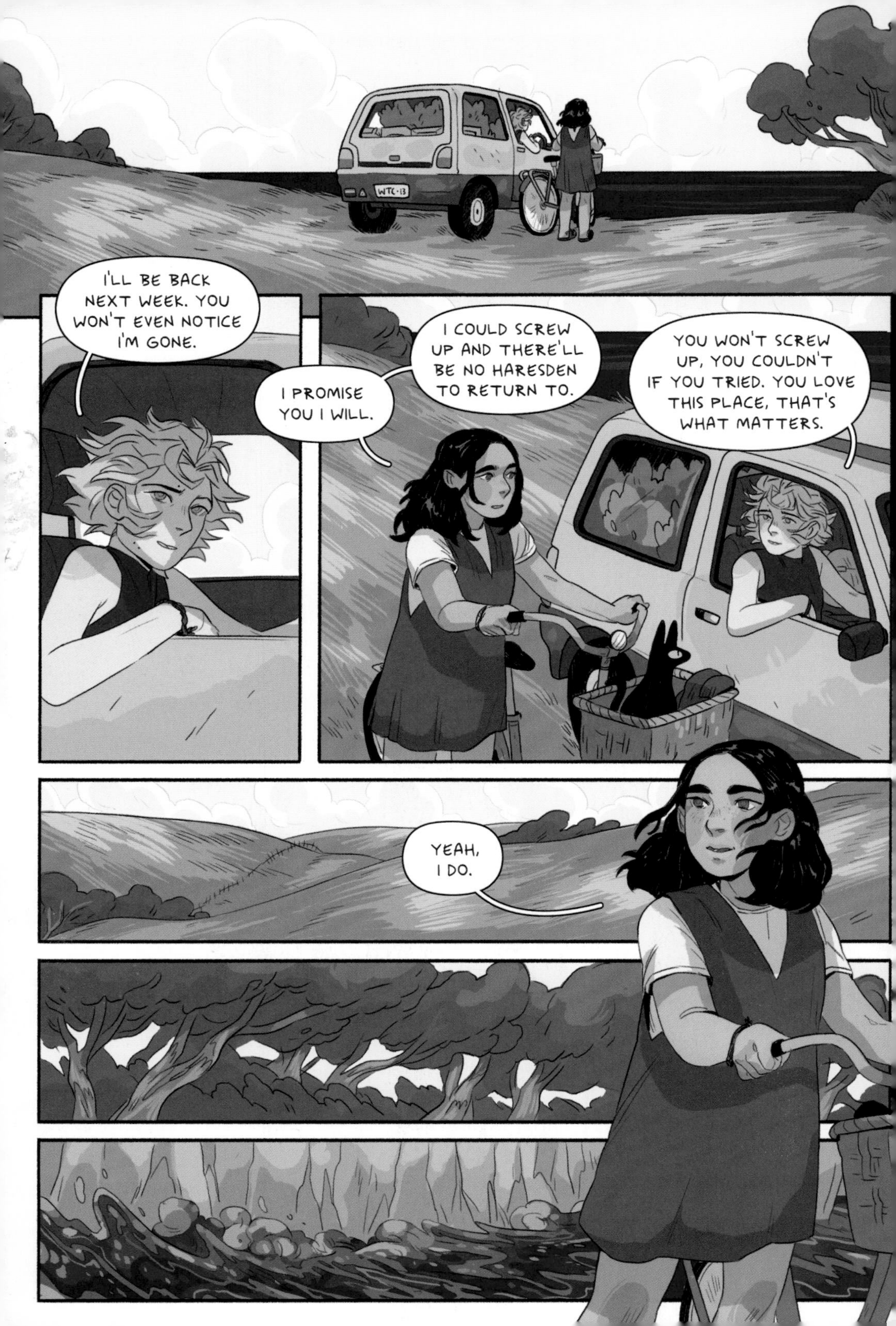
I'LL BE BACK NEXT WEEK. YOU WON'T EVEN NOTICE I'M GONE.
I PROMISE YOU I WILL.
I COULD SCREW UP AND THERE'LL BE NO HARESDEN TO RETURN TO.
YOU WON'T SCREW UP, YOU COULDN'T IF YOU TRIED. YOU LOVE THIS PLACE, THAT'S WHAT MATTERS.
YEAH, I DO.

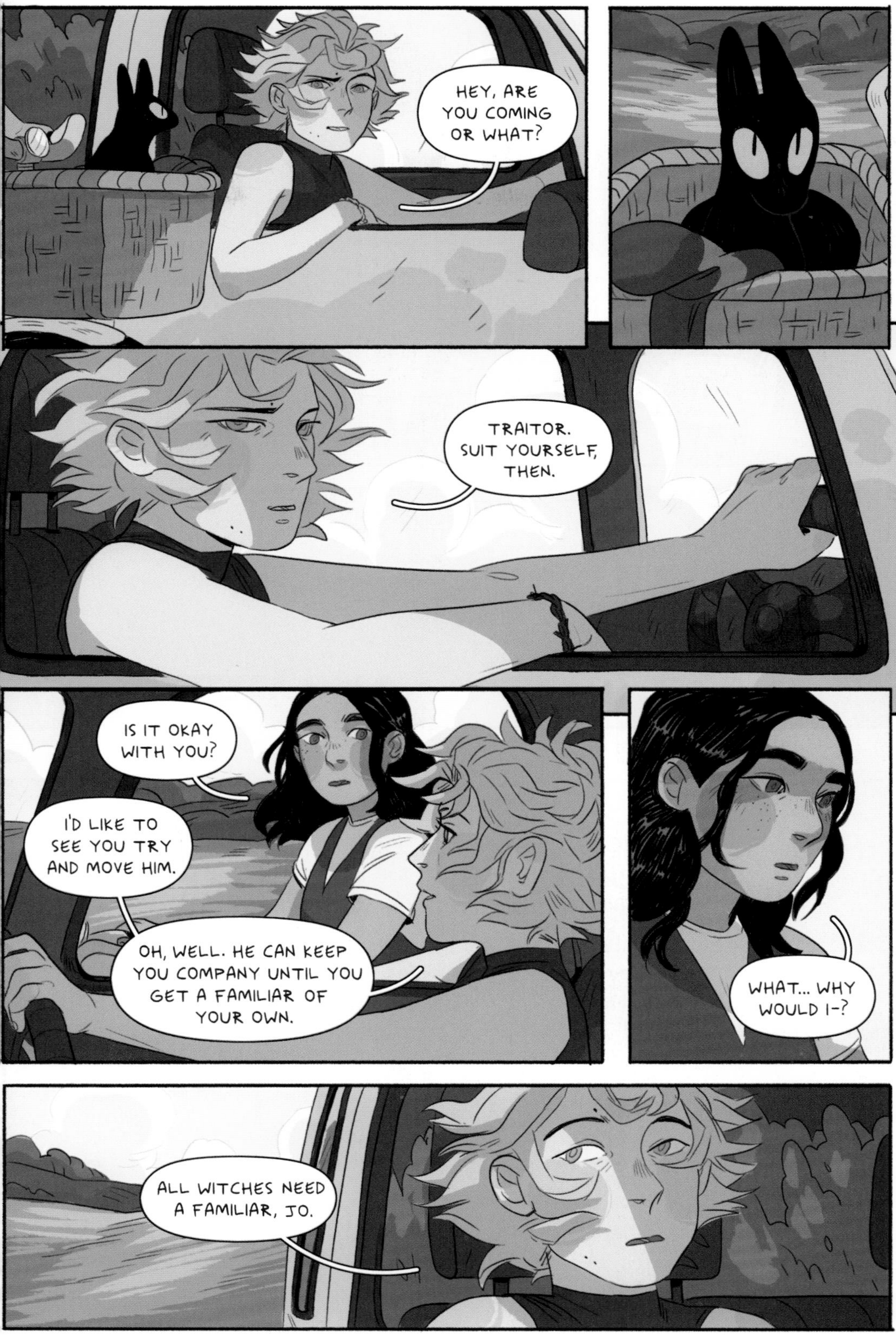
HEY, ARE YOU COMING OR WHAT?
TRAITOR. SUIT YOURSELF, THEN.
IS IT OKAY WITH YOU?
I'D LIKE TO SEE YOU TRY AND MOVE HIM.
OH, WELL. HE CAN KEEP YOU COMPANY UNTIL YOU GET A FAMILIAR OF YOUR OWN.
WHAT... WHY WOULD I-?
ALL WITCHES NEED A FAMILIAR, JO.

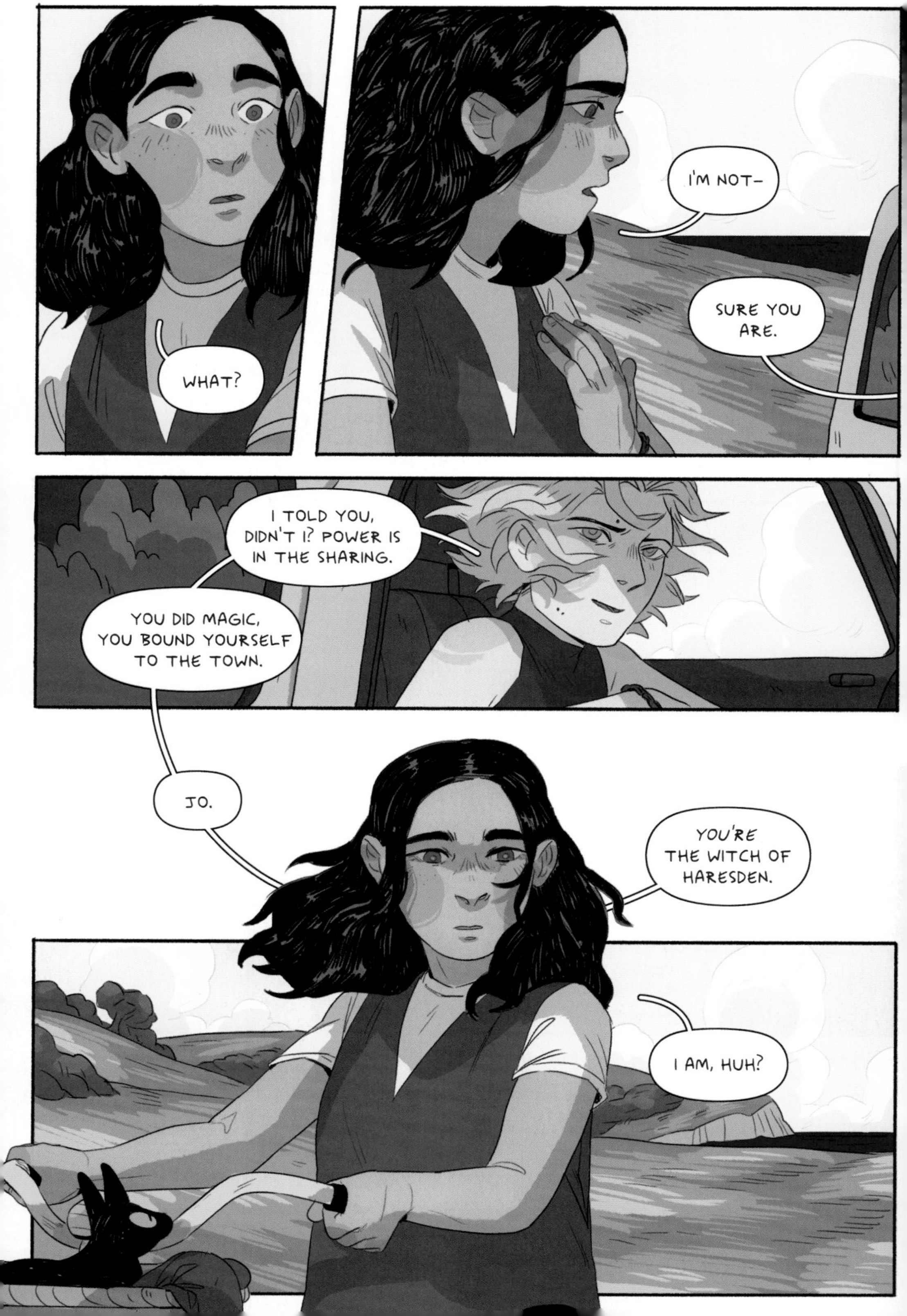
WHAT?
I'M NOT-
SURE YOU ARE.
I TOLD YOU, DIDN'T I? POWER IS IN THE SHARING.
YOU DID MAGIC, YOU BOUND YOURSELF TO THE TOWN.
JO.
YOU'RE THE WITCH OF HARESDEN.
I AM, HUH?

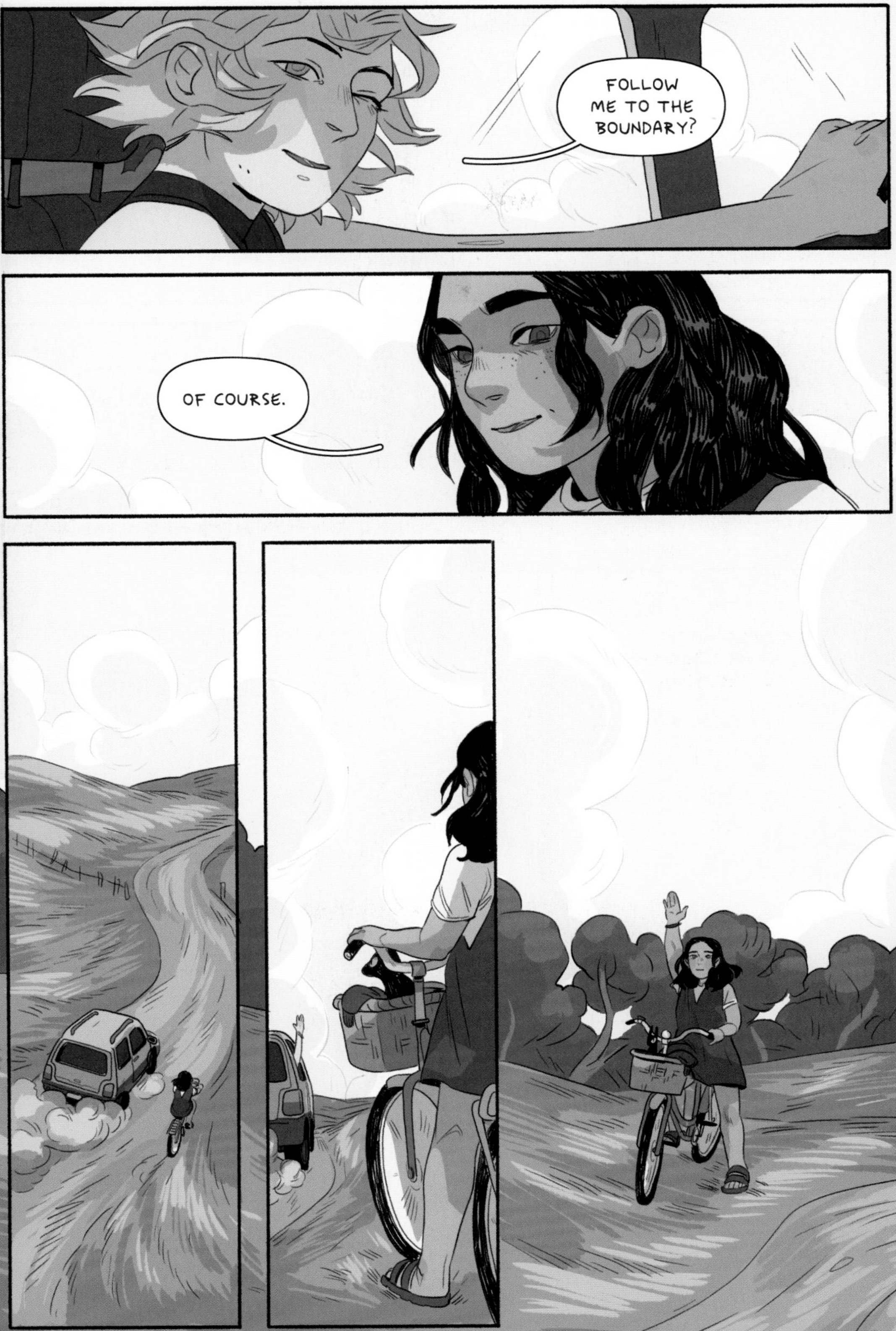
FOLLOW ME TO THE BOUNDARY?
OF COURSE.

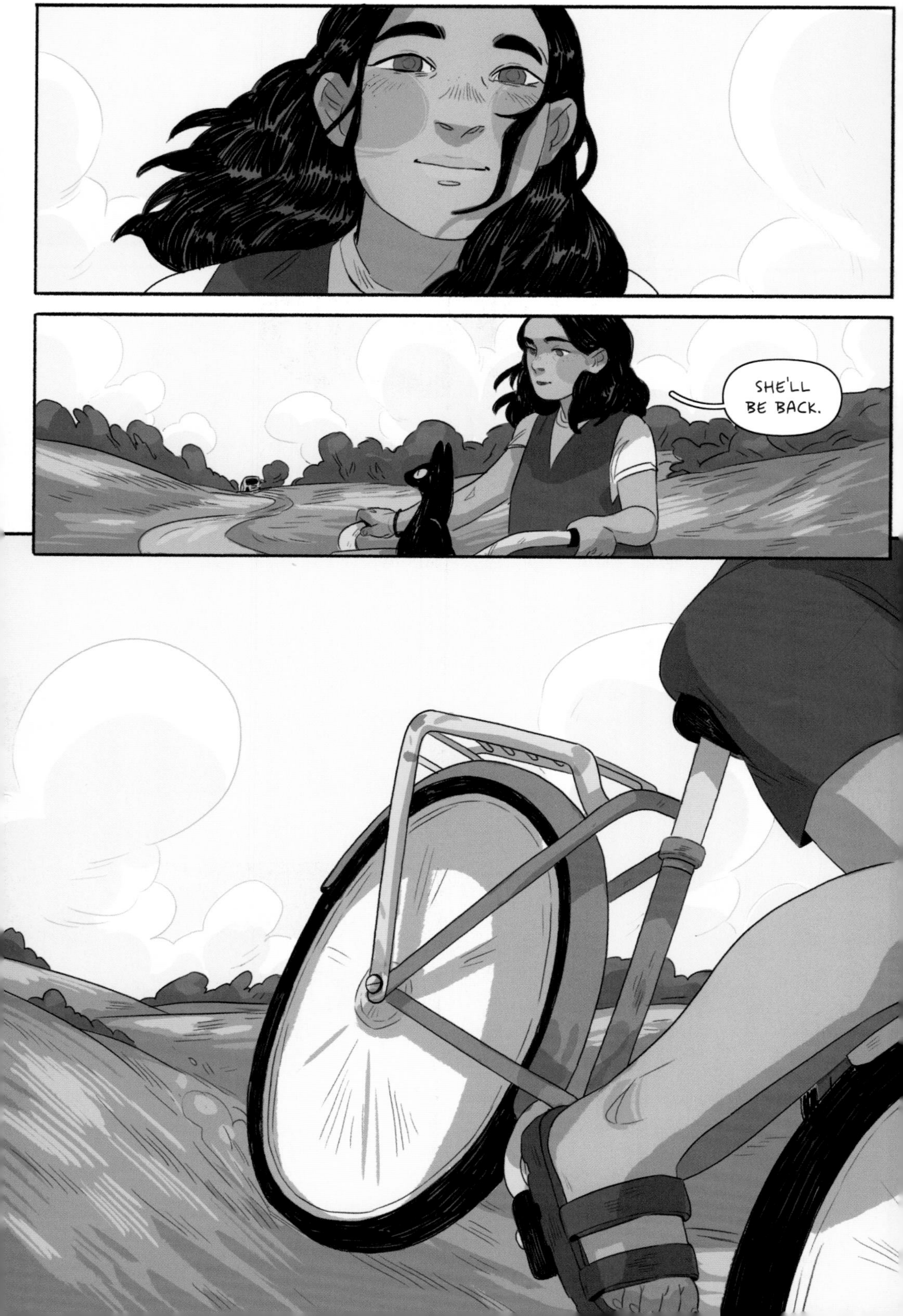
SHE'LL BE BACK.

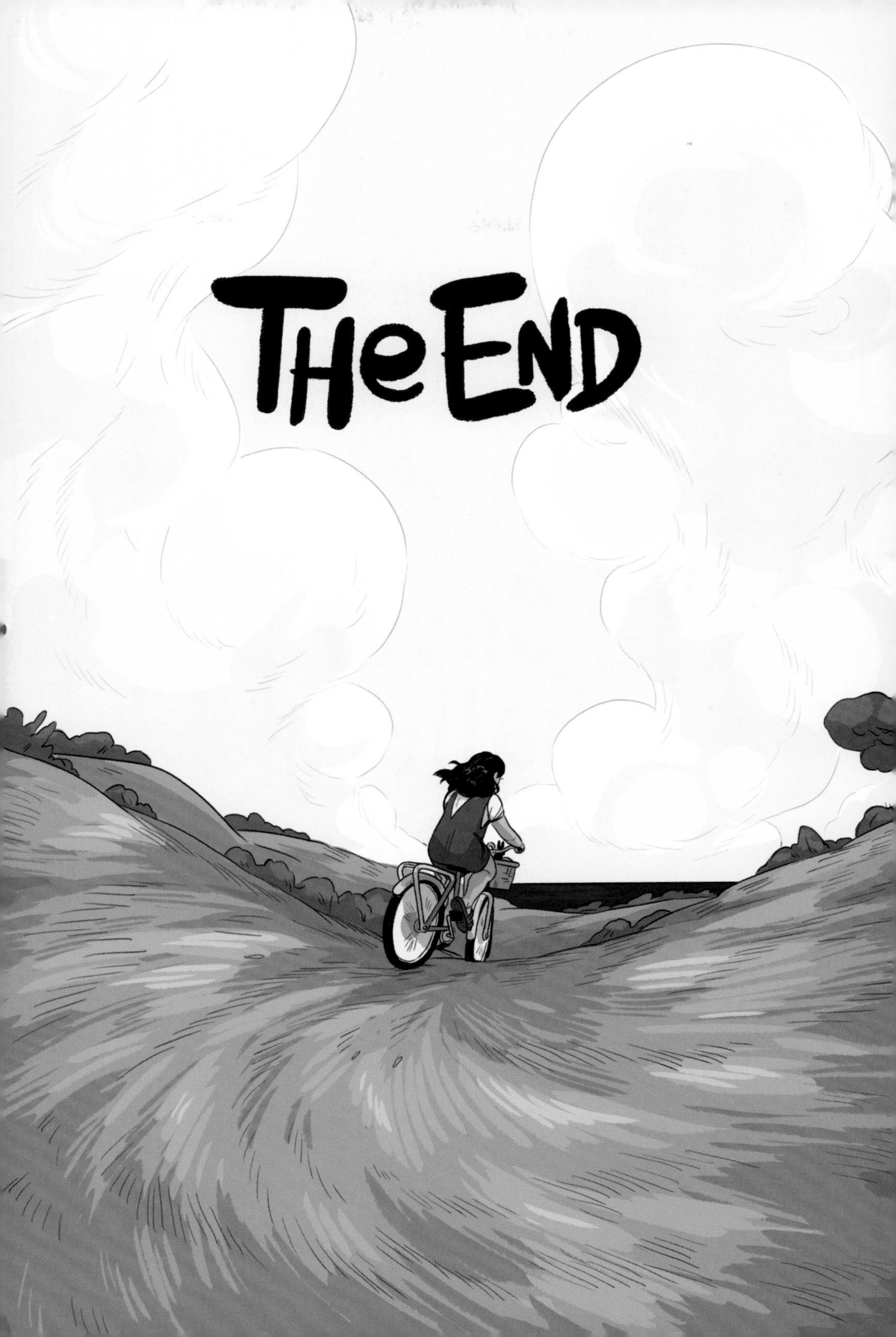
THE END

Cover
Gallery

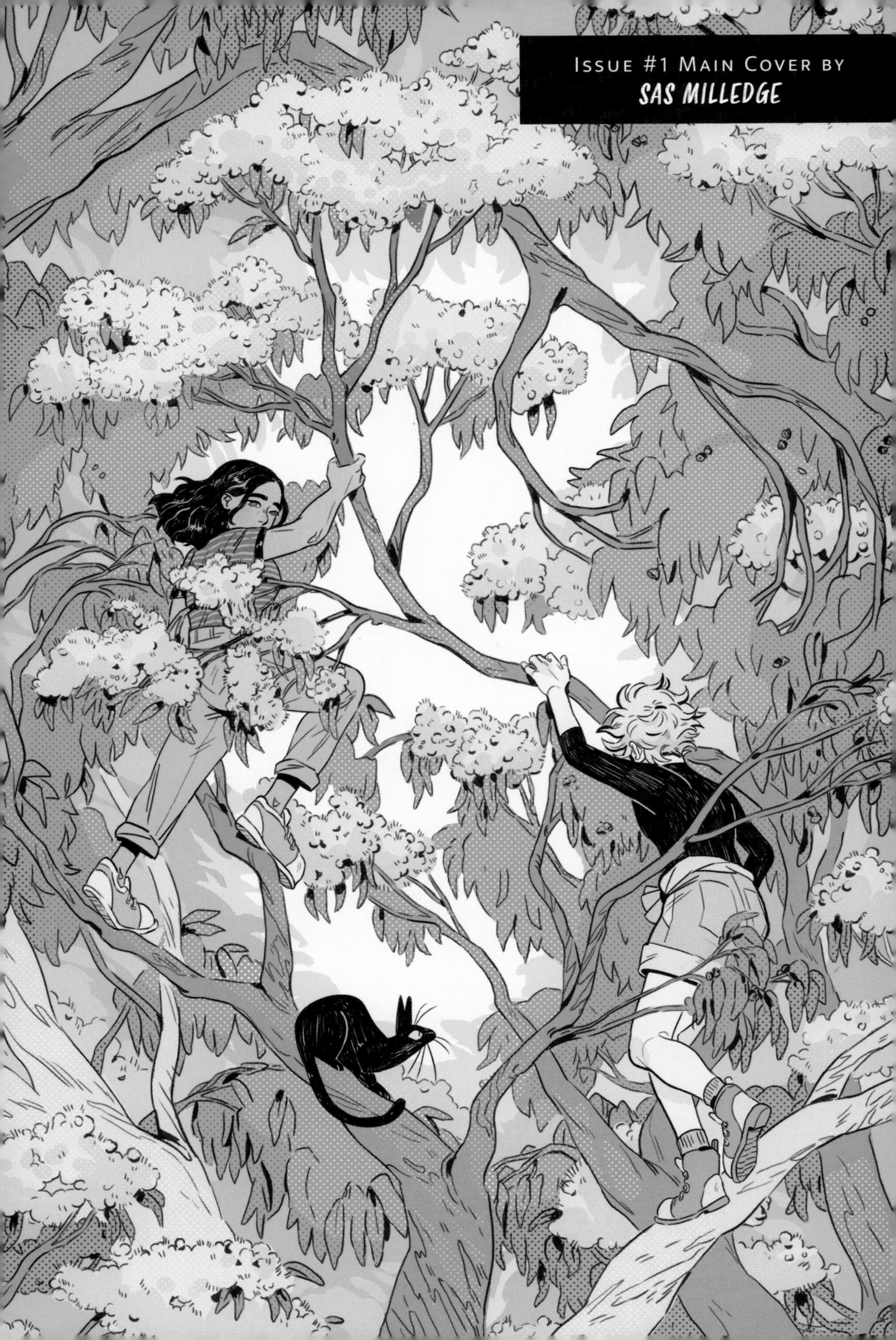

Issue #1 Main Cover by
SAS MILLEDGE

Issue #1 Variant Cover by

Trung Lê Nguyễn

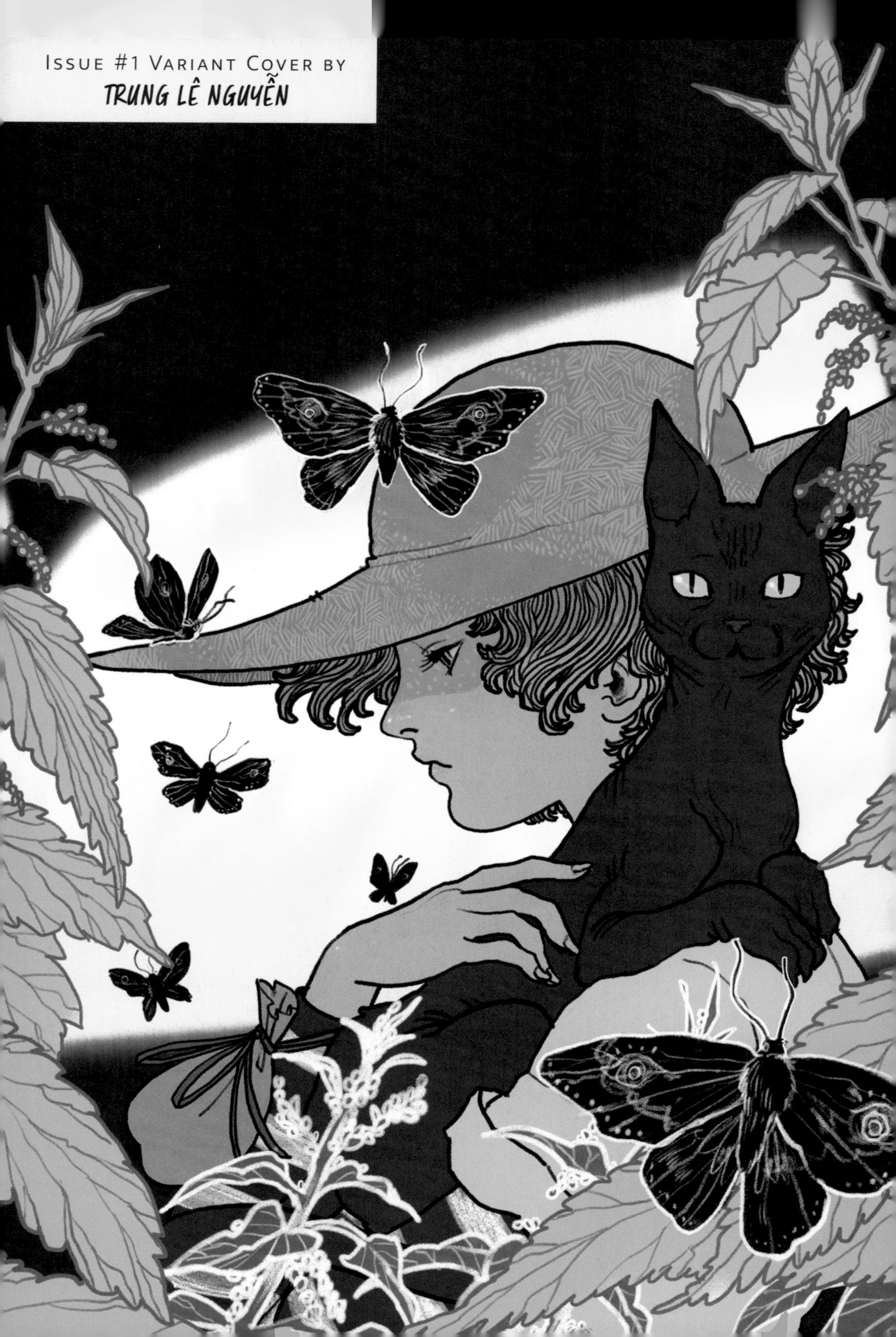

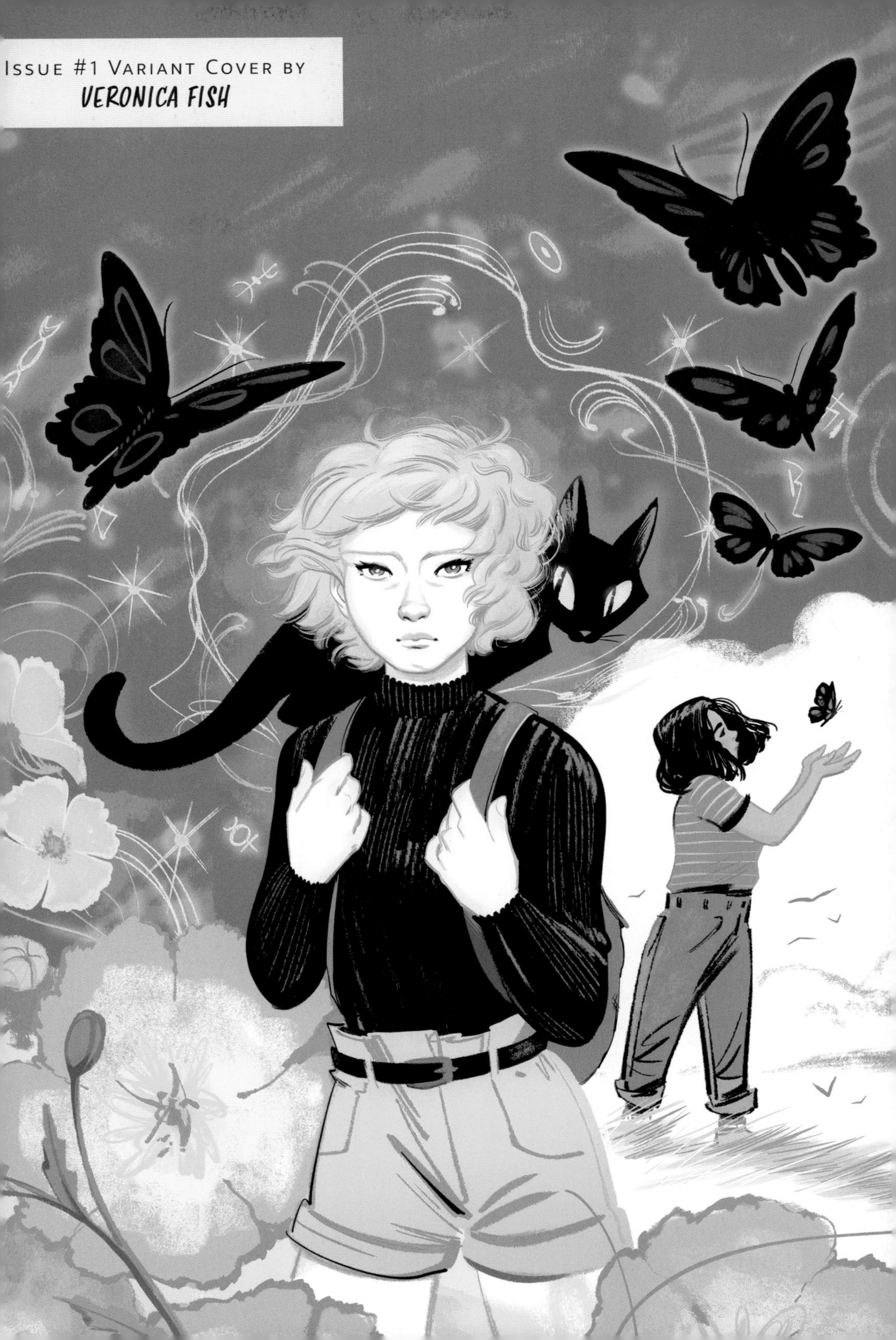

Issue #1 Variant Cover by
VERONICA FISH

Issue #2 Main Cover by
SAS MILLEDGE

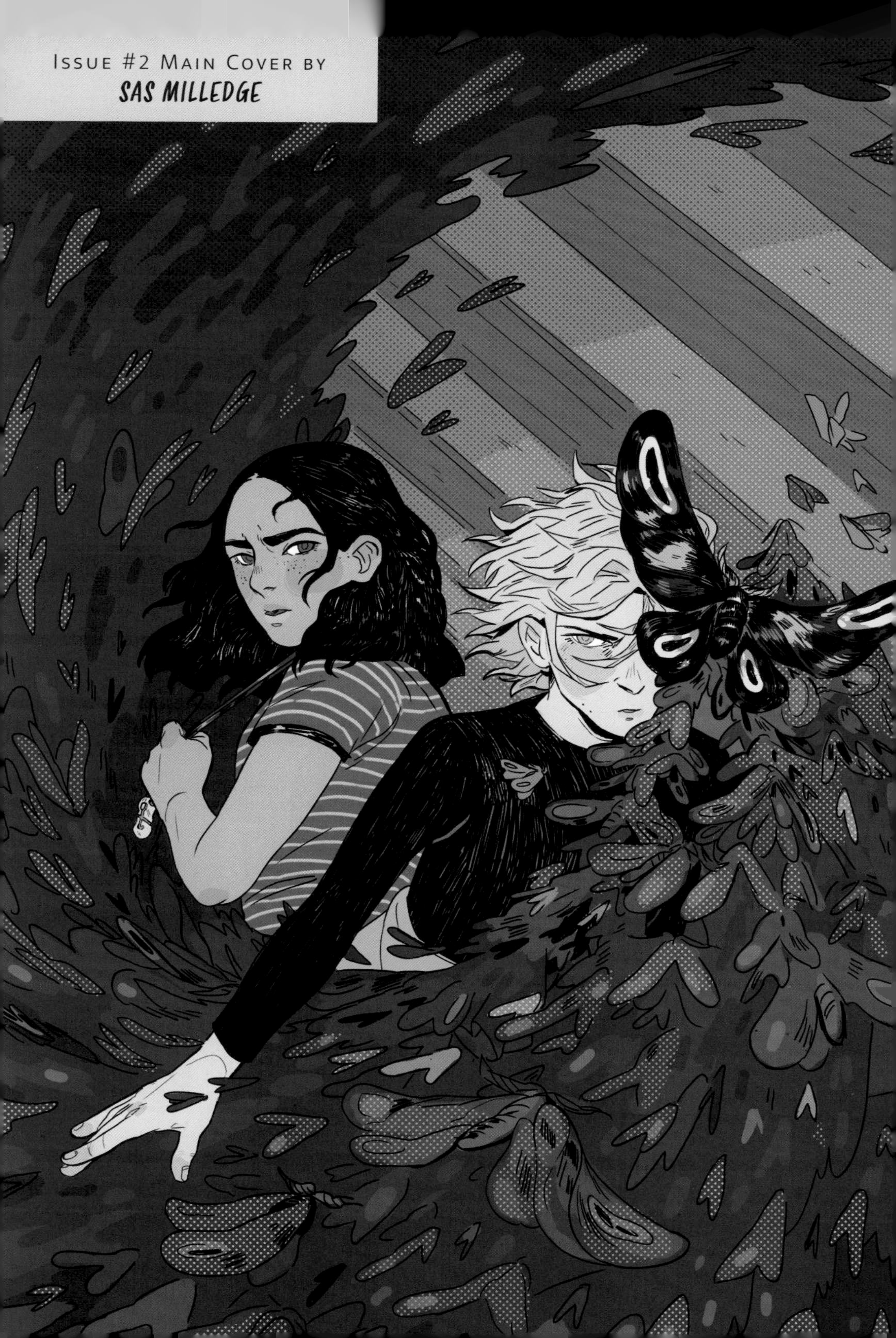

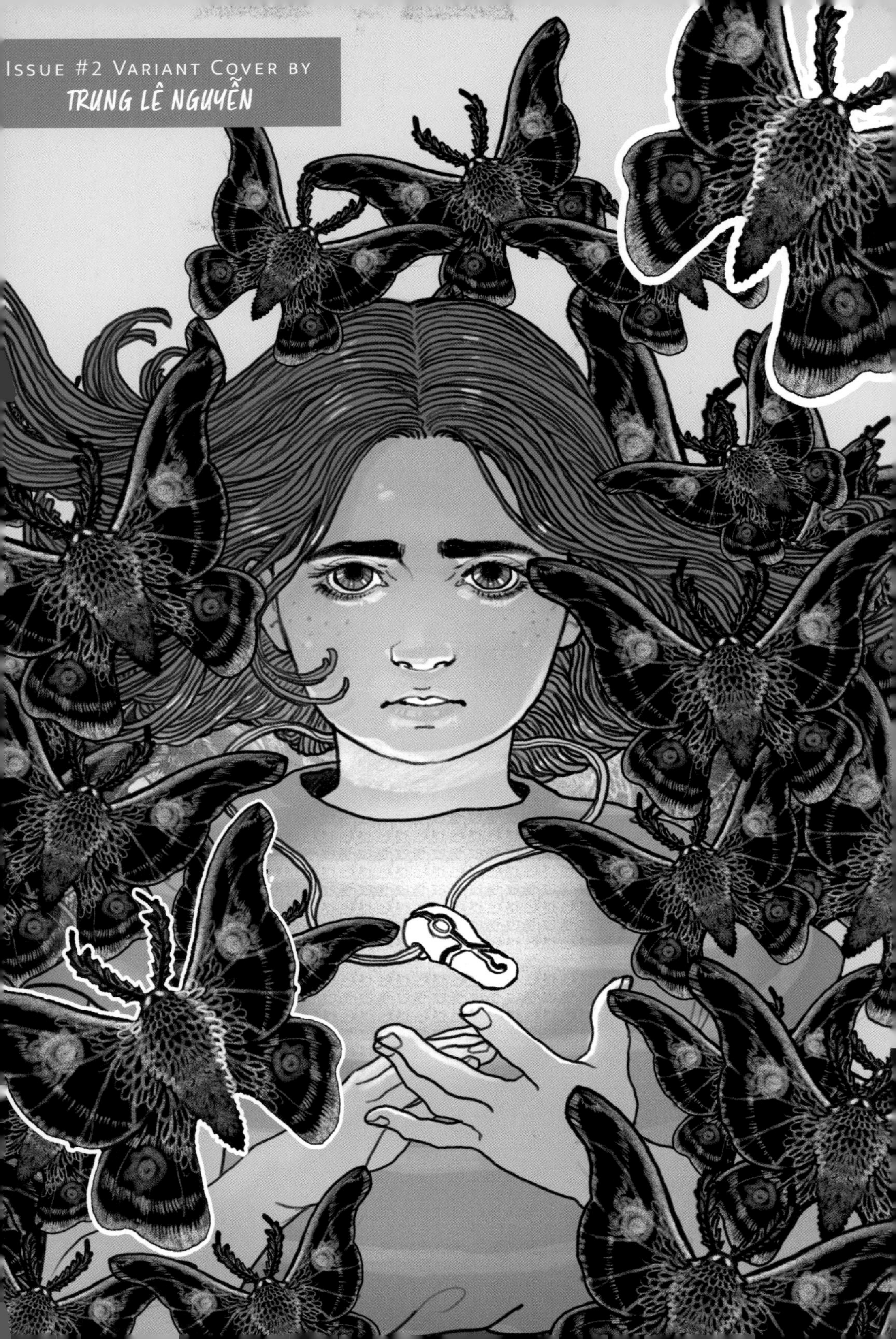

Issue #2 Variant Cover by
Trung Lê Nguyễn

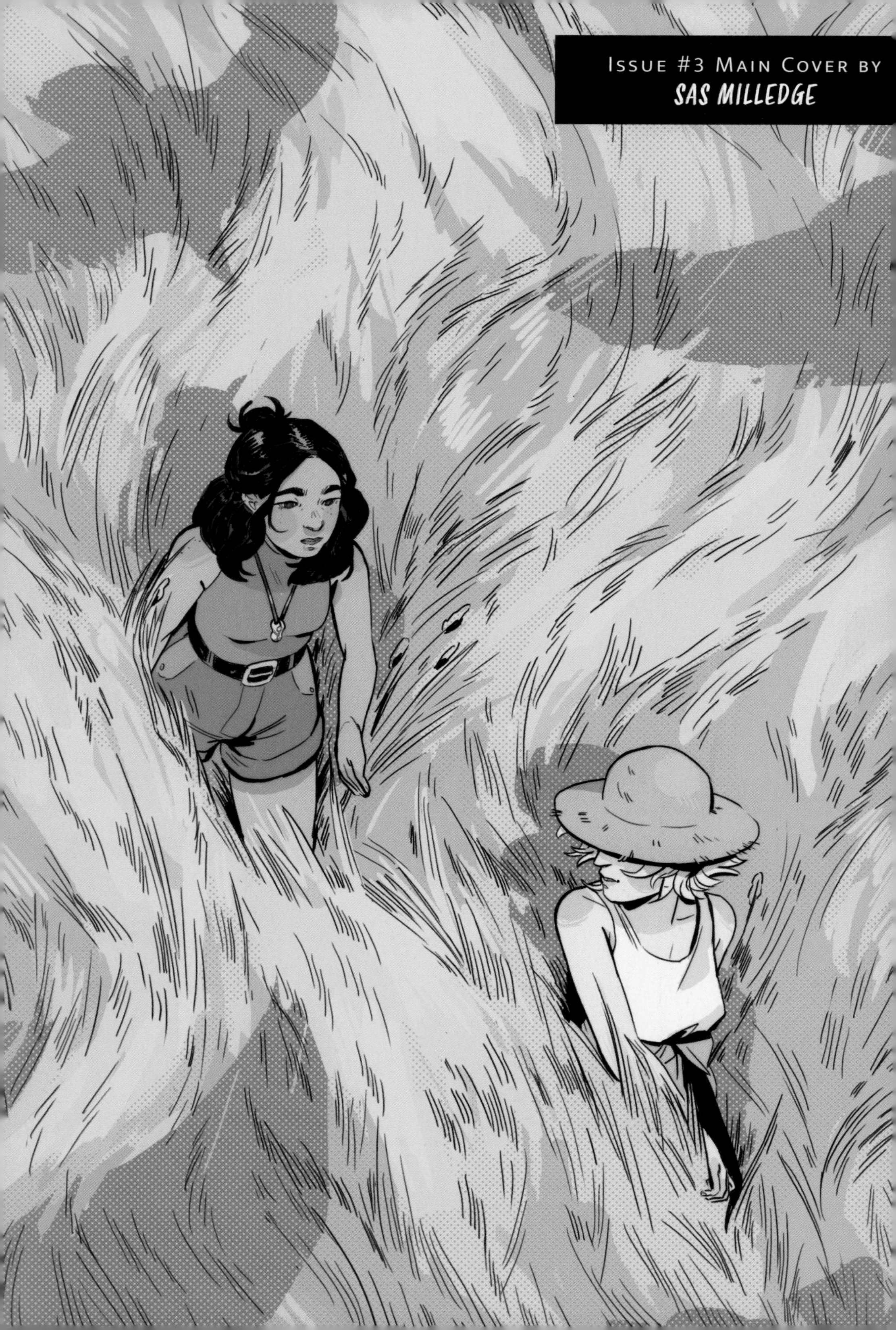

Issue #3 Main Cover by
SAS MILLEDGE

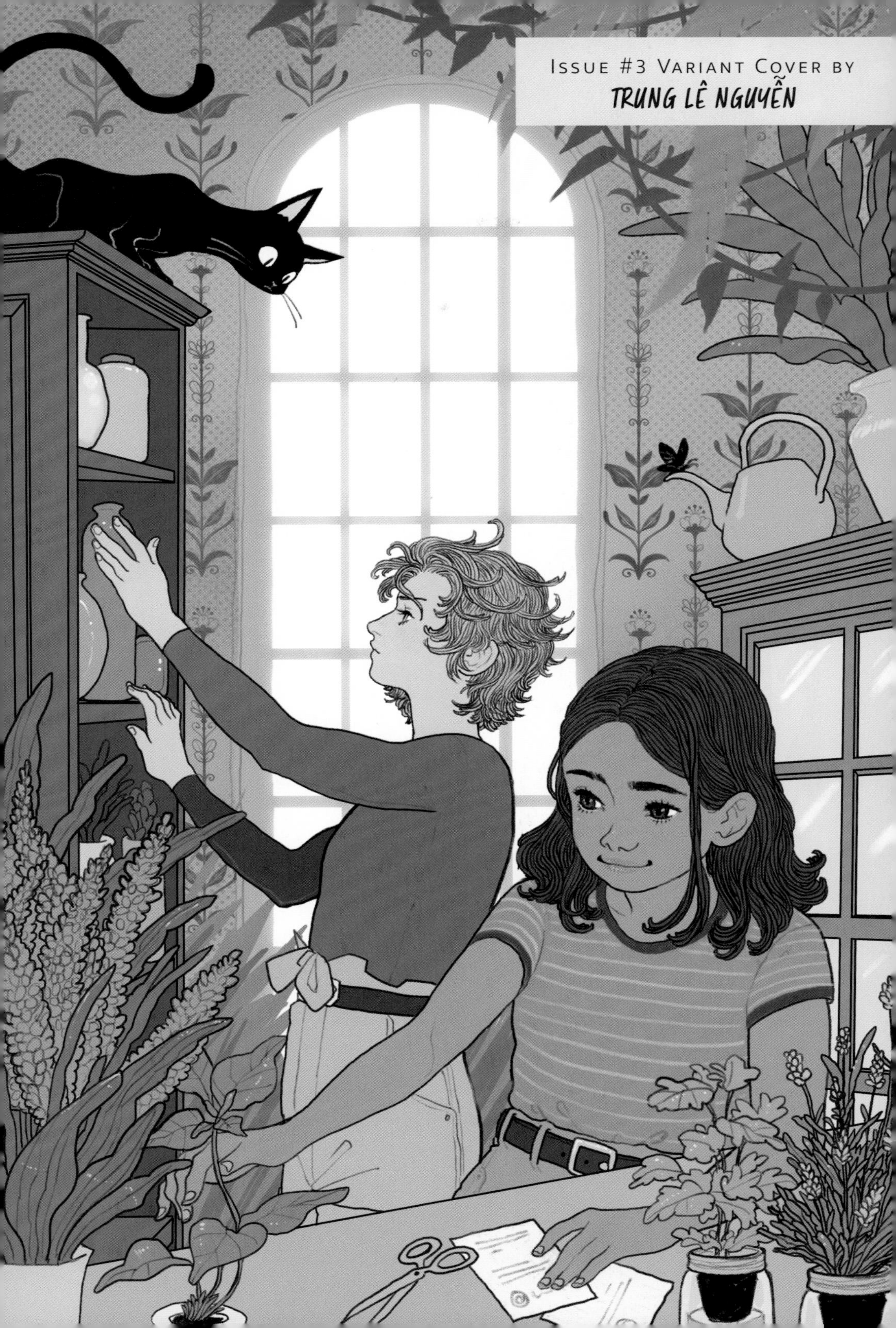

Issue #3 Variant Cover by
Trung Lê Nguyễn

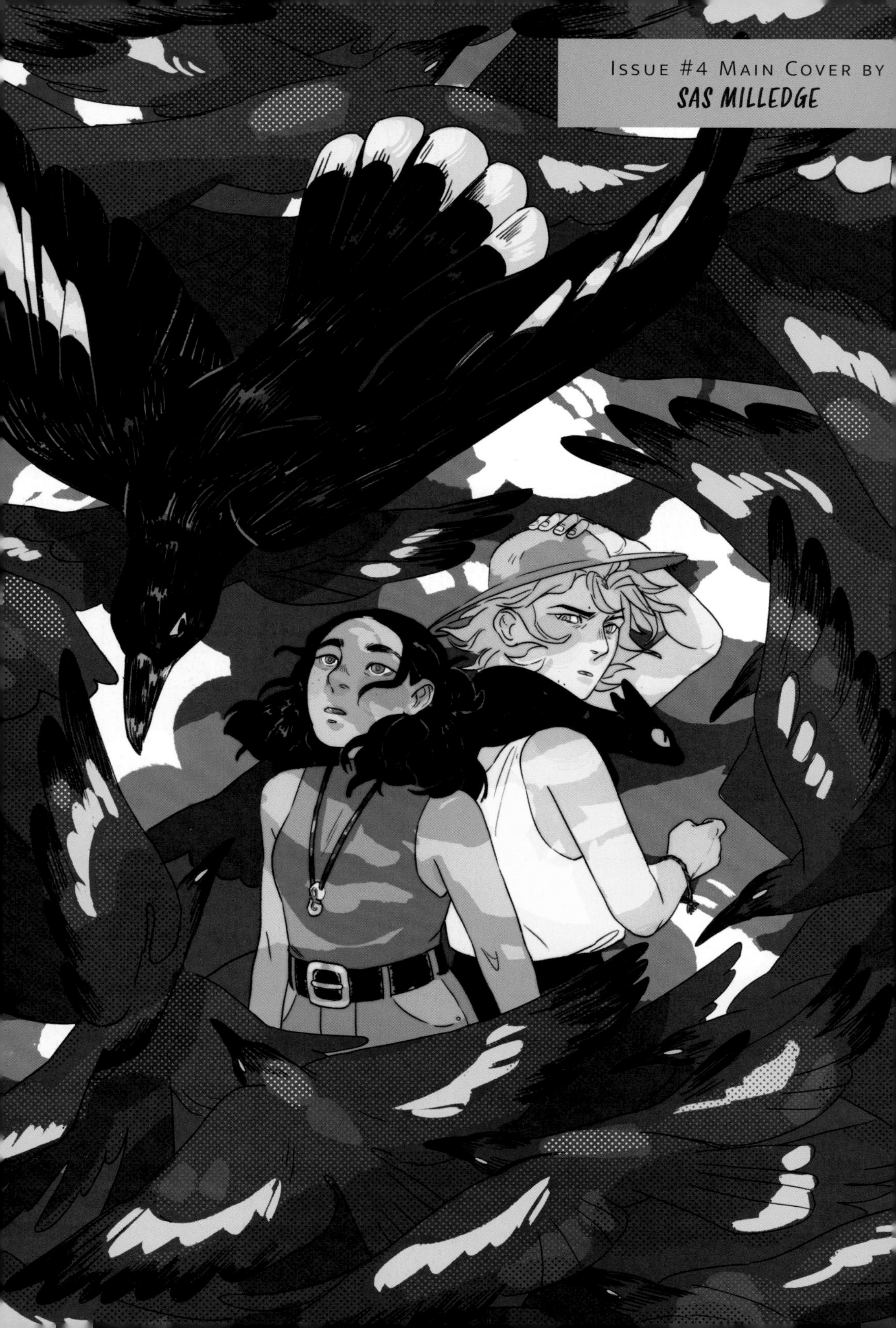

Issue #4 Main Cover by
SAS MILLEDGE

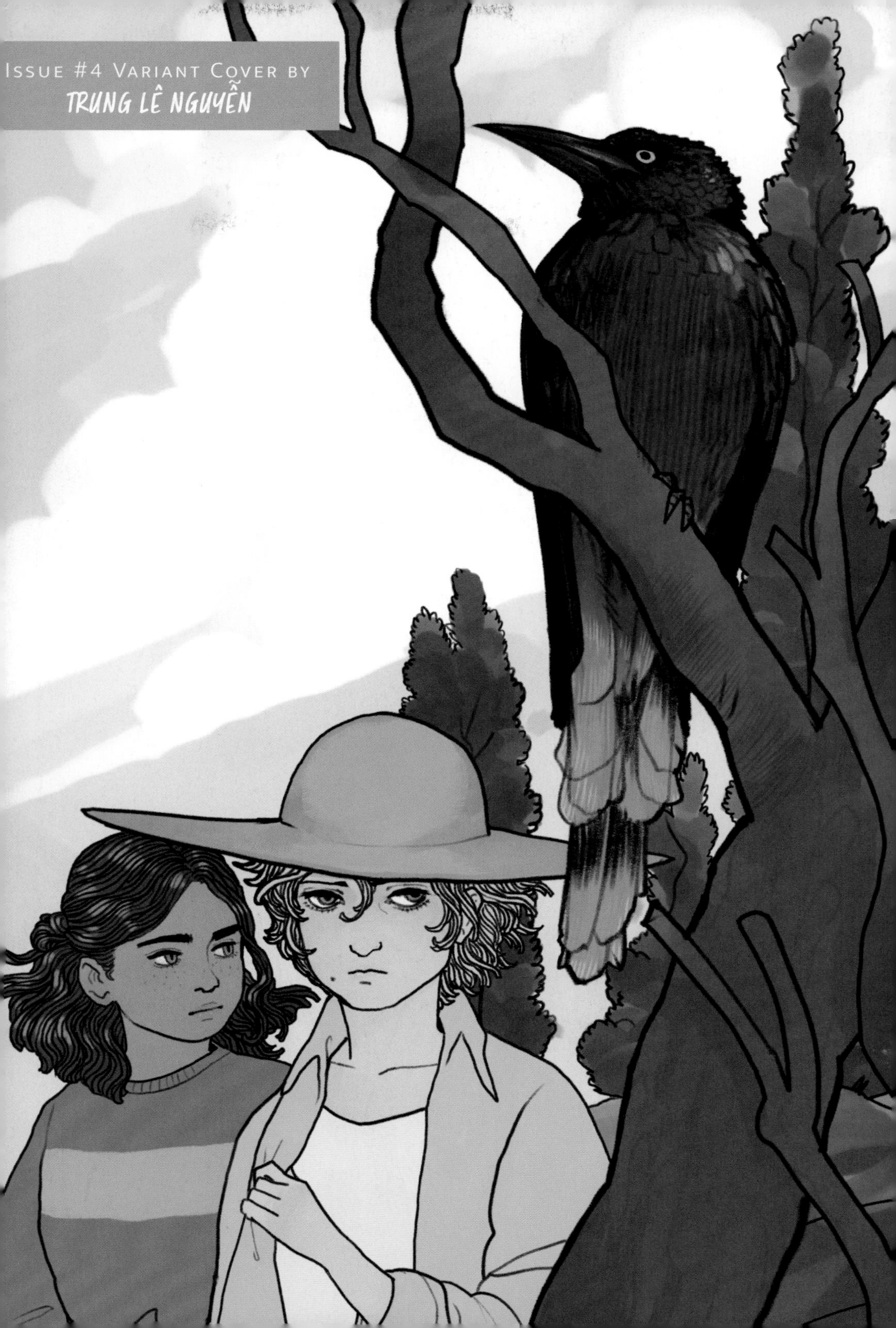

Issue #4 Variant Cover by
TRUNG LÊ NGUYỄN

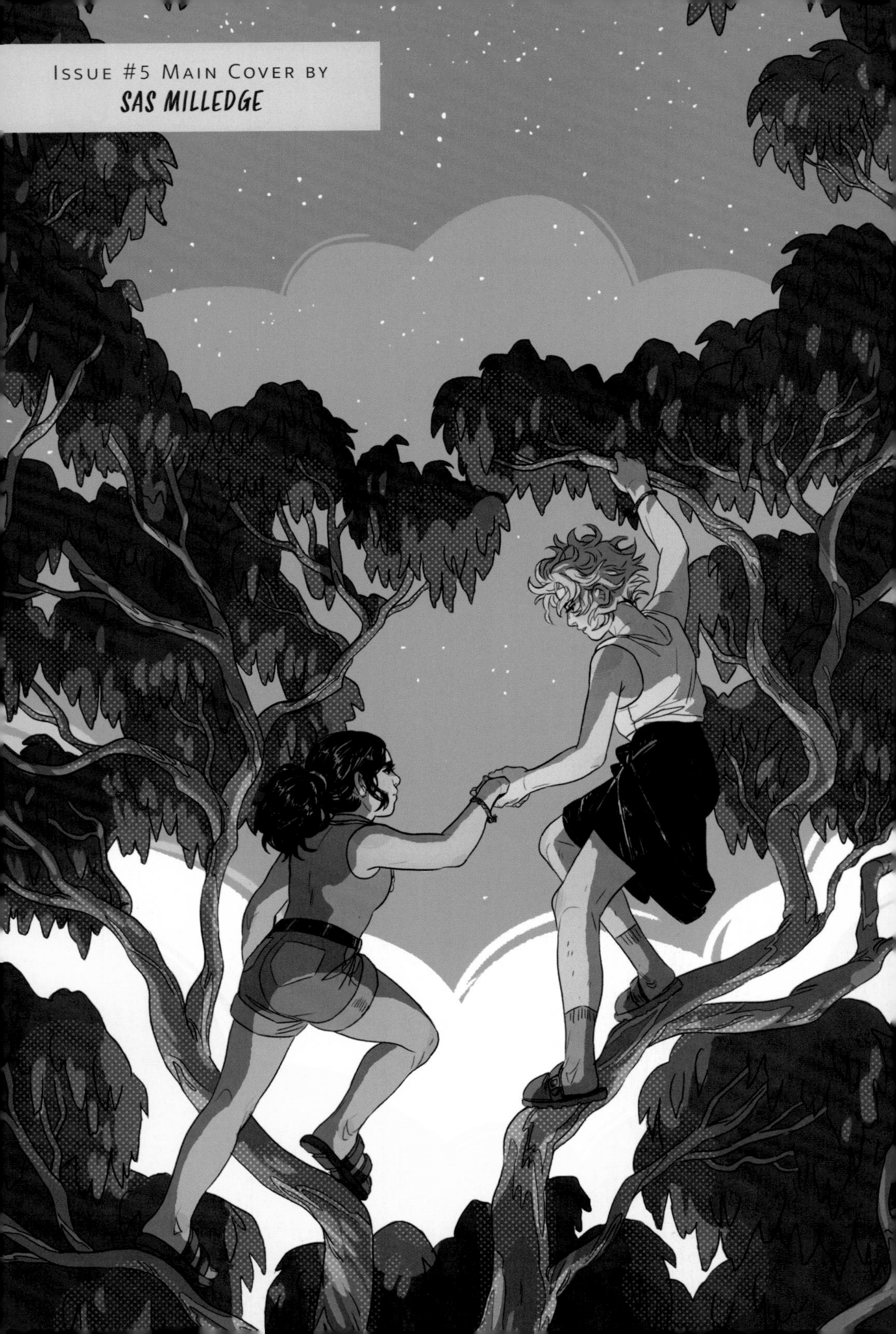

Issue #5 Main Cover by
SAS MILLEDGE

Issue #5 Variant Cover by

Trung Lê Nguyễn

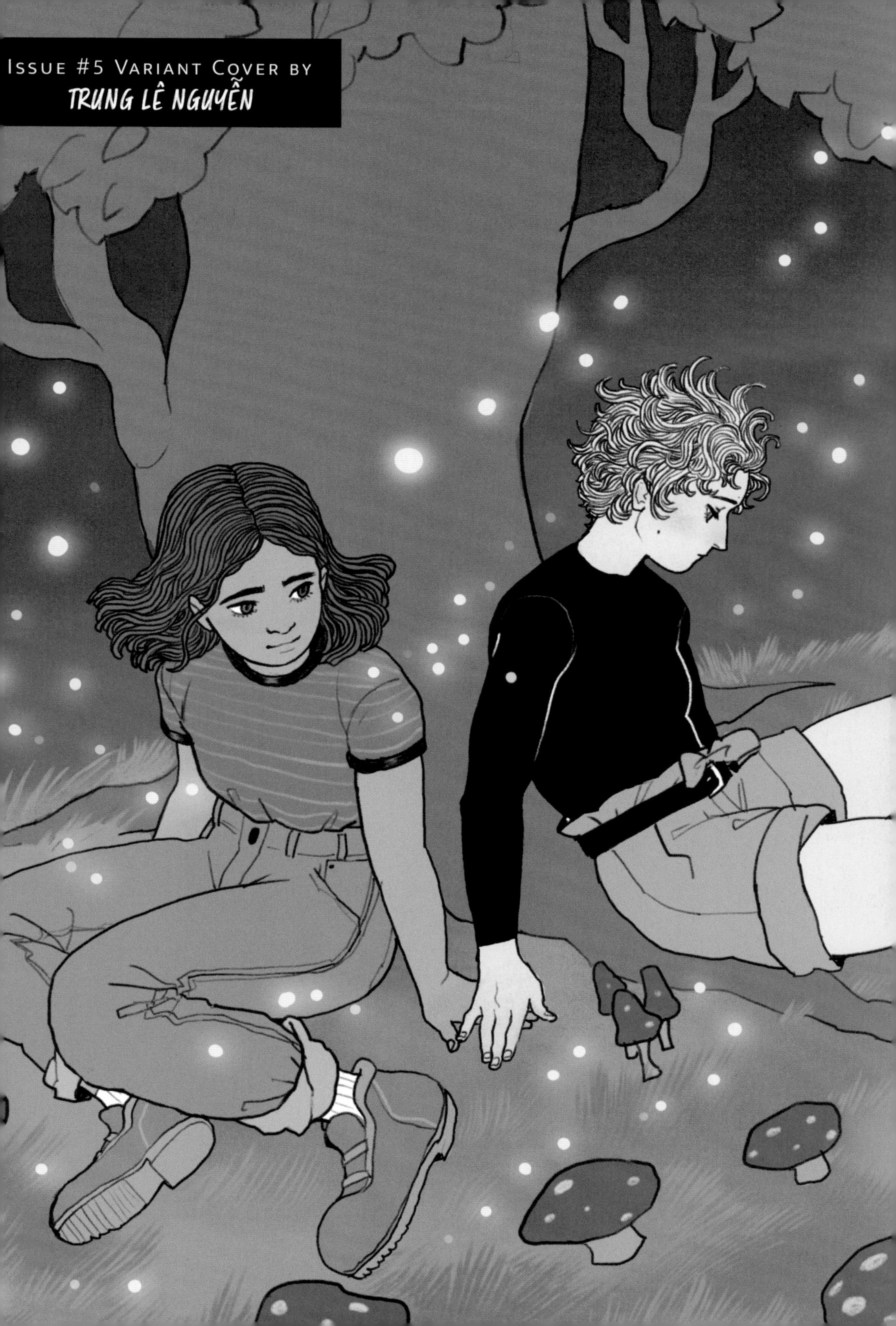

Sketches and designs by

SAS MILLEDGE

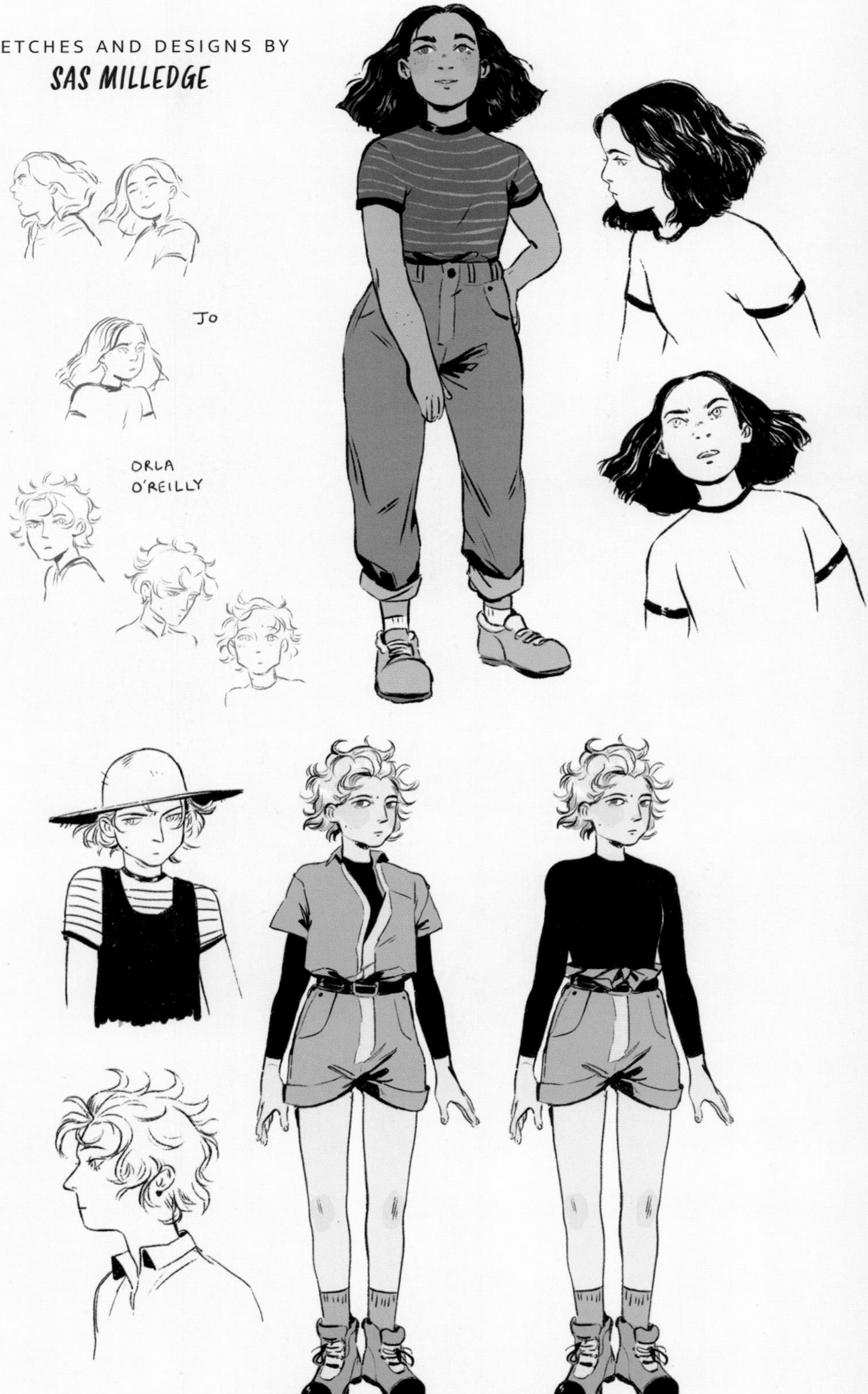
JO
ORLA
O'REILLY

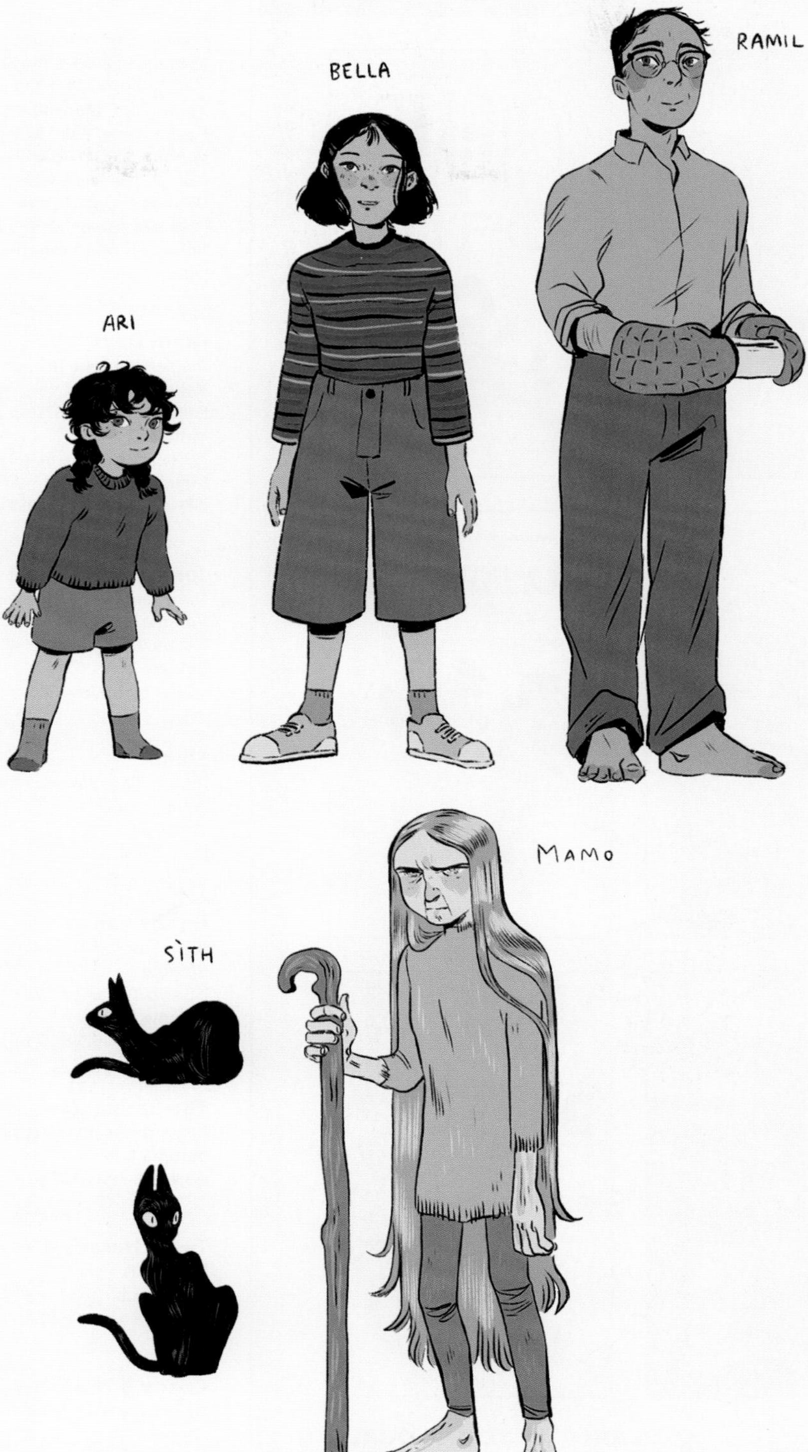
BELLA
RAMIL
ARI
MAMO
SÌTH

DISCOVER ALL THE HITS

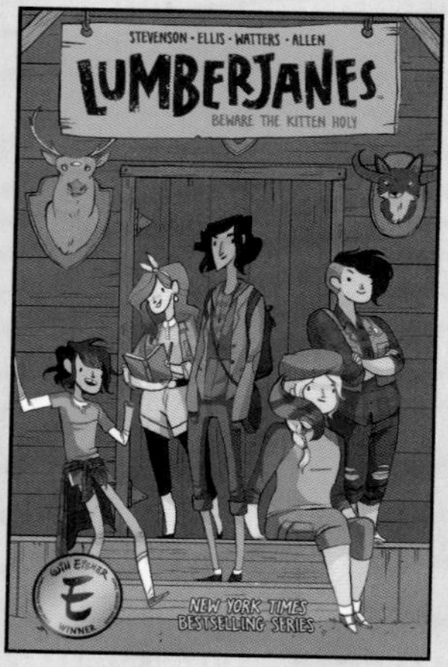
STEVENSON • ELLIS • WATTERS • ALLEN
LUMBERJANES
BEWARE THE KITTEN HOLY
NEW YORK TIMES BESTSELLING SERIES

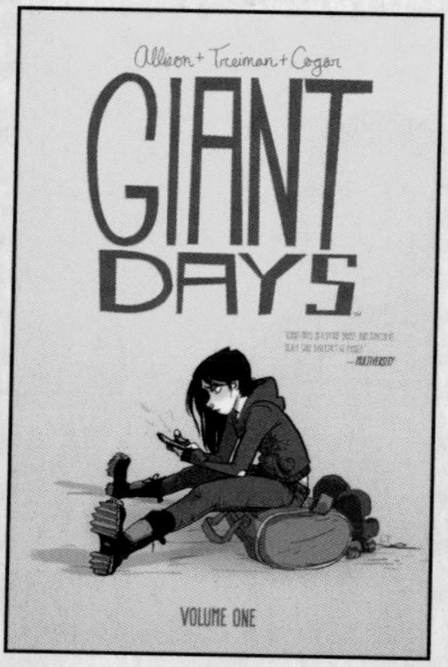
Allison + Treiman + Cogar
GIANT DAYS
VOLUME ONE

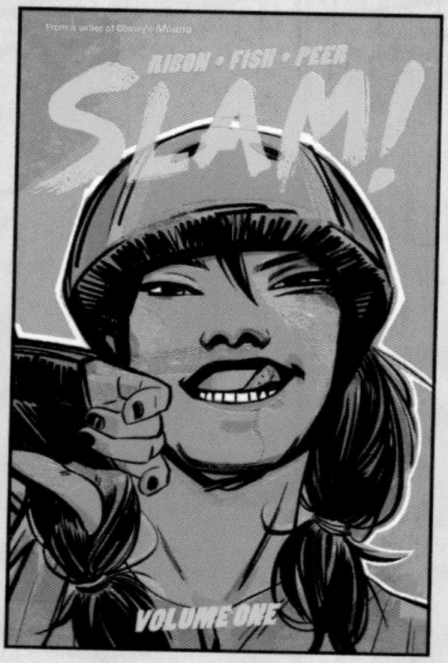
From a writer of Disney's Moana
RIBON • FISH • PEER
SLAM!
VOLUME ONE

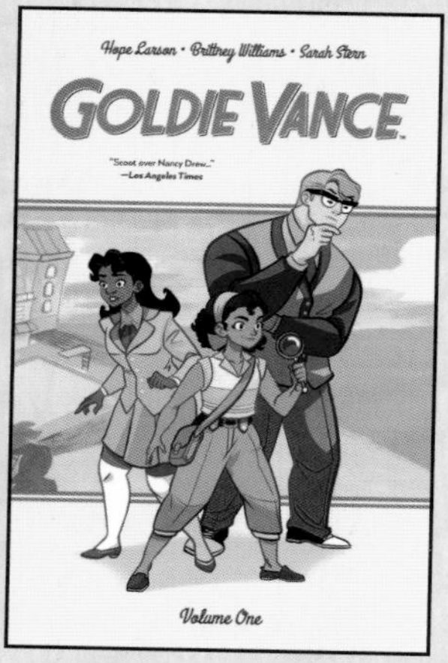
Hope Larson • Brittney Williams • Sarah Stern
GOLDIE VANCE
Volume One

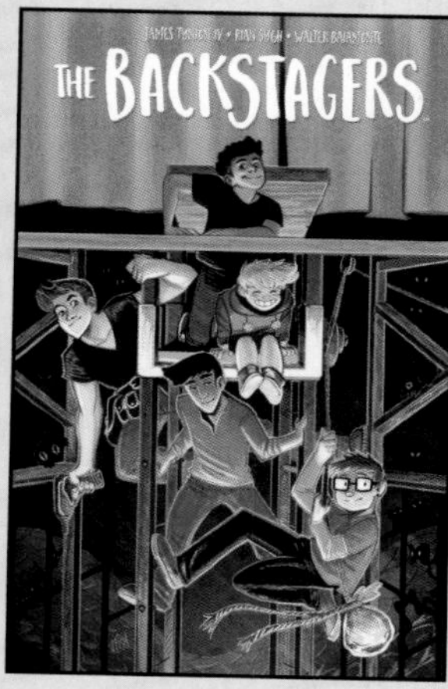
THE BACKSTAGERS

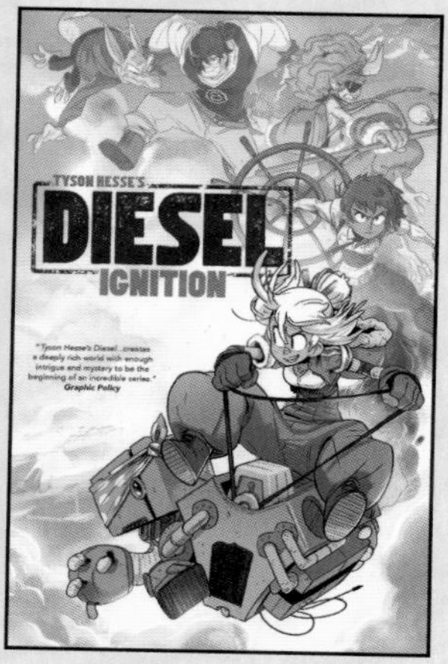
TYSON HESSE'S
DIESEL
IGNITION

Lumberjanes
ND Stevenson, Shannon Watters, Grace Ellis, Gus Allen, and Others
Volume 1: Beware the Kitten Holy
ISBN: 978-1-60886-687-8 | $14.99 US
Volume 2: Friendship to the Max
ISBN: 978-1-60886-737-0 | $14.99 US
Volume 3: A Terrible Plan
ISBN: 978-1-60886-803-2 | $14.99 US
Volume 4: Out of Time
ISBN: 978-1-60886-860-5 | $14.99 US
Volume 5: Band Together
ISBN: 978-1-60886-919-0 | $14.99 US

Giant Days
John Allison, Lissa Treiman, Max Sarin
Volume 1
ISBN: 978-1-60886-789-9 | $9.99 US
Volume 2
ISBN: 978-1-60886-804-9 | $14.99 US
Volume 3
ISBN: 978-1-60886-851-3 | $14.99 US

Jonesy
Sam Humphries, Caitlin Rose Boyle
Volume 1
ISBN: 978-1-60886-883-4 | $9.99 US
Volume 2
ISBN: 978-1-60886-999-2 | $14.99 US

Slam!
Pamela Ribon, Veronica Fish, Brittany Peer
Volume 1
ISBN: 978-1-68415-004-5 | $14.99 US

Goldie Vance
Hope Larson, Brittney Williams
Volume 1
ISBN: 978-1-60886-898-8 | $9.99 US
Volume 2
ISBN: 978-1-60886-974-9 | $14.99 US

The Backstagers
James Tynion IV, Rian Sygh
Volume 1
ISBN: 978-1-60886-993-0 | $14.99 US

Tyson Hesse's Diesel: Ignition
Tyson Hesse
ISBN: 978-1-60886-907-7 | $14.99 US

Coady & The Creepies
Liz Prince, Amanda Kirk, Hannah Fisher
ISBN: 978-1-68415-029-8 | $14.99 US

BOOM! BOX™

AVAILABLE AT YOUR LOCAL COMICS SHOP AND BOOKSTORE
To find a comics shop in your area, visit www.comicshoplocator.com
WWW.**BOOM-STUDIOS**.COM